MW01502679

DAMNED IF YOU DO

Also by Pat Leonard:

PROCEED WITH CAUTION

DAMNED IF YOU DO

A NOVEL BY PAT LEONARD

GOLDEN
PHEASANT
PRESS

MT. FREEDOM, NJ

Published in the United States of America
by Golden Pheasant Press, a division of Leonard Publications, Inc.
of Mt. Freedom, New Jersey.

Library of Congress Catalog No.: 93-090854
Damned If You Do / by Pat Leonard. — 1st ed.

ISBN 0-9632933-2-X

Printed in the United States of America
by BookCrafters of Chelsea, Michigan

First Edition 1994

1 3 5 7 9 10 8 6 4 2

To my children's grandparents,
Eddie, Peggy and Florence,

and to the memory of their departed grandfather,
James Stanley

Acknowledgments

Thanks to all the people who gave of their time and
expertise to help me get this book into print, including:
Mary Dempsey, Joanne Donnelly, Dave Evans, Ann Huber,
Margaret Leonard, Frank Pinto, Renée Rewiski, Janet Slivovsky,
Bob Sudela, Gary Walsh, Marianne Willis, and the staff
of the Randolph Township Public Library.

And, of course, my deepest appreciation to my *erudite* editor,
Julie Aberger.

DAMNED IF YOU DO

NO REASON

1

IF YOU HAD SUDDENLY FELT IT, hard and cold against the back of your neck, maybe you would have known what it was. Maybe you would have sensed the danger. But it was my neck, and I didn't know, and that's probably why I'm still here and he's not. It was my neck, and his gun. My ignorance, his death. Believe me, I've been over this at least a hundred times, and it hasn't begun to make any sense.

I can still hear his voice. My eyes were on his wife's battered and bloodied face when he came up behind me, silently. Her eyes, or rather the sudden terror in them, gave him away. But not before I felt that alien pressure against the base of my skull.

"Is this the guy?" he growled at her.

Tell me, how dumb am I? There I was, uninvited in their house, kneeling over her, when all at once I felt something blunt and metallic an inch below and behind my ear. Then I heard his agitated voice carrying such a question. Don't you think it should have dawned on me?

To be honest, a realization did come to me just then, but not the critical one, the one that would have gotten me killed. No, my initial insight was that he was drunk. He had noticeably slurred his question, and I could now smell the bilious odor of exhaled alcohol. Fleetingly the absurd notion crossed my mind: maybe that frigid circle of metal I felt against my neck was a bottle cap, and this was his way of offering a beer. Ah, nothing for me, thank you.

"Is this the asshole you've been fucking with?"

Isn't it peculiar how the mind works? From those eight angry words, which he snarled in her direction, I should have finally grasped the fact that I was in considerable peril. Instead, I noticed the dangling participle. Um, fellow—whoever you are, what you meant to say was "the asshole with whom you've been fucking." But let's not quibble; I've never seen this woman before.

"It don't surprise me, Angie," he continued. "You could be screwing some guy with class, but instead you pick a shithead in crummy sneakers. Some stupid *schmuck* from the rescue squad. It don't matter, though, 'cause I'm gonna..."

Gonna what? I still don't know, I can only suspect, because he never finished that sentence. Or any other sentence. Two things happened just then, causing my thoughts and his intentions to dash off in separate directions. For my part, I at last started to understand my predicament. I at last realized he was holding a gun, and that he suspected me of a transgression far less forgivable than the crime I had actually committed.

You see, I was in that house as a first aid volunteer, responding to a call for help. My role in that scene was that of the good guy, the selfless hero, but I had broken the first rule of first aid in taking the part. I had forgotten to look after my own ass. So instead of tending to her several injuries, I now found myself trying to negotiate, in my own mind, the cheapest possible payment for my mistake. At that moment, anything less than a bullet through my throat was starting to seem reasonable.

For his part, he had heard a sound behind him. He was drunk, he had been speaking, and yet he managed to hear something I had not. Without removing the gun from my neck, he turned to look at the front door, the door through which I had passed, foolishly alone, just three minutes before. What he saw made him jerk the gun away from me, rather swiftly for a drunken man, I thought, but perhaps not for a man who perceived danger far more readily than I did.

Turn around, my instincts told me. *Turn around and see what the hell's happening.* That's what my instincts were saying, screaming, but my actions were still trailing my thoughts, and my thoughts were still bouncing about without direction. Instead of concentrating on getting me out of that situation, they were tauntingly reminding me of how I'd gotten into it. I don't know; maybe they bear repeating.

Ten minutes earlier, I had nothing on my mind but a pepperoni pizza. I was walking out the door of my apartment, on my way to *Luigi's,* when I heard the signal tones of my police scanner coming from the kitchen. It was a call for the Dayfield Police, so I stopped for a moment to listen. The dispatcher signed on and asked for a patrol car. Then he and I both waited another fifteen seconds until a unit radioed back.

"Dayfield-three," a voice answered simply, and I smiled to myself in recognition. It was "Skip"—Sergeant Barry Skipinski—responding to the dispatcher's call. I've known Skip for a few years.

"Ah, three, could you take a run over to 712 Kilbourn? Gary and Angie Greer are at it again."

Skip apparently knew what the dispatcher was talking about, because he didn't hesitate before asking: "Did Fay call it in?"

"Who else?" the dispatcher replied, without emotion, before adding: "He must be slamming her around pretty good this time. Fay says she thinks Angie is hurt bad. I'll get you some backup in a minute, after I tone out the squad."

"I'm on my way," Skip answered.

Again I hesitated, just for a moment, before grabbing my rescue squad pager from my desk. I was halfway down to my car when the pager came bawling to life.

Bee-bee-bee-bee-bee-bee-bee!

"Dayfield dispatch to the Dayfield Rescue Squad," the dispatcher intoned, "you have an emergency call at 712 Kilbourn Avenue, that's in the Hilltop section, for a woman with multiple injuries. Repeating, Dayfield dispatch to the Dayfield Squad, please respond to 712 Kilbourn Avenue for a woman with multiple injuries. Time is 20:22. Out."

Go ahead and say it, because I won't argue with you now: I should've minded my own business. I wasn't on duty, and I knew that a half-dozen other hopeful heroes on the Dayfield Rescue Squad would, just then, be jumping in their cars, flipping on their blue lights, and driving like moonshine runners to 712 Kilbourn. And I knew that the Sunday night duty crew would be there with the ambulance in ten minutes or so. They could certainly take care of a battered woman without my help, and I had a pizza waiting for me at *Luigi's*.

But I couldn't resist. I was already in my car, and 712 Kilbourn was only two blocks away. Besides, there's something about a domestic call that brings out the *voyeur* in all of us. I've known guys on the squad who wouldn't cross the street to help a stroke victim, but who would leave their own wedding and race clear across town to see a man beating up his wife...or vice versa. Hell, I've been accused of having similar priorities myself. I threw my squad identification plate on my dashboard and sped to the call.

The first thing I noticed when I got to the house was an older woman standing on the driveway. She was holding an oversized, shaggy sheepdog on a leash, and the two of them were fidgeting and pacing nervously. When I drove up with my blue light flashing, they quickly came over to my car.

"Can you hear her in there?" the woman demanded, just as I was pulling my first aid kit from my trunk. "Can you hear her?"

I listened for a moment, and indeed could hear a woman inside the house, sobbing and shrieking. But I didn't hear a man's voice, or any other sound.

"Go help her," the older woman commanded me, gesturing repeatedly at the house. "Go help that poor creature."

"Who are you?" I asked the old woman as I put on my squad jacket.

The woman stopped gesturing and pulled her dog closer to her side, as though she felt threatened by my simple question. She looked around uncertainly.

"Me?" she asked vacantly. "Who am I?"

The woman seemed, momentarily, at a loss for words. Now that I think back, her confusion was the first of several warning signals I didn't notice, or chose to ignore.

"My name's Fay... Fay Johnson," she answered finally, "and this is my dog Bailey. She's an English sheepdog, you know. We live next door."

I pointed at the house. "Is her husband in there?" I asked Fay Johnson.

"Husband? Oh, no. Bailey doesn't have a husband, and neither do I. Never have. We're a couple of old maids, just getting by on my pension—"

Maybe it was the injured woman's repeated and pathetic cries for help that made me do what I did next. And I wish I could say I regret it, but I can't. I grabbed Fay Johnson's wrist and put my face three inches from hers. My action seemed to have the effect I wanted. She stopped fretting and dithering, and looked at me as squarely as I was looking at her. I even got the impression, staring into her faded eyes, that a light went on somewhere inside.

"The injured woman," I said slowly and deliberately. "Is there a man in there with her?"

Fay shook her head. "No," she answered clearly. "Just as I got off the phone with the police, I saw Gary, her husband, coming out the side door. His car was parked right there, where yours is now. He got in and drove away."

"Are you sure?"

Fay looked hurt, and then offended, by my question. She sharply pulled her wrist away from me. Her dog barked at her quick movement.

"I may be a bit older than you are, young man," she snapped, "but I still have two good eyes in my head. I know what I saw. I was out here walking Bailey when I heard Angie screaming, and his car was parked right there. I went in my house and called the police, as I always do when he starts hitting her. Then I looked out and saw him come from their house. He drove away, I tell you."

"Oh, God, I'm... I'm bleeding to death!" the woman in the house screamed. "Please, oh please, somebody *help* me..."

I left Fay, went up on the front porch, and looked in through the storm door. On the left was a small dining room, completely dark. On the right I could see part of the living room, but couldn't see the woman who continued to sob for help. There was an overturned chair on the floor, but no other sign of activity, past or present. I guessed that the woman was just out of my sight, at the far end of the living room. Tentatively I tapped on the door.

"Rescue squad," I called through the glass.

"Help me!" the woman cried again, although I couldn't say for certain she was responding to me. I looked around, hoping to see someone else arriving. In the distance I could hear the approach of a police siren. I turned back, opened the storm door, and stepped inside. I held the door open behind me.

"Hello? Where are you?" I called, hoping for an invitation. The woman just continued to cry. I cautiously poked my head around the corner and saw her, against the far wall.

I've seen battery victims before. Once, a year ago, I responded to a call when a man had taken a baseball bat to his brother-in-law, and had gotten in a dozen good licks before breaking the bat on a door frame. But I had never, outside of the movies, seen anyone looking quite so thoroughly abused as Angie Greer did at that moment. Now that I think back, I should have taken the awful sight of her for what it was: another warning signal. Instead I took it as sufficient proof that my assistance was needed.

I let the door close behind me and rushed to her side. I did a quick assessment of her vital signs, and had barely gotten my first aid kit opened, when I felt the nozzle of her husband's pistol burrowing into my neck. Maybe now you can understand why I had no inkling of the danger I was in.

"Gary! Drop the weapon!"

The sharpness of Skip's shouted command jolted me back to the present, while the clear urgency in his voice instantly shocked and panicked me. In the years I had known Sergeant Skipinski, I had never seen him lose his cool, or even raise his voice, though I'd often seen his composure tested.

"Put it down, Gary! *Now!*"

Another voice, equally urgent, bordering on shrill, followed

Skip's. I didn't recognize it, but it was exactly what I needed to get my sorry ass moving. I twisted sideways and dove, headlong, away from Angie and Gary Greer. As I hit the cheap carpet on their living room floor, I turned to look back at my assailant, just as he spun around to confront my would-be rescuers.

Skip had come through the door first, followed by another, younger patrolman. Neither had anticipated the situation they were facing, though both were now working furiously to unholster and draw their handguns. They obviously weren't expecting their shouted orders to be obeyed. Skip was crouching down, moving for cover, but the younger patrolman stood erect, just inside the door. He made a better target and, in the last act of his life, Gary Greer went for him; his gun exploded and the bullet, which seconds before had been poised to tear through my spine, hit the young patrolman square in the chest.

I know very little about firearms. I have never even held a loaded gun, let alone used one. And I'd certainly never seen one fired at a human being before. So you could reasonably say I was unprepared for what was happening. In fact, I still find it difficult to comprehend or recount.

With his eyes bulging, the young patrolman staggered and fell back against the wall, and then slid down, awkwardly and heavily, onto the carpet. I stared in disbelief and horror at his crumpled form. Behind me, Angie Greer was screaming louder than before. Less than a second later, her screams were drowned out by the rapid, repeating fire of another handgun. Skip emptied his service weapon into Gary Greer. Greer slumped to his knees and then fell, most assuredly dead. His arm came to rest against the back of my leg. I squirmed away. Or at least I think that's what I did.

"Scott! Are you okay? Scott Jamison!"

Three or four minutes later I realized someone was calling my name. I shook my head a few times, and tried to focus. The room was now full of people, all dashing around, all trying to do what I couldn't—to make some sense of what had taken place. Four people on the floor, including me, and a half-dozen more, crouching, kneeling and standing. I took a moment to rub my eyes, half expecting to wake up from this strange nightmare. Then I noticed someone crouching over me. His fingers were against my left wrist. It took me another moment to recognize him, and to figure out what he was doing. He was taking my pulse.

Miles, I thought. Miles Coates. One of my best friends in this world, a fellow rescue squad member. His black face broke into an easy smile as I gazed up at him. I guess my expression answered his question. Now I was hoping he could answer a few for me.

I didn't have to ask about Gary Greer. His bullet-riddled body still lay at my feet, surrounded by an oozy red swamp. My shoes, the "crummy sneakers" he had remarked on, were splattered with his blood. I flinched momentarily before turning to look at his wife, still leaning against the wall, now being tended to by two more first aiders. The Dayfield Rescue Squad had turned out in force for this call, just as I had expected.

I hesitated before turning my head back the other way, toward the front door. When I did, I wasn't surprised to see a crowd of uniforms—police and rescue—surrounding the fallen patrolman. But it did surprise me to see the young man sitting up and speaking to the crowd. He was completely alert, and only winced occasionally as he inhaled through an oxygen mask. My spirits climbed as I watched him.

Skip was among the crowd tending to the young patrolman. After a moment, he glanced over at Miles and me. Then he stood up and walked over to us. I felt a wave of apprehension come over me as he crouched down beside Miles.

"How you doing, Scott?" he asked evenly, with a minimum of concern.

"Okay, I guess."

He looked down at Gary Greer's bloody corpse, and back at me. Then he said what I had been thinking: "That could easily be you lying there, you know."

"I know. I'm glad you guys showed up when you did."

Skip nodded at my meager expression of gratitude, but said nothing.

"How's your partner doing?" I asked, motioning to the group by the door. "I thought he was a goner when he went down."

Skip looked again at Gary Greer's body before answering my question.

"He'll be okay—just a helluva bruise. He's lucky he had his vest on."

Of course; why hadn't I remembered? We on the squad had often joked about the Dayfield Police's mandatory use of bullet-proof vests, here in the peaceful, quiet suburbs of New Jersey where nothing ever happened. Even in my semi-dazed condition, I realized we would joke no more.

"Yeah…lucky," I agreed.

"What were you doing here?" Skip asked suddenly, with no trace of his previous concern.

"Responding to a call, just like you," I said.

"How did you get here so fast?"

I looked at Miles for a moment before answering. I debated whether to mention hearing the initial call on my scanner.

"I was already in my car when the tones went off. I live just two blocks from here."

"Did you know it was a domestic?"

Again I looked at Miles, who—uncharacteristically—was saying nothing. Something told me to lie.

"I wasn't sure what it was—the dispatcher didn't say, did he? There was a woman out on the driveway when I got here–"

"Fay Johnson?" Skip interrupted.

"Yeah, I think that's her name, and she told me…" I glanced over to where my fellow squad members were bandaging Angie Greer's head, and lowered my voice before continuing: "…she told me the woman's husband had left."

Skip gave me one of his famous, sardonic grins. "And you *believed* her?" he asked.

His questioning was making me uncomfortable, though I couldn't tell why. "I had no reason *not* to believe her," I answered defensively.

Skip shook his head. "You don't know Fay Johnson," he said. "She's as loony as they come. She called us one time, a few years ago, to say the Russians had invaded, and that an armored tank was patrolling the neighborhood. Her 'tank' turned out to be a street cleaner."

Miles laughed at Skip's anecdote, but I didn't find it humorous. The erratic workings of Fay Johnson's brain had nearly left me with a hole through mine.

"We're going to want you to come back to headquarters, Scott," Skip told me as he stood up, "and make a statement about what happened here. Are you up to it?"

I avoided looking at the Greers—one dead, the other being lifted onto a stretcher—as I answered Skip's final question. "Yeah, I'm up to it."

"Good," he replied. "Help him up, Miles, and don't touch anything." Skip walked back to the group near the front door. Miles took my arm and hoisted me to my feet. We waited until Angie Greer was taken, still sobbing, on a stretcher, and then we walked around the crimson puddle in which her dead husband lay. As we passed the group near the door, I smiled weakly at the young patrolman who had stopped the bullet with my name on it. He nodded back.

"You want me to drive you to the police station?" Miles asked when we got outside.

I shook my head. "No, I'm okay," I answered bravely. "Just give me a minute to get my bearings."

"Well, when they get done with you, I'm gonna want to hear all about it. I'll come by your place later."

"Not tonight, Miles," I said wearily. "Maybe tomorrow."

"Okay," he answered, "but don't go inventing some story that makes you the hero of this tale. I *know* better. I saw the look in your eyes while you laid there, staring at that dead guy. I'm surprised you haven't pissed yourself dry."

"Thanks, Miles. I love you too."

He laughed crisply, as always, before walking over to the ambulance that would take Angie Greer to the hospital. I glanced around, noticing the bystanders that had gathered just outside the police lines. Fay Johnson was nowhere in sight.

The chief of the Dayfield Police was waiting for me when I arrived at headquarters. He offered me a cup of coffee, which I accepted, before leading me to a small interrogation room. He turned on a cassette recorder and explained that this was just for the record—standard procedure for whenever a officer had discharged his weapon. He identified himself for the cassette recorder and asked me to do likewise. Then the questions began.

He asked for a lot of details, beginning with the moment I entered the house. His main concern, so it seemed to me, was if Gary Greer had *clearly* been told to drop his gun, and if Skip had *clearly* been faced with a life-threatening situation. I answered both questions affirmatively, several times each. Then I waited while a stenographer typed up my statement. I signed it without hesitation.

By the time I returned to my apartment, I was starting to feel sick. My hands were shaking as I pulled out my key to unlock the door. Inside, the first thing I noticed was the message light on my answering machine, blinking twice. I correctly guessed who had left one of the two messages.

"Hello, H.B.," Pam's recorded voice greeted me. "Call me if you get in before 10:30. If I don't hear from you, I'll assume we're still on for tomorrow evening. I'm looking forward to it. Bye."

It was barely ten o'clock, but I decided not to call Pam anyway. She'd understand. I was feeling terribly, terribly nauseous. I barely made it into the bathroom, and over the bowl, before the vile contents of my stomach came rushing up and out. Over the echoing sounds of my heaving guts, I couldn't hear the second message from the answering machine. It took me a couple of minutes to get myself settled. Then I slowly walked out of the bathroom and over to the machine. I replayed the second message.

"Yeah, Scott, this is Luigi," a gruff, obviously irritated voice repeated. "When you gonna get in here and pick up this pizza?"

NO REST

2

LUIGI, MY ASS. HIS REAL NAME, WHICH admittedly would not be much of an asset in the pizza business, is Fred Schimmer. Fred's a German Jew, and when he took possession of his parlor a few years back, he didn't know olive oil from axle grease. The *story* he likes to tell is that he acquired the place as payment for a gambling debt. The *truth* is that it was left to his wife by a bachelor uncle, and Fred got it under their divorce agreement—an otherwise unremarkable document that notably failed to mention that she had been keeping company with two other individuals—one male and one of indeterminate gender—prior to her break-up with Fred. Not that any of this matters, of course, but it helps explain why "Luigi" always retreats to the kitchen whenever a customer actually addresses him in Italian.

I had difficulty sleeping that night, and more than once I found myself rubbing the spot on my neck where Gary Greer, the drunken wife-beater, had impressed the muzzle of his pistol. When I finally fell asleep, I had the same dream I've had off and on for the past two years. It's a stupid dream, and one I'm mostly bored with anymore, but I will admit it kept my attention the first few times.

Probably rooted in an old movie I saw but don't remember, or a book I had to read in high school, the dream takes place in ancient times, aboard a galley ship tooling around the Mediterranean. I'm a slave on board this ship, five rows back, second seat on the right. After two years of faithful but fruitless rowing, I think by now I should have earned a window seat, but the dream never varies. We haul on the oars for a while, then we engage the enemy in battle, and then we get sunk. Being mere slaves, of course, we're shackled to the floor boards, so we're doomed to go down with the ship. Understandably, this causes us some distress. The first couple of times I screamed the loudest as the swirling waters rose and rushed over us.

As I said, the dream never varies, but it wasn't until the third or fourth time that I noticed a hand—a woman's, slender and delicate—holding the key that can free me. Just as the waters are about to engulf me, the hand descends, presumably to unlock my now-submerged shackles. I used to follow the hand downward, thinking it mattered whether or not it reached its destination. Now I know better. Now I know I'm going to wake in the next instant, so instead of watching the hand descend, I look up and try to see the face of the woman who is coming to my rescue. But it never happens; I never get to see her face.

This time, however, I was privileged to hear her voice. She brought her hand back up from under the water, but she was no longer holding a key. Rather, in her slender and delicate hand was a telephone. Cordless, of course. And then, just before I awoke, I heard her speak for the first time.

"It's for you," she said.

"This is Scott," I said into the receiver, as my eyes rebelled against the sunshine streaming into my bedroom. I was alone, and for the moment amazed that I had been able to reach and answer my phone while still residing in the dream, going down with the galley ship.

"Well, good morning, sir!" came back a voice that was familiar, and cloyingly derisive. "I *hope* I didn't wake you." It was Arnie, my boss, and as my eyes adjusted and my head cleared, I realized he wasn't apologizing; he was expressing his extreme disfavor. I glanced at the clock, and the four numbers on the digital display confirmed what I had feared: I was on his time now. Had been for the past sixty-eight minutes.

"Well, yes… er, no…" I mumbled back, debating whether to confess, or lie. I lied. "I'm not feeling so well, Arnie. I may not make it in today."

"And when were you going to tell me that?" he replied coolly. "We did have a meeting scheduled for this morning, you know."

Rub my nose in it, why don't you?

"Yes, I know," I whined, groveling like the dog he suspected I was. "Can we reschedule for tomorrow, Arn? I'm sure I'll feel better by then."

Silence for a minute. A cold, penetrating mass of dead air. Then: "Who's Dorothy?"

"Who?"

"Dorothy! A young woman called for you a few minutes ago. Said her name was Dorothy. Acted like she knew you."

"You sure it wasn't Pam?"

The derisive tone returned. "Pam. Now, gee, why didn't I think of that? She said her name was *Dorothy*, but she obviously meant to say *Pam*. Maybe she forgot to look in the mirror this morning, and wasn't sure just *who* she was."

I hoped he was only trying to be funny, and not funny at Pam's expense. That's off limits, even for my boss.

"I don't know a Dorothy," I said defensively.

"Yeah, well, she seems anxious to get in touch with you. I said I expected you at any minute, but she wouldn't leave a number. Said she'd call back. Do I tell her your tummy is hurting you? Or what?"

I was tiring of this abuse, so I lashed out: "Tell her whatever the fuck you want. Tell her I'm taking a 'personal' day. I still have two coming this year."

"You *had* two coming," he shot back. "But you didn't give adequate notice. You didn't give *any* notice. And the next time you use that kind of language with me, Mr. Jamison, it won't matter if you have two *dozen* personal days coming, because you'll no longer have a job to skip out on!"

The sound of his phone being slammed back into its cradle reverberated through my skull for a few seconds, and then there was just the vacant hiss of a broken connection. I hung up the phone and lay back against my pillow. Great.

Already the day was trashed. Then I noticed I had a headache. It wasn't one of those hammer-pounding-on-anvil, bring-you-to-your-knees headaches, but a headache nonetheless. I took a perverse pleasure in it; it gave me some justification. I hadn't lied to Arnie after all; I *wasn't* feeling very good this morning.

Maybe, I thought, I could get back to sleep for an hour or two, and then start the day over again. Maybe I'd have better luck the second time around.

But five minutes later, the phone rang again. I hoped it was Arnie, giving me a chance to apologize. If I told him about my brush with eternity the previous evening, I was sure he'd be forgiving.

"Hello," I said, sounding appropriately miserable.

"Is Scott Jamison in?" It was a woman's voice, totally unfamiliar.

"Speaking."

"Mr. Jamison, my name is Dorothy McCrae. I'm a reporter for *The Dayfield Dispatch*." She hesitated for a second, perhaps allowing me to surmise the purpose of her call. I said nothing, so she continued: "I understand you witnessed a shootout last night between the Dayfield Police and a suspected drug dealer. Is that right?"

Drug dealer? The drunk who thought I was tapping his wife was a drug dealer?

"I don't know if 'shootout' is an accurate description of what I saw, Miss…"

"McCrae."

"…Miss McCrae, but, yes, I was there when it happened. Who told you?"

She ignored my question.

"I was wondering when we could get together, so I might ask you a few questions about the incident."

"What would you like to know?"

"Would tomorrow evening be good for you? Say, around six o'clock?"

Was my phone broken? Or hers? Why wasn't she answering me?

"Miss McCrae..."

"I understand you work for DataStaff Corporation, in the Hilltop section of town. There's a diner just down the street from your office, isn't there? How about if we meet there?"

"Miss McCrae..."

"I'll be wearing a red baseball cap, and carrying a newspaper. How will I know you?"

"I'll be wearing pantyhose, and nothing else."

"Excuse me?"

Yes, it was cheap. But it got her attention.

"Miss McCrae..."

"Dorothy."

"Okay, Dorothy. Did you say you're going to ask me a few questions about what happened last night?"

"Yes, Mr. Jamison..."

"Scott."

"Yes, Scott, of course I'm going to ask you a few questions. I'm a reporter. That's my job." She was patronizing me, but something in her voice told me she wasn't as tough as she was trying to sound.

"Are you going to expect me to answer your questions?"

For the second time, she hesitated. I could almost hear the wheels turning. Finally, she said, brightly: "I get you."

"You get me?"

"Yes. Why should you answer my questions, when I'm refusing to answer yours?"

Smart girl. Probably the type who routinely guessed the punch line when the joke was only three-quarters told.

"Why are you refusing?"

"It's a habit," she said, and I could imagine her shrugging. "I'm better at asking questions than answering them."

"It's a *bad* habit," I said.

"Yeah...maybe. So will I see you at the diner tomorrow? Six

o'clock?"

"I don't own a red baseball cap."

She laughed. A rich, warm laugh that originated in her chest. Honestly, I could tell that, even over the phone. I'm something of an expert on laughter, and especially on its various points of origin. Mouth laughs I detest; if it starts no deeper than that, it's usually phony. Throat laughs are better. Chest laughs are the best. Anything deeper is overkill—belly laughs should be left to Santa Claus. Ho, ho, ho.

"That's okay," she said. "I'll trust you to spot me."

"Let's make it seven o'clock instead. That's when I get off duty."

"Off duty?" she asked.

"Rescue squad."

"Oh, yes, that's right. You're on the squad. Will you have your uniform on?"

"Do you want me to?"

"Suit yourself," she said. "Seven o'clock, tomorrow, at the Hilltop Diner." She hung up.

My headache had diminished somewhat, so I decided to get out of bed. I ate a quick breakfast, shaved, and then jumped into the shower. That's usually where I do my best thinking, so I took my time under the steaming water, considering the significance of what Dorothy McCrae had said about Gary Greer. He was a suspected drug dealer. For the moment, it didn't appreciably alter my outlook on the previous evening's incident, but it did make me imagine the phone calls Dorothy McCrae would be making this morning had the police not arrived when they did.

"...Hello, Mr. Arnie Rosensteel? I'm a reporter, and I'd like your reaction to the shooting death of your employee, Scott Jamison. You say he was a highly valued associate, and you're deeply shocked and saddened, and you'll miss him dearly, both personally and professionally? Thank you, Mr. Rosensteel. ...Hello, Mrs. Billie DeMarino? I'd like your reaction to the shooting death...what's that? You say Scott was a highly valued associate, and you're deeply shocked and saddened, and you'll miss him dearly, both personally..."

What else could anybody say? At age 33, I'd be leaving behind the usual assortment of parents, siblings, friends, co-workers, former classmates, fellow rescue squad members, and a girlfriend—all attesting that I was a helluva guy, callously gunned down while trying to help a stranger in need. My obit, naturally, would contain most of the pertinent data: born in New York City, second son of an executive with General Electric, educated at various private schools, graduate of M.I.T., talented computer programmer, etc., etc.

As I turned off the water, I remembered Dorothy McCrae's laugh. My headache was gone now, and all of a sudden I was overwhelmed with an appreciation for all that had nearly been taken from me. I smiled to myself. Nothing like a near-death experience to open one's eyes to one's blessings. I pulled back the shower curtain and Pam was standing there.

She studied me from head to toe—at least I think her gaze went down that far.

"You don't look sick to me," she commented in a matter-of-fact voice. "And what's that silly grin for?"

WHAT CAN I TELL YOU ABOUT PAM Healy? We've been on-again, off-again for nearly six years, both of us madly in love with the other—well, I *think* she feels that way too—and both of us too smart or too stupid or too scared to take the relationship to another level. She went through a personal crisis about seven months ago—something to do with her thirtieth birthday, no doubt—but has since settled back into the routine we established in an earlier "on-again" phase. Which is to say we call each other daily, see each other two or three times weekly, and get *very* intimate maybe half that often, which isn't often enough for me. All in all, though, we have a comfortable arrangement, which we both know can't last.

I hesitate to describe Pam physically because invariably I get myself in trouble when I try. For starters, I'll say that someone who doesn't really know her might be inclined to call her a bimbo. Hell, *I* call her a bimbo sometimes—there I go, asking for trouble—but only in her presence, and usually in jest. You see, Pam's a knockout. She's tall, naturally blond, athletic…and has a body that visually defines the word *curvaceous*. I gaze at her every once in a while and marvel that a veritable goddess like her could have any interest in an ordinary mortal like me.

That's the good part. The not-so-good part is that Pam often comes across as being, well, ditsy. God knows she's not dumb—she graduated from Bucknell in the top third of her class, and she holds a good job that requires considerable brainpower—but occasionally Pam says and does things that make her appear... *confused*. You could also say she's naïve. Her willingness to believe anything she's told has enabled others to take advantage of her, on more than one occasion. But the beauty of it is, she's invariably come out of those experiences feeling that the *other* person had a problem that needed fixing, and not her.

That's how the world sees Pam Healy, and even if that were all I could say about her, you might understand why I'm so attracted to her. After all, it's not like I'd be the first male of the species who listened only to his hormones when selecting a mate. And it's not as if I couldn't do worse—even if I let my nobler, intellectual self do the choosing.

But, believe me, there's more to Pam Healy than meets the eye. It's not readily apparent, but she possesses this rare quality, a certain inner...*grace*—a loveliness beyond description. It's like the sweet innocence of a smiling three-year-old, the warm compassion of your dear departed grandmother, the steadfast loyalty of a lifelong friend. It's, well, as I already said: it's beyond description. But whenever I see it—whenever Pam's internal goodness shines through, and momentarily dazzles me—even her physical beauty pales by comparison. And that says a lot.

I've never told this to anybody, and our mutual friends would be stunned to hear me say it at all. "Scott," any one of them would remark, "I can remember times when you've ridiculed Pam in public, when you've made fun of her gaffes, when you've said she's 'as shallow as vapor on a mirror.'"

Those, regrettably, are my words, saying far more about me than the woman they were meant to demean. Why did I say them? It shames me to confess it, but it's jealousy. It's my childish way of protecting her, by diminishing her value in the sight of others. I don't want anyone else to discover, to realize, how deep her beauty really goes. I don't want to lose her.

"Don't I always smile when I see you?" I asked, wrapping a towel around my waist.

"You were smiling before you even knew I was here."

"And why *are* you here?"

"You didn't return my call from last night. I tried you at the office earlier, but Arnie said you were out sick today. I came over to see if I could do anything for you."

I stepped closer, and started to slide my arm around her waist. She planted her palm in the middle of my chest, and pushed me away.

"You're all wet," she said simply. "Dry off. I'll wait in the living room for you." She turned and walked out of the bathroom.

"Not the bedroom?" I whined.

"No, H.B., the living room," she called back.

I toweled off, and applied the usual combination of lotions and potions to my face, underarms, and assorted body parts. When I finished, I walked out of the bathroom, but didn't go directly into the bedroom. I glanced around the corner into the living room to see her sitting in a chair, paging through a magazine. She looked up and smiled.

"So, how sick are you?" she asked.

"Not sick," I said, "just shaken up. I was nearly killed last night."

That would get her out of that chair, I thought. I retreated to the bedroom, expecting her to follow. She didn't.

"Too much to drink?" she called, casually. Then: "Again?"

"No, not a drop," I called back.

"Then what?"

I didn't answer right away. I started getting dressed, debating with myself just how to relate the story to Pam. Did I want her to be sympathetic, enthralled, or what? The phone rang just then, and I sat down on the edge of the unmade bed to answer it.

"Yo, Scott," the voice on the phone addressed me. It was my buddy Miles, following up as promised. "Feeling better today? Ready to tell me what went *down* in that house last night, other than you and Gary Greer?"

Miles made it sound like he knew the dead man—the suspected drug dealer. That interested me. "Had you ever been in that house before, Miles?"

"Yeah, I was there on a domestic call a few months ago. Cops told me that guy beat up his wife on a regular basis, but she would never file a complaint against him. Guess she won't be filing any this time, either."

"No, I guess not," I said.

"So tell me, what happened?"

I recounted the entire story for Miles, failing only to mention that I didn't realize, at first, that Gary Greer had been holding a gun to my head. In the midst of my recital, Pam came into the bedroom. Her face darkened with concern as she listened, and then with dismay as I repeated Greer's last words. She gasped aloud when I described the young policeman's physical and cognitive reactions to being shot. By the time I finished telling of Greer's flopping onto the living room carpet, Pam was sitting next to me on the bed, anxiously holding my hand. At that point, Miles pushed the "pause" button.

"Wait a minute, Jamison," he said abruptly. "One thing I don't get. Where were the cops when Greer came up behind you?"

I thought I had made this point clear, but apparently Miles hadn't been listening. So I repeated: "They hadn't arrived yet."

"They hadn't *arrived* yet?"

Was he hard of hearing? "No."

"And you had *already* entered the house? Alone?"

"Yes. Just as I told you."

Miles let out a low, slow whistle. "Scott," he said finally, "that's pretty damn stupid. Even for a white know-nothing from Sunnybrook Farm, that was just plain stupid. It's also against squad regulations."

Squad regulations. There I sat, literally shaking as I retold the single most harrowing experience of my young life, and Miles was quoting chapter and verse from a mimeographed manual that no one's *looked* at in twelve years. As if it even mattered. Meanwhile, Pam was softly stroking my upper arm, trying to comfort me. It was time to end this conversation.

22

"Say, Miles, can I call you back later?"

"Sure, sure," he answered. "Say hello to Pam for me. Tell her she's sleeping with a dumb shit." He hung up.

When I set the phone down, Pam wrapped her arms around me, and cuddled her face against my chest.

"My God, Scott," she murmured. "You could've been killed."

Exactly. I pressed my fingers against the small of her back, and deftly massaged her lower spine. She seemed not to notice. Then she pushed away from me, and fixed her brilliant blue eyes upon my dull gray ones.

"That policeman..." she stammered, pleaded. "Is he...?"

"He's fine. His body armor stopped the bullet, left him with just a bruise."

"Oh, good!" she exclaimed, jumping up from the bed. "You have to give me those policemen's names, so I can thank them for saving your life!"

Their names? Thank *them*? What about *me*? Get back on this bed, I wanted to tell her, and show *me* some gratitude that I'm still here. But she was already out in the living room, digging in her purse for a pen and note pad. I gave her Skip's name and confessed, sheepishly, that I didn't know the young patrolman. She frowned, then indicated she'd call the police station and get it herself. Finally, she approached me and put her forearms on my shoulders, linking her fingers behind my neck.

"So, you're okay?" she asked softly.

"Want to come back in the bedroom and see for yourself?"

She smiled, removed her arms, picked up her purse, and turned for the door. "No, thanks. Maybe later."

"When later?"

"Later."

I was about to go after her when the phone rang again. She waited in the doorway while I answered it. It was Peggy Nowicki, the captain of the Dayfield Rescue Squad. When Pam heard me say Peggy's name, she waved and closed the door behind her. I felt a sudden, hollow ache at her departure.

"Yes, Peggy," I said into the phone. "What can I do for you?"

"I didn't think you'd be home. I was just going to leave a message on your machine." Peggy almost sounded apologetic, which is not her style. She's a tough broad, who neither expects nor grants much compassion.

"I took the day off. Do you need something?"

"Well, sort of, Scott. It has to do with the call you were on last night."

I wasn't surprised. "Yes?"

"Well, I've already received a couple of phone calls about it. Two or three board members would like to have a special meeting to discuss it. Sort of a 'debriefing', if you will. Could you make it, if we hold the meeting Wednesday evening?"

Did I have a choice? "Can you hold the meeting without me?"

"There wouldn't be much point."

"Okay, what time Wednesday?"

"Board meetings are usually held at 7:30. If you don't hear otherwise, assume that's when we'll get started. Get there early if you want to get a cup of coffee or something from the kitchen."

"Thanks, Peggy. I'll see you then." I hung up the phone. An interview with a newspaper reporter on Tuesday evening, and a "debriefing" with the squad's board of directors on Wednesday evening. My, wasn't I suddenly the popular one? Who else, I wondered, would be calling to schedule an appointment with the township's most sought-after eyewitness?

Less than two hours later—as I was intently watching Maxwell Smart outmaneuver a whole squadron of KAOS agents—I got an answer to that question. Billie DeMarino called, no doubt following a conversation with her friend, Peggy Nowicki.

"Mind if I help you check the rig tomorrow?" Billie offered.

"Hell, no, Chief," I answered. "You can do it by yourself, if you want. I won't be upset."

"It's not my turn," she kindly reminded me. "I just thought you'd like some company."

"Don't expect me to be much of a conversationalist at that hour."

"You're not much of a conversationalist at *any* hour," she replied, but still just as warmly. "I'll see you at 6:50. Bye."

NO WARNING

4

BILLIE DEMARINO IS MY PARTNER on the Tuesday day crew of the Dayfield Rescue Squad. She's another one of those do-gooders who got into EMS to save the world, or at least their corner of it, and only later tasted the unflavored truth. *Which is:* first aid volunteers are primarily hack drivers in unstylish jumpsuits, who do the on-scene grunt work for little or no recognition, and afterwards are permitted to mop up the festive assortment of bodily fluids that strangers leave behind in the back of the ambulance. If it was blood yesterday, it'll be puke today and piss tomorrow.

Well, maybe that's not an entirely accurate appraisal of Billie *or* of the work we do, but it's a reasonable start for an irritable EMT who would rather be anywhere else at seven in the morning.

Actually, it's not a fair description of Billie at all. If anybody ever walked into this avocation with their eyes open, and with a sober understanding of the first aider's second-class status in the world of modern health care, it was Billie DeMarino. In fact, it has often occurred to me that my partner—an attractive, long-married redhead who's ten years older than I am but who looks ten years younger—is patently out of place in the EMS environment. She has no business being here, although every week I thank God she is, and that I'm riding with her.

Out of respect, mainly, I call her "Chief."

Billie has a different outlook on emergency care, and thus she takes a different approach to it. While most of the squad's yahoos typically look for what's wrong and try, wrongly, to fix it, Billie holds on to what's right and tries to enhance it. The yahoos love it when a patient codes—i.e., goes into respiratory and/or cardiac arrest—but she despises it. The yahoo puts himself at the center of the picture, and sees another's tragedy as his chance to be the hero. Billie sees the reality of the moment. She sees a human being in pain, or perhaps in danger of death or permanent disability, and she feels for *them*. She has earned her share of *Save* pins over the years, but I doubt she's ever enjoyed receiving one. In other words, she's just too damned compassionate.

My partner has an adequate sense of humor, but has trouble applying it to EMS; I can usually joke with her about anything except the patient we just took in. In the five years we've worked together, we've traded insults about politics, career choices, sex lives and significant others. Regarding that last topic, I'd say we're about evenly matched. I'll readily concede that Billie's husband, the Italian attorney, has more smarts than my Pam. But thus far, every search party that's been dispatched to find Mark DeMarino's personality has returned empty-handed.

Tuesday mornings, Billie and I take turns inspecting the ambulance we'll be driving that day. When it's her turn, invariably I sleep in. When it's my turn, she'll occasionally show up to give me a hand. That's what she did this Tuesday morning, although I know her curiosity about the "Sunday Evening Episode" was at least partly the reason for her early appearance at the Hilltop ambulance bay. Not that she'd admit it, of course, but she did bring up the subject within five minutes of our bleary-eyed greeting.

I've found that each time I tell someone about that call, about that whole incident, I get further removed from it. I become more of a spectator, less of a participant. In the version I told Billie, I made sure to repeat the point that Miles had missed—that I had entered the Greers' house before the police arrived.

Billie listened silently until I finished. Then she asked just a few innocuous questions. She seemed more interested in Sergeant Skipinski's role in the drama than in mine, which didn't entirely surprise me. She and Skip have always had an affinity for one another, an attraction that I find fascinating because they won't even admit it, let alone act upon it. For one thing, she's married...if not happily, at least comfortably. For another, we've all been instructed in EMS training that working professionals are supposed to keep other working professionals at a respectful distance. That's the mandate, anyway, but it fails to allow for the heat that emergency work often generates—heat that's been known to cause unexpected chemical reactions.

Then again, maybe I'm reading something into their coy remarks and lingering glances that doesn't really exist. Maybe the occasions when Billie and Skip rub up against one another, while carrying a patient or when switching an oxygen line, are purely accidental. Maybe they're just good friends, and neither has any interest in the other beyond friendship.

And maybe Madonna's still a virgin, too.

At any rate, Billie didn't just lap up the details as I dished them out, she weighed and considered them. And she had the most insightful commentary of any I had yet heard on the subject.

"I remember," she started to say, "an incident very similar to yours, from when I lived in Milwaukee. As I recall, it resulted in a lawsuit against the police officer involved.

"The incident took place in a tavern just outside the Milwaukee city limits. A bartender was having problems with a loudmouthed drunk one night, so he cut him off. The drunk got belligerent and started breaking things. Somebody—not the bartender—got to a phone and called the police. Whoever made the call didn't realize, though, that the bar was in a suburb, so he called the Milwaukee cops.

"In the meantime, an off-duty cop from that suburb happened to be in the bar. When the drunk started smashing bottles and glasses and whatnot, the off-duty cop pulled his service gun out and subdued him. So when the Milwaukee police came rushing in, they saw one patron kneeling on the back of another patron, while holding a gun to his head. Pretty much what Skip encountered when he came upon you and Gary Greer, wouldn't you say?"

The situations were similar, I admitted, except in Billie's case it wasn't the drunk who was holding the gun.

"So what happened?" I asked.

"The Milwaukee police didn't know the off-duty cop. They yelled at him to drop the gun. And he, *being* a cop—in his own jurisdiction, no less—wasn't about to give up his weapon to somebody shouting at him from behind. He spun around and pointed his gun at the Milwaukee police.

"Now that's an action which will reduce your life expectancy to three seconds, at best. The Milwaukee cops riddled the poor guy. They were gracious enough, though, to credit him with the collar."

I pondered Billie's story for a minute, wondering for the first time if Skip might be in any trouble for having "riddled" Gary Greer. I quickly rejected the notion.

"One big difference, Chief," I said. "Greer shot at and hit Skip's partner. I would think that justifies his using whatever force necessary to take out Greer."

Billie nodded. "No doubt about that, Scott. But the question a lawyer might ask is whether Skip and his partner had reasonable cause to enter the house without first identifying themselves and requesting admittance. Just because a neighbor reported a domestic argument doesn't give them *carte blanche* to stroll in and start blazing away. Gary Greer had the right to assume some degree of privacy in his own home, even if he was bashing his wife.

"Besides...if, as you say, Skip and the other Dayfield cop didn't unholster their weapons until *after* being confronted with an armed Gary Greer, they can't very well claim that they knew of a life-threatening situation within. If *you* couldn't see into the living room from the front porch, neither could they. All the more reason they should not have entered unannounced."

Billie's husband, the lawyer, couldn't have done a better job at summarizing a possible case against the Dayfield Police. But where did that leave me? If the police had violated Gary Greer's rights, wasn't I better off—i.e., alive—because of it? Besides, who could possibly want to reopen the subject? Gary Greer was certainly in no condition to complain, and Angie Greer was, in all probability, better off a widow. That left...nobody. Didn't it?

"I assume you've talked to Peggy," I said.

"Yes."

"So what does the board want from me?"

Billie shrugged. "It's probably just routine. They want to know the details of the call, in case anybody should ask. Don't be too concerned about it, unless..." She hesitated. I could tell she knew more than she was saying, and I could guess why she was reluctant to continue. Peggy had told her something as a friend, and had requested that it go no further.

"Unless what?"

"Well, unless someone on the board wants to make an issue about how you handled the call. I didn't know—until you just told me—that you had entered the house first, before Skip arrived. Of course, it may not matter. But if it comes out at the board meeting, they might vote to slap your hand."

"Slap my hand?"

"Reprimand you for not adhering to squad regs. Although I'd assume you've learned your lesson."

Bee-bee-bee-bee-bee-bee-bee!

"Oh, shit!" We hadn't even finished checking the rig when our pagers sounded the familiar, irritating tones. I wasn't ready for this, not without a morning cup of coffee, and not in place of the discussion Billie and I were having.

She motioned for me to drive, while she climbed into the passenger's side of the ambulance. When the tones ended, the dispatcher called us: "Dayfield dispatch to the Dayfield Rescue Squad, please respond to a possible D.O.A. at 1572 Applecross Lane. Victim is male, age 48. Repeating Dayfield dispatch to the Dayfield Squad, please respond to a possible D.O.A. at 1572 Applecross Lane. Time is 7:12. Out."

Billie frowned and shook her head before picking up the radio handset to respond to the dispatcher. I knew what she was thinking: this was not going to be a fun call. A "possible D.O.A." usually means a corpse, discovered by a relative or a neighbor hours—and sometimes days—after the lights had gone out for good. We couldn't assume that, of course, so we went into service as always, with lights and sirens. On most such calls the police usually cancel us—tell us to go home—before we even reach the scene. They know dead as well as anybody, and are eminently capable of phoning the coroner.

On this occasion, we weren't canceled en route, although the police arrived at the house long before we did. Two patrol cars were in the driveway when we pulled up. Billie gave me a puzzled look before she grabbed the first aid kit and went in the house. I parked the rig and followed a minute later. The lack of information from within was troubling.

One thing more I should tell you about Billie before I continue: She knows damn near everybody in town. Between her job as a travel agent...and her numerous church and club affiliations...and her husband's law practice...and her son's activities, she has probably met and charmed every resident of Dayfield at least twice.

Does that matter, you ask? You better believe it. It matters because—contrary to all the evidence—some people still think that the arrival of an ambulance is proof positive the grim reaper is close behind. Patients with relatively minor ailments often panic, and aggravate their conditions, when the guys in the white jumpsuits show up.

But when the person in the white suit has a familiar and friendly face, the opposite effect can be expected. Frightened patients calm down; troublesome bystanders back off. On dozens of occasions I can remember, Billie has brought a scene under control just by walking in the room. If this work was important to me, I'd probably be jealous of her capability. But I'm too much of a pragmatist: Her high recognition factor simply makes my job easier.

This call was no exception. The man for whom we had been summoned was most assuredly deceased. "As dead as Elvis," as my friend Miles would say. He had gone the way most of us would prefer, I imagine, if given a choice. He had died in his sleep, in his bed, after complaining the night before of nothing more than feeling "a bit under the weather." His wife had come to the unpleasant realization of his current condition when, having failed to wake him by shouting and shaking the bed, she had touched his arm and found it disagreeably cool. She was now our patient.

Certainly, I can't imagine what it would be like to discover, without warning, one's mate of twenty-five years cold and stiff and gone forever. Nor could I guess how I would react—what thoughts I would have, what fears and regrets would burst to the surface. As foreign as these considerations are to me, they had probably been just fifteen minutes before to the woman Billie was now attempting to console.

She had been given no cause for concern. Her husband was healthy, and active, and needed. To find him dead this morning was simply outside the realm of possibility. She was devastated completely. When the police had arrived, she was incoherent, wandering about the house, shaking her arms and even slapping herself as if to end this awful nightmare. That's why they had allowed us to continue to the scene.

When Billie entered the house, she and the woman recognized each other at once. The two of them had worked together a few years before, on a project their children in high school had undertaken. As Billie would tell me later, their paths had crossed a few times after that, and they had always been pleasant and congenial to one another—something less than friends, but more than acquaintances. The woman's name was Vicki. When I came into the house, a minute later, Vicki was in Billie's arms, sobbing uncontrollably. Of course, I didn't know it at the time, but it was the catharsis the woman needed, to help her prepare for the empty and bewildering times ahead.

Billie's the absolute best in circumstances like these, and I'm among the worst. I never have a clue what to say or do. I mean, I know better than to ask: "Where's the stiff?", but I also *don't* know whether to sympathize or empathize. So usually I just dematerialize—get the hell out of the way and let my partner do her thing. There's no doubt: She's going to be emotionally exhausted by the time we leave, and upset—or depressed, maybe—for the next few days, but Billie wouldn't have it any other way.

Sometimes, EMS has nothing to do with blood and bandages. I wouldn't know that from first-hand experience, but—as Yogi Berra would say—you can observe a lot just by watching. And I've watched enough.

When the clergy arrived, about twenty minutes later, Billie gave me the signal to pack up. I waited outside for her, and held the rig's passenger door open while she wearily climbed in. We returned to the Hilltop bay in silence.

Just after I parked the rig, I turned to my partner. I couldn't help but say it: "You know, Chief, I've been meaning to ask you something for a few weeks now. If you don't mind…"

She shook her head, so I continued: "In a former life, did you ever serve aboard a slave ship?"

Billie stared at me impassively. She knew that *I* knew that she was in no mood for riddles. So she gave me the benefit of the doubt.

"A slave ship?" she verified.

"Yeah, you know, a *galley* ship, with the long oars and the fat guy in back beating the drum and the incentive managers strolling around with whips—a slave ship."

Again, she shook her head slowly, not in answer to my question, but with a mild disbelief that I had asked it. To what length would I go, she must have wondered, to find humor in a humorless situation?

At last she replied: "Scott, in my former lives—all four of them—I stayed on dry land, and rode horses, and sat with knights and ladies and court jesters. I never saw a ship, let alone served on one, until long after slavery was abolished. So you must be thinking of someone else."

"Yeah," I said, nodding in agreement. "Must be someone else."

Not so many years ago—two, maybe three—I honestly enjoyed my job. The pay was good and the benefits decent. More importantly, the working conditions were ideal for a malcontent like me.

My boss, Arnie Rosensteel, was a laid-back kind of guy who let me know what needed to be done, and then gave me the time and the tools necessary to do it. He assumed I was a professional and treated me like one. Ergo, I willingly busted my ass to affirm his assumption. We got along admirably.

It's not easy to describe the type of work we do at DataStaff Corporation, because it changes from week to week, from year to year. The common denominator of the projects we handle is that they involve statistical analysis of some sort.

When Arnie started the company, about fifteen years ago, he was an accomplished number-cruncher with a smattering of close contacts in the right places. With time, he developed an uncanny ability to sniff out money-making opportunities lurking in the most unlikely combinations of raw data and raw nerve. He'd pick up the phone and—as if by magic—get himself connected with a mid-level functionary at a major corporation who was about to launch a new product or enter a new market or otherwise undertake some risky venture. Typically, Arnie would ask a few insightful questions, using just the right mix of industry buzzwords that he'd learned the day before, and then extrapolate a plausible-sounding scenario of such virgin-pure bullshit that the sucker—er, prospective client—had no choice but to invite Arnie in to discuss the matter further.

At that point, Arnie would shift into high gear. He'd work non-stop for days, assembling interrelated bits of empirical evidence into a stunning presentation package that could, and did, convince even casehardened skeptics that they'd be ruined—financially and otherwise—if they embarked on their major ventures without retaining DataStaff Corporation to survey the unconquered lands awaiting. Once retained, Arnie would hand such projects off to underlings, like me, who would somehow fulfill the lofty promises on which said projects had been secured, or at least give the appearance of fulfilling same.

Now, I don't have Arnie's imagination, but I can stay with him when it comes to analyzing data, and I've been known to make stale, pallid information sing and dance, after running it through a few of my custom-made software programs. So that's what I do, mostly. I take data that's readily available—or dig it out, if I have to—then I massage and re-wrap it, and induce it to tell clients what they already know, or should know, but are nonetheless happy to pay for because it gives them a credible alibi in case something, anything, goes wrong.

It sounds like a shady racket and in some cases it is. But I *can* say, without shame, that we've never misguided or harmed a client, and have occasionally provided a true, valuable service. In at least two instances that I know of, our work actually proved to be of greater value than even Arnie himself could have stipulated, much to the delight of the fortunate clients who benefited by it. Arnie continues to use their glowing letters of recommendation, which he authored, in his new business presentations—although I'm sure he regrets not having charged the lucky bastards more in the first place.

Those were the glory years, when companies and county governments and assorted think tanks had money to spend on services like ours. My current job dissatisfaction, no doubt, is at least partly due to the austerity of more recent times. The budgets are smaller and the projects less innovative and interesting.

Worst of all, Arnie isn't the same, carefree guy he was a few years ago. He's become fanatical about meeting deadlines, and staying within budgets, and finding more efficient ways to get jobs completed and out the door. We use less "color" in our reports, and less original research. Whereas three years ago he'd send me off to Chicago or St. Louis without a second thought, just to track down a few elusive facts, now I'm lucky to get an afternoon at the local library. The pressure to produce just keeps building, while the rewards continue to shrink.

Yes, this ongoing recession has caused me some personal frustration, but at least I don't have to worry about where my next meal is coming from. If Arnie decided tomorrow that DataStaff could survive without benefit of my software wizardry, I could fall back on my inherited assets.

You see, my father did exceedingly well in the years before he retired, and—out of generosity or to avoid taxes, I'll never know—he passed a sizable portion of his holdings on to my brother and me. Forgive me for not divulging my net worth; suffice it to say I could survive on the interest alone if necessity dictated. Someday, I'll figure out what I want to do with the money, but in the meantime I have it squirreled away in the care of a trustworthy investment banker. Well, as trustworthy as any of them are, anyway.

A slight digression...

A few weeks ago, I received an ornate, personalized prospectus from a nearby country club, informing me that its board of managers was accepting applications from a "carefully selected group of successful, upwardly mobile achievers." After digesting that tidbit of pure puffery, my head had hardly begun to swell before I realized what it meant. *In effect,* my portfolio balance had qualified me to be on a list that the Walnut Grove Country Club had bought, at a premium, from a source that had no qualms (nor scruples, either) about renting out names like mine.

Pardon my candor, but *that* pisses me off. For a number of reasons, I prefer to keep my financial status to myself. Only my family and a few close friends know that I'm not living from paycheck to paycheck, and I like to keep it that way.

Yet, here these pompous country club goofs—who wouldn't have wasted the postage, let alone the prospectus, if they only knew me—had somehow ascertained my approximate worth, and were thus enticing me with their slathering descriptions to join their cherished establishment. They had apparently lumped me in with those self-aggrandizers who respond in a big way to tacky phrases such as "indulge yourself" and "reward all your hard work" and "let the world know that you've arrived, by becoming one of our elite associates" and so on, ad nauseam.

As I said, this invitation arrived a few weeks ago, but I can clearly remember the subsequent conversation I had with the blowhards. It went something like this:

"Good morning, and thank you for calling Walnut Grove Country Club. How may I direct your call?"

"I'd like to speak with your membership director, please."

"That would be Mr. Oswald. May I ask who is calling?"

"Yes, you may."

As I recall, this last statement of mine was followed by ten or fifteen seconds of silence. When the receptionist finally realized I had merely answered her question, she asked the appropriate follow-up: "Your name, sir?" Her voice was tinged with annoyance. I can't imagine what I had done to irritate her.

"Scott Jamison."

"And may I tell Mr. Oswald what this is in reference to?"

"Yes, you may," I answered again.

This time, she recovered much more quickly. The woman was no dummy. "What *is* this in reference to?"

"It's in reference to the prospectus I received in yesterday's mail."

All at once she became noticeably more attentive: "Oh! I'll connect you right away, Mr. Jamison."

From the receptionist's instant change of tone, I gathered that not just any schmoe had received an invitation to join the Walnut

Grove Country Club. Unlike those sweepstakes packets from Publishers Anonymous, that congratulate you for being one of a lucky few to have won a magnificent prize, and that arrive bulk rate.

I imagined the conversation then taking place between the receptionist and the membership director, Mr. Oswald. Though I'd spoken with her, I had formed no image of the woman. But I could already picture the fellow whose calls she was paid to screen. Mr. Oswald would burst onto the line in a moment, bubbly and gracious and finely humored, a salesman who can pretend—who is *encouraged* to pretend—that he's not merely a salesman. I was ready for him.

"Mr. Jamison! How nice of you to call! How may I be of assistance to you this fine morning?"

His voice told me that he was all that I expected, and then some. In my visualization, Mr. Oswald went from 5'10" to an even 6'0". From Brooks Brothers to Armani. From Duke to Yale. From the Rotary Club to the Athletic Club. Sometimes, you can tell a lot from the first twenty words.

"Well, I received your prospectus yesterday, and I must say it's aroused my interest–"

"Whetted your appetite, eh?"

"You might say that–"

"Good, good. But let me *also* say, Mr. Jamison, that the prospectus doesn't do justice to the total ambience of Walnut Grove. You simply *must* come down and have a look around. We're only fifteen minutes from your home in Dayfield, and we can schedule a tour of the facilities at your convenience."

Wasn't this interesting? I had phoned him, out of the blue, yet he knew immediately where I was calling from. Now my visualization expanded, to include a personal computer at his fingertips. He was running a database that had just been prompted for my name. I wished I could peek over his shoulder, to see what program he was using, and to see what else was in my file.

"Uh, could I get back to you in a minute, Mr. Oswald? Something just came up that I have to take care of." I hoped he would bite.

He did. "Of course! How about if I call you?"

"Yes, please do. Give me five minutes, and call me at my work number."

He confirmed the number without my giving it to him. I hung up, and quickly cross-tabulated the personal data that the Walnut Grove Country Club had likely accessed before deeming me worthy of an invitation. I jotted down a few questions to ask Mr. Oswald—in all apparent innocence—that would help me determine the source of his information. Being in the data business, this was a game to me. And since I felt my privacy had been invaded, and/or a confidence betrayed, it was a game I intended to pursue in all earnestness.

My first move was to call our receptionist, Francine Hufnagel. I prayed she wasn't gossiping with one of her lady friends when I punched the "0" button on my phone.

"Yes, Scott?" Fran answered, knowing from her control module who was calling. There's no privacy left in the world, is there?

"Fran, dear," I said in the sweetest voice I could manage, "would you do me a favor, please?"

"Depends what it is," she answered simply.

"I'm expecting a call in the next five minutes from, ah, a possible client–"

"Who's the prospect?" she interrupted.

"The Walnut Grove Country Club."

"Nice place," she commented. "A little on the snooty side, but the food's okay."

"You've been there?" I asked, with perhaps too much surprise in my voice. Bad move on my part.

"Yes, Mr. Big Shot," she replied, sounding miffed. "You don't raise four kids these days without hosting and attending a couple dozen private social affairs. I was there for a wedding reception—no, it was a bat mitzvah—a few years ago."

"But I thought it was a new place."

"Nah," she scoffed. "I heard it was recently taken over by a group of investors, but it's been around for awhile. I hope the new owners replaced those awful drapes in the main dining room."

"Well, anyway, Fran, the call I'm expecting will be from a Mr.

Oswald–"

"How do you spell that?"

"I don't know. Like it sounds, I guess. You can ask him when he calls. If a secretary places the call for him, try and get her name–"

"*Try?*" Fran mimicked me, as though insulted. Of course Fran would get her name…and her age, weight, and sexual proclivities, if I wanted them. Maybe even if I didn't want them. Fran is the absolute best at wheedling information out of people, strangers especially, while ostensibly just making small talk.

"Okay, get her name," I continued, "but don't make a big deal about getting Oswald on the line before putting the call through to me."

"You don't have to tell me that," she sniffed.

"I know…just making sure. But if you *do* get Oswald on the line, don't mention their shitty drapes, or anything else about the club. Act like you've never even heard of the place–"

"Why?" she interrupted again.

"I don't have time to explain now," I said, not having a handy excuse to toss her. Then, thinking of one, I added: "We may be doing an awareness study for them, and it strengthens our case if they perceive they're not well known."

"Oh," she said. "Well, then, do you want me to mention the names of a few other clubs—like Millbrook, and Calais, and Misty Mountain—so he doesn't just think I'm some ignorant *putz*, as you apparently do."

I winced at this. "Fran," I said consolingly, "I never said you were ignorant–"

"But you *think* I am," she snapped.

"That's not true. Now, look, are you going to help me with this guy, or not?"

"What do you want me to find out?" she pouted.

What did I want her to find out? "Well, first of all," I groped, "don't start pitching DataStaff to him. He doesn't know, yet, that we're, ah, seeking to do business with them, and I don't want–"

"You don't want him to find out from the likes of me."

She could be so exasperating. "Fran, stop being so defensive, and just listen for a minute, will you?"

Her silence told me she got the message. I continued: "If you can, find out how long he's been working there. See if you can learn anything about his background: if he's been in marketing, or the hospitality industry, or sales. Also, if you can do it without being a noodge—"

"A *noodge?*"

"—find out if he's from the area, or if he moved here from somewhere else. Do you have all that?"

"So you think I'm a noodge, do you?"

"I think you're a wonderful person, Francine, and I'm fortunate to be working with you." It was bullshit, and she knew it, but it nonetheless softened the bite of my earlier comment.

"I'll get back to you," she said, hanging up.

Six minutes later, she buzzed me. I knew enough to have a pad and pen ready when I picked up the phone. "Yes, Fran?" I answered.

"Your Mr. Oswald is on line four. I told him you'd be with him in a minute. He said he'd wait.

"His secretary's name is Jill Polet. She's worked there for five years, and doesn't seem too impressed with the new owners. I'd say she's in her early thirties—thirty-five, tops. No kids, lives five minutes from work.

"Oswald came on with the new regime. Used to have a similar position somewhere in Connecticut. Went to Dartmouth, but I don't think he graduated. Loves to play golf; says he's a five handicapper—whatever that means. He used to live in Jersey...grew up in Rumson, but only moved back here with the job, four months ago. He was *very* interested in what I had to say about the other private clubs in the area, especially Calais. Didn't seem to believe me when I said I'd never heard of Walnut Grove, so I said I wasn't sure if I had or not..."

I was writing furiously, trying to keep up with Fran's verbal barrage. Arnie had done well when he hired her; she could learn more about a prospect's background in five minutes than a private investigator could in a week.

"...he's married, two kids, one of each. Wife works part time. Can't stand his mother-in-law—welcome to the club. He's a firm believer in direct mail, says it increased membership–"

"Hold it, Fran," I interrupted. "What was that again?"

"What? That Oswald doesn't get along with his mother-in-law?"

"No, just after that."

I waited while she reviewed her notes, which must have been in shorthand. Then she said: "He's big on doing direct mail campaigns. Said something about 'pinpoint marketing' and 'demographics'. That's the kind of stuff we do here, isn't it?"

"Yeah, sometimes," I answered absently.

"Well, he says a recent campaign increased membership applications by twenty-two percent. He seemed real proud of that."

"I'll bet," I murmured.

"Yes, well, that's about all I got from him, on such short notice. Give me some warning next time, and I'll do better. You should pick up now. You know how Arnie hates to keep clients on hold."

"Okay. Thanks for all your help, Fran."

"No problem," she replied. "Should I copy Arnie on the report?"

Uh oh. "What report?" I asked.

"A prospect report, dummy. Arnie always has me type up one for his files. Won't you need one for yours?" A suspicious tone had crept into her voice.

"No, no, that won't be necessary, Fran," I said. "We're not likely to get any work out of these people. I'm just following a lead."

"All the same..." she responded, her voice trailing off. I knew what *that* meant: she wasn't going to be held responsible.

"Tell you what, Fran," I offered. "Let me see how the call goes. If there's any potential there, I'll let you know. Then you can do the prospect report."

She grunted a half-hearted assent. I pushed the button for line four. "Mr. Oswald! So sorry to keep you holding," I said.

"No problem," he answered cheerfully. "I'd rather wait for an industrious man than speak with an idle one."

How many times had he used that line before?

"Business must be booming there at DataStaff," he ventured.

"Oh, we've had our share of good times," I answered vaguely.

41

"What sort of work is it that you do, if I might ask?"

"A little of this and a lot of that," I replied, even more vaguely. I wanted to be asking the questions here, not answering them. Somehow, I had to get back in the driver's seat. I did it clumsily: "But let's not talk about me, Mr. Oswald, let's talk about Walnut Grove."

"Yes, let's," he agreed.

"You know Groucho Marx's old line, don't you?" I was reasonably certain I didn't have to specify *which* line.

"Oh, yes," he laughed, a laugh that came from his throat. "Groucho said he wouldn't belong to any club that would accept someone like him as a member."

"Yes, exactly," I said. "I couldn't help but think of it as I read through your prospectus."

"And why is that?" he asked.

"Well," I replied, "I'm curious to know why you contacted me. Why did you select me, of all people, to receive your prospectus and invitation?" I started with the *why*, hoping that the *how* would follow.

Mr. Oswald answered: "Offhand, I can't say why…"

Which was bullshit.

"…but in all probability you received an endorsement from one of our current members…"

More bullshit.

"…or you've been recognized in your community, or among your peers, for your contributions to society—or to the industry in which you work. We don't invite just anyone to become a member of Walnut Grove, Mr. Jamison. We take great pains to attract only those individuals who've distinguished themselves in some way, and whose association with Walnut Grove would enhance their prestige, as well as ours."

I wondered if he was reading from a script. If not, he could certainly sling it. Not even by inference did he introduce the subject of financial resources. I guessed that would be my job.

"Um, how much does a membership cost?" I asked, as though speaking with the desk clerk at the local YMCA.

He sounded offended when he responded to my tactless query:

"Mr. Jamison, it would hardly be appropriate to discuss our fees and bond considerations at this point, over the phone. Why don't we schedule you for a personalized tour—say, next week?—at which time we can answer all your questions. I'm sure you'll be very impressed with everything we have to offer, for an investment that is most reasonable."

"I just don't want to waste your time, if it turns out I can't afford it."

His patience was starting to flag. "I don't see that as a problem, Mr. Jamison."

What didn't he see as a problem? That I would waste his time? Or that I couldn't afford it? Only one way to find out: "Why not?" I asked.

"Mr. Jamison, trust me. We've done our homework. We wouldn't be having this conversation right now if we felt you couldn't meet *all* the requirements for membership at Walnut Grove."

Bing-o. Mr. Oswald had just answered the first of the two big questions. Now, was he ready for the second one? If he was the marketing maven he imagined himself to be, the answer could probably be found in the next active field on his computer screen—right after the code that had reported to him my estimated assets. I asked the question with all the tact and diplomacy I could muster: "Who told you I had money?"

For the first time, I left him speechless. I immediately realized that—with my blunt, profane approach—I had blown any chance that I might get an answer to my question. But, if only for the moment of silence purchased by my candor, it had been worth it.

"I–I'm not sure I know what you mean," he stammered at last.

"Mr. Oswald," I said brusquely, "let's not play games. I don't know any of your members, and I haven't discovered a cure for AIDS. So—if I might borrow your phrase—the only reason we're having this conversation is because you've learned of my personal wealth. I'd just like to know how you got that information."

Another glorious moment of dead air. Then: "Mr. Jamison, it's been a delight to speak with you. I'm sorry that our services and your needs are not mutually suitable. Have a pleasant life." With that, he hung up.

I had hardly replaced the handset in its cradle when the phone buzzed with an internal call. And I had hardly brought it back up to my ear when Fran asked, abruptly: "Well?"

"Just as I thought, Fran," I said, faking a sigh. "A dead end. No chance for business there."

"Mm-hmm, okay," she answered. "Just do me a favor, would you, Scott?"

"Sure, Fran."

"From now on, let Arnie handle the sales work. No offense, but you couldn't sell cold beer to a thirsty sailor."

NO RESPECT

6

BEFORE I TELL YOU ABOUT MY interview with Dorothy McCrae, ace reporter, let me tell you what I know about *The Dayfield Dispatch*, the paper that employs her. In three words, it's a rag. It serves its purpose, I guess, if its purpose is to stroke the egos of the town's social climbers, and to cheerlead for the local sports teams. You can also count on it for the usual birth and death announcements, and detailed listings of all the poor sons-of-bitches clocked doing 48 in a 35 m.p.h. speed trap.

But as far as serious journalism goes, you'll never mistake *The Dispatch* for *The New York Times*. Which isn't all bad, of course, but which might tell you why I was somewhat reluctant to meet with Ms. McCrae and, once again, retell the story of Gary Greer's final few minutes. If reported accurately—a remote possibility—the story wasn't going to do me any good. If botched, it could very well do me harm. Nevertheless, I had agreed to meet Dorothy McCrae on Tuesday evening, so I showed up at the Hilltop Diner, only ten minutes late, and started looking around for her red baseball cap.

Nearly every seat in the diner was filled, but I had no trouble spotting her. She was in one of

45

the two corner booths, sipping a cup of tea and reading a newspaper that was laying flat on the table. It was not *The Dispatch*.

The front of her cap sported an unmistakable logo: the intertwined letters of the St. Louis Cardinals. The rest of her garb was even less stylish. She wore an oversized, faded denim shirt—open three buttons from the neck—a pair of torn jeans, and paint-splotched deck shoes. A well-traveled but nondescript pocketbook sat beside her. She was apparently not seeking to impress me or anyone else with her wardrobe.

"Dorothy McCrae?" I asked as I approached her table. I received no reply. For a moment, she didn't even move, making me think I was implausibly mistaken. I glanced around for another baseball cap. The Cincinnati Reds, maybe? Then, she raised her index finger, while continuing to study an article in the paper. She held the finger aloft for ten or fifteen seconds, in effect asking me to wait while she finished reading. I was annoyed by her rude behavior, but waited anyway. Then, before she even acknowledged me or my question, she took a pen from her breast pocket and circled several paragraphs in the article. I looked at my watch.

"Scott Jamison," she said finally, setting the pen down and extending her hand my way. I regarded it momentarily before shaking it. No jewelry, no nail polish, no nothing. "Thanks for coming. Have a seat."

As I slid into the booth, Dorothy McCrae gave me the once-over, not even trying to disguise her appraisal process. Her eyes wandered all over me as she checked out my features, my hair, my clothes—everything—making mental notes as she went. I half-expected her to examine my teeth, as one does to a horse they're thinking to buy.

"So how long have you been on the rescue squad?" she asked directly, making no attempt at small talk.

I ignored the question, and started looking at the menu. Two could play at this game. "What would you recommend here?" I asked.

She shrugged. "Order what you want," she said. "It's on me."

"That's not necessary."

"Good. I've already maxed out my expense account."

"Four years," I said flatly, hoping to catch her off-guard. I didn't.

"Was this the first shootout you witnessed?"

"On or off the squad?"

"Either way," she said, producing a small cassette recorder from her pocketbook and, without asking permission, switching it on.

"Either way," I answered, "yes."

"Was Sergeant Skipinski justified in shooting Gary Greer?"

"Absolutely."

"Six times?"

"Was Gary Greer a drug dealer?"

She regarded me with narrowed eyes. Hazel, I noticed, and managing quite well without benefit of mascara or shadow. Maybe because I was evaluating them it took me a few seconds to fathom her problem. She had taken my last question the wrong way, although I had just been playing her irritating little game—asking instead of answering. I hadn't expected our queries to collide.

"There's such a thing as *due process*, you know." Her voice had a touch of irritation in it, though her face remained neutral.

"Let's start over, shall we?" I offered. "Pleased to meet you, Dorothy."

"What were you doing in the Greers' house?" She took off her baseball cap and shook her hair free. It was pale blonde, but not naturally so. Considering her total lack of make-up, or any other embellishments, that surprised me.

I paused, and then motioned for the waitress. After requesting a hamburger and a salad, I asked Dorothy if she wanted anything. She ordered a bagel, toasted. The waitress took our menus and left.

"I was responding to a call for help. It's what we do."

"Had you ever known or met the Greers before?"

"Not to my knowledge, no."

"The police told me that Gary Greer was holding a gun to your head when they arrived. Did he think you were an intruder?"

"From what little I heard from Greer, he suspected his wife was having an affair. Something made him think I was the guilty party." I eyed the cassette recorder, uncomfortable that it was preserving words I might later regret having said.

47

"Was she *having an affair*?" Dorothy McCrae altered her tone slightly when repeating the euphemism, as though mocking my use of the sanitized expression. I wondered, briefly, what she would have preferred. Fucking around?

"You'd have to ask Angie Greer that question. I have no idea. Besides, is it really relevant to the article you're writing?"

Dorothy shrugged again, as if she wasn't sure herself. Then she looked at me evenly. "In your own words, Scott," she said, with a warmth I hadn't detected before, "tell me what happened from the moment the police entered the house, until Gary Greer was dead. I've read the official report, but I want to hear it from you."

And so, once more, I repeated the story. This, I assumed, would be the version most people would learn, once Dorothy's article was printed. So I was very careful in providing the details. She interrupted me two or three times to clarify minor points. I will admit: she was very thorough. She assumed nothing, and refused to let me gloss over details that I considered insignificant. Thankfully, though, she didn't seem to know that I should have waited for the police before entering the house. Naturally, I didn't volunteer the information.

I finished my recital just as the waitress brought our orders. Dorothy switched off the cassette recorder and turned her attention to her bagel. We sat like an old married couple for a few minutes, saying nothing as we seasoned and sampled our dinners.

"So, are you a Cardinals fan?" I asked finally.

She squinted at me, perplexed. "Who?"

"The St. Louis Cardinals. The baseball team. That's their cap you're wearing."

She picked up the cap and studied it for a moment. "Oh, so that's what those letters mean. I never knew. Never cared, really. A friend gave me this cap a few years ago. I don't wear it often."

"Only when meeting someone you want to impress, I take it."

She actually smiled. "Are you impressed, Scott?" she asked, with a mouthful of buttered dough.

"With your journalistic talents, somewhat. With anything else, no. Which, I would bet, is just as you want it. You work very hard at being unimpressive."

"Maybe too hard," she answered. Then she turned the cassette recorder on again. I'd only had two bites of my hamburger, and she was already preparing to resume the interview. Quickly I took another bite and washed it down. I didn't want my voice recorded through a filter of semi-cooked, semi-masticated ground beef.

"What condition was Angela Greer in?" she asked, less concerned than I was, apparently, about her dinner's effect on her enunciation.

"At what point?" I countered.

"At any point. When you arrived, when it was over." She wiped her mouth—with her napkin, no less—before she started writing again. The woman was an enigma to me.

"When I arrived, she looked terrible. The human face, as you may know, is loaded with capillaries. Facial trauma tends to result in excessive effusion."

"Could you spell that?"

"Yes. B-l-o-o-d. Lots of it."

Dorothy stopped writing and, for the second time, smiled at me. Her hazel eyes twinkled. I continued: "But by the time it was over, I imagine she wasn't worrying about her appearance. Neither was I, actually."

"You think you're pretty clever, don't you?" Her smile lingered.

"Never thought about it," I replied brusquely. "Next question."

Her smile disappeared and, for just a moment, I regretted being so curt. She looked down at her notes. While she formulated another question, I finished off my hamburger.

"What would have happened," she asked at last, "if you hadn't responded to Mrs. Greer's call for help?"

A good question—one that I'd asked myself numerous times in the two days since. The trouble was, I didn't like the answer I invariably came up with: Gary Greer would probably still be alive.

"You're a journalist, aren't you?"

Such a sleazy way to fend off a legitimate inquiry. Dorothy frowned at me before she answered: "I consider myself one, yes."

"Then why are you concerned with what *might* have happened? Isn't it your job to report what *did* happen?"

She refused to back down. "There's a fine line here, Scott, one that you've obviously missed. I'm not interested in knowing what *might* have happened. I'd just like to know what *should* have happened. Something went wrong in that house. The police and rescue squad had been there on several previous occasions, and no one had ever pulled a gun. Why this time?"

Another good question. But since I had no idea what the answer was, I merely shrugged. "Accidents happen," I said lamely.

Her eyebrow shot up. "So that's how you would classify Mr. Greer's death? An accident? He absorbed six bullets by accident?"

What did she want from me? "From that standpoint, no. Skip shot him deliberately, in self-defense. But nobody planned for it to happen. What are you looking for, anyway? A conspiracy? These things happen all the time, Ms. McCrae. People get drunk, people get pissed, people get shot. It happens all the time."

"Not in Dayfield, it doesn't."

"Well, so now you have something to write about, don't you?" I glanced at my watch. "Is there anything else you wanted to ask me?" I hoped we were finished.

"Yeah, one more question, Scott. I want to know how this affected you. It's a popular theory these days that people have become inured to violence, because they see so much of it on the tube. What about you? Did it upset you to see another person shot to death, right in front of you?"

"I don't watch much TV."

"Answer the question, wouldya?"

"I thought I did."

She pondered this for a second, then wrote something else on her note pad. "So it *did* bother you, huh?" she asked.

"I went home and threw up. Is that what you wanted to hear? I never claimed to be Clint Eastwood."

She nodded slowly. "Can I quote you on that?"

"On one condition," I said flatly. "Answer a question for me."

"Shoot."

"You have such pretty blond hair…" I hesitated.

"Yeah? You think so?"

"Yeah, I think so. So why do you dye the roots dark brown?"

NO DECISION

(7)

AMONG FRIENDS. THAT'S WHERE I assumed I was, the next evening, and thus I assumed the questions would be a bit more cordial than the ones Dorothy McCrae had thrown at me. As it turned out, my assumptions were completely groundless.

The seven members of the Dayfield Rescue Squad's board of directors nodded at me as they came into the meeting room from the adjacent kitchen. Most of them did, anyway. One by one, they gingerly carried their cups of coffee or cans of soda, and sat down behind two long tables that had been placed end-to-end. I was already seated, alone, at a small table facing them.

"Would it be all right if Billie and Miles sat in?" I asked, not sure who among the group I should be addressing.

Six sets of eyes turned to...Karen? Carol? I always get the two of them mixed up. The one who spoke—Carol, I think—is the board's parliamentarian. "You can call them in if you need corroboration on a particular point. But otherwise, no, they'll have to wait outside."

I turned to my friends and lifted my hands, palms up. Miles did likewise in response.

"Catch you later," he said, as he and Billie left the room and closed the door behind them.

Hank Cindrich, the squad president, picked up a small gavel from the table. He held it aloft for a moment and twirled it, impatiently, between his thumb and his forefinger. Noticing his action, Karen, or Carol, pulled a cassette recorder from her squad jacket, set it on the table and turned it on. Yet again were my words on *The Greer Call* to be preserved on tape for future examination. Hank tapped the table lightly with the gavel. "This board meeting of the Dayfield Rescue Squad is now in order," he said. "Carol, would you please call the roll?"

If I'd had any doubts before, I realized at this point they were going to do this by the book. Immediately the back of my left hand started to itch. I scratched it with the side of my pen.

"Peggy Nowicki."

"Present," Peggy said, sounding bored, as usual. Peggy has been squad captain long enough to know when a special board meeting is of any real importance, and when it's just a bitch session. If her opinion of this evening's proceedings could be discerned from the tone of her voice, we were in for a bitch session.

"Jerry Boronski."

"Present." Jerry, one of the squad's two lieutenants, has always been a standup fellow. He takes himself a little too seriously, perhaps, but usually knows what he's talking about. Does his job quietly and effectively. In high school, I would bet, he wasn't voted most popular, best-looking or wittiest, but he was probably a damn good partner to have in chem lab. Thorough, efficient, detail-oriented. Someone once told me he's an engineer by profession, which makes perfect sense.

"Mike Marder."

"Present." Now the back of my right hand started to itch too. From the day I met him, Mike Marder has never been one of my favorite people, on or off the squad. And since he was elected lieutenant—a position of some authority—he has given me even less reason to like him. If anyone was going to hassle me this evening, it was going to be Mike.

At some point in your life, you've probably worked with or

lived next door to Mike. He's the guy who knows it all, or at least thinks he does, and tries to prove it by finding fault with everything that anyone else says or does. I think he's employed by a marketing firm, but I'm not sure about that; he's changed jobs once or twice since I've known him. Mike has a few redeeming qualities, no doubt, but outside of a passing resemblance to yours truly, I've never noticed any.

"Hank Cindrich."

"Here." Depending on your viewpoint, Hank is either the best president the Dayfield Rescue Squad has ever had, or the worst. He runs a lean operation, with no time for long-winded discussions, no inclination for pomp or ceremony, no interest in extracurricular activities, and no patience for matters of marginal importance. He's a long-time worker for the road crew in town, so he's not accustomed to meetings and memos and other forms of corporate bullshit. Some complain that Hank pays no attention to details, but I've always liked his quick, to-the-point proceedings. With any luck, Hank would get this ordeal behind us with minimal pain and wasted time.

"Joshua Menzel."

"Who?" Having never attended a board meeting before, I didn't know that "Who?" was the usual response Joshua gave when his name was called. I also didn't know his name was Joshua; he's always been "Stick" to me. Stick Menzel is easily distinguished in a crowd of EMS personnel because of his unique body shape: he's the thin one. He probably weighs less than his IQ, though he's by no means brilliant.

Stick works in a hardware store in Ironport, a town adjacent to Dayfield. He's a harmless, nervous, eager-to-please type who became vice president because no one else wanted the job. Nonetheless, prayers are regularly offered by most squad members that Hank doesn't get hit by a bus.

"Karen Weyrich."

"Present."

"And Carol Hartshorne is present, too." said Carol, completing her roll call.

If you could see the two of them—Karen and Carol—seated

side-by-side, you'd know why I have such difficulty remembering which one is which. If you would describe Karen, the squad treasurer, as plump, then you would have no choice but to say that Carol, the secretary, is obese. They both have medium-length, non-descript brown hair. They talk alike, they ride together, they live together…and they're lovers. Seeing Karen without hearing Carol nearby is like seeing lightning and not hearing thunder. It happens, but only under special circumstances.

As far as their relationship goes, it's generally known and *almost* generally accepted by the squad. A few old-timers grumble about it on occasion, but since both women are excellent EMTs, to say nothing of dependable volunteers, even the bible-thumpers among us have learned to keep their opinions to themselves. Me, I really don't care. If some people prefer to bed down with members of their own sex, or with orangutans or watermelons for that matter, it's okay with me. As long as the orangutans don't mind.

My only problem—and it *is* a problem, I admit—is that I'm occasionally afflicted with a mental image of the two of them, Karen and Carol, grappling and groaning between the sheets, and I have to distract myself to make the image vanish. Thinking about orangutans usually helps.

"Okay, let's get started then," said Hank. "Mike, I believe you requested this meeting, so let's hear what's on your mind. Do you intend to bring charges against Scott, or what?"

Charges?

Mike Marder hadn't expected Hank to reveal, so abruptly, what this meeting was all about, but he was no more taken aback than I was. Had I heard the word *charges?*

"Well," Mike began slowly, looking at Carol, or Karen, for help, "I don't know if that's the proper, er, procedure in this instance, but there are a few irregularities about how the call was handled on Sunday that we, ah, the board, should look into. For one…"

Mike was just beginning to get his stride when Stick interrupted him. "Which call was that, Mike?"

Peggy rolled her eyes and Hank buried his face in his hands. "The shootout, Stick, on Kilbourn Avenue," Hank said from behind his palms. Then, lifting his head free, he added: "Didn't you hear about it?"

"Oh, yeah," Stick remembered. "I was *on* that call." Turning to me, he asked: "Were *you* on that call, Scott?"

"I scrambled to the scene, Stick," I said obligingly.

"Oh. I didn't see you there."

"Anyway," Mike Marder continued, "I think there's a problem that we should, ah, try to resolve tonight. I'm hoping Scott will be able to help us."

He didn't even look at me as he said it, so he didn't see me scratching my forearms. Rather, he walked over to the chalkboard on the wall behind him and started to draw something. I noticed Hank glancing at his watch, but everyone else was paying close attention to Mike's drawing.

Mike showed some artistic talent with the chalk as he sketched the general layout of the Greers' house, driveway, yard and immediate neighborhood. It wasn't perfectly to scale, but close enough. When he finished, he turned and calmly asked me where I had parked upon arriving. He drew in a rectangle representing my car when I told him. Then he asked me where the police had parked.

Of course, I hesitated. Just long enough for Hank to break in. "Does this really matter, Mike?" he asked.

"I think it does," Mike answered.

"Well, then, let me ask you this before we get off the subject. Are you planning to assert that Scott rendered improper care on this call?"

Mike Marder tilted his head, as though he didn't understand Hank's question. Carol—I'm sure it was Carol—came to Mike's assistance.

"Actually, Hank," she offered, "Scott rendered *no* care on this call. I think that's what Mike is leading up to."

Mike didn't verify or dispute the assumption. Rather, he said: "Why don't we just let Scott answer my question. We'll get into the matter of patient care shortly."

I knew damn well what Mike was looking for, and so did he. Somehow, he had learned that I had entered the house before the police arrived. It was going to come out sooner or later anyway, so I figured it would be best if I just admitted it and faced the consequences. As Billie had said, they would probably just slap my hand and be done with it. They'd reprimand me, or suspend me for a week or two. I could certainly live with that, couldn't I?

But something made me stall.

"Well, Mike, as you know, I arrived at the scene before the police did. Then I got into a conversation with the woman who lives next door. She was the one who called the police, I think." Again I hesitated, hoping someone would ask another question, one that would get us off this track. But no one spoke. Mike merely nodded once.

"I don't remember the woman's name…"

"Fay Johnson." It was…Karen?, reading from a sheet of paper, who filled the gap in my memory.

"Yes, Fay Johnson. Thank you,…" My benefactress smiled slightly, but offered nothing more. I continued: "…and she was standing on the front lawn with her sheepdog. She and the dog were both upset; we could hear Angie Greer in the house screaming for help. I'm not sure where the police parked."

There. I slid it in as unobtrusively as I could, but I definitely answered the question. I noticed Peggy Nowicki's eyes narrowing slightly, and Jerry Boronski making a note on a scrap of paper. Otherwise, my statement caused no discernible reaction. Now I could only hope Mike would leave it at that.

"What made you ask Fay Johnson if there was a man in the house?"

If he had touched me with a live wire, Mike couldn't have done a better job of shocking me to my shoes. Until now, I assumed he had been guessing at what had happened that night. And if push came to shove, I figured I could fabricate whole conversations, and invent numerous mitigating factors, to reduce my exposure. That's what I had figured, but Mike's question suddenly made me feel as if my pants were down. My bare ass was exposed for a whipping.

I could hardly form the words, let alone say them: "Did I?"

"She says you did."

She says I did. But *who* had talked to her? And why did it matter anyway? Why were my arms, and the back of my neck, and the bridge of my nose, itching so furiously? After all, it wasn't like my *career* was on the line. This was a *volunteer* activity, one that I had gotten into almost on a lark. And over the years, I had often been tempted to tell these people to take their precious rescue squad and shove it. Now, at least two of them were practically begging me to say it. A large part of me wanted to do just that.

But my instincts were instructing me otherwise. Maybe a lingering sense of guilt, or of self-righteousness, was compelling me to be acquiescent, and to ride out the storm. One thing was becoming clearer to me: There was more going on here than I could grasp.

"Well, Fay gets confused," I answered. "She once called the police and told them an armored tank was patrolling her neighborhood. What she thought was a tank was a municipal street sweeper." That got me a couple of smiles, but no time.

"Let's not impeach the source, Scott. Just answer the question. Why did you ask Fay Johnson if a man was in the house?" Now the squad secretary—Carol, definitely—wanted an answer.

I wasn't going to tap dance my way out of this jam, so I had to think. The precise chalk drawing...the question about the cops' arrival...an accurate knowledge of my words to Fay Johnson—these things all had meaning. Or they did to Mike Marder and Carol Hartshorne, at least. Did anybody else know where this was going? I looked from face to face, searching for clues.

Hank and Peggy were expressionless, and Jerry was either writing or doodling on the same scrap of paper as before. Karen was gazing at Carol. Stick was, was—oh, shit, why do these things happen to me? I didn't mention it before, but Stick Menzel has this annoying habit: he frequently picks at something in the corner of his eye and then, when he's finally able to capture it, he brings it out about six inches in front of his nose and examines it—whatever it is—thoroughly. Like an entomologist examines a bug. Whenever I witness this exercise, I can't help but wonder: what the hell is he looking at? So when I noticed him at it again as I glanced at each of the squad officers, I broke into a grin.

Peggy and Jerry followed my glance, and immediately deduced the cause of my amusement. They smiled themselves. But Carol Hartshorne, unfortunately, did not realize I had been distracted. She saw only my grin, in response to her question.

"Do you find this amusing, Scott?" Her voice was testy.

"Oh, no, Karen…" I blurted.

"Carol," she corrected, even more curtly.

"No, Carol, I was just…thinking about something else. I'm sorry. What was the question again?" I had honestly forgotten. My thanks to Stick for the comic relief.

"Why did you ask Fay Johnson if Gary Greer had left the house?"

Carol rephrased the question Mike had originally asked, and Mike winced slightly when she did. Like a teacher winces when her star pupil misspells a simple word. Like a coach winces when his quarterback fumbles the ball. Like a prosecutor winces when the eyewitness admits he's myopic. It wasn't much, but it was significant…

Then it hit me. In following Mike's lead, Carol had overplayed her hand. They weren't interested in the answer to the question; they just wanted me to admit that I had asked it of Fay Johnson. If I was going to be nailed for anything that had happened at the Greers' house that night, it wasn't my actions, but my *words*, that were about to be hammered.

You see, I had been fooling myself, dancing around the issue of when the police had arrived. Mike Marder knew for certain I had broken the rules, and also knew he could prove it. What he needed to establish first, however, was that I had prior knowledge of the regulation I had trashed. He knew, and I knew, that the board could forgive ignorance. Hell, if it was a crime to be ignorant, several yahoos on the squad would be serving life sentences. But the board *couldn't* forgive deliberate disobedience. If I had asked Fay Johnson if there was a man inside, I must have *known* there was a risk in entering the house alone, and that I had no business taking it.

"I don't remember asking Fay Johnson that question." It was a lie, and a gamble to boot, but it seemed to be my only choice. Gauging the dumbfounded reactions it caused, it seemed to be a good one.

"What do you mean, you don't remember asking Fay Johnson that question?" Mike recovered quickly enough to challenge my memory lapse. "She says you *pointedly* asked her if Angie Greer was alone in the house."

I shrugged. "I don't remember, Mike. And you certainly can't trust anything she might have said. She's loony. Just ask anybody who knows her. Besides, what difference does it make?"

In an instant, I had reversed the momentum. Not only had I compromised Fay Johnson's credibility, but I had effectively admitted my ignorance of the applicable regulation—without *actually* admitting it. So I had overlooked one of the squad's countless regs. Slap my hand, somebody. Tell me to be a good boy from now on, and let's get the hell out of here.

Hank tapped his fingers on the table, waiting for Mike to proceed. But Mike didn't know *how* to proceed. Carol had knocked over his first domino, but had tipped it the wrong way. I was feeling pretty smug at this point.

Then it happened. Stick Menzel raised his hand, tentatively, perhaps fearing the question he was about to ask had already been answered.

"Excuse me, Hank?" Stick hesitated, waiting for Hank to give him the floor.

"Yes, Stick?"

"I think I may have missed something here." Smiles greeted that admission, but Stick continued bravely. "I don't understand, Scott, why you can't remember where the police parked. Didn't you see them drive up?"

Ouch. "No, Stick, I didn't."

"Oh," he answered, but only partially satisfied. Then: "You hadn't already gone inside the house, had you?"

Ouch, ouch. "Yes, Stick, I had."

"You had? But that's...that's against squad regulations. Isn't it?" He looked at the other members of the board for corroboration. Most nodded in agreement. Two, at least, grinned while doing so.

I was dead. If Stick Menzel—who had trouble distinguishing a weed whacker from a toilet plunger, though he sold them both on a daily basis—knew of the rule I had broken, I couldn't very well claim ignorance myself. I saw Mike Marder's eyes light up; Stick had given him fresh ammunition to renew the fight.

They say the best defense is a good offense. With that in

mind—and considering that my *only* defense had just been demol-
ished—I quickly decided to get in my own licks, before Mike or
Carol or anybody else could capitalize on Stick's revelation. It
would be a risky tactic, I knew, to renounce the statutes these people were sworn to uphold, but I felt I could make an acceptable
case for my actions if I immediately took the initiative.

So, just as Mike Marder opened his mouth—to bring the appropriate charges against me, no doubt—I lashed out: "You're right,
Stick, what I did was against regulations. And I knew it at the
time."

This admission got the expected stares of astonishment. It also
gave me uncontested control of the proceedings, for the moment.
If I wanted to hang myself, no one in the room was going to prevent me. One or two would gladly hold the chair steady, until I
was ready to kick it out from under me.

I plunged ahead: "But none of you were there. None of you
heard that poor woman crying for help, fearful for her life. I was
alone, and I had to decide what was more important under the circumstances: an obscure squad regulation, or the well-being of my
patient. If this board wishes to discipline me because I made a
decision to help someone in need, then go right ahead. I'll stand by
my decision."

For twenty seconds, at least, no one said a word. Hank Cindrich
scratched his chin and nodded, as though in approval. At last,
Carol Hartshorne broke the silence, but only barely. Her voice was
soft as she observed: "But your decision, Scott, led to a man's
death–"

Peggy Nowicki cut her off: "That can't be verified, Carol. That
man—Greer, is it?—might have shot at the police regardless of
anything Scott did or didn't do. You can't blame Scott for another
man's actions."

Mike Marder waved his hand, as if to dismiss Peggy's statement. "That's not the point, Peggy. If the lawyers start digging into
this, which they probably will, they'll want to know that every
uniform on the scene acted by the book. Scott has just admitted
that he disobeyed regulations. If we, as the board, do not make
him accountable for his actions, then we, by extension, could be

held liable—joint and severally."

"Joint and *what?*" Stick Menzel asked. When Mike didn't answer him, he looked from one board member to another, totally perplexed.

Again the room became silent as everyone—except Stick, perhaps—pondered Mike's assertion. Nearly a minute passed before Jerry Boronski spoke for the first and only time of the evening: "Are you suggesting, Mike, that we disassociate ourselves from Scott, and hang him out to dry?"

A very good question, I must say. It brought the issue into sharp focus. All eyes went promptly to Mike Marder. I wish I could say his response surprised me, but it didn't.

"I don't see that we have any choice, Jerry. It's him or it's us, and we're not the negligent party. Rules are made to be obeyed, and whoever breaks them must accept the consequences. In this case, a suspension would not be sufficient. Our only option is to dismiss."

Hank Cindrich shook his head, and then looked at me. "Scott," he said, "I'm going to ask you to leave the room for a few minutes, while we discuss this. And I think it would be best for everybody—you included—if you didn't say anything to Billie, or Miles, or anyone else just yet."

"I don't get to defend myself?" I asked sharply.

Peggy answered me: "You had your chance, Scott, and you admitted that you willfully disregarded a squad regulation. There were mitigating factors, and we'll take them into account. But it's out of your hands now. Give us a couple of minutes to decide what we're going to do. We'll come get you once we've voted."

"Okay," I said coolly. I stood and left the room.

As they had promised, Billie DeMarino and Miles Coates were waiting outside for me. They were sitting at a picnic table that an appreciative Dayfield resident had donated to the squad a few years before. I felt gratified that the two of them, my crew chief and my best friend, had chosen to stick by me. Miles slid over on the bench as I approached, making room for me to sit down.

"Well, beam me up, Scotty," Miles said, "tell us what's going on in there."

"I can't, not yet," I answered simply.

Billie raised her eyebrows, but said nothing. Miles remarked: "That bad, huh?"

I shrugged. "Well, it's not exactly Nuremberg, but they're not pinning any medals on me, either. They'll decide in a few minutes what they're going to do with me."

"You got a will made up?" Miles asked, without even a smile.

I eyed him disdainfully. "No, why?"

"Well, if they decide to send you to the chair…" He paused to imitate an electrocution victim, kicking and twitching and bulging his eyes out. "…I hope you'll leave me your stereo system. I'll think of you every time I crank up my *Public Enemy* CDs."

"That shit won't play on my system. I've programmed it to spit out anything recorded by Neanderthals who wear their hats backwards."

"Then I'll take your car, man."

"Miles," Billie interjected quietly. "Let's not start laying claim to Scott's possessions just yet. If worse comes to worst, I'm sure Peggy will hold out for life imprisonment. With time off for good behavior, who knows?"

"Yeah, Peggy *did* seem to be on my side in there," I admitted. "But when the sharks get the scent of fresh blood…" I stopped before saying more than would be appropriate.

"I'll bet the dyke duo gave it to you good," Miles ventured. "When it comes to squad regulations, they're a couple of heavy hitters. Pun intended."

Again I shrugged. It would do me no good, at this point, to feed or satisfy Miles' curiosity.

"You know," Miles continued, "if I were you, I'd tell them *all* to go fuck themselves. I'd walk away from it. You don't need these assholes."

I looked at Billie for a moment, and then back at Miles. Of course, I had already considered that option. There certainly was some sense in it.

"Are you telling me this as a friend," I asked, "or as a member of the Dayfield Rescue Squad?"

"What difference does it make?" he countered.

What difference, indeed? No difference, really. His advice had its merits either way. Still, that voice inside told me again to reject it. "No, I'm going to see it through," I replied, closing off the subject. Billie nodded in agreement.

The three of us made small talk for another fifteen minutes. Billie asked me if I'd join her, Peggy, and possibly a few others for a drink when the meeting broke up. I took this as a good sign, but told her I wanted to hear the board's decision before I accepted or took a pass on the invitation. She understood.

At last, Stick Menzel came out to fetch me. I waved to my friends and followed him back inside.

I had assumed that I would know—just by the expressions of two or three key players—what my fate would be. If Mike Marder appeared satisfied, I was history. If Peggy Nowicki was smiling, my penance would be reasonable. However, to my bewilderment, nobody seemed happy. Hank Cindrich appeared especially agitated when he looked up at me.

"Scott, in the finest traditions of this esteemed body," he said, his voice just dripping with sarcasm, " we've decided *not* to decide what to do with you, just yet. We're at an impasse, so we're going to table this matter until our next meeting.

"We *did* manage to agree that, in the meantime, you're to consider yourself warned not to say or do anything that might harm the reputation of the Dayfield Rescue Squad. Which—if I might express my own opinion—is the most mealy-mouthed resolution ever issued by this or any other *supposedly* intelligent group of elected officials. This meeting is adjourned."

Hank slammed down his gavel, abruptly picked up his personal belongings, and—without saying another word—stormed out of the room. I assumed he was annoyed.

A few moments of silence ensued. And, as it turned out, they were revelatory seconds. Considering the extreme state of confusion I was in just then, I'm proud to say I managed to put that brief period of time to good use. For starters, I kept my mouth shut. That was a difficult and intelligent move on my part, but not nearly so productive as the other action I took...or didn't take.

I ignored Peggy Nowicki and Mike Marder and Carol

Hartshorne for the moment, and studied the faces of Jerry Boronski, Stick Menzel and Karen Weyrich. On the matter of suspending or even dismissing me, I presumed to know the yeas and nays among the former three officers: Peggy was in my corner, while Mike and Carol had led the opposition. Hank Cindrich, who had walked out, would have also voted on my behalf.

That left Jerry, Stick and Karen. Either all three of them had abstained from voting—an unlikely possibility—or one of the three had abstained while the other two had split their votes. I spent the period of silence trying to read in their faces which way each had gone.

Jerry Boronski, in addition to being a good engineer, is probably a helluva poker player. His face told me nothing. In my absence, he could have defended me before the board, or condemned me, or never said a word—and there was no clue to his actions in his expression. I doubted, though, that he had abstained from voting.

Stick Menzel's bias was equally difficult to discern, but for a totally different reason. He was gaping, openly, at every person in the room, looking for reassurance that what he had done in the closed meeting—whatever it was—had not been the cause of Hank's displeasure. In all probability, I thought, it had been his inability to make up his mind that had led to the *no decision*. I made a mental note to get on Stick's good side in the near future. I considered stopping by his hardware store to buy a snow blower.

Karen Weyrich's expression seemed to verify my estimation of how each officer had voted. Her glare was fixed on me, and she did not return the smile I offered. Though nobody in the room—including me—was pleased by the outcome of the meeting, Karen appeared especially hostile. I couldn't imagine what I had said or done to offend her so severely.

The silence was finally broken by the most silent of all the squad's officers. "Well, it's getting late," said Jerry Boronski, glancing at his watch. "I'm going home." As he stood to leave, Peggy Nowicki approached him and said something to him in private. He looked at her for a moment, then shook his head. "No, thanks," he said to Peggy, before picking up his note pad and departing.

One by one the other officers filed from the room. I watched them go, still searching their faces for clues. Then I felt a hand on my back. I turned to face Billie. She had entered the room as the officers had left. Looking behind her, I could see Miles out in the hallway, speaking with someone who was out of my view.

"Hank says you're still in limbo," Billie confirmed. "A waste of a perfectly good evening, huh?" As she said this, Peggy came over to where I was sitting.

"That's for sure," I said.

Billie looked up at Peggy and the two of them nodded at each other. It was a signal that meant something, but only to them. Then Billie turned back at me. "So, are you going to join us?" she asked.

I glanced around. "Us" apparently meant just the two of them, and perhaps Miles, who was now coming into the room.

"Where we going?" I asked.

"Just for a drink. To *Dimitri's*, I guess." Billie answered.

"Okay, Chief, you go ahead; I'll be there in a few minutes. I have a phone call to make right now."

"Sure," said Billie. Then, to Miles, she added: "Would you like to join us?"

Miles frowned, uncharacteristically. "Just for one," he answered.

I waited until the three of them—Billie, Peggy and Miles—had left before I picked up the phone to call Pam. After ten or twelve rings, I gave up. I tried not to imagine where she might be.

As I was about to leave the building, I heard voices coming from the "ready room"—a small, furnished chamber that serves a number of purposes. The door to the room was slightly ajar. I crept close and peered in, curious to see who had stuck around after the meeting, and hoping to find out why. Through the narrowest of openings I was able to see Carol Hartshorne and Mike Marder. They were seated side by side, talking to someone who was out of my sight. I listened—eavesdropped, really—and soon determined that the third person in the room was Stick Menzel. I couldn't make out all the words, but it seemed that Carol and Mike were trying to talk Stick into something.

The thought struck me: a snow blower wasn't going to be enough. I wondered for a moment how much a lawn tractor might cost, and how much commission Stick would make selling one.

Then I saw Mike looking toward me. He started to rise—in all probability to make sure they were not being overheard—so I scampered away.

Ten minutes later I was strolling into *Dimitri's Tavern*, a quiet, dimly-lit bar on the border of Dayfield and Ironport. It took me a few seconds to locate my friends. They were seated at a table in a far corner, with drinks already in front of them. The waitress who had just served them was walking my way, so I stopped her and placed an order, asking her to bring it to the table. She smiled fetchingly when I paid and tipped her in advance.

As I approached the table, I could tell right away that the topic of conversation had to do with the squad. Peggy was telling Billie and Miles about a call she had been on recently. Momentarily, I hoped the point of her story would be humorous; I needed a good laugh about then. But the tone of Peggy's voice, and the somber expression on Billie's face, told me that there would be nothing funny in this particular recollection. I pulled the fourth chair out from the table and sat down quietly, barely nodding at Miles as I did so.

"...to us, he was just another old guy," Peggy was saying as I tuned in, "looking like they all do when the pump stops. His mouth was hanging open...his skin was gray...his eyes all glazed over. We knew he was a goner, but we did our thing—thumped and bagged him all the way, until they pronounced him at the hospital. I more or less forgot about him after I wrote up the call sheet.

"Then, a few days later, I saw his obit in the newspaper. Turns out the old guy was famous—an artist of some kind. Escaped from Poland during the war. Knew the pope personally. His works hang in galleries all around the world.

"They had a picture of the guy in the paper, a file photo of him accepting an award of some sort. An international award, if I recall, that's given to noted humanitarians. He had a big smile on his face, posing for the camera with this enormous trophy. He looked so dignified, so...joyful. I was amazed to see that it was the same guy."

Peggy paused to sip her drink, and then went on: "Because, at the moment he went down, when he stopped retching and...contorting, there was no dignity, no pomp, no glory. There was just…drool."

Again Peggy paused, this time taking a full swallow from her glass. I waited, expecting something more to her story. It took me a minute to realize she had finished, and that her only point was the pronounced contrast between her patient's most treasured moment in life, and his last one. This puzzled me, because it was out of character for Peggy. It was the type of story that Billie—who is far more sensitive—might tell. But for Peggy, the squad's original tough nut, this anecdote was much too sentimental.

Just then the waitress delivered my drink, and Peggy seemed to notice my presence for the first time. She smiled ever so slightly. Then she returned to her usual form.

"What did you ever do to Mike Marder?" she asked me, pointedly. "I'm not one to talk out of school, but it's clear he's got it in for you. He wants you off the squad, permanently. And he might get the votes to make it happen."

I couldn't help but turn my head to look at Billie, and she couldn't help but look away—while trying to suppress a smile. That lifted my spirits, momentarily, to find that she could now see some humor in the incident. I turned back to Peggy.

"I decked him once," I said flatly.

Peggy flinched. "You did what?"

"You heard me. My fist had a collision with his face, and it knocked him on his ass. I did it right in front of his girlfriend, too. Or at least someone he was dating at the time. Maybe that's why he's not so enamored of me."

Peggy frowned and shook her head, like a parent expressing disapproval of an unruly child. She sipped her drink, set it back on the table, and stared at me, expressionless, for just a moment. She's good at that kind of thing.

"You want to tell me *why* you hit him?"

NO REGRETS

WHAT'S TO TELL? THE BASTARD had it coming, that particular morning, and if I had it to do over again I'd not only deck him, I'd kick him while he was down. With his girl-friend sitting nearby or otherwise.

It wasn't even his call; he had no business being there. Billie and I had responded with the rig, and the paramedics were on their way. Our patient was an elderly woman, and she was complaining of severe abdominal and back pains. I say "complaining of" because that's the terminology we're conditioned to use, but actually the old woman wasn't complaining at all. It wasn't in her nature. Even as she lay there—at the edge of a single bed in a neat little room on the first floor of her daughter's house—she was actually apologizing for causing us an inconvenience.

Billie apparently knew the woman, because she addressed her by name as soon as we entered her bedroom. I had brought the litter in the house with me, but left it in the hallway due to the cramped quarters.

"Where does it hurt, Grace?" Billie asked in her usual, cheerful-yet-comforting voice.

Grace smiled at her, though it was obviously

an effort. She pointed at her waist, on the near side, and then ran her hand around to her back. She winced repeatedly as Billie assessed her.

Grace's daughter, a distressed-looking woman of about forty, was standing at the foot of the bed, trying to be helpful while also trying to stay out of our way. It's a difficult dual role; few bystanders ever master it.

Next to the bed sat a young boy, a seven-year-old if I remember correctly. He was Grace's grandson. He was gently holding his grandmother's hand, and speaking too softly to be heard. Later, one of the paramedics told me he was praying, but I can't be sure about that. What I *was* sure about—what was evident to everyone—was that the boy was very close to his grandmother. He knew she was in a perilous condition—children have a way of knowing these things, sometimes—and he was doing all that he could to comfort her in her agony. She turned and smiled at him occasionally, and squeezed his hand in appreciation.

As Billie took the woman's vital signs, I stepped into the hallway with her daughter. I introduced myself, and she did the same. Her name was Rita. She started to fill me in on her mother's history: how long she had been bedridden, her medications, her ailments of the recent past. I could tell by Rita's voice that something different was happening this time. That she was afraid for her mother and probably had good reason to be.

It was about then that the MIC unit arrived, and we—Rita and I—stood back against the walls of the hallway to let the paramedics pass. Less than a minute later Mike Marder showed up, wearing his squad jacket. He barely nodded at me as he strode by, and then he squeezed into the little, make-shift bedroom.

As I've said, there was nothing for him to do, but since he was a squad officer and I was just a grunt, I wasn't about to tell him he wasn't needed. At least, I told myself, he couldn't do any harm.

The paramedics started an IV line, and took an ECG. They were acting more businesslike than usual, and that didn't give me a warm feeling. I turned back to the daughter, Rita, to keep her occupied with small talk.

"So how long has your mother lived with you?" I asked.

"Two years," Rita answered simply. "She had gotten to the point where she couldn't take care of herself, so we invited her to move in with us. This used to be my husband's office, but we converted it into a bedroom for her. The past few months she's gone downhill rapidly. Thank God, Steven is so good with her. He's been a big help to me since she's been here."

"Steven is your husband?"

She gestured into the room. "My son," she said. "He's grown up so much since my mother has been here."

I nodded, and we stood in awkward silence for a few moments. The paramedics were on their portable radio, discussing the case with the hospital. Billie was giving the woman our usual pre-departure briefing. This was my cue to get the litter ready.

Looking into the bedroom, while trying to determine the least disruptive way to get Grace from the bed and onto the litter, something about her position struck me as odd.

"Why," I asked Rita quietly, "does your mother have herself scrunched over on the side of the bed like that? Does she have a problem with lying in the middle?"

My question did not surprise Rita, but the expression she gave me made me regret having asked it. She hesitated a few moments before answering, and then I noticed a hint of tear in her eye.

"Usually she does lie in the middle, Scott," she said softly. "But last night, just before I retired for the night, I found her like she is now, right at the far edge. 'Move over, mom,' I had said to her. 'You'll be more comfortable in the middle of the bed.' But she had said to me: 'No, he's here tonight, Rita, and that's his side of the bed.' And I had said, 'Steven's in his own room, mom. He's been asleep for two hours. Move over.'"

Now there wasn't just the hint of a tear in Rita's eye, it was starting to overflow. So was the other one. But she managed to continue.

"'I'm not talking about Steven,' my mother said to me. 'I'm talking about your father. Your father is here tonight, and I have to make room for him.'"

"Your father?", I asked, not even wanting to consider the forces acting upon the older woman's consciousness.

"Yes, Scott, my father...who has been dead for sixteen years. My mother hasn't talked about him much in all that time, but last night she *insisted* he was here with her. She still thinks he's here now."

Now, true, the story is just a bit poignant, but not all that unusual or maudlin under the circumstances. Thinking I was the only one who had heard it, I nodded—with just the right dose of empathy, I hope—at Rita. Then I turned and saw Mike Marder standing there, grinning at the two of us. He had overheard our conversation, and was now conveying his impression of Rita's touching little story. He mockingly dabbed at his eyes, and then shook his head with mild disdain. I was suddenly angered and embarrassed by his actions, but just as suddenly I forgot them. In the little bedroom behind us, the worst was starting to happen.

Grace was crying out in her pain. I didn't know it, and the paramedics could only suspect it, but it was later confirmed she had suffered a "triple-A", which is the abbreviated term for a ruptured abdominal aortic aneurysm—which is usually as deadly as it is painful. Billie was giving her full-flow oxygen, but Grace's vital signs began to deteriorate rapidly. Nonetheless, she continued to hold onto her grandson's hand, and he, very bravely, kept speaking to her in a soothing voice.

No one likes to be faced with a situation like this. We couldn't let little Steven stay there, while his grandmother's condition became increasingly more desperate, and while our efforts to stabilize her became increasingly more invasive. Yet, we also knew—all but one of us, as it turned out—that his presence was sustaining her as much as the oxygen and the IV and anything else we could do for her in the field. So you might say we were all dancing around the decision to remove him, giving Grace every opportunity to pull out of her nosedive, when the decision was abruptly and irrevocably made for us.

"C'mon, kid," Mike Marder said, grabbing Steven by the wrist. "You don't belong here. I'm not gonna have you on some shrink's couch for the next ten years just because we let you watch your grandma die."

And with that, Mike forcibly removed the child from the room, turned him over to his mother—who was still standing anxiously in the hallway—and closed the door.

You can guess what happened next. With her grandson's removal, and Mike's callous remark—which I'm convinced she heard—what little strength Grace had held in reserve instantly drained out of her. Her vitals went to zero, and her ECG went flat. We continued to work on her for a few more minutes, but she was out of our hands.

When I walked outside, minutes later, Mike was still there, standing next to his car. He was recounting the squad's noble heroics, failed though they were, for a curious neighbor. It was then I noticed a woman sitting in his passenger's seat, trying very hard to be inconspicuous, or to appear bored.

I can't put my finger on it, and I'll admit my displeasure with his earlier actions may have colored my judgment, but something wasn't right about the scene before me. And then I realized just what was bothering me: Mike was posturing for the woman in his car, hoping to gain her esteem by intimating, in his story, that he had fought valiantly to save Grace's life.

That's when I got angry.

"Hey, Mike," I said as I approached him, as though I was about to ask a favor.

"Yes, Scott, what is it?" he answered, as though he was going to graciously grant it.

"Just this," I said, leaning back and delivering a right hook, square and solid to the side of his grinning face. The grin disappeared, I noticed, just as he went on his ass, and just as his ladyfriend bolted upright in the passenger's seat, with an expression of shock that contrasted so vividly with her earlier *ennui*.

I turned and walked back to the rig, and climbed in next to Billie. If she had noticed the brief and one-sided altercation between Mike Marder and me, she pretended otherwise.

WHEN I CAME HOME FROM WORK TWO days after my hearing with the board, I found the door to my apartment ajar. I stopped in the hallway and stared at it for a minute. I wasn't positive, but I was reasonably certain I hadn't left it that way in the morning.

My first thought was of Pam. Aside from my landlord, she's the only person who has a key. But Pam would *never* leave an unlocked door behind her, let alone an open one. She's so security-conscious, she locks the door behind me when I go downstairs, in my bathrobe, to get the morning newspaper. Then she makes me say a special code word before she'll let me back in.

Without touching anything, I examined the door and the jamb for a sign of forced entry. Nothing. Then I put my ear to the opening and listened for any sounds inside. Nothing. I cleared my throat.

"Pam?" I called softly. Again, nothing.

The police will tell you, in a circumstance such as this one, *not* to enter the residence. And the police are right; it's better to get help and possibly embarrass yourself, than it is to be brave and possibly get hurt, or worse. Besides, I was already in trouble for having walked into a home I should have stayed out of. So you might think I would have known better.

But I didn't. I pushed the door slowly open, ready to bolt the other way at any sign of peril. I figured I could tell if the place had been burglarized by just looking in. I certainly wouldn't enter if I could see that someone had been inside during my absence. The door gave a muffled groan as it swung away from me.

Everything was in its place. I bobbed my head back and forth, trying to see around corners that were six and ten feet away from me. "Hello?" I called loudly, thinking maybe the landlord was checking…who the hell knows *what* he might be checking? Aren't landlords supposed to check *something* from time to time?

I kept hoping for a sign, or a sound, or anything that would tell me what to do, but the situation remained neutral. No evidence there was trouble ahead, and no evidence there wasn't. I had to make a decision. Heads I go in, tails I call 9-1-1? It seemed like a ludicrous choice, so I walked in.

I looked around one corner into the kitchen, then around another one into the living room. Nothing was missing, nothing was moved. I shrugged my shoulders and started down the hallway to my bedroom, walking right past the bathroom door. It came open swiftly behind me, and someone stepped out and stuck a finger into the back of my neck.

"*Bang!* You're dead!" Pam squealed, and I nearly shit myself. I spun around, throwing my hands up, while sucking in all the air in the apartment. My eyes bulged, my legs went rubbery, and my guts imploded. Yes, I was scared. Wouldn't you be?

Pam squealed again, with laughter, and she clasped her hands together in delight. "The paper was right!" she chirped. "The paper was right!"

"What the hell…" I protested—relieved, angry and confused all at once. "What are you talking about? Don't you *ever*…"

"Oh, shut up!" she blurted cheerfully, while stepping up to me, wrapping her arms around my neck, and locking her lips against mine. It was all so unexpected, yet—I had to admit—*damned* exciting. And as I could quickly tell, she was as pumped-up as I was. I could feel her pulse racing at pressure points I would *never* presume to palpate on an emergency patient. Hiding from and then surprising me like that had apparently gotten her blood up, and she squeezed and twirled me around and around in the hallway.

Of course, I had to try to take advantage of her momentary passion, so I directed our impromptu tango toward the bedroom door. As I crossed the threshold, though, she caught hold of the doorknob, throwing me off-balance in mid-spin.

"Hold on, H.B.," she said breathlessly, while neatly extricating herself from my embrace. "We have all night. Come, I want to show you something."

She walked back down the hallway and, naturally, closed and bolted the front door. It deflated me to think that her bounding heartbeat had been brought on by nothing more than the suspense of waiting for me in an unlocked apartment. She winked and smiled my way as she beckoned me into the kitchen.

The weekly newspaper was sitting on a chair, where I often left it, and Pam took it and laid it flat on the table. She opened it, and presented an inside page for me to read. I got a hollow ache in my stomach when I saw my own picture staring out from the page, just beneath a headline that read: *"'I'm no Clint Eastwood,' local first aider confesses after witnessing shootout."*

"Oh, shit," I moaned, seeing Dorothy McCrae's byline at the top of the article. "This isn't going to help my self-esteem."

"Actually," Pam said soothingly, while draping an arm over my shoulder from back to front, "it's not a bad article. It makes you sound like a decent, caring individual."

"Who happened to be in the wrong place at the wrong time, I imagine."

"Mmm. Yeah, sort of." Pam kissed me on the neck, and then wandered over to the refrigerator. While she found a piece of fruit to munch on, I sat down at the table and started reading:

Dayfield Rescue Squad volunteer Scott Jamison was simply doing his duty when he got caught in the middle, literally, at the township's first drug-related shootout on Sunday (see main story, page 1).

I turned back to the front page and scanned the first few paragraphs of the issue's lead story. There were three accompanying photos, including one of Sergeant Skipinski. Credit for the article, and for another related story below it, were given to Dorothy McCrae. As I flipped back to "my" article, it occurred to me that the incident represented quite an opportunity for the brash young reporter. Big city editors, I've heard, are impressed by dramatic stories involving guns, drugs and innocent bystanders. Such articles show that a reporter can handle the territory, I imagine. I was also struck by Dorothy's use of the word "first" in describing the shooting, as though more were to be expected...

Responding in his own car to what seemed to be a routine first aid call at the home of Angela and Gary Greer, Jamison was mistaken for an intruder by Mr. Greer, who crept up behind the surprised first aider and put a loaded pistol to his head. According to Jamison, Greer had just expressed an intention to use the gun when he was confronted by the police.

"At first, I was too confused to be scared," says Jamison. "I was concentrating on my patient (Mrs. Greer), and it took me a while to comprehend that another person...might want to do me harm. I suppose that when you look at the situation from (Gary) Greer's point of view, you can understand why he considered me a threat."

Of course, no one will ever know what Mr. Greer's point of view was, exactly. He was killed in the shootout with police that followed immediately. Jamison was a witness to the exchange of gunfire, and his recollection of events mostly corroborates the details provided by the Dayfield Police Department.

In contrast to the police report, however, Jamison's version introduces an emotional element into the story. As an emergency medical technician (EMT), Jamison's function at an emergency scene is normally a helping and healing one. He says that witnessing a fatal shooting at close range conflicts directly with his usual orientation, and he admits to a high level of discomfort with what happened.

"I blacked out, just after Greer hit the floor. I was feeling a combination of emotions: relief, certainly, but also an overwhelming sense of remorse, that two people had been mortally shot for no good reason. (Jamison didn't find out until later that Officer Saporta had been wearing a bullet-proof vest, and had sustained only a minor injury.) It didn't seem real. I just couldn't deal with it. I never claimed to be Clint Eastwood."

The article went on from there, mostly with background information about the squad and my years of volunteer service. Dorothy McCrae had not misquoted me, per se, but the slant she had chosen for the article didn't feel right.

I looked at my photo in the newspaper. It appeared to be a mug shot—minus the identifying numbers across the bottom. Judging from the length of my hair, I guessed it had been taken four or five years earlier. Then I noticed just the tip of a silver badge above my left breast pocket. The shirt I had been wearing for the photo was my dress white squad uniform, which I haven't worn since the picture was taken, which was shortly after I had become an active member. Dorothy McCrae had recovered the photo from my personnel file at squad headquarters. I wondered, briefly, who had released it to her.

"So, what do you think?" Pam asked, with a mouth full of fruit. She walked up behind me and leaned over my back, resting her forearms on my shoulders and snuggling her cheek against my ear. I could smell her faint but aromatic scent, and I could feel her breasts pressing against my back. I quickly forgot about the newspaper article.

"About what?" I asked, turning my face to her cheek, which I kissed lightly.

"About the article, H.B. You're the only one who seems to care that the man was killed. I think that's sweet."

"The man who would have killed me, and who tried to kill a policeman," I reminded her. "The man who had beaten his wife to a pulp."

Pam frowned. "He wasn't a very nice guy, was he?"

I stood up, turned around and embraced her. Maybe, I hoped, I could recapture some of our earlier excitement. "No, he wasn't very nice," I said absently. I started stroking her back, running my fingers along her spinal column, on the outside of her blouse. As my hand crossed her bra strap, I paused, feeling for the clasp. There was none, which meant that it hooked in front. Such knowledge could prove valuable, if the evening progressed as I desired.

"Did you read in the front page article that he had been arranged three times on drug charges?" she asked.

"Arraigned," I corrected her, which I tend to do too often. "No, I didn't read that. But it doesn't surprise me." My hands were starting to get away from me. My brain would soon follow.

Pam still felt like talking. "So, how did your meeting go last night?" she asked. "Did the board of directors expend you?"

"If you mean *suspend* me, no. They haven't made up their minds what they want to do. They deferred the matter."

Again she frowned. "Deferred?"

"Put it off, postponed it."

"Oh. Are you happy about that?"

"Frankly, my dear..." I said in my best Clark Gable imitation. Then I nuzzled her neck.

She pushed me away, gently. "Frankly, my dear, *what?*" she asked. She honestly didn't know, or remember, Rhett Butler's famous rejoinder. There wasn't much point in completing it.

I paraphrased: "I don't give a shit."

She grinned. "Please don't swear. There's a lady present."

"A lady, really? Isn't that great: a lady with a *woman's* body." Again I wrapped my arms around her. Taking hold of her firm derrière, I interposed my thigh between hers, and rocked forward, on my toes, gently. There was no sense being ambiguous about my intentions, was there?

She sighed, but didn't resist. "Is this all you ever think about, H.B.?" she asked.

"You mean there's something else?"

"Yes!" she answered, taking me seriously. "There's...music, and art, and...and walks along the beach. There's dancing..."

"Mere diversions," I suggested, while rocking forward again. The friction was delightful. "Distractions. Poor substitutes for the one, true human interaction. Or, at best, preludes to it."

"Preludes?" she asked. "Like the car?"

"Yes, like the car," I answered, while starting to undo the top button of her blouse. Still, she wasn't resisting. "Sleek, and racy. Built for the curves. Or just built, *with* curves, like you are."

She giggled at this, and then looked over my shoulder. "Is the door locked?" she asked. A marvelous question, that. Tantamount to foreplay.

"You locked it," I said, now working on the third button. One more to go, and my immediate goal—that front clasp, nestled in her cleavage—would be within reach. "And nobody can lock a door like you can."

I almost had her convinced. In fact, she *was* convinced. She had "The Look" in her eyes, the look that means "get ready, fella, your dreams are about to come true." I *love* that look. But then, for God knows what reason, she glanced up at the clock. The look disappeared, and was replaced by yet another frown.

"Oh, *fiddle!*" she exclaimed, stepping back from me.

Fiddle? What the hell does *fiddle* mean? I wasn't sure, but whatever it was, I knew I wasn't going to like it. She started to redo the buttons I had undone. That elusive clasp vanished from view.

"Now what's wrong?" I cried, literally.

"I'm sorry, H.B.," she said consolingly. "I almost forgot. Kelly asked me to stop over at her place tonight. She said it was real important. I've got to be there in fifteen minutes."

"*Kelly?*"

This wasn't happening. Kelly Perniciaro is one of Pam's friends at work. She's somewhat of a busybody—a shrewd operator who likes to get her own way—but generally she's tolerable. On the plus side, Kelly looks out for Pam. She's been with their company long enough to know the players from the pretenders, and she helps Pam steer clear of the numerous hazards and obstacles that lurk in most corporate settings. On the minus side, Kelly demands complete loyalty in return. Pam wouldn't *think* of telling Kelly no—not if Kelly really wanted Pam to do something. I knew it was hopeless to try and talk her out of leaving at this moment.

"Can you come back later?" I moped.

She winked as she gathered her belongings and started towards the door. "We'll see," she said promisingly. "I might be back sooner than you suspect."

Expect, I thought, but dared not say.

"Well, at least let me walk you to your car," I whimpered.

"You're sweet," she said softly, as I unlocked the door. She placed her hand on my hip, and let it glide down the front of my thigh. I looked at her and again she winked. Then she grabbed the door knob, swung the door open, stepped out into the hall and headed for the elevator.

I caught up with her just as the elevator doors were opening. We embraced, once, on the ride down, but the spark was noticeably absent. Her mind was on her destination—Kelly's place.

It was just getting dark outside as we emerged from my apartment building. Arm in arm, we crossed over to the parking lot. She had parked in a far corner, just so I wouldn't have seen her car earlier. I was quietly pleased that she had incorporated that small detail into her plan. She had actually thought it through in advance, so as not to spoil her surprise.

That's what I was thinking when a set of headlights—high beams—went on in my face. The sudden, unexpected brilliance startled me, and I stutter-stepped in my distraction. Which means: I tripped over my own feet. Pam—always graceful and athletic— caught me before I fell. She laughed: "You're such a klutz, H.B."

It was a forgettable little anecdote, but because I was mildly embarrassed, I scowled in annoyance at the offending vehicle as we walked by. It was an ordinary gray van. In the gathering darkness, I couldn't see the driver, but I hoped he or she could see me—and took note of my expression of displeasure.

Pam unlocked her car door, kissed me on the cheek, and climbed into the driver's seat. She started the engine and put it in gear.

"Hurry back," I said.

"The wait'll do you good," she smiled. Then she pulled away.

She was wrong about that: even five minutes would be too long to wait. And had I known how long it was actually going to be until I saw her again—and had I even suspected what I would go through in the meantime—I would have run after her and…and…

I'm not sure what I would have done, but if ever there was a moment when I should have done *something* differently in my life, that was it. I just didn't know it at the time.

I walked back to the building. The gray van, I absently noted, was still in the same spot. Its headlights were out. I climbed the stairs to my apartment, went in the kitchen and, deflated, sat down to read the articles written by Dorothy McCrae.

NO RETURN

10

FOR THE NEXT SEVEN DAYS, MY LIFE was graciously uneventful. A few friends called with the usual, insipid comments about the newspaper article— I must have heard *"Go ahead, Scott, make my day"* at least twenty times—but otherwise my daily existence returned to what passes for normal. Tuesday came and went without a single emergency call, and I heard *nada* from the squad's board of directors. I figured they had given up on reaching an agreement, or had lost interest, and thus were going to drop the matter of my supposed transgressions.

Better still, Arnie was out of town most of the week. His absence made my working hours at DataStaff somewhat more agreeable.

My biggest concern was the perceptible cooling of my relationship with Pam. Or, more accurately, of her relationship with me. She didn't return that evening—she only called with a brief and distressingly vague apology. After that, we spoke on the phone a few times, but I couldn't entice her to spend any time with me—not even with promises of candlelight dinners at expensive restaurants or front-row seats at her favorite comedy club. She always had an acceptable excuse, but her excuses didn't diminish my escalating level of frustration. By week's end, I was reduced to savoring memories of our past liaisons. In fact, that's what I was doing—savoring—when Francine, our receptionist at DataStaff, paged me to the front desk. It was Thursday afternoon, a week to the day later.

I wasn't expecting anyone, so understandably I was hoping Pam had stopped by the office to surprise me, to tell me she hadn't been feeling well but was now ready to pick up where we had left off. It was a possibility, you know.

Instead, there was a man waiting for me. I didn't know him, and he didn't look like the typical sales rep who might drop in unannounced. He was a worn and tired old guy, wearing an equally worn and tired overcoat. It was a little much for a warm, summer afternoon.

The man had an official look about him, or at least a bureaucratic one. In his left hand was a large manila envelope. A tiny voice in my brain told me the envelope was for me, and that it was not something I wanted.

As I approached, the man turned from Francine to face me. "Mr. Scott Jamison?" he asked. I nodded. "Mr. Jamison, I'm from the county sheriff's office, and I have something for you. Mrs. Hufnagel?"

Francine looked from the man to me and back to the man. "Yes?" she replied.

The man pulled a folded sheet of paper from inside his overcoat and gave it to her. As his hand came out, I noticed a badge on his breast pocket. "Would you please sign and date this, Mrs. Hufnagel, attesting that you witnessed my delivery of this package to Mr. Jamison?" He handed me the manila envelope.

Francine took the sheet of paper and, with a distrustful expression, studied it for a moment. Then she looked up at me, as though seeking my approval. I just shrugged. She signed the paper and returned it to the man.

"Thank you," he said to Francine, and then to me: "Have a nice day." He gave a half-ass, half-hearted salute, and then turned and left the building.

When the door had closed behind him, Francine voiced the question I was asking myself: "What was that all about?"

"I'll tell you in a minute," I said, taking a letter opener from her desk and sitting down in a nearby chair. I slit open the envelope and spilled the enclosed document onto my lap. Francine craned her neck to see, but I didn't think she could.

The word *Summons* jumped off the first page at me. I scanned the rest of that page, and the next few, before I could make myself believe what I was seeing. Angela Greer, of 712 Kilbourn Avenue in Dayfield, New Jersey, was bringing suit against me for being *an aggravating cause of her late husband's wrongful death.* Against *me*— the kind-hearted soul who had come to her aid when she desperately needed it, and who had nearly paid for his charitable act with his life!

I tried to read the document, there in the reception area, but my vision went blurry. My hands started to shake, and all at once I could feel my own clammy presence beneath my shirt.

"Well?" Francine demanded.

I looked up at her blankly.

"What is it?"

"Oh, it's...ah..."

Thankfully, the phone interrupted her as I stammered about. She gave me a sharp look as she answered it.

Don't tell her, the tiny voice inside my skull was saying. *She's a yenta, and she'll have this all over the company and half the civilized world before you even get off your ass. Don't tell her!*

Francine directed the incoming call and turned back to me, just as I finished sliding the document back into the envelope.

"Well?" she asked again.

I absently tapped the letter opener on my knee for several moments, as though lost in thought. Then I looked up at Francine. "Oh, it's just a notification. My, um, aunt passed away a few months ago, and left me some property. It has to do with that."

I wouldn't have believed me if I was her, and I'm not nearly as suspicious as she is.

"Property?" she scoffed. "For *that* they send out a deputy, and deliver it to you in person?"

"Well, there's some dispute about land rights...that sort of thing. It may end up in court, in a lawsuit or something." I tried to sound cavalier, as if I had no real interest in the matter. Which was easy enough to do, considering there was no aunt, no land, and no lawsuit. Not on this issue, anyway. My explanation seemed to satisfy Francine, for she instantly stopped glowering at me. I should have guessed why.

"Do you have a good lawyer?" she asked brightly. "My son's a lawyer, you know. One of the best in the county. Here, let me give you his card." She fished in her desk drawer for no more than three seconds and came out with a plain white business card. I took it without hardly glancing at it, and stuffed it in my shirt pocket.

"Thanks, Fran," I mumbled. "If the need arises, I'll give him a call." I wanted to get back to my cubicle, to examine the document in my hands, and to think.

Francine continued her sales pitch. "He's a fighter, my son is. Those people who sent you that summons won't know what hit them, when he gets through with them. You call him today. He'll take care of you."

I waved over my shoulder as I left the reception area. Obviously, Francine had been able to see the heading on the document's first page; she knew it was a summons. I couldn't imagine, though, that she had been able to read anything else.

When I reached my desk, my phone was ringing. I could tell by the cadence of the rings that it was an internal call. I set down the envelope and the letter-opener before I answered: "Scott here."

It was Francine, again already. "Oh, Scott," she said, "one other thing I forgot to mention. A man stopped in earlier and asked if you work here. I didn't know what to tell him."

"So what *did* you tell him?"

"I asked if he had an appointment." In other words, she said yes.

"Was it the same man who brought this, ah, document?"

Her voice turned acidic. "I'd have *told* you if it was. No, this was a younger man. Very big, with lots of facial hair. He looked like a professional wrestler."

A professional wrestler. Now there's an oxymoron.

"Did he say what he wanted?"

"No, he just smiled and walked out. Didn't give me a name or anything. Do you think it has anything to do with your aunt's property?"

"I'm sure it doesn't. But if he stops by again, let me know. Okay?"

"Certainly. Oh, by the way, right now would be a good time to catch Geoffrey. Afternoons are usually best."

"Who?"

"My son, Geoffrey. Should I put the call through for you?"

Was this woman working on commission? "No, Fran, thanks anyway. I don't think I even need a lawyer. Let me see what's what, first."

"Whatever you say. Oh, and one other thing..."

"Yes?"

"Arnie called in while you were out to lunch. He says you're to have those numbers ready for him when he gets back next week."

"What numbers?"

"*What numbers?*" she mocked me. "How am I supposed to know what numbers? *You're* the numbers guy around here, or so I'm told. Arnie seemed to know what numbers he wants, so I'd suggest you figure it out.

"And, before you forget, get my letter opener back out here." She hung up.

Whatever numbers Arnie wanted would have to wait, because my mind certainly couldn't focus on them just now. The summons on my lap had promptly replaced Pam's absent affections as my primary concern. Also, there was the puzzling, somewhat bothersome element of the "professional wrestler" who had come looking for me.

On that matter, though, I acquiesced to the suggestion I had denied in Fran's presence: the big guy who had asked about me was probably related, somehow, to the pending lawsuit. He might even work for the lawyer—James Pressman, I noted—whose name was listed on the summons as attorney for the plaintiff, Angela Greer. How else would the sheriff's office have known where to find me during the day?

It took me fifteen minutes or better to fully examine the papers I had been served. A lot of it was legal gobbledygook, but I took special interest in three items, using a blank piece of loose-leaf paper to write notes to myself.

First, the complaint filed by Angie Greer, via James Pressman, specifically mentioned the squad regulation I had disobeyed. Not surprisingly, the plaintiff claimed that my action constituted "gross negligence" and "reckless endangerment." On the loose-leaf paper I wrote: *How did Pressman get a copy of the squad's regs?*

Second, the judgment being claimed by the plaintiff was to be "contingent on a thorough, independent examination of the defendant's personal assets." This concerned me. On the loose-leaf paper I wrote: *How much could Greer/Pressman expect to make from this?*

Finally, the summons informed me that I had twenty days to file a written answer to the plaintiff's complaint. I checked my calendar and then scribbled the deadline date on the loose-leaf paper. Twenty days seemed like plenty of time to find a competent lawyer and formulate a response to Angie Greer's complaint. But I wondered, as I idly played with Fran's letter opener, if it would be enough time to learn why she had filed it in the first place.

I needed an ally, someone with some investigative skills. I reached for the phone book, found the number I wanted, and dialed it.

A young man answered: "Good afternoon, *Dayfield Dispatch*."

"Dorothy McCrae, please."

"She's not in right now. Could I take a message?"

"Yes, have her call Clint Eastwood."

"I'm sorry, sir, I must not have heard you correctly. Could you give me your name again?"

"You heard me correctly," I said, and then hung up the phone.

CHANCES WERE GOOD, I KNEW, THAT I'D
catch Sergeant Skipinski if I made it
to the municipal building before five
o'clock. That's when the Dayfield
Police Department changes shifts, so
better than half the force is either coming or going at that hour. For once, I lucked
out: Skip was coming off duty and heading
home. He walked right by me on the way to
his car.

"Hey, Skip, you have a minute?" I called,
running after him.

He stopped and looked back at me, as
though noticing me for the first time. "For
you, Scott, ninety seconds," he answered flatly,
glancing at his watch. "But no more."

"Can I buy you a drink?"

"No. Eighty-five seconds."

"Oh, cut the hard-ass routine, wouldya? I
have to ask you a few questions."

Skip smiled, much too sweetly. "Why not
have your girlfriend ask them for you? I'd be
happy to talk to *her*. All night, if necessary."

A warning siren started to blare from someplace nearby. I looked around for its source,
mystified that Skip hadn't seemed to have
heard it. He just kept smiling. Then I realized
the siren was only inside my head. The green

monster was loose, because Skip had been talking with Pam.

"My girlfriend?" I asked, probably sounding as dazed as I was.

"Yeah, your girlfriend. She came by a few days ago to thank me and Saporta for saving your ass. She's one *fine* looking woman. Nicely proportioned. What's she see in you?"

I noticed the name he said—Saporta—before the siren grew louder. "How is Saporta?" I asked, acting like I'd known the young patrolman's name all along—and hoping to get Skip onto another subject. I failed.

"He's floating on a cloud, ever since Pam kissed him."

Pam? *Kissed* him?

"Yeah," Skip continued, "I think he'd stop a *howitzer* shell, for just another taste of her luscious lips." For a reason I couldn't fathom, Skip was trying—successfully—to get under my skin.

"Seriously, Skip," I whined, "I have a problem on my hands. Can you help me out here?"

He quit smiling and simply stared at me for a moment. Then he looked at his watch again. Finally, he walked past me, back into the building. "C'mon," he said. "I can give you ten minutes."

I followed him past the entrance to the police headquarters and down a main corridor. He stopped at a door near the front of the building. On the wall beside the door was a small plate inscribed with the words: COMMUNITY ROOM. Skip cracked the door, looked inside, and then pushed it all the way open. He flipped on the lights to reveal a small conference room, with a utilitarian table and a half dozen mismatched chairs.

"What is this?" I asked, as I followed him in. "An interrogation room?"

"Hardly. It's supposed to be a meeting room for local service groups. It doesn't get much use, though, 'cause no one knows it's here."

"Our highly efficient municipal government at work," I said, trying to be flip.

Skip ignored my comment. He sat down in a chair and pushed another one out from the table with his foot. I hesitated, not sure whether he intended the second chair to be my seat or his footrest. When he put his feet up on the table, I sat down.

"So what's your problem?" he asked curtly. "Don't like what that bitch from *The Dispatch* wrote about you?"

That bitch, huh? Was Skip irritated about Dorothy McCrae's slant on the shooting? I had thought her article to be even-handed—an accurate if somewhat dramatized account of the event. She hadn't portrayed Skip as a hero, nor Greer as a villain. They had just been two characters in a play, as had I.

"No, she quoted me fairly. What about you?"

Skip regarded his fingernails, as if to say that a lingering hang-nail was of greater interest to him than my question, or this conversation. He shrugged and said: "I have no complaints. I just didn't like her attitude.

"But we're not here to talk about some reporter, are we?" He stopped looking at his nails and stared impassively at me.

"No. We're here to talk about my legal problems, stemming from the death of Gary Greer."

Skip smiled again. "Yeah, I heard you're getting some grief from the squad, for entering the house before—"

"I'm not talking about the goddamn squad, Sergeant. I'm talking about a liability suit filed by Angela Greer. A suit that blames *me* for her husband's death."

I cut Skip short, and raised my voice in doing it. Maybe I over-acted, but I got his attention. He squinted at me as though disbelieving what I had just said.

"That makes no sense," he mumbled.

"Maybe not to you, and certainly not to me," I agreed, "but it apparently makes sense to Angie Greer and her lawyer."

"What's the lawyer's name?"

"Offhand, I don't remember. Does it matter?"

Skip shrugged again. "Just thought it might be the same asshole who was nosing around here last week. Guy by the name of Presser, or Pressler—something like that. Looking for an angle. Even when a low-life like Gary Greer gets what he asked for, you can expect some bottom-feeding attorney to show up and cause trouble.

"This particular clown didn't pursue the matter, though, once he learned that Greer had fired first."

Skip's comment raised three questions in my mind. I debated which of the three to ask first, and settled on the safest one.

"Tell me what you knew about Gary Greer."

"What I knew, or what I suspected?"

"Both."

Skip exhaled and looked at the ceiling. "Well, I *knew* he was a heavy drinker, a wife beater, and a lazy, no-good bastard. He somehow glommed onto Angie in one of her weaker moments, and for years he made her pay for that weakness. Dearly.

"What we *suspected* was that he was a part-time dealer of controlled substances. We nicked him on possession charges—two or three times—but never caught him selling. The word was that he supplied most of the druggies in the apartment complexes, and made enough doing it to keep himself in booze. Angie works, and she probably paid for everything else—food, rent, car and clothes. You'd think she would have thrown him out long ago, but she wouldn't even press charges against him when we had him *dead to rights* for abuse. And that happened several times."

Skip paused. He brought his feet down from the table and looked at me. His voice was noticeably lower when he continued.

"But I'll tell you, Scott, I was surprised as hell that Gary had a gun that night, and even *more* surprised that he used it. He always struck me as a coward, as the kind of scum who could pummel a defenseless woman, but would cower and whimper if you got the upper hand on him. We still don't know why he shot Saporta."

I prepared my second question. An answer would probably not help my defense against Angie Greer's lawsuit, but I needed to know it anyway. I guessed that Skip was as likely to have the answer as anybody.

"Before you and Saporta arrived, Greer accused me of, ah, having had relations with his wife. It didn't seem like he had any doubt about *whether* she'd been, you know, doing it with another guy; his only question was *who*. Do you know if Angie Greer was, um, fooling around?"

Tell me, how do you ask that question, without sounding like a priss, or an oaf?

Skip gave me his cold stare. "I'm sorry, Scott," he said in an emotionless tone, "but you've obviously mistaken me for someone who gives a damn. If Angie Greer was, or is, screwing the mail-man, or the paper boy, or the neighbor's golden retriever, I wouldn't know. Nor care. It wouldn't surprise me, though, consid-ering the shit her husband was."

Well, so much for Skip's help in that matter. He not only didn't *answer* my question, but made it clear he had no interest in the topic. He looked at his watch, which made me jump into my third question before I'd completely thought it through.

"Did someone in your department tell Angie Greer's lawyer that I made a mistake on that call?"

As soon as the question left my mouth, I knew I hadn't done an admirable job of phrasing it. Hell, why didn't I just accuse Skip and his colleagues of tossing me to the wolves?

Yet Skip took no offense at my flawed sentence structure. His lack of polish notwithstanding, I must admit he's a pretty sharp guy. He had, apparently, already figured out how and why Angie Greer's lawyer had determined to implicate me.

At this point, you see, I still believed that Skip might come to my assistance—if I didn't get him pissed off with my crass ques-tions and banal comments. He'd pulled my chestnuts out of the fire once already; maybe he'd do it again. Maybe he disliked bot-tom-feeding attorneys as much as he disliked cop-shooting drug dealers. Maybe...

"You know, Scott," he said slowly, "you have no one but your-self to blame for your troubles. If I were you—and I'm glad I'm not—I'd get myself a lawyer. He'll tell you what's going on here, and what a judge will see if it gets that far.

"He'll see a grieving widow. He'll see a police force that did nothing wrong, but was forced to take out a guy because some *dumb* shit of a first aid volunteer disobeyed his own squad's regu-lations, and thereby jeopardized three or four lives.

"Maybe, if you're lucky, a judge will see the lawsuit for what it is—a dipstick lawyer's attempt to capitalize on your mistake and Angie Greer's misfortune. Maybe he'll let you off the hook. But I wouldn't count on it."

O-kay. So maybe Skip wasn't going to be much help. Maybe he

was feeling an occasional twinge of guilt about shooting Gary Greer, and maybe he blamed me for being the catalyst. If that was the case, I couldn't really blame him.

"Then again," he added, after a moment's reflection, "maybe a judge will look beyond the lawyers' arguments, and see this incident for what it really was. If that happens, he just might give you a medal, for helping to rid the world of a slime like Gary Greer."

NO RELIEF

12

THE NEXT MORNING WAS HOT, AND the afternoon hotter still. As Miles Coates would say: "'Twas hotter than the hammers of hell." The air conditioning at DataStaff provided adequate relief, but I'd have preferred a bracing dip in somebody else's pool.

I thought about taking a drive the next day, Saturday, to drop in on my older brother, David. His property in Westchester County just happens to include one of those aquatic conveniences.

David's daughters—my darling nieces—certainly wouldn't object to an unexpected visit from their Uncle Scott. They're still at an age that permits them to horse around and splash water and do silly dives, and I'm still at that age too. In fact, if it was only the two of them I had to contend with, I'd have packed my flip-flops, sun tan oil, and inflatable raft—and scheduled my departure for mid-morning.

But, unfortunately, I can never travel to my brother's without paying due homage to the lords of the manor: David and his wife, Donna. He's my only brother and she, thankfully, is my only sister-in-law, and the two of them are both royal pains in the ass. To give you a minor example: one time, when I stopped by uninvited, David introduced me to a neighbor as his "younger bother." Dropping the "r" was so clever, he thought, that he still manages to repeat it at least three times an hour while I'm there. He says it with a smirk.

That I can handle. What I can't handle is the rarefied air of superiority he and Donna breathe, and the unctuous sweat of disdain they exude. If pompousness could be bottled and sold—like, say, spring water—they'd be running three shifts up there and employing a fleet of trucks to haul the shit away. Hell, they'd corner the market in a week.

But there was still another consideration that, ultimately, made me decide against the trip. Pam would not be coming, and showing up without her would make the visit even more painful than otherwise. Maybe I should explain why.

First of all, my nieces—bless their hearts—just adore Pam. She plays games with them and admires their clothes and laughs at their stupid jokes. She's more like an older sister to them than a surrogate aunt. They'd be somewhat disappointed if I arrived alone, and I don't like disappointing them.

Conversely, if I showed up on their veranda without Pam along, my sister-in-law would be pleased—and I try not to do *anything* that pleases Donna. She wouldn't be overjoyed to see *me*, of course, but she'd be greatly relieved that Pam had not accompanied me. Donna makes a point of rolling her eyes when Pam misses a punch line, and she frets when her daughters emulate Pam's mannerisms and malapropisms. I think her main problem with Pam, though, is physical. The first time I brought Pam with me, for an impromptu pool party, David's jaw hit the pavement when Pam innocently removed her beach robe to show off her new, hot pink maillot. It was so new, in fact, the price tag was still affixed to the shoulder strap. Not that David noticed that particular detail, of course; he was too busy rubbing his ear, the one Donna had caught with a swift backhand.

Finally, if I journeyed solo to my brother's place, I'd spend the better part of the afternoon answering questions about Pam. Questions I couldn't or wouldn't want to answer. *Why isn't she here? Did she forget you had a date, again? Are you two having problems? Are you two getting engaged?* And so on. For that reason alone, the trip simply wouldn't be worth it, so I started to think of alternatives. It pains me to say that my options were few, so I picked up the phone and dialed the number for Miles Coates' beeper. Ten minutes later, he called back.

"You got a problem?" he asked, rather abruptly.

"No, I just wondered if you had any plans for this weekend."

"Whatsamatter," he taunted me, "did Pam finally wise up and toss you over?"

"Something like that."

"Well, maybe I can grab a beer with you this evening, but I'm outta here tomorrow and Sunday. Going to see my folks–"

Bee-bee-bee-bee-bee-bee-bee!

My squad pager, which had been sitting silently—until now—on the corner of my desk, cut off Miles' recitation of his weekend plans. He heard the squealing tones, over the phone, almost as clearly as I did just four feet away.

"Is that your squad pager?" he asked, just before the dispatcher signed on.

"Yeah. You don't have yours with you?"

"Nope," he replied. "I'm on a job right now, and I need the cash. Can't be running out on paying customers just to fix somebody's bloody nose. I got a mound of bills that all say *past due.*"

The dispatcher came on, more animated than usual: "Dayfield dispatch to the Dayfield Rescue Squad, please respond to a possible drowning at 601 Rosewood Drive—the DePasquale residence. Victim is male, age 70, not breathing. Repeating Dayfield dispatch to the Dayfield Squad, please respond to a possible drowning at 601 Rosewood Drive—that's in the Canal Bridge development. MICU is being dispatched. Time is 14:46. Out."

"A drowning, huh?" Miles said as the pager went silent. "Some poor fellow trying to beat the heat, and ending up with flooded lungs. That's why you'll never see me in water above my ankles. I'd rather sweat than swim."

"You're better at it," I observed.

"You got that right."

"Do you know who's on duty?" I wondered.

Miles scoffed at my question. "There *is* no duty crew, man. We're low on daytime help to begin with, and half the squad is away on vacation. Or haven't you heard?"

"You can't scramble?" I asked.

"No way," he answered definitely. "I gotta get back to work. I'll call you later. No—better still—I'll meet you at seven at *Jason's*. Gotta go." He hung up before I could say another word.

I brought the pager up to my ear, waiting and hoping to hear a squad member report that a crew was going into service. When—after a few minutes of silence—there was no such response, the dispatcher put out a second call. Another minute passed before I heard a female voice, very faint, responding.

"Um, this is ambulance 84...at the Canal Bridge bay?" the woman said, nervously and with considerable hesitation. I didn't recognize her voice at all. "We have two probationary members standing by. Um, could you tell us what we should do?"

"Hold on a second, 84," the dispatcher responded. He was not sure himself what to say to a pair of rookies.

I shook my head, knowing that what I was about to do would probably be judged improper, according to some obscure regulation. But *something* had to be done. I picked up my phone and dialed the dispatcher. He answered on the second ring. He didn't disguise his annoyance at being interrupted in the midst of mobilizing an emergency response team.

I got directly to the point. "This is an active squad member in the Hilltop part of town. Tell the probationary members to roll; I'll get to the scene as quickly as I can."

The dispatcher seemed relieved as he acknowledged my instructions, and relayed them to the probies standing by. I grabbed my pager and started out.

As I dashed through the reception area, I told Fran I had to step out for a few minutes. She frowned at me. "Where you going?" she asked, picking up a pen to make a note of my answer.

"On a squad call," I replied tersely. I thought: What's it to you, anyway?

Her frown deepened. "You're not on duty," she reminded me. "Let somebody else handle it."

"There *is* nobody else," I replied, pushing the door open.

She yelled after me as I went down the stairs: "Aren't you in enough trouble as it is?"

Her words reached me just as I went through the outside doors. In combination with the sweltering humidity that quickly enveloped me, they forced me to pause and catch my breath.

Trouble? What could Fran know about my difficulties with the squad, or with Angie Greer's lawsuit? I hadn't told her—or anybody else at DataStaff—about those annoyances. Then, as I ran through the parking lot, another disturbing possibility needled me: maybe Fran hadn't been referring to the problems that I had on my plate. Maybe she was tuned in to some office talk that had somehow circumvented my cubicle. I made a mental note to quiz her about it later.

My car, which had been sitting for hours in the broiling sun, was like an oven. I started it up and turned on the air conditioner, full blast, before finding my Dayfield street map in the glove compartment. I had no idea where I was going. The Canal Bridge section of town was several miles from where I sat, and Rosewood Drive—in all probability—was an obscure little side street that couldn't be accessed without a dozen stops and turns. If, as the dispatcher had reported seven long minutes before, an elderly man had been dragged from his pool in respiratory arrest, there was almost no chance I could do him any good. I only hoped the police had arrived quickly enough, and that the responding patrolman had kept his CPR skills sharp.

It took me nine more minutes to get to the scene, a large white colonial at the end of a cul-de-sac. A patrol car and the ambulance were already there. I parked in the street. Though my clothes were already damp with sweat, I pulled on my squad jacket as I made my way to the back of the house. I opened the gate of a six-foot stockade fence and immediately found what I was seeking.

At the far end of an average-sized, in-ground swimming pool were five people. Two of the five, both women, were standing apart from the other three. The remaining three were in uniform, and they were crouched down, apparently working on the patient. As I drew closer to them, and got a better view of what they were doing, I corrected myself: It wasn't a patient they were tending to, it was a corpse. At least, there was no doubt in *my* mind that the drowned man was absolutely, positively dead. I could tell—by his skin's pallor, the amorphous arrangement of his limbs, and the bloated condition of his thorax—that life wouldn't be breathed back into his body. Nevertheless, I did a quick evaluation—a pulse and pupil check (non-existent and fully dilated, in that order)—before appraising the resuscitation ritual already in progress.

The three people in uniform were a police officer, whom I did not know, and the two probationary squad members, whom I knew only slightly. The patrolman's clothes were soaked from the chest down; I assumed he had pulled the body from the pool. Both of the squad members were women, both were young, and both nervous as hell. With the patrolman's assistance, they were performing a reasonable approximation of CPR on the pallid victim. They were ventilating him with a bag-valve-mask, with oxygen attached, and compressing his sternum. If any of the three knew that their efforts—at this point—were simply for show, none let on. I offered nothing but a few words of encouragement.

According to protocol, I should have relieved the patrolman and taken charge of the patient's treatment. But since the officer seemed content, and competent, working with the two young probies, I didn't interfere.

The two other women at the scene were standing together about twenty feet away. I approached them, guessing that the older of the two was the victim's wife. She looked the part: confused, apprehensive, irritated. Her companion, a neighbor, was doing a fair job of keeping her calm. Both women looked at me expectantly as I came near. But, knowing better than to offer hope where there was none, I simply reached into my jacket pocket for a note pad and pen. The paramedics would be arriving soon, and they would do the dirty work of pronouncing. In the meantime, I'd confirm the man's name and medical history for the record.

His name was Philip DePasquale, and he had a history of heart problems. His wife, Meredith, told me that he had come out to the swimming pool about an hour earlier to swim a few laps. When she came looking for him later, she had found him floating "in a most peculiar manner—face down."

As I asked my questions of Meredith DePasquale, she kept glancing over my shoulder at her lifeless husband and the three-some working on him. Each time she did so, she frowned disapprovingly. After the third or fourth time this occurred, I turned to look at the rookies and the cop performing CPR, expecting to see something amiss. For the most part, however, their resuscitative efforts were acceptable—though fruitless.

Finally I had to ask: "Is something wrong?" It was a stupid question, I'll admit, but I think she understood why I asked it.

She glanced again. Then she whispered to me, as though not wanting her neighbor to hear: "Why is Philip naked?"

I turned again and looked at her lifeless husband. Silly me, I hadn't noticed before that Philip didn't have a stitch on. Now how could I have missed that? I turned back to the woman. "Isn't that how you found him?" I asked, innocently enough.

She stared at me in shock, as though I had accused her husband—and her, perhaps—of something indecent. "Certainly not!" she snapped. "Those two young women removed his swim trunks when they got here!"

They did, did they?

"Hold on a second," I said to Meredith DePasquale. I walked back to the group of three, still performing CPR. I could hear the wail of the MICU's siren, just up the street. Crouching down next to one of the probies, I quietly asked her and her partner: "Did you two strip this guy, or is this how you found him?"

The one probie glanced at the other one, who glanced up at me. She continued to compress the man's chest as she replied: "He looked so uncomfortable. I thought he'd breathe better if we took off his shorts. Isn't that what you're supposed to do, to do CPR?"

Actually, no. A bare chest is necessary, a bare bottom is not. But I didn't want to chastise the young woman for simply doing what she thought was right. I said nothing.

As she returned her attention to her work, I stood up straight and gazed down at Philip DePasquale. After five years as an EMT, and roughly six hundred emergency calls, I've become accustomed—indifferent, even—to the sight of patients in various stages of undress. In fact, after observing my first dozen or more nude victims, I started to notice a somewhat perplexing yet undeniable trend. At some point, I codified my findings into a truism, which I've humbly entitled *Scott's Law*. My truism is this:

Most people, alive or dead, are far more attractive with their clothes on.

Philip DePasquale, I noted on this hot afternoon, was no exception to *Scott's Law*.

I glanced around and spotted a towel on a nearby lounge chair. Unobtrusively I took the towel and draped it over the dead man's lower regions. The two probies flinched slightly at my implied rebuke. Again I gave them a word of encouragement, and returned to Philip's wife.

She nodded appreciatively at me, but nonetheless raised an eyebrow as though expecting an explanation. Isn't it funny, I thought, the things that some people consider important, even in a crisis? Or maybe, *especially* in a crisis?

"They were concerned your husband may have injured his pelvis," I said to Meredith DePasquale, "so they exposed the area to check it out."

"Did he hurt himself?" she asked.

Did it matter? "I don't believe so," I mumbled.

My lie seemed to satisfy her. She nodded again, contentedly. Then she asked a question that made me wish I had joined in the thumping and pumping, and left the public relations work to the patrolman. "Will you have to take him to the hospital?"

There was a possibility—a possibility that I nurtured for a second—that the woman knew her husband was dead, and she simply wanted to avoid carting his body from one facility to another. But I couldn't just assume that.

"I'm not sure," I said simply.

"Well," she continued, "if you *must* take him to the hospital, I hope they don't have to admit him. I have something special planned for this evening, and I wouldn't want him to miss it."

Forget the possibilities; this was full-scale denial. The woman had not even entertained the notion that her husband might already be wafting his way to the great beyond. Apparently, she couldn't understand why he wasn't already up, kicking and sputtering and ordering us off his property.

From there, the situation went downhill. The paramedics came jogging onto the scene just then, carrying their advanced life support equipment. There were two of them: a woman I had never seen before, and a man I wish I could say the same of. I'll tell you why in a minute. As they approached Philip DePasquale, I could see in their eyes that they were both arriving at the same conclusion I had. Still, they knelt down and started the usual procedures.

Meredith DePasquale nudged me on the shoulder. "Who are they?" she asked suspiciously. She noticed how readily the two probies and the patrolman had released Philip into their care.

"They're paramedics from St. Gregory's Hospital," I answered simply.

"Paramedics, huh? Well, if *they're* paramedics," she said, even more suspiciously, while turning to face me, "then what are *you?*"

"An EMT," I answered, trying not to sound defensive.

"A *what?*"

"An emergency medical technician. I'm a volunteer."

Meredith DePasquale crossed her arms in front of her, and stared at me in silence for a moment. I knew what was taking place in her mind. Once again, Hollywood's influence had compromised the effectiveness of the volunteer EMS community.

On the few occasions when I've watched prime time television dramas, or even a soap opera, I've noticed what happens whenever an actor dials 9-1-1 and breathlessly requests an ambulance. Invariably, it's the *paramedics* who show up—promptly and impressively—in the very next scene. Her frame of reference thus defined, Mrs. DePasquale was no doubt wondering why her husband had been afforded something less in his moment of distress.

As she looked at me, and then at the two most recent arrivals in uniform, she was probably building a mental hierarchy of the entire EMS world in general, and, specifically, of the six responders now on the scene. Briefly I wondered if I had landed at the bottom. Then Roy spoke up, and her imagined hierarchy came crashing down.

"Roy" is the male paramedic's first name; I'm happy to say I don't remember his last. Let's just call him Roy Shit-For-Brains, and take it from there.

It's a well-known fact that many paramedics in the field did *not* deliberately choose their profession. More than a few are wannabe doctors, and many just drift into the business and surprise no one when, a year or two later, they drift right back out of it. Some just love the occasional gore, and some are simply indifferent to it. I've known paramedics who are gracious, caring and highly-skilled—and I've encountered a few who are the meanest bitches and bastards ever to don a stethoscope. Yet none that I've met can compare with Roy Shit-For-Brains.

Roy's not a total incompetent; I'll say that much for him. He obviously made it through the required training, and probably did an adequate job on his boards. I'd trust him, for example, to know the difference between a nosebleed and a broken leg—provided the patient in each case was alert and could at least point to the problem area.

No, Roy's biggest handicap isn't that his medical expertise is on a par with Doctors Moe and Larry, it's that his level of common sense is several notches below that of Doctor Curly. And what makes the entire package even less palatable is his insufferable manner with patients and their next-of-kin. On more than one occasion I've cringed while Roy—within seeing and hearing distance of an anxious loved one—has made a sorry attempt at gallows humor, at the expense of the mortally ill or injured. At this call, on this broiling afternoon in Philip DePasquale's backyard, Roy Shit-For-Brains did it again.

This time, it was Groucho Marx that Roy chose to become. After performing a quick inspection—and instructing the probies and the police officer to cease CPR—Roy grasped an imaginary cigar in his right hand, flicked away some imaginary ashes, and rolled his eyes a few times. "Either this man is dead," he pronounced, the impersonation close enough only to be painful, "or my watch has stopped." He paused, hoping for a laugh, I suppose, but only an uncomfortable silence ensued.

Meredith DePasquale turned slowly to me, an expression of absolute shock on her face. "What...what did he say?" she asked, her voice trembling slightly. "Did he say Philip was...*dead?*"

I wanted to tell her to ask Shit-For-Brains himself what he had said. It would have been appropriate to let him be the one to confirm, and perhaps explain, his coarse pronouncement. But there was no sense subjecting the poor woman to any more abuse.

"Yes," I responded somberly. "I'm afraid your husband is dead, Mrs. DePasquale."

She shook her head, as if she knew better than we did. "No, no, he can't be dead," she assured me. "He just can't."

I looked at the woman paramedic. Though I had never met her before, I confidently assumed that she had more sense than her partner. She shook her head at me. There was no doubt that Philip DePasquale was no longer with us.

I asked myself: what would Billie DeMarino do in this case? Answering my own question, I took Meredith DePasquale's hand in both of mine, squeezed it, and looked her in the eyes. It wasn't too difficult to be compassionate.

"Your husband is dead, Mrs. DePasquale," I repeated. "There was nothing we could do."

That's when she started to lose it. She kept shaking her head, as her eyes filled with tears. "He just *can't* be dead," she said again. "He can't. Today's his birthday, and I have a cake in the oven for him right now. Our...our children are on their way. They'll be here in a few hours. One's driving from Pennsylvania, with our grandchildren. The other's flying in from Texas. Philip can't be dead. He *can't.*"

She broke down and wept. Thank God her neighbor was there to hold her, because I wasn't up to the job. When I released her hands, I strode immediately over to Shit-For-Brains, my anger rising with each step. He stepped back as I came near, his hands in front of him.

"Calm down, jerk-off," he told me defiantly. "It isn't my fault the old guy's croaked. Can't you take a joke?"

I managed to control myself. Barely. "If there's nothing else for you to do," I hissed, "then why don't you just get the hell out of here? Go find another audience to practice your sick routines on."

Shit-For-Brains shook his head, arrogantly. "Can't," he said. "Can't leave until the M.E. releases us. We got an unwitnessed death here. But you—you and your fellow incompetents—you can take off any time you want. Go back to your squad building, and put in some time with your Annie dolls. You could use the practice. I've never seen such a poor excuse for CPR as I saw here a minute ago. I've seen *foreplay* performed with more vigor."

"I'm sure you have," I shot back. "And I'll bet you wanted to put another quarter in the machine to see it again, but your hands were all gooey."

"Guys. This isn't the time, or the place." The woman paramedic was trying to restore some semblance of decorum to the scene. Her censorious tone silenced the both of us, though we continued to glare at one another.

Finally I turned to my two fellow squad members, who were still kneeling next to Philip DePasquale's corpse. Their eyes were averted. They were waiting for some signal, some instruction on how to proceed. The situation had suddenly become very awkward, very uncomfortable. Now it was up to me to get us out of there, as gracefully as I could.

"Gather your equipment, girls. We've been relieved by a higher authority. You did your best. Let's go now." I tried very hard to keep my voice even as I said it.

"A higher authority," Shit-For-Brains sneered. "That's the first thing you've gotten right."

"Roy, knock it off," his partner warned.

Like ducklings, the probies followed me away from the pool and out of the yard. We could hear Meredith DePasquale wailing behind us, even as we reached the front of the house. As I passed the MIC unit, parked on the driveway, I held back an urge to smash a headlight, or dent a fender. It wouldn't have done much good.

The two young probationary members were quite shaken. I helped them complete their call report, and again praised their efforts, before I sent them on their way.

"They can't all have happy endings," I mumbled to myself, as the ambulance drove away, silently.

NO TOMORROW

13

MILES BOUGHT THE FIRST ROUND, and I paid for the next two or three. Not that I minded, though. With Miles Coates, I need not pretend that the cost of a few imported beers will clean me out. We've been close friends for several years, since shortly after I joined the squad, so by now he knows the score. And—without dwelling on the fact that his one-man landscaping business has been struggling of late—it's the least I can do to pick up our bar bill.

After the events of the last two days, I needed some cheering up. That's something I can normally count on Miles to manage. His wry comments about the crowd that frequents *Jason's* on a Friday evening are usually worth the cost of his company. We typically sit at a booth far from the dance floor and, in asides to each other, skewer our fellow patrons. It's not difficult to do.

Jason's is a curious place. It's not a nightclub and it's not a tavern and it's not a family restaurant by any means, but it has elements of all three. If you can stand the constant ambient noise—thought to be music by those who don't know any better—the establishment can be counted on to serve a decent sandwich, a cold beer, and the opportunity to observe at least four distinct social animals at play.

For starters, the remnants of what used to be a yuppie clan occasionally hang out at the long tables next to the bar, trading stories of investments and ventures that haven't quite lived up to expectations. A few years back, these guys and dolls were bona fide worldbeaters—they partied loud and long and threw money around like there was no tomorrow. Well, they were right about that: tomorrow has yet to arrive. Now they're a smaller, more conservative group. I get a certain perverse pleasure when I see one of them glancing surreptitiously into his wallet, hoping for reassurance he can cover his tab for the evening.

The bar itself is usually occupied by sunburned construction workers in grimy t-shirts and jeans, who snicker at the yups when not comparing notes on housing developers who've fallen behind on their accounts payable. A generation ago, this faction would have been known as the shot-and-a-beer crowd, and its members would have included local factory workers and iron miners. The factories are gone, of course, and the mines have long since closed. Also, it's rare these days that a shot glass keeps company with the frosted bottles that arrive and depart in groups of four or six.

On occasion, one or two rednecks among this group will get rowdy or even belligerent—Miles attributes such behavior to too many hormones, suspended in too much alcohol, acting upon too little brain matter—but it's rare that actual hostilities break out. There's always the chance, though, so we keep a hopeful eye on these fellows.

Surrounding the dance floor, mostly, are the members of a third distinct species: the single and recently-divorced working women who, for lack of anything better to do, sip at spritzers and sweet drinks between dances with each other...or with anyone else who's willing. Dancing, I'm convinced, has become a lost art, but fond memories of their senior proms and best friends' wedding receptions keep these girls—don't call them ladies, yet—from giving it up altogether. A boogie-woogie called *The Electric Glide*—or something like that—is a current favorite, though it seems to be on its way out.

Finally, at the perimeter of the establishment are the rapidly-aging married couples who munch on burgers and greasy fries while trying to remember why they came here in the first place. Miles and I usually sit among this last group, comfortably ignoring their glances and presumptions that we're anything other than two friends sharing a few beers and simple conversation. I think we're often estimated to be a pair of off-duty vice cops, probably because he's black and I'm white and people have come to expect that particular combination of undercover partners—though in actuality the police departments of most suburban communities are far less integrated than Hollywood would have us imagine. Perhaps we even encourage that mistaken impression by the way we sit with our backs to the wall, hardly glancing at each other while sizing up and cutting down our fellow patrons.

Okay, okay... so it's not the most stimulating use of a Friday evening. But it beats sitting home with a rented video, or doing the laundry.

Miles didn't seem surprised—or even interested, for that matter—when I told him about my recent difficulties with Pam, and about the pending lawsuit.

"You knocked over the first domino," he dryly observed. "Now you just have to hang in there until they stop falling." That was, in fact, his total commentary on my personal problems of the moment. Which just goes to show: When one's best friend can offer such insights, who needs a shrink? And this I was getting for the bargain price of three or four beers...

We were on our fourth, actually, when I noticed a young woman, standing alone near the bar, looking our way. She smiled and waved, which caused Miles and me to glance at one another, each of us expecting the other to identify her. I raised my palms and he shrugged, which meant, if nothing else, that our fourth round tonight should also be our last. We both waved back, weakly, confirming that neither of us had a clue who she was.

As we feared she would, she approached us. It didn't seem possible—to either of us, apparently—that the young woman was a total stranger who simply desired some male companionship, and was boldly seeking it from one or both of us. As if the offerings near the bar did not suit her tastes. We squirmed in our seats, racking our muddled brains for the occasion on which we had met this woman before. She was at our table, still smiling, before a glimmer of something recognizable appeared in her face. But it was only a glimmer, which made me even more ill at ease.

"Hello, Scott. How are you?" she said amiably, if a little formally. And though I was staring at her, smiling stupidly, I could see Miles exhaling in relief. He was off the hook; I had to pretend.

Now, it would have been easy enough to simply confess my lapse of memory, if the woman wasn't so appealing. I don't meet many people from one week to the next—unless you count accident victims, which I don't—so it was unlikely I could have previously spent any time with this woman and not remembered her. Three beers do not impair my recognitive abilities *that* severely.

It wasn't polite, but I had no choice: I surveyed her from top to bottom, searching for some identifying feature. At least it was a pleasant exercise. She was of medium height, dressed in a stylish—if somewhat provocative—outfit. She wore a pair of form-fitting culottes, and a silky white blouse, open to the waist. Beneath the blouse was a tight, black-and-white-striped, thin-strapped top. Her shape was—shall we say—*shapely*, which means that the striped top and the culottes curved in all the desired directions. She had several gold bracelets on her wrists, and the last two fingers on each hand were adorned with single, elegant rings. She held her hands together in a ladylike fashion while she waited for my reply.

The features of her face and head only confounded the mystery. Her hair was brunette, full, and curled forward at her shoulders. Her lips, colored a glossy magenta, were parted slightly, revealing a gleaming white set of teeth. Her cheeks were rouged and her eyes made up as though she had just been visited by an overeager Mary Kay saleswoman. Her entire visage, in fact, seemed completely out of place in *Jason's*, and more appropriate for the pages of a glamour magazine. Overdone, perhaps, but not garishly so.

She must have sensed that I did not recognize her, because she cocked her head and opened her eyes wider—as though reproving me for my ignorance. When she did so, I got a better look at her eyes—hazel—and that's what finally tipped me off.

"Dorothy?"

I shouldn't have phrased my greeting as a question, but I couldn't help it. Though I knew I was right, even before she nodded, my subconscious self was rejecting the match-up. The image currently reaching my brain could not simply, could not plausibly, be an updated version of the bitch with the ball cap, Dorothy McCrae.

Miles was greatly amused by my perplexity, which must have shown on my face. Then again, maybe he mistook my momentary confusion for something else. "Let me guess," he offered, knowing an introduction was not immediately forthcoming. "Miss Lovely here is an old flame from high school that you haven't seen in twelve years. Am I right?" He smiled up at Dorothy and winked. She winked back, ever so charmingly.

"Twelve years?" I murmured in a stuporous undertone. "No, more like twelve days."

"Ten," Dorothy corrected politely. "But who's counting?"

This amused Miles even more. "Well, then, Miss Lovely," he proclaimed, "you'll have to excuse my friend. He must have been tanked on that occasion, ten long days ago."

Smiling again at me, Dorothy responded: "No, not at all." Then, turning to Miles, she asked in a sweet yet authoritative tone: "Could I speak with Scott in private, please?"

Now Miles was nonplused. He raised his eyebrows and looked at me. I smiled back apologetically.

"Miss Lovely's not shy, is she?" he asked. Then, without waiting for an answer, he slid from the bench seat and stood up. "I can find my way out," he added crisply. "Catch you later, Scott. Miss Lovely." He bowed slightly and started walking away.

"Miles!" I hollered. "I'll call you later."

"Oh, joy," he said, caustically. "I'll wait by the phone." He kept walking.

I turned back to Dorothy. I was still having difficulty reconciling her present, made-up countenance with her former, unadorned appearance. But then, the presumptuous manner with which she had shooed Miles confirmed she was the same person beneath the paint. Briefly, I wondered if our meeting here had been a coincidence, or if she had sought me out. I didn't ponder the question for more than a moment because—as I quickly convinced myself—it didn't really matter.

I expected her to sit down across from me, in the seat Miles had vacated. She didn't. Rather, she sat down next to me, and slid right up against me on the padded bench. Like the gentleman I occasionally pretend to be, I made room for her by moving closer to the wall, several inches away. For the moment, she remained where she was.

Since she had invited herself, I didn't feel compelled to buy her a drink. At least not until I determined the purpose of her visit. Damned if I was going to keep her tongue lubricated just so she could flay me with it. Again.

She turned and gazed at me, and batted her hazel eyes two or three times. "I got a message you called for me, yesterday," she said smoothly. Then she added a perfect *non sequitur:* "You're looking good, Scott."

"Yes, I called. Your hair's different," I said, indifferently.

Nimbly, she tossed the soft curls from her shoulders. "It's my natural color."

"But not your natural hair."

Her eyes twinkled at my remark, and then she laughed. It was the full, uninhibited laugh that I remembered from our first conversation, over the phone—but which had been notably absent during our meeting at the diner.

"You're very observant," she said when she finished laughing. It was then I noticed that the four-inch gap I had left between our hips had disappeared. It was also then I noticed her hand resting lightly on my leg, just above the knee. And, I think, it was also just about then I noticed her scent, which reminded me of fresh-cut evergreens. I hate the smell of evergreens.

"What were you calling about?" she asked, her voice lower, warmer.

"I need some help. I need to learn a few things about Gary Greer's widow, and I thought that you–"

"Hey! Scott! Mind if we join you?"

Another woman's voice, one that I almost recognized, brought me out of Christmas tree forest. I looked up to see a young couple approaching our table. It was Kelly Perniciaro—Pam's friend and co-worker—and her wealthy beau, what's-his-name. Kelly had hailed me in a cheerful tone, but she was eying Dorothy coldly. Kelly has always been very protective of Pam—and she knows I don't have any sisters. I could tell, immediately, that she was going to want an explanation.

"Kelly!" I said brightly, as though overjoyed to see her. "Sure, have a seat!" I gestured magnanimously to the empty bench across the table.

As she and what's-his-name sat down, Kelly remarked, wisely: "You remember Jonathan, don't you?"

That's-his-name, Jonathan.

"Certainly! How've you been, Jonathan?" I offered my hand across the table, but he only smiled dumbly and nodded. Not that Jonathan's a snob, mind you. Rather, I assumed that he had gotten his hand under Kelly's bottom, and didn't want to remove it merely to shake hands with me.

Pam and I have double-dated with Kelly and Jonathan a few times, and we're always bemused to see how persistently he gropes and paws at her in public. If I had a quarter for every time she's removed his hand from her thigh, or some other portion of her ample anatomy, I could ride the supermarket's mechanical horse for a week, non-stop.

Speaking of hands on thighs, by this time Dorothy's fingers had progressed to a point superior to my knee—but still inferior to my crotch—on the medial surface. That's EMS terminology, meaning she was stroking my inner thigh. Had we been alone, I would have been amused by, or perhaps ambivalent about, her unexpected aggression. But under Kelly's suspicious glare, I was becoming decidedly uncomfortable. Kelly couldn't see what was going on, of course, but she certainly noticed that Dorothy's hands were not topside.

"Um...Kelly...Jonathan, this is Dorothy," I said simply. There was no need—was there?—to provide any more detail than that.

Dorothy didn't even bother to extend her hand, as I had just done to no avail. Kelly nodded without expression. Jonathan continued to smile dumbly. He gazed at Dorothy and, after licking his lips, said flatly: "Pleased to meet you." Which, I must admit, was one of the wittier clumps of conversation I had ever heard from him.

"So…Kelly…Jonathan, what's new with you two?" I asked in all earnestness, though I really didn't give a damn.

"*Pam* hasn't told you?" Kelly rejoined, with the emphasis on *Pam* just a bit heavy-handed.

"Told me what?"

Kelly brought her left hand up from under the table, which, she knew, would leave her defenseless against Jonathan's forays. In a preemptive strike, she bashed his ribs with her elbow, stalling him long enough for her to dramatically display the hand, back side up, for my inspection.

It only took me a few seconds—I'm no dummy—to comprehend the point of her presentation. Her ring finger was weighted down by a rock—a diamond, I suppose—the size of a grape. She wiggled the finger with practiced skill, to capture and refract the light for maximum effect.

Oh gee, I thought, ain't this just nifty? Old what's-his-name, Jonathan the rich kid, had finally managed to assemble and enunciate those four fearsome words, and Kelly had apparently responded in the affirmative. After four-plus years of coping with his groping, Kelly would soon be exploring the facets of his assets. Seemed like a fair trade to me.

It was commonly assumed, by those of us who didn't know the whole story, that Jonathan had inherited a sizable fortune. I, for one, refused to believe that he—especially he—could have earned the kind of wealth he apparently had. He was constantly lavishing Kelly with expensive gifts, or flying off with her to some distant, exotic locale.

Kelly had decided some time ago, I guess, that social grace isn't all that it's cracked up to be. Wit and charm count for something in a mate, but there's nothing like a bank balance in seven figures to make the old heart go pitty-pat.

"Hey, that's great! Congratulations!" I blurted, speaking at first to Kelly, but then—recovering my own sense of social propriety—to her fiancé. "You're a lucky guy, Jonathan!"

He was now grinning broadly, though I wouldn't assume in response to my good wishes. The effect of Kelly's warning shot had faded, and there was little she could now do to protect her flank. Her left hand was still on the table, detained there by Dorothy, who was examining the oversized diamond. If I live to be ninety, I'll never understand why some women suddenly turn into master appraisers when exposed to another woman's engagement stone.

"Nice," Dorothy said without emotion, as her fingers recommenced their northward march on my inner thigh. Then she added: "But who's Pam? And why should she have told Scott that you two are engaged?"

Kelly withdrew her hand, but not to its former defensive position. It wasn't necessary. Even Jonathan noticed—how could he have *not* noticed?—the immediate effect Dorothy's question had on his fiancée. Hell, even I felt the chill that suddenly pervaded the room, as if somebody had thrown open a window to Nome. Kelly fixed Dorothy with an icy stare.

"You don't know Pam?" she asked, icicles forming on the words. Then she slowly turned her head, and shifted the stare from Dorothy to me. "Who is this woman?" she demanded.

I was astounded. Jonathan had actually brought both hands to the table top, and was now rubbing them together—as though to stave off frostbite. He was also staring at me, but more out of perplexity than irritation.

"Oh, calm down, Kelly," I chided, taking a high-handed approach. Dorothy's fingers stopped traveling. She took a half-inch of tender thigh flesh in her grasp, and waited. "Dorothy's a reporter for the Dayfield newspaper..." She squeezed, forcefully enough to get my attention, but I plunged on. "...and she just came by to say hello. She's the one who wrote the article about me in last week's paper. Ow!"

Dorothy pinched me, hard, but I don't think Kelly or Jonathan noticed.

"Oh, yeah!" Jonathan gushed. "I saw that article! You wrote

that?"

"Yes," Dorothy answered demurely.

"Clint Eastwood!" Jonathan continued. "Yeah, I'll agree: Scott's no Clint Eastwood."

"Nor Cary Grant," snapped Kelly. "Nor Fred Astaire. Nor Jimmy Stewart or Gene Kelly, for that matter."

Perfect gentlemen, all four. Simply amazing, I thought, how she rattled the names off without hesitation. I imagined the walls of Kelly's bedroom, from maybe twenty years gone by, and saw posters of those matinée idols, dressed in crisp black tuxedos (except Stewart, perhaps), their handsome faces smiling down at her. Kelly had made it her life's ambition to ensnare a wealthy aristocrat, and now she was halfway there.

"What's your point, Kelly?" I asked, playing dumb. She just gazed out over the dance floor, as if she hadn't heard me.

"Well, I must be going," Dorothy announced, patting my thigh consolingly, and then sliding out of the seat. "Nice meeting you both," she said flatly to Kelly and Jonathan. "Give me a call, Scott," she said as she strode away.

Kelly watched her depart, then hissed at me: "What do you see in her, anyway? She doesn't hold a candle to—"

She stopped in mid-sentence, glared at Jonathan, and nailed him again with her elbow. "If you don't quit that…" she yelled, causing a couple at the next table to turn our way. She inhaled deeply, composing herself, while Jonathan just smiled sheepishly. It was all that I could do to not burst out laughing.

When calm was restored, I prodded Kelly: "You were saying?"

"About what?" She was too flustered to recall.

"About holding a candle."

"What? Oh, yeah. That painted bitch doesn't compare to Pam— no way, no how. So why are you playing grab-ass with her?"

I shrugged. "Pam hasn't been returning my phone calls. Maybe you can tell me why."

Again Kelly looked out to the dance floor, promptly avoiding the issue. It was obvious: she knew something she wasn't telling me.

"C'mon, honey, let's go home," Jonathan whined. His hormones were killing him, I could tell.

Kelly smiled at him, and gently stroked his cheek—like a mother consoling a tired child. "In just a minute, sweetie..." she cooed.

Honey. Sweetie. I was starting to feel nauseous.

"Don't forget, we have that appointment tomorrow morning," she added, glancing my way. She paused, obviously hoping I would inquire. Who could it be?, I wondered for a moment. The caterer? Her pastor? His broker?

"What appointment is that, Kelly? If you don't mind my asking..."

She didn't mind. She smiled brightly and told me: "Jonathan was invited to join a new country club. We're getting a guided tour of the facilities tomorrow." Her pride was touching.

"Oh. Well, good for you," I said. Then, quite innocently, I asked: "By any chance, would it be Walnut Grove?"

Kelly gave her fiancé a concerned look, but he just shrugged. She turned back to me and answered, tentatively: "Yes, it is Walnut Grove. How did you know?"

Or, rather, how would the likes of you know about such things?

"Just a lucky guess."

THE FOLLOWING TUESDAY, BILLIE AND I had only one emergency call during our entire shift. But it was enough. In fact, it was the type of incident that nags me to take Miles' advice—to walk away from this volunteer bullshit. I'm just an EMT, you know. No one's paying me the big bucks that a surgeon pulls down to deal with acute trauma, so why should I subject myself to the shock and anxiety and occasional nightmares that sometimes come with the territory?

Give me a good reason, if you can, because I'm fresh out of them myself.

It started innocently enough. I was in my cubicle, extracting and assembling those "numbers" Arnie wanted from me upon his return. It was my responsibility to make a case for a client that planned to turn a wooded hillside into a strip mall, and I was halfheartedly wrestling with population densities and traffic projections and environmental impact statements—mundane things like that—when my pager sounded.

Actually, I welcomed the break from the tired and twisted statistics. It wasn't my fault—was it?—that a higher, civic responsibility was calling. Even Fran didn't seem to mind: she barely looked at me as I dashed through the reception area, pulling on my duty whites as I went.

I even welcomed the dispatcher's initial report, which I heard as I went out the front door. We were being summoned to treat a dog bite victim—exact details still to come. In my ignorance, I imagined a hapless delivery boy with a few gnaw holes in his pant leg, complaining about a nick or two. You know, superficial wounds similar to those I inflict on myself when shaving with a new blade and a hangover. Still yapping at her prey—as I envisioned the scene—was one of those ugliest of all God's four-legged creatures: a Pekingese bitch, weighing in at about twenty-two pounds.

I all but congratulated myself on my good fortune. No coronary patient to defibrillate and no grieving widow to console. Just a strip of gauze, a piece of tape, and a minimum of paper work to complete. A walk in the park.

If only I had been so lucky…

When the dispatcher came back on, I had just started my car. He now knew more than he had a minute before, but nothing of what he had learned was good. Our patient was a five-year-old girl, and the dog that had attacked her was a full-grown Japanese Akita. The image I'd had of a pug-nosed Pekingese was instantly transformed into a raging man-slayer—right out of the pages of a Jack London novel. I managed to avoid thinking about the little girl. For the moment at least.

Dogs are, in my estimation, essentially worthless creatures. They eat, they shit, they slobber, and they howl when you're trying to sleep. They pass gas, piss on your furniture, and chew up your new sneakers—even when they've been provided with a perfectly good bone to grind their molars on. I suppose some canines have a few good points—I'm always impressed by dogs that escort the blind—but the guy who determined that the species deserves the title of "man's best friend" was probably short on friends of any other variety. I'll guarantee you one thing: he had never seen the likes of Trish McDaniel, at least not in the condition the child was in when I encountered her on this Tuesday afternoon.

As I pulled out of the parking lot at DataStaff, I realized that the address of the emergency call—on Cumberland Turnpike—was closer to me than was the Hilltop ambulance bay. Since my crew chief, Billie DeMarino, could be counted on to realize that as well, I sped directly to the scene. The number painted on the curbside mailbox confirmed I had found the right location.

I was the first to arrive.

It was a small house, set well back from the road. An unpaved, circular driveway wound past a number of shaggy shrubs and overgrown pine trees. As I coasted to a stop near the front porch, I could hear a dog barking from within the house. It was a heavy, excited snapping noise—not the menacing growl I would have expected—but it nonetheless filled me with an apprehension that I couldn't ignore. I climbed out of the car and started looking about for a stick or a board or anything I might use to defend myself, if the dog was still free to cause more damage. It was then that I saw the blood.

There were a few drops on the walkway leading to the porch. On the steps were two or three large splatters. On the porch itself, just outside the door, was a red puddle the size of a medium pizza. I'll never forget how vividly it contrasted with the slate gray color the porch had been painted.

I opened my trunk and pulled out my first aid kit. Then I lifted the floor matting and grabbed the tire iron that accompanied the car's jack. It occurred to me, just then, that I had never used the jack, nor the lug wrench in my hand. I hoped I wouldn't use it this day, either.

Looking up, I saw a young woman—a teenager, actually—staring vacantly at me from inside the storm door. As I came closer, she slowly opened the door to receive me. Her eyes were glassy, as though she was in shock.

"In here," she said in an eerie, lifeless monotone.

I hesitated. Wasn't I already in trouble for entering a victim's home before the police arrived? I strained to hear an approaching siren. Nothing.

"In here," the girl said again, in the same monotone.

"Where's the dog?" I demanded.

"What?"

"The dog! Where's the dog?"

"I put him in the basement," she said, without emotion.

"Are you sure he can't get out?" As soon as I asked the question, I realized how poorly I had phrased it. If she answered "no," would that mean "no, he can't" or "no, I'm not sure"?

"Yes," she answered, trance-like.

"Yes, what?"

"Yes, I'm sure he can't get out. The door's latched."

Okay, the scene was presumably safe.

"Where's the little girl?" I asked.

"In here," the teenager said for a third time, still in a monotone. "She's laying down."

I peered over her shoulder into the house. Immediately I saw the little girl, sitting on the floor in the hallway, leaning back against the wall. She had a towel—a blood-soaked rag—wrapped over her face. She was sobbing beneath it.

Now I could hear a siren, still in the distance.

"What's her name?" I asked the older girl.

"Patricia. We call her 'Trish.'"

"And what's your name?"

The older girl cowered, as though I was going to hit her. "Laura," she answered meekly. "I'm…I'm the babysitter."

"Okay, Laura, I want you to do something." I took a note pad from my pocket, ripped off a sheet, and wrote a phone number on it. As I handed it to her, I said slowly and distinctly: "Go call this number. Let it ring until someone answers. It'll probably be a woman. Tell her that Scott is already at the scene, and she can roll the rig. You got that?"

Laura shook her head. "She can do what?"

"Tell the woman to bring the ambulance. Now."

Laura nodded, staring dumbly at the phone number. Then she turned and ran into the next room. The dog, wherever he was, barked louder.

I caught the storm door before it closed. The siren behind me was much closer now. Taking a good grip on the tire iron, I entered the house. At this point, I wasn't much concerned about squad regulations. I was just worried about the damn dog.

I hastened to the little girl's side. There was blood everywhere:

on the floor, the wall, and all over her clothes. Most of it, I assumed, had come from a wound, or wounds, that the babysitter had hastily covered with the towel. The only other damage I could see was a gash on the little girl's forearm. The gash was ugly, but not very serious.

"Trish?" I said softly, kneeling down beside her.

"Yes," she murmured between sobs.

"My name is Scott. I'm with the first aid squad, and I'm here to help you."

"Yes," she said again, weakly.

I set down the tire iron and opened my first aid kit. Two rolls of gauze, tape and scissors—I grabbed them all and set them down next to the girl. Then I found a few sterile dressings and tore off their wrappings.

"Trish?" I said again.

She didn't answer.

I swore to myself. Reaching down, I took hold of her uninjured arm, lying limply at her side. Her skin was cool, clammy and pale. I searched for her pulse. It took a second, but I was able to find it: rapid and weak. The appropriate but disagreeable phrase entered my mind, direct from the EMS textbook. Hemorrhagic shock. Like everyone else, little girls can spare only so much blood. When the volume dips too low, the entire system starts to collapse.

"Trish, I want to look at your face now," I said quietly. I had to assume she could still hear me. "You let me know if it hurts when I take off the towel. Okay?"

Still she didn't answer. I took hold of the soggy towel, where it overlapped in the back, and slowly, carefully, started to remove it. As I lifted it away from her face, I clenched my teeth. It was one of the smarter things I did.

As the towel came off, Trish's left cheek came with it. The skin and flesh had been gouged, just below her eye, and then ripped downward to the level of her mouth. The avulsed tissue flapped forward, inside out, and released a fresh trickle of blood. I was staring at the little girl's exposed cheekbone—white streaked with red.

That was awful enough. But then it got worse. As I caught my breath, and refocused, I saw that Trish was gazing—mournfully yet hopefully—into my eyes. Though she was on the verge of losing consciousness, an inner strength had enabled her to remain alert just long enough to seek reassurance from the stranger who had come to help her. Her resolve, at that moment, hung on the reaction she saw in my eyes. If I were to grimace, or even flinch, she would probably have been overcome with despair.

I did my best not to let my initial feelings—of revulsion and pity—show on my face. Though my guts were churning, outwardly I acted unaffected. Like Hawkeye Pierce on *M*A*S*H*, I even nodded slightly. I wanted to make Trish believe that I'd seen this injury many times before, and that I knew exactly what to do for her.

Did I imagine what happened next? Did I actually see her attempt to smile? That's how I remember it, now, but I can't be sure because, just then, I realized how much Trish McDaniel looked like my brother's younger daughter, Melissa. Even with the lower half of her face partly torn away, the resemblance was remarkable. The similarity was in the eyes, I guess, though just at that point Trish's eyes began to fade.

A hand touched my shoulder. I glanced up to see Marty Gustafson, a veteran patrolman on the Dayfield Police Department, looking down at us.

"What do you need, Scott?" he asked calmly.

I looked back at my young patient. She was fighting to remain conscious. "Get me the oxygen," I answered, just as calmly. "And find out if the MIC unit has been dispatched."

"I don't think so," he said. Then he went back outside.

Using an oversized gauze pad, I gently lifted the flap of Trish's torn cheek and eased it back into place. I covered it with another sterile pad, and then started wrapping it with a gauze roll. I worked quickly, and was just securing the dressing when Officer Gustafson returned with his portable oxygen kit.

"No MIC unit," he said. "Should we call for them now?"

Outside, I heard the distinctive wail of our ambulance approaching. The babysitter had apparently conveyed my message to Billie. I could also hear the dog, still barking behind the basement door.

"No, Marty. Let's just get going." I found a child's oxygen mask in his kit, and gently fitted it on Trish's bandaged face. "Here, Trish," I said softly, "breathe this in. It will help make you feel better." I was surprised, yet gratified, when Trish nodded in response. With great effort, she brought her hand up from her side and placed it on the oxygen mask.

"That's a girl, Trish," I said.

Billie DeMarino came in the door. She glanced about, at the red-stained walls and floor, and then looked at me.

"Chief, this is Trish," I said to my partner, as I gathered our patient up in my arms. "She's a brave little girl, and we're going to take her to the hospital. Right now." I said this more for Trish's benefit than Billie's.

Billie looked around. "Is there an adult here?" she asked.

"The babysitter's around somewhere. I don't remember her name."

"Laura," Trish said, just above a whisper.

"Yes—Laura," I repeated.

"Laura!" Billie shouted.

After a moment, the babysitter came back into the hallway. Her head was down. "Yes?" she said, her voice quavering.

"Can you get in touch with Trish's parents?" Billie asked.

"Yes. No. I don't think so. Maybe." The babysitter was completely rattled, and very fearful. It seemed clear to me: she was blaming herself for Trish's injury.

"Did they leave you a number to call?"

"Maybe. I'm not sure." The girl started to cry.

"Where would they have left it? By the phone?"

"I think so. Oh, God, I'm so sorry! Trish, I'm so sorry!"

Billie's patience is legendary, but the babysitter was trying it. "Show me, Laura. Show me where the phone number is."

"I'm taking Trish out to the rig," I said to Billie. "Don't be long. We gotta roll."

"I'll be right there," Billie called back to me as she followed Laura into another room. The dog started barking again.

"Come on, Marty," I said to the officer. "Carry the oxygen kit."

I had left one of Trish's eyes uncovered when I bandaged her. As I carried her onto the porch, she opened it and looked at me. "What's your name?" she asked through the oxygen mask.

"Scott," I answered. "And my partner's name is Billie."

Trish closed her eye and nodded, as if this satisfied her. "She's pretty," she said.

Marty helped me get the little girl secured onto the litter in the back of the ambulance. Her bleeding had stopped, and the oxygen seemed to be helping.

In a minute, Billie came from the house. As she climbed into the rig, she said to Trish: "I just spoke with your mother. She'll meet us at the hospital."

Trish just nodded. Then Billie turned to me. "Do you want to drive, Scott?" she asked, knowing I usually preferred her to stay in the back of the rig with our pediatric patients. She's better with kids—much more comforting to them—than I am.

"Sure, Chief," I said, patting Trish's hand lightly. I squeezed by my partner and stepped down out of the rig. Marty followed me.

As I was closing the rear doors, Marty asked if there was anything else he could do. I considered requesting an escort, then rejected the idea. Traffic is usually light at that hour.

"Yes, Marty," I said. "I left my first aid kit and a tire iron in the house. Could you get them and toss them in my car?"

"A tire iron?"

"Yeah. And if you have a minute, go shoot that damn dog."

I drove just a little bit faster than usual to the hospital, lights and sirens the whole way. Trish remained conscious for the trip. As always, Billie did a great job of keeping the little girl's spirits up.

After we released Trish into the care of the emergency room staff, I went back outside, ahead of my partner. I was returning the litter to the back of the rig when I noticed a woman running towards me from the parking lot. When she reached me, she stopped and placed her hand on my arm.

"You're from Dayfield?" she asked, out of breath.

I nodded.

"I'm Trish's mother," she continued. "How is she?"

What could I say to the woman? I began: "Well, the doctors are looking at her now–"

"But how *is* she?"

What could I say? That her daughter had bled all over the house? That part of her face had been torn off? "Well, it could have been worse," I said somberly. "The dog just missed her eye."

She shuttered as I told her this, then shook her head. "I thought I was doing the right thing," she said, her voice shaking. "We needed the money, so I went back to work…" She stopped talking, looked at me plaintively for a second, then ran into the emergency room to find her daughter.

When our duty shift ended, and I returned home, I was physically and mentally drained. I ignored the blinking light on my answering machine for at least ten minutes. Then the glimmer of hope that the message was from Pam got the better of me. I tapped the play button and listened. A woman's voice spoke to me. It was Peggy Nowicki. Oh captain, my captain.

"Ah, Scott," Peggy said, hesitantly. "We had an impromptu board meeting this evening, and it seems we've reached a decision. It was only a preliminary vote, but in light of, um, recent events, it's probably a good indication of how a formal vote will turn out. Anyway, we'll be doing that tomorrow night, at the scheduled meeting, and I'd suggest you be there. Give me a call if you have any questions.

"Oh, and good work on that call this afternoon. Billie said it was a tough one, but you handled it quite well.

"See you tomorrow. Bye."

NO CHOICE

15

PEGGY NOWICKI HAD NEWS SHE didn't want to tell me. When the meeting was called to order, with me facing the seven board members as before, she did her best to put their most recent decision in a positive light.

"You have a few problems to deal with, Scott, and they're not going away by themselves. So, we've talked it over and, in your own best interests, we think you should consider taking some time away from active duty."

"Oh hell, Peggy, stop coddling him. You make it sound like he's got an option. The fact is it's not your choice to make, Jamison. You're suspended—immediately and indefinitely. We can't risk you acting as a squad member, not while there's a lawsuit pending against you."

Of the eight people in the room, I probably cared the least about the board's decision. A suspension from active duty was of scant concern at this point. But Mike Marder, in his caustic rephrasing of Peggy's polite suggestion, had thrown down the gauntlet. I couldn't help but take it up.

"So what happens," I asked acidly, "when you get another life-threatening call—like the one on Friday—and there's no one in town but a couple of rookies?" It was a weak comeback, but the best I was capable of at the time. My heart simply wasn't in it. I had become very weary of this sniping and squabbling.

"What call is he talking about?" Mike asked, looking at Peggy.

"I'll take my chances with the rookies," Carol Hartshorne interjected.

"What call?" Mike asked again.

"The drowning, over on Rosewood Drive," Peggy replied.

Mike turned and looked at me accusingly. "*You* were on that call?"

I didn't answer, so Peggy did: "Yes, Scott ran the call until the MIC unit showed up." Which was an exaggeration, but I didn't dispute it.

"Oh, that's just great!" Mike shouted. "Just fuckin' *great!* This is all we need. A squad member is under investigation—being sued for wrongful death—and two days later he's got his nose in another fatality. What is it with you, Jamison? Why is it that every time you show up on a call, someone ends up in cold storage? How'd we ever get saddled with an incompetent like you?"

"That's enough, Mike," Peggy said quietly.

"*Enough?*" Marder steamed. "No, Peggy, that ain't the half of it. Do you know the particulars of that drowning? Are we at risk? If some sharp lawyer gets hold of this case, and Jamison so much as misspelled the victim's name, they're gonna take us *all* down. No goddamn Good Samaritan law is going to protect us, because we let *him* stay in uniform. I told you people: we should have canned him two weeks ago…"

Peggy raised her voice, but no more than necessary: "I *said* that's enough, Mike. There's no indication Scott did anything wrong on the drowning call, and—as for the pending lawsuit—it isn't a conviction. He's innocent…"

"Yeah, yeah…until proven guilty," Karen cut in. "So then why are we suspending him? Doesn't that indicate a lack of confidence on our part?"

I decided to get bold. "Good question…Karen," I said, and she nodded slightly at my correct guess. "But what *I'd* like to know is: if this lawsuit doesn't just go away, can I count on you to support me? Will the squad back me up?"

"Back you up? *Back you up?*" Marder roared incredulously. "Hell, no! We're not on the hook for that one, Jamison, and you're not putting us there! You entered that house at your own risk, and in *direct* violation of squad policy. You're on your own, completely. And if you want *my* opinion, Angie Greer has a good case against you. A *damned* good case."

Marder's vindictive rantings were getting awfully tiresome, so I turned to Peggy for the straight line. But there was little she could offer me.

"Mike has a point, Scott," she said flatly. "You knew better, or *should* have known better, than to have entered that house before the police secured it. Also, you should be aware of something. If the widow subpoenas our call sheet, or a copy of squad regulations, we have no choice but to turn them over to her. Confidentiality laws don't apply in this instance."

Somehow, I had the feeling that Peggy was merely justifying a *fait accompli—ex post facto.* Angie Greer's attorney had already seen the documents in question. How else could he have quoted them in his summons?

"Tell me, Peggy," I said slowly, trying to think of the best way to phrase my next question, "have we *ever* had a case before, when a squad member entered a domestic scene before the cops arrived?"

"That's not the issue," Carol answered quickly. "Our regulations have an uncharacteristic clarity on this point. What someone else may or may not have done before has no bearing."

Without even looking at Carol, I said: "Let the captain answer my question, please."

Peggy paused to think. "Yes," she said finally, "I seem to recall that it's happened once or twice. Offhand, I don't remember who or when, but I'm almost positive that it's happened."

I didn't hesitate: "And *when* it happened, was the offending squad member disciplined in any way?"

It suddenly became clear to everyone just what I was looking for. Peggy smiled slightly. Mike scowled. Carol took the matter in hand: "Again, Scott, that's not the issue..."

"That's *precisely* the issue, Ms. Hartshorne, at least as far as *this*

board is concerned. I'm not pleased—nor surprised, for that matter—that you're going to hang me out to dry. But considering what
Peggy just said, you have *no right* to make things more difficult for
me, by adding your own charges to those I'm facing."

My mind was frantically searching for a few more clods of
specious logic to toss, for I fully expected a rebuttal from at least
one board member. But to my immense surprise, no one said a
word. Two or three heads actually nodded; one or two sets of
shoulders shrugged with indifference. Incredibly, it appeared that I
had won this point.

Then, Mike Marder clarified the issue for me. For all of us.

"Jamison," he said, with an annoying tinge of arrogance, "we're
not looking to hang you. You're doing an admirable job of that
yourself. Speaking for a few of us in this room, and others on the
outside, we just don't want you to do any more damage to the
squad's reputation. *That's* why you're being suspended. And if
Angie Greer wins her lawsuit against you—if a judge or a jury
finds that *your negligence* was a cause of her husband's death—
then we'll have no choice but to make your suspension permanent.
I think we're all in agreement on this point, aren't we?"

He looked from face to face, and mostly found what he was
looking for.

"Fair enough," I answered. "But by the same token, if Mrs.
Greer drops the suit, or if it gets thrown out, then you people get
off my back, and we put the matter behind us. Okay?" I didn't
wait for a vote, or even a dispute, before adding: "And since
you've already said that Angie Greer can have access to the
squad's records, I expect the same consideration. If I need to
review or copy any document—a call sheet, board minutes, anything—I'm assuming I'll have your complete cooperation. Is that
right?"

Jerry Boronski, the more rational of the squad's two lieutenants,
spoke for the first time: "Don't press it, Scott. You're not calling the
shots here. Personally, I don't have a problem with giving you
access to anything pertinent, but only as a matter of courtesy. It's
definitely not your prerogative."

Courtesy, prerogative—who the hell cares? Did I get access or didn't I?

"I think he should have to submit a list of what he wants, and we should have to vote on it before he gets it," Carol Hartshorne suggested. Her friend, Mike Marder, nodded in agreement.

Peggy shook her head. "Oh, come off it, Carol. Our records don't contain any state secrets. Let Scott look for whatever he wants. Just don't let him take an original out of the building. The same goes for Mrs. Greer. That's my motion."

"Is there a second?" Hank Cindrich quickly asked.

"Seconded," said Stick Menzel, who probably hadn't followed the discussion, but was more than pleased to help end it.

"All in favor? Opposed?" Hank called for the roll, while Carol dutifully recorded it. By a four-to-two vote, with one abstention, I was granted access to all squad reports and records. Not that I knew if they'd do me any good. Not that I was seeking anything in particular. But it was the first break that had gone my way in some time, and, for twenty seconds anyway, I was satisfied with my victory.

NO EXCUSES

16

"So, Scott, have you called Geoffrey yet?"

Francine Hufnagel, the part-time receptionist at DataStaff and full-time referral service for her son's legal practice, stopped by my cubicle the next morning. Her timing was impeccable. I had just been thinking about contacting a lawyer.

"No, Fran, I haven't. Maybe I'll give him a call this afternoon."

"Why wait until then? Why not call him this morning?"

"Didn't you say afternoons were the best time to reach him?"

Francine smiled innocently. "Did I say that? Well, today's Wednesday. I think he told me once he's in his office on Wednesday mornings. Or was it afternoons? I don't remember, but it's worth a try either way, isn't it? I mean, if your late aunt's property is worth fighting for…"

She let her voice trail off, either suggesting that I wasn't showing sufficient interest in the matter, or that she was aware my problem had nothing to do with property. Or both.

"You're right, Fran. I'll call him in a few minutes." I made a quick, superficial search of my pockets and desk drawers. "I think I have his card around here someplace…"

As if she conjured it from thin air, Francine was suddenly holding another of her son's business cards in her fingers. She handed
it to me, still smiling innocently. "Call him when you get out of
your meeting with Arnie," she said.

"Meeting?" I asked, taking the card and slipping it into my shirt
pocket. "What meeting?"

"The one Arnie wants to have with you right now," she
answered, walking away.

Great. Arnie had been out of town for ten days—on business or
pleasure I couldn't say—and now he was back, looking for
progress reports. It was time to put on my dancing shoes. I
grabbed three or four project files from my desk and headed for
my boss's office.

Arnie Rosensteel was at his desk, signing checks, when I tapped
on his open door. He looked up and smiled at me—a good sign—
and motioned to a chair across from him. He appeared tanned, but
not rested. As I sat down, I noted to myself that his appearance
reflected his lifestyle of recent years. He had forgotten how to
relax. He carried his business problems with him everywhere,
including, it seemed, on vacation. His body had gotten a break, but
his brain had never left this room.

"How's it going, Scott?" he asked amiably, while continuing to
sign checks.

"Not bad."

"Any difficulties with your current assignments? Anything I
should know about?"

I hated when he did this. I could never be sure what he was
leading up to. Sometimes, he was just being a good boss, giving
me an opportunity to air my troubles. But other times—I had
learned the hard way—he was setting me up for a verbal thrash-
ing. This time, the advance signals were mixed. The smile said it
was to be a friendly meeting, but his refusal to suspend the check-
signing task said otherwise.

I shrugged. "No, nothing I can't handle."

He stopped with the checks and looked at me. Or through me—
I couldn't tell which. I tried to smile back, but the corners of my
mouth weren't cooperating.

"Any reason your throughput figures are down twenty-three percent?" He asked the question in a monotone, as though reciting from a script...and expecting a scripted response.

"That much, huh?" I was surprised. Throughput figures are weighted measurements of productivity, and usually don't vary much from an established norm. A drop of twenty-three percent demanded an explanation, which I didn't have.

"Yes, that much." Again the monotone.

"Well, business has been off from the last quarter..."

"By *four* percent," he interjected. There was life in his voice now.

"Yes, *overall,* but the input I've been getting..."

Arnie waved his hand, dismissing my argument before I could even put it into words. "Let's be candid, Scott. Okay? You're simply not pulling your weight..."

Uh oh. I'd heard those words before. From a former employer, just before the ax fell.

"...and I think I know why. You're too distracted. You're...what is it—34 years old?—and you're not sure..."

"I'm 33," I interrupted, which wasn't smart.

"Would you let me finish, please? You're 33, and you feel like you've hit a wall. The work here isn't as much fun as it used to be, you're not getting ahead, and you're feeling pressure from Pam to make a purchase or get out of the store. Am I right?"

Christ, everybody's a goddamn shrink.

"About the work here, yes, you're right, Arnie. Maybe we should talk about that. But as for my relationship with Pam, I don't see where that's any of your business."

He lifted his hand, conceding the point. "Perhaps it's not my business. But your performance here is. I've put a sizable investment into you over the years..."

"That cuts both ways," I said, again interrupting. Why couldn't I keep my mouth shut?

"...and I'd like to think we can solve your problems together. Maybe it's time for you to rethink your priorities. For example, maybe you should give up your involvement with the rescue squad."

Was I hearing right? "But, Arnie, *you're* the one who suggested I volunteer in the first place. You thought it was a socially responsible thing to do." Which was true. I would never have considered joining the squad if Arnie hadn't urged his employees to become more involved in community activities. He squirmed slightly in his chair as I reminded him.

"Yes, Scott, I did. But that was then, when business was better and I could afford to be more generous with my associates' time. Times have changed, as I'm sure you've noticed. And since you're not keeping up with your workload as it is, something has to give. The squad managed without you before; I'm sure they can do without you now."

I couldn't argue with that point. "Well, they must think so, anyway. I was suspended from active duty last night."

Arnie continued to stare at me blankly. I could tell he didn't really care about my troubles with the squad, but—knowing him as I do—I figured he would act like he did.

"Anything you want to tell me about?" he asked.

"The squad's not the problem, Arnie. It's the lawsuit I'm facing that stems from a squad call."

"Lawsuit?" Now his interest was genuine.

I gave him an up-to-the-minute recital of recent events. And, yes, it's possible that I embellished it in spots. I had a career to protect, you know, and if a correlation could be made between my deteriorating job performance and my recent tribulations as an EMS volunteer, it was certainly in my best interests to make it. Since Arnie had originally encouraged me to join the squad, he might feel some responsibility now that my involvement had gone sour. Some.

"It sounds to me," he said at last, "like you've got a shakedown suit on your hands. Mrs. Greer doesn't want this to go to trial any more than you do. Her lawyer has probably convinced her that you'll buy her off before it gets that far."

That possibility had occurred to me, but its likelihood rested on one improbable factor. Angie Greer and her lawyer would have to know that my pockets were far deeper than they appeared to be. I could count on one hand the people who knew the extent of my personal assets, and Angie Greer certainly wasn't one of them. I'd never told Arnie, nor Billie, nor even Pam. Only Miles Coates, whom I'd sworn to secrecy and whom I could trust, knew about the funds my father had bequeathed me.

"I don't intend to buy anybody off, Arnie. Even if I could, I wouldn't. I don't feel that I've done anything wrong, and I want to clear my name."

"Excuse me, Arnie?" Francine's voice was on the intercom.

"Yes, Fran?"

"Is Scott still in there with you?"

"Yes."

"There's a policeman here to see him."

NO CLUE

17

SERGEANT BARRY SKIPINSKI SHOOK hands with Arnie Rosensteel, in the DataStaff reception area. I made the introductions. Skip was polite, but cool as ever. Arnie turned on the charm he usually reserves for clients. He invited Skip to join us in his office, and offered him a refreshment. Naturally, Skip declined the invitation, and refused the offer.

"I've been asked to have Scott come down to headquarters with me," Skip said.

"Is he under arrest?" Arnie asked.

"No, we just have a few questions to ask him, pertaining to the Greer incident."

"I see," Arnie said reflectively. "Would you mind if I accompanied him?"

Skip hesitated, just long enough for Francine to get a plug in. "Officer," she asked, "should Scott have an attorney present?" Arnie turned and shook his head at Francine, who pretended not to notice.

Skip answered both questions with one reply. "We'd prefer to speak with Mr. Jamison alone. I'll have him back in less than an hour."

Francine persisted: "Has he been informed of his rights, officer?"

"Fran," Arnie said in a soft but firm voice, "please mind your own business."

Skip nodded to Arnie, then turned to me. "Are you ready?"

I looked at Arnie, who raised his hands in resignation. I was on my own.

"Scott." Francine called to me, holding out yet another business card.

I tapped my pocket. "I still have the one you gave me, Fran."

"You're allowed one phone call," she yelled, as we went out the door. "Use it!"

We had barely reached the parking lot when Skip stopped me. "Don't ask me any questions," he warned, "because I can't tell you anything. You'll find out soon enough what's going on. If you don't already know."

I was listening to Skip, but I wasn't looking at him. My attention was drawn to a gray van that was slowly pulling from the parking lot. I wondered: could it be the same one that had been outside my apartment on Monday? I squinted, and made out its license plate. Over and over I repeated the number to myself, until it was committed to memory.

"No, I don't know what's going on, Skip. I'm trying to get on with my life, but everybody keeps hassling me about that call two weeks ago. Last night, the squad suspended me indefinitely."

"Yeah? On what grounds?"

"They're covering their asses. They want to get as distant from me as they can, in case Angie Greer's lawsuit takes me under."

"*Semper fi*," Skip said.

"What's that mean?"

"You don't know?" Skip grinned at me mockingly.

"I was never in the Marines."

"Obviously," he snorted. "They don't take..." He stopped himself before the damning word got out. Would he have said *sissies*? *Slackers*? *Cowards*? One thing was certain, Skip was more than just annoyed with me at this moment. He couldn't tell me why the police department had a sudden desire to question me again, but he was nonetheless letting me know that it was something distasteful. To him, anyway.

Skip led me to a conference room that was at least twice the size of the neglected little "community room" where we had met before. He walked over to a chair against the room's far wall and sat down. I started to pull a chair out from the side of the long conference table. Skip cleared his throat, loudly, gaining my attention. "Not there," he said. He pointed to the seat in front of him, which was at the foot of the table. "There."

For a moment, I considered defying him, simply to show that I wasn't going to be ordered around like a child, or a thief on parole. I tapped my fingers against the back of the chair I had selected. Then I reconsidered. I took the seat at the foot of the table. Skip remained seated behind me.

We waited for four or five minutes, mostly in silence. My attempts at small talk went nowhere. Finally, a door opposite from the one we had entered came open, and two men walked in. I recognized the Dayfield police chief from the night of the shooting. The other man—a trim, neatly-groomed fellow in a dark, pinstriped suit—was not familiar. He was holding a briefcase. The two men separated and walked down opposite sides of the table until they reached the chairs on my immediate right and left.

The chief spoke first. "How are you today, Scott?" he asked, but didn't wait for an answer. Instead, he motioned at the gentleman who accompanied him. "I want you to meet the county's assistant prosecutor, Theodore Jones."

I stood and extended my hand to Jones, who gave me a politician's smile as he took it. "Pleased to meet you, Scott," he said in a voice that almost sounded sincere. When he let go of my hand, I turned to shake also with the chief, but he was now behind me, quietly conferring with Skip. Then he returned to the chair at my right and sat down, ignoring my outstretched hand. Jones said hello to Skip and sat down as well, on my left.

Immediately I could see why Skip had positioned me in this chair. The prosecutor and the chief could make eye contact with each other, and me, and Skip—all at the same time. But I had to swivel my head to see either one of them, and was obliged to turn completely around to see Skip. They would be able to exchange glances and gestures out of my sight, while I could only see and address one of them at a time. They had deployed themselves according to a manual of tactics I had never read, and had put me at a disadvantage.

"Scott," said the prosecutor, cheerfully, while opening his brief-case, "we have a few nagging loose ends—pertaining to Mr. Gary Greer—that we're having the damnedest time trying to reconcile. We thought you might be able to help us. *Will* you help us? If you can?"

He asked so politely, and so solicitously, that for a second I thought I might have a choice. Stupid me. "Of course I'll help you, Mr. Jones."

His smile broadened. I wondered, briefly, how much a gleam-ing set of uppers and lowers like his might cost. "I thought you would, Scott." He reached in the briefcase and pulled out a cas-sette recorder, which he placed on the table and switched on. Yet another conversation of mine was about to be preserved for the ages. Lately, it seems, everybody's been so intent on capturing every word I say, I'm beginning to believe that one of these days I might actually utter something of lasting value.

Theodore Jones reached again into his briefcase, and this time came out with a clear plastic bag. Inside the bag, with a small tag attached to the trigger guard, was a handgun. He placed the gun on the table next to the cassette recorder. Then he looked at me. Actually, he studied me, impassively searching my face for a reac-tion.

Something made me turn and look at the chief. He wasn't just searching, he was scowling. I got the feeling that, had I turned around, I would have found a similarly disagreeable expression on Skip's face. I turned back to face the prosecutor.

"Tell me, Scott Jamison," he commanded in a far less friendly tone than before, "do you recognize the weapon I've laid in front of you? Take your time before you answer."

Why take my time? "No, I don't recognize it," I said flatly. Calmly, even.

"No? Well let me tell you this: It's the gun Gary Greer was hold-ing your head when Sergeant Skipinski and Patrolman Saporta arrived at the Greers' house that Sunday evening. *Now* do you rec-ognize it?" Jones had quit the friendly politician act altogether.

Now he was the tenacious interrogator.

"Oh, that's what it is? Well then, as Skip can tell you, it was not in my line of sight at that moment. So there's no way I could recognize it. Unless you want to hold it against my neck, as Gary Greer did, and see if I can identify it that way. I would prefer if you didn't, though."

Sure, I was being cynical. But I didn't like the direction this conversation was taking. I had thought this had to do with Angie Greer's lawsuit.

"How did Mr. Greer come to have possession of it?"

"Excuse me?"

"The gun is registered to a Mr. Ray Keegan. Do you recall that name?"

"Not offhand, no."

"Mr. Keegan lives here in Dayfield. He had an automobile accident about eight months ago. The rescue squad was called, and you were on the crew that responded. Do you remember that?"

An MVA call? From eight months ago? I was going to need more information than that. "Give me some details."

Jones looked behind me at Skip, who spoke up long enough to jog my memory: "It was that Saturday morning accident, Scott, over on Cumberland Turnpike. The car hit a tree, and went into the ditch. Keegan was trapped inside."

Oh, yeah. An *early* morning call. The driver was drunk.

"Yes, I remember now."

NO CHANCE

18

How could I forget?

It was eight months earlier, as the assistant prosecutor had said. Billie DeMarino and I had been scheduled for the dreaded Saturday day shift, which meant that late night partying on the preceding Friday was out of the question. Pam and I had gone to a movie that particular evening, then to *Luigi's*, but not back to my apartment. She had declined my invitation to stay over.

"I'd like to sleep in tomorrow morning," Pam had told me, "but you go on duty at seven o'clock. That dumb pager of yours will probably wake us both up at 7:10."

How do you argue with a woman who can call a passion-prohibiting, tryst-terminating pocket pager *"dumb"*? The modifiers I might have chosen just then were infinitely more colorful, but not outside your imagination.

"Will I see you tomorrow night?" I had whined.

"Maybe," she answered, radiantly. "Call me during the afternoon. I'll try to pencil you in."

Pam's prediction had been right—almost to the minute. The clock radio said 7:07 when my pager blasted me out of bed the next morning. I jumped into my whites, yanked on a pair of sneakers, and ran out, still half asleep. Billie was waiting for me at the bay, with the ambulance ready to roll.

"Morning, Chief," I mumbled as we went into service. "What do they want us for?"

"An MVA on Cumberland Turnpike," she answered, "with a man trapped inside. The crash truck is already en route."

Oh, golly, the crash truck. The most *macho* of all emergency vehicles. The ark of the covenant for that supremely exalted piece of rescue equipment: the vaunted Jaws of Life. Though everyone on the squad is trained in extrication procedures, only a chosen few—all guys, of course—are ever permitted to actually heft the hydraulic tools at a motor vehicle accident.

And, Christ almighty, do those guys *ever* get into it. To bust out a car's windshield, and snap its support columns, and peel back its roof like the lid on a sardine can...hell, that's more stimulating than sex for some yahoos. When else can a semi-reformed vandal make Swiss cheese out of a late model import, or break its hinges, or snap its steering column, while the police stand by and simply watch in admiration? Talk about a sensation of *power*...nothing else even compares.

Some of those guys get a hard-on just firing up the goddamn generator. Their eyes glaze over, their pulses quicken, and...well, you get the idea.

When Billie and I arrived at the scene, the yahoos with the crash truck were already there, unloading their equipment. The object of their anticipation—an older Buick or Oldsmobile, I don't remember which—was off the road, perched at an angle over a drainage ditch. The area was wooded, and the car had sustained significant damage bouncing off a few trees. Its windshield was already caved in. But it was still salvageable...for the moment, anyway.

I noticed all this as I climbed out of the rig and did a half-hearted survey of the scene. Two patrol cars were also on hand. One cop was out in the road, diverting the sparse, Saturday morning traffic, while the other—Sergeant Skipinski, of course—was on the hood of the wrecked car. Skip had his portable oxygen kit with him, and he was reaching in through the collapsed windshield, attempting to revive the driver, who was sprawled across the front seat.

The yahoos, whose identities were concealed by their helmets and face masks, were shouting at one another as they prepared their tools to take apart the Buick. I approached the nearest one and knocked on his hard hat to get his attention.

"How's our patient?" I yelled above the roar of the generator. He gave me an uncomprehending look, as though I was speaking Swahili.

"Who?" he shouted back.

"Our patient! The driver! What's his status?"

The yahoo shrugged his shoulders. "How the hell should I know?" he said, and then turned back to his equipment.

I glanced at the other two yahoos, and determined that neither of them could tell me any more than the first one had. So much for assessing the patient first. For all these guys knew, they could be dismantling some poor son-of-a-bitch's vehicle just to remove his corpse. I walked over to the car and tried the two doors on the near side. Neither would open. Give the yahoos that much credit.

I shouted to Skip, still up on the hood: "How is he?"

Skip raised a palm. "I can barely reach him. He hasn't moved since we got here."

Well, that sealed it. It was up to me to determine the driver's condition. I fished in my jacket pocket and found a small tool that, until that moment, I had never used except in practice. Please don't ask me its name; I can only describe it and tell you what it does. It looks like a slightly oversized ballpoint pen made of brass, and it works on the same principle. It has a tip that retracts inside, and then shoots out when a release is pushed. An instructor once told me that, when fired, it exerts 2000 pounds of pressure—but only for a moment.

I placed the tip of the device against the bottom corner of the driver's window, turned my head, and hit the release. The window crumbled into a half-million fragments. The yahoos, I guessed, were immediately resentful. I had drawn first blood. Well, tough shit.

The car's tilted position over the ditch raised the height of the driver's side about a foot above what it would normally be. The base of the window frame, which on level ground would be at my waist, was chest high. I reached in through window opening and attempted to open the door from the inside. No chance. None of the doors were locked, they had just been jammed shut by the force of the collision. Giving them the benefit of the doubt, I assumed the yahoos had already discovered that.

I couldn't just crawl through an opening that was four-and-a-half feet off the ground, so I took the only option that time and circumstances would allow. I grasped the window frame and vaulted through, landing on the legs of our supine patient. He didn't seem to notice.

"Can you get a pulse?" Skip shouted down at me.

The driver was a middle-aged guy, dressed in well-worn work clothes. His head was resting against the far door, and his eyes were closed. For a second I thought he might be sleeping, but then I considered all the noise, as well as Skip's efforts to pump him up with pressurized oxygen. He was definitely out, if not gone. I reached down to his neck and groped around for his carotid artery. I thought I detected a slow, faint *thump*, but with all the confusion and motion and my awkward position I couldn't be sure what I was feeling.

"Get this blanket over you, Scott! We're comin' in!" One of the yahoos threw a nylon tarp in the window, which I grabbed and quickly attempted to spread over my patient and me. When the sawing and the smashing began, it would be the only protection we'd have from the hurtling fragments of his car.

By now, I suppose, I was fully awake. Underneath the tarp, I was doing my best to determine if our efforts this morning were going to be for naught. I peeled back one of our patient's eyelids, but in the dim light I couldn't be sure just how dilated his pupils were. I placed my cheek next to his nose and mouth, and placed my hand on his chest, hoping to feel the suggestion of respirations. It was then I noticed the smell of alcohol. That discovery certainly helped explain a few things. Like why this guy had abandoned a dry road in broad daylight, in favor of a tree-lined drainage ditch. Like why his vital signs and reactions to stimuli were practically non-existent. Only the truly dead can give a more convincing appearance of *being* dead than can the dead drunk.

What happened next might well be blamed on all of us rescuers, with the exception of Billie. She was still in the rig, so she can hardly be faulted for not making sure that the scene—that is, our patient's vehicle—was secure. As I was trying and failing, mostly, to find some sign of life in the body beneath me, and as the yahoos were noisily making a convertible out of what had been built and sold as a hardtop, the edge of the drainage ditch realized its present payload was in excess of its design specifications, and it collapsed. Not all at once, thankfully, but rapidly enough that the yahoos were able only to remove themselves from the path of the sliding vehicle, and not their precious equipment.

Inside the car, I only noticed that the disconcerting angle of my surroundings was becoming more so. I can't say that I was aware of the car's downward motion, at least not until the motion halted. Then I heard a straining, crushing sound, as two pieces of extrication gear—which had been blissfully engaged in dismembering the Buick—were dispassionately dismembered by it.

The following five minutes are faint in my memory. A lot of shouting and scrambling about ensued, which abated only when Billie—a woman, mind you—took control of the scene and refocused the yahoos' attention on the reason we were all there.

"Scott!" she yelled to me. "How's our patient?"

"I have no idea!" I hollered back. "Can you get us out of here?"

That's what Billie did, with the help of two humbled yahoos using humble hand tools. We extricated the patient, immobilized him, and stabilized him in the back of the ambulance. Only then were we able to properly assess his condition. He was bruised up, and had suffered some internal injuries, but we knew for certain he would recover.

We were just as certain his car would not.

That's all I remember from that call and—considering how soundly I had been sleeping when it began—I'd say it's a wonder I remember that much. Billie took care of the paperwork. The yahoos, I assume, cleaned up the scene.

What else was there to tell?

NO SECRETS

19

THE ASSISTANT PROSECUTOR, Theodore Jones, listened quietly while I recounted all that I could remember about my actions at the accident scene, eight months earlier. Once or twice, he glanced behind me at Skip, as though to confirm a detail in my story. Occasionally, he jotted a note on a scrap of paper. His expression never changed.

When I finished, he tapped his pen on the table a few times, then held it still while he continued to stare at me. "Is that all?" he asked at last.

"All that I remember."

"And you never saw this?" he asked, gesturing at the gun between us.

I shook my head.

"Does that mean *no?*" His voice was even less pleasant than before.

"It means *no,* I never saw that gun. What's your point, anyway?"

Jones made another note before he continued: "Two days after he got out of the hospital, Mr. Keegan—your patient on that call—contacted the Dayfield Police and reported a handgun was missing from the glove compartment of his car. This gun. It was properly licensed and registered in his name. And it remained missing until the incident at the Greers' residence."

Jones paused, apparently expecting me to comment on his revelation. I said nothing, so he prodded: "Do you see where I'm going with this, Scott?"

"No, I don't."

"Well, we find it rather coincidental that the gun disappeared from Mr. Keegan's car at about the time *you* were in it, on a squad call, and then reappeared eight months later at the Greer residence, when *you* were there, again on a squad call."

"Well, that *is* a coincidence, Mr. Jones. But that's *all* it is. How could I have gotten the gun from Keegan's glove compartment in the first place? Skip was staring right down at me while I was in the front seat with Keegan—"

"You were under a tarp, Scott. I couldn't see what you were doing. And I jumped off the car before it started sliding into the ditch." Skip was hardly sticking up for me.

I continued my defense: "And if you'll recall, Mr. Jones, the gun was not in *my* possession when the two officers showed up at the Greers. Gary Greer was holding it. Isn't it more likely that he stole the gun from Keegan's car, before or after the accident? I don't know much about handguns, but I'd assume it's preferable to be pointing one at somebody else, than to have one pointed at you."

"Yes, that's a correct assumption, Jamison, but your guess that Gary Greer stole the gun from Mr. Keegan is just as certainly *incorrect*. Greer was being held in the county jail at the time Mr. Keegan's gun disappeared."

"Oh," I remarked, not knowing what else to say.

"What seems far more plausible, in my opinion, is that you had the gun on you when you entered the Greer residence, and Gary Greer somehow took it away from you. Perhaps while you were *tending* to his wife."

Jones deliberately emphasized the word *tending*. I noticed the inflection, but was far less bothered by that than by his ludicrous assumptions. First, he speculates that I'm Wyatt Earp, packing a six-shooter while running out for a pizza. Then he infers that I'm Barney Fife, letting some drunk take it away from me.

And I'd never even seen the weapon before.

"It may be plausible to you, Mr. Jones, but it's not true. I've never touched that gun."

Did he smile when I said that? Maybe not, but his mood seemed to brighten when he asked: "Would you mind if we fingerprinted you?"

"Why?"

"Because there's a print on that gun we can't identify. It's not Keegan's, and it's not Greer's."

"So you think it's mine?"

Jones shrugged. "Is it?" he asked.

Could it be? I wouldn't think so, but then I couldn't be sure what happened in those few minutes when I blanked out, after Skip had shot Greer. Greer had fallen onto my leg, and I had squirmed away. Had he still been holding the gun? Had I, reflexively, pushed him away? Could I have touched the gun then?

I turned around and looked at Skip. Maybe he would remember. Maybe he could help me resolve this question. But, as usual, his expression said nothing.

"Let me ask *you* something, Mr. Jones. The unidentified fingerprint on that gun—can you tell if it was put there *before* the gun was fired? Or was it put there afterwards?"

I watched Skip while I asked this question, and Jones followed my gaze. He seemed to contemplate the matter before he replied: "I know what you're driving at, Jamison, but I can't answer your question right now."

I turned to face him. "Then I can't answer yours," I said calmly.

"In that case," he shot back, "I'd suggest you get yourself a lawyer, because it's likely we're going to have to discuss this in greater depth, some day *real* soon." And with that, he gathered up his belongings—including the gun—and left the room.

The chief remained a minute longer, still scowling at me. "I thought you had more brains, Scott," he said, derisively. Then he departed as well. Skip and I were alone again.

To my surprise, he walked around from behind me and sat down where the chief had been, so that I could see him and he could face me. He exhaled, audibly, and shook his head. "You're not being very helpful, Scott. Why don't you wise up? If you're connected to that gun, we're going to find out sooner or later. And we'll make it *very* rough on you, because that gun damn near killed one of our guys. If you're *not* connected with it, then why give Jones the runaround? He's just trying to get to the bottom of this. If you can help us, it would certainly make your legal problems a damn sight easier to solve."

Skip was not very convincing as the good cop; he and the chief should have switched roles.

"Tell me, Skip, what do you think? You were at the accident on Cumberland Turnpike, and you saved my life at the Greers' house. Do *you* think I could have been holding that gun, all that time?"

Again he shook his head. "I wouldn't have thought so, but then I wouldn't have thought Greer could shoot a cop, either. Maybe I don't know you assholes as well as I thought I did."

Being lumped into the same classification—assholes?—as the late Gary Greer made me wince. "That wasn't necessary, Skip," I pouted. "Look at my situation, would you? I'm being sued by Angie Greer...the squad has me up on charges...my girlfriend's all but abandoned me...my boss is on my case...and now you people are accusing me of, of stealing a handgun from someone—"

Skip waved his hand to cut me off. "Don't cry to me, Jamison," he said curtly. "If we find out you're fucking with us, let me assure you: You'll learn what *real* problems are."

Well, I should have known better than to ask for his sympathy. So now there was only one thing left I might ask of him. What the hell, the worst he could say is no.

"Do you think you might do me a favor, Skip?"

He actually smiled. "You never give up, do you?"

"I don't have much choice." I took a piece of scrap paper Jones had left on the table and, fortunately, found that I had a pen in my breast pocket. I wrote down the plate number I had been repeating to myself. "Could you find out who belongs to this license plate?"

Skip took the scrap of paper and studied the number on it, frowning. "Why should I?" he asked.

Good question. Certainly deserving of a better answer than the one I gave: "Because you're a public servant, and I'm an upstanding citizen in need of help. That's why."

"Fuck you," he said, crumpling up the paper and tossing it back at me. Then he stood up and walked out.

The rest of the workday was an utter waste and I was utterly worthless—Arnie's pep talk notwithstanding. I sat in my cubicle and doodled on a note pad, trying to make some sense out of my predicament. I wanted to call Pam—it had been two weeks since I had seen her—but a misdirected sense of pride kept me from dialing her number. The last time we had been together, she had chided me about the newspaper article. She certainly wouldn't want to hear me whine about my mounting problems now.

At last I picked up the phone and, taking his business card from my breast pocket, I called Fran Hufnagel's son, the lawyer. Geoffrey P. Hufnagel, Attorney-At-Law. The phone rang for nearly a minute. I was about to give up when someone at the other end of the line picked up the handset and immediately dropped it. I held the phone away from my ear, flinching at the noise as the handset I couldn't see clattered from desk to chair to floor. Then a male voice, out of breath, came on.

"Attorney's office," the voice gasped.

I hesitated, listening to a staccato panting sound, like that of a pregnant woman practicing her Lamaze breathing. "Geoffrey Hufnagel, please," I said at last.

"Speak-ing," the voice wheezed. "What can...I do...for you?"

"You can catch your breath," I answered. "Look, if this is a bad time, I can call–"

"No, no...please...hold on," the voice asked. "Just give me...a second." The line went completely silent, as though he had covered the mouthpiece with a towel. Twenty seconds later, he came back on. His breathing was almost normal now.

"Excuse me," he said. "I was...busy, in another room. I had to run to catch the phone. Who's calling, please?"

I debated whether to hang up. We hadn't even spoken, and already I was getting bad vibes about this guy. Yet I decided to give him the benefit of the doubt.

"Mr. Hufnagel, my name is Scott Jamison. I work at DataStaff Corporation with your mother. She–"

"Oh, yes! Mr. Jamison! Mom said you might be calling!" He was positively ebullient. "Something to do with an emergency call, and a shooting you witnessed? Is that right?"

Is that right? That's more than adequate, considering what I had said to Fran.

"Um, yeah, I guess," I stammered. This clown, this unknown quantity, was already a step ahead of me. I wasn't sure whether I liked that or not. "Didn't your mother say anything about an inheritance from my late aunt? And a property dispute?" Didn't I fake her out at all? Had I no secrets left?

"Mr. Jamison," came back the voice, warmly, "how long have you known my mother?"

"Three, four years," I said.

"Then you should know by now," he chuckled, condescendingly. "She's not easily hornswoggled."

Hornswoggled? I didn't like the sound of that. But before I could protest, he continued: "No offense intended, Mr. Jamison. I've tried to feed my mom a line on many occasions, and have rarely gotten away with it. And I'm a pretty fair lawyer."

A pretty fair lawyer. He said it matter-of-factly, not as though he was pitching me. "Your mother says you're the best in the county," I informed him.

Again he chuckled. "What mother wouldn't?" he asked. Then, as though assuming we had progressed beyond the introductions, he added: "I read the article in the paper, Mr. Jamison. And I nosed around a little, after my mother called me. Let me guess what your problem is. The widow of the man who was shot—Greer, wasn't that the name?—is suing you for causing the circumstances which led to her husband's death. Am I close?"

What, had he read the summons? Or had he considered soliciting Angie Greer himself, only to be beaten to the punch by Pressman? Or were all these lawyers working together?

"You're *very* close," I said tersely.

"Well, then, let's do this: You send me a copy of the complaint, and a copy of your first aid squad's rules and regulations. And if you don't feel that the newspaper article quoted you accurately, write me a single page report on what happened.

"I'll check with the police, and see what they can give me. In all probability, you have nothing to worry about. This is a nuisance suit, and I bet we can get it dismissed in a heartbeat, under the state's Good Samaritan Act. You can't be held responsible for the man's death."

"You think so, huh?" Now I *did* feel like I was being pitched, and it made me uncomfortable. Also skeptical.

"Well, I'm not guaranteeing it, Mr. Jamison. But I've handled far more difficult cases than this one, and come out on top."

"Give me a *for instance*," I challenged him.

A moment of silence ensued. Was he trying to invent, or—worse—remember one? "I get the impression you don't trust me, Mr. Jamison," he said evenly.

"You're a lawyer, aren't you, Geoffrey? Why should I trust you, when I don't even know you?"

"So much for the family referral," he reflected bitterly. "Well, then, maybe you should find yourself someone else–"

"No, no, don't mind me," I interrupted his noble gesture. "I'll make copies of the materials you want, and send them over by messenger. When do we get together?"

"Let me check my calendar," he said.

Yeah—do that, I thought.

"Today's Thursday. Give me the weekend to review what you send me, and to study up on the subject. Let's meet Monday afternoon. Can you come here, say, around four?"

"Will do," I answered, jotting myself a note.

"The door will be open," he added. "If I'm not in the front office, just keep walking—to the back of the building. You'll find me eventually."

That sounded odd. "What kind of a building are you in? An airplane hangar?"

"Something like that," he answered vaguely, and then hung up.

Great. My crackerjack attorney: a one-man, one-phone operation, with offices in an abandoned warehouse. The best in the county, his mother had assured me. I wondered if I should have shopped around in another part of the state.

NO CIGAR

20

A DAY LATER...ANOTHER FRIDAY NIGHT, alone. I had tried to reach Pam at work, earlier, but she had been "unable to come to the phone." Or so I had been told. To my disappointment—but not to my surprise—she didn't return the call. I finally admitted the probability that she was avoiding me, though I wasn't ready to consider why.

Later in the day, Miles had turned down my half-hearted suggestion that we meet at *Jason's* for the second week in a row. Rather frostily, he had told me: "I'd rather drink alone than spend the evening with you. You ain't much fun these days, Jamison."

Right. Like I'd never listened to him cry in his beer.

So there I was with a TV dinner in the oven, looking forward to a late-night trip to the laundromat. Another swinging Friday evening. The excitement was unbearable.

Then the phone rang. I jumped on it, desperately hoping Pam was feeling as lonely as I was. "Hello!" I blurted cheerfully.

A pause, then a male voice: "Is this Scott Jamison?"

"I think so."

Another pause. Then: "Oh, good evening,

Mr. Jamison. You don't sound like a man who's being sued for everything he's got." It was Geoffrey Hufnagel, my esteemed barrister. The notable attorney I had never met, but whom I had nonetheless retained to defend my reputation and my wallet from those who wished to plunder both.

"Yes, Geoffrey," I said wearily. "What is it?"

"I was just calling to say I received those materials you sent over today. Some interesting stuff here, but nothing to be concerned about. I'll work on it over the weekend. Anyway, I wanted to confirm our meeting for Monday, at four o'clock—"

My estimation of my as-yet-unseen attorney had just started to rise when the phone beeped in my ear, signaling another incoming call.

"Could you hold on a second, Geoff?" I pressed the buttons to take the other call, and answered it flatly. My mind was on the coming Monday.

"Hello, Scott. How are you?"

I knew the voice as soon as I heard it, but it took me a few seconds to believe what I was hearing. Yes, it was Pam. But no, it *wasn't* Pam. I mean, it wasn't Pam's usual bubbly voice. She had called me *Scott*—not H.B.—and she sounded very serious. I don't like Pam very serious. A little serious, sometimes, but this was much *too* serious.

"Fine, Pam. And you?"

"Okay. Can I come over for a few minutes?"

Just for a few minutes? For the evening, certainly. For a lifetime, perhaps. But just for a few minutes? That was ominous. But what could I say? That I had laundry to do?

"Hold on, just a sec, Pam. Let me get rid of this other call." I quickly punched the buttons to bring my lawyer back. "Yeah, Monday at four, Geoff. Your place. I'll be there."

He could tell I wanted to get rid of him. Thankfully, he didn't resist. "Make it five," he said. I agreed, and he hung up. I punched back to Pam.

She was talking to someone else when our lines reconnected. All I heard her say was: "He's on another call." But though I strained to listen, I didn't hear anybody speak back to her. Then she spoke into the phone. "Scott?"

"I'm here."

"Are you alone?"

"Yes. That was my lawyer on the other line." If this announcement meant anything to her, she didn't let on.

"Uh-huh. So, can I come over? Just for a few minutes?" She kept hammering the *few minutes* aspect of her pending visit. So as not to get my hopes up?

"Anytime, Pam. It'll be good to see you. I've missed you."

"Okay, I'll be there shortly." There was no promise in her voice. She hung up.

I sat staring at the phone in my hand, while a feeling of emptiness started gnawing at my insides. Pam was on her way over. I had been pining for her for two weeks, and now she was coming. You would think I'd have been overjoyed. But I knew better.

Twice before this had happened. And twice before, Pam had thrown me over—just this way. She was not the cowardly type; she would never just send me a *Dear John* letter or, worse, leave a parting message on my answering machine. It was a point of honor with Pam Healy: she would look me in the eye and tell me it was time for us to part ways. To move on. She had already done it twice. This evening, I felt—even before I saw her—I was going down for the third and final time.

I hung up the phone and made a pitiful attempt at tidying up the place. In the bathroom, I glanced at myself in the mirror, and shook my head at what I saw. Age 33, living alone, and about to be dumped. And that wasn't the only depressing aspect of my reflection. My outfit, such as it was, was fine for the laundromat, but hardly suitable for this long-awaited reunion. An old work shirt and sweatpants. But I didn't have time to change, or anything to change into, for that matter. Why else would I be going to the laundromat?

Pam rang the doorbell, but didn't wait for me to answer it. She used her key to let herself in. It would be easier to surrender it to me, no doubt, if she didn't have to fish in her pocketbook for it when she was ready to leave. That's what I was thinking as I stepped into the hallway to greet her.

God, she was gorgeous. After fifteen days of being deprived of the sight of her, I was simply overcome by her beauty. The thought of losing her, for good, panicked me.

Ask her to marry you, the voice inside my brain whispered. *This is your last chance, shithead. The worst she can say is no, and that's no worse than what she's about to say, anyway. Go for it!*

"Hi," I said weakly. "Boy, you look great."

She did. She was wearing a simple pink blouse, and a pair of navy slacks. But it wasn't the clothes that made her so appealing, it was her. Pam looks good in anything.

She said nothing, but stepped up to me, leaned forward, and kissed me. She didn't even put her arms around me. She barely closed her eyes.

It was, I thought, the kiss you get from your sister-in-law, when she and your brother are leaving their kids in your care, just before they hop on a plane to the Bahamas. Perfunctory—that's the word. Not really worth puckering for.

Her lips lingered on mine, longer than I expected. I also didn't expect, or even notice, at first, what her hands were doing. My sister-in-law's hands had never attempted the action...at least not with me. Pam had undone three buttons on my shirt, and was working on the fourth, before I had a clue what was happening.

She saw the change in my expression. She stepped back, smiling coyly, while pulling my shirt front open. She seemed pleased to see my chest naked beneath the shirt. Of course I was naked: all my undershirts were in the laundry basket. Gently she ran her hand from my neck to my navel.

Then, locking her eyes with mine, she undid the buttons on her cuffs. Next went the buttons on the front of her blouse, which she deftly pulled off and dropped on the floor. Her smile never wavered.

I stood transfixed, afraid to move, afraid to breathe, lest I cause this dream to evaporate—like the dreams of Pam I'd been having for the previous two weeks. But she was absolutely, perfectly real. I knew it for sure when she grasped the clasp in her cleavage, when she unlatched her bra, when her magnificent breasts fell free, and when my undershorts—just like *that*—became much too constricting.

Now, there are three reasons why this sudden expansion/ restriction occurred, all of which might not be obvious. The first cause, of course, was visual: the welcome and welcoming sight of Pam, so quickly in a state of partial undress. To date, that particular stimulus has never failed to get a reaction.

The second cause of my sudden discomfort was mental. Like most intimate couples, I imagine, Pam and I have developed, over time, a few non-verbal indicators of how we anticipate our carnal encounters to progress. The manner in which we disrobe is a key indicator. Undressing ourselves is okay; undressing each other is better. When I have to do the work for both of us, it's a reliable clue she'd rather be watching Letterman. But when Pam takes the initiative—and all I have to do is watch—my entire body gets tingly with anticipation. On those occasions, she usually makes it a night to remember.

The third and final cause of the sensation of cramped quarters was material. Or, more accurately, due to a *lack* of material. Certainly, I hadn't expected company this evening; otherwise, I would have dressed appropriately. But the selections remaining in my underwear drawer had been slim—literally—when I had earlier gathered up my laundry. All I had left to wear, beneath my sweatpants, was a pair of bright red bikini briefs, two sizes too small. I had been given them as a gag gift some years before. Not wishing to venture out in public, not even to the laundromat, without some semblance of support beneath the sweatpants, I had sucked it up and squeezed myself into the scarlet briefs. They had been tight before; now they were pressurized. Something had to give.

Pam stopped undressing, took both my hands in hers, and led me to the bedroom. She walked backwards the whole way, something I could never do without tripping. Hell, I stumbled as it was. I forget how to perform complex tasks—like walking—when I'm gazing at her breasts.

When we reached the bedroom, Pam knelt down and undid my laces. In less time than I could have done it myself, she removed my shoes and socks. She tossed them aside, stood up, and reached for the tie on my sweatpants. I grasped her wrists to stop her, or at least slow her down.

"What's your rush?" I asked.

She didn't answer, just winked and reached again for the tie. In a flash, she undid it, took hold of the sides of my sweatpants, and dropped them to the floor. It was then she noticed my fire-engine-red briefs, stretched to the bursting point.

Seductively she raised her head, raised her eyebrows, and gave me a sly grin. "Were you expecting someone?" she asked, as she slipped a finger, or two, inside the waistband. It was a tight fit.

"No," I gasped, sucking in my stomach. I couldn't wait another minute to be free of the binding garment. Fortunately, Pam didn't keep me waiting. She stretched the waistband forward and stripped me. The relief was wonderful. Then she leaned forward and kissed me again, sensuously this time. Any second, I expected to wake up.

I reached for her, but she evaded me and walked around to the opposite side of the bed. Still smiling at me, she undid the top button on her slacks and—in a single, fluid motion—removed them and her underwear at once. Then she put her hands behind her and stood still for a moment, her legs slightly apart, letting me just look at her. I nearly fainted.

Previously, I mentioned the truism that I call *Scott's Law*, which stipulates that most people are far more attractive with their clothes on. Just for the record, allow me to say that *Scott's Law* does not apply to Pam Healy. No sir.

"Come," she said, kneeling on the bed and moving across it towards me. "Let's not waste any time."

I wasn't about to argue with her, though I was becoming somewhat perplexed by the hurried approach she was taking to our love-making. Did she have an appointment to keep, and could spare only ten minutes with me?

Pam reached out her hand and, when I took it, she pulled me onto the bed and—almost before I realized it—on top of her. Now I was totally baffled. It had been less than five minutes since she had walked in the front door, yet here we were, poised on the threshold of making it happen. Like rabbits in the woods. It was exciting—and intensely stimulating—but it just didn't *seem* right. We were moving much too fast.

Not that I wasn't ready for her, mind you. And—as I soon discovered—not that Pam wasn't ready for me either. I would never have guessed she could become so excited, so aroused, in such a short time—but she clearly was not putting me on. Though part of me wanted to hold back, to slow down, I got caught up in her urgency. My heart went into overdrive. I plunged ahead.

It was how she wanted it, I guess, because she maintained, and maybe even accelerated, the breakneck tempo. It wasn't intimate intercourse to be sipped and savored—like wine; it was outright passion to be gulped all at once—like tequila. I've since decided I wouldn't want a steady diet of such frenzied encounters, but as it was happening, I couldn't imagine anything more thrilling. We both climaxed in less than a minute. Like rabbits in the woods.

Then she got weird. She grabbed my face with both hands, kissed me hard, then rolled me off of her. She jumped out of bed and, without saying a word, strode out of the room, still stark naked. I watched as she left, and then I slapped myself. I still wasn't certain I hadn't dreamed all of the foregoing.

Then my nostrils flared—I could smell something burning. I suddenly remembered: the TV dinner in the oven! I'd forgotten about it since Pam had called. I jumped out of bed and ran to the kitchen.

I should have noticed—as I raced down the hall—that the bathroom door was open. It was dark in there. I had assumed that was where Pam had gone in such a hurry. But I was so intent on getting to the oven before my dinner went completely up in flames that I overlooked that detail. Into the kitchen I dashed, too late to save my dinner, but in plenty of time to save the building.

I had just removed the scorched pan and its blackened contents from the oven when I heard Pam's voice, in the living room. Peeking around the corner, I saw that she was on the phone, her bare back to me, speaking in a muffled tone. Apparently, she thought I was still in the bedroom. But hadn't she smelled my dinner burning, too?

I crept into the room. I felt guilty about eavesdropping on her, but my curiosity, at that moment, was stronger than my scruples. What was so urgent that she had rushed our reunion to make this call?

"Yes," she was saying, "I'm positive. Sorry if I interrupted you, but that was the bet. You can pay me on Monday. Gotta go."

She quietly hung up the phone, turned, and ran right into me. Not expecting me there, she gasped in fright. Her eyes were as wide as silver dollars.

I held her at arm's length, and relished the view. "What was that about?" I asked.

Pam's a lousy liar, and she knows it. Standing naked and startled in my living room, she wasn't going to deceive me—though she probably wanted to try.

"That was Kelly," she said, which didn't surprise me. Pam can hardly change her nail color without first clearing it with Kelly.

"Yes. And?"

She looked away from me, and for just a moment I almost felt sorry for her. She didn't want to tell me whatever it was she and Kelly had been discussing. But she knew—and I knew—that she would tell me anyway. Like a child caught with her hand in the cookie jar, Pam always felt guilty when she did anything even slightly improper. And she apparently felt that she'd committed some unbecoming act. She would have to confess to purge the guilt.

"Well," she stammered, glancing at me, and away again, "Kelly and I stopped for a drink after work, see, and we got to talking. Mostly about you and Jonathan–"

"Kelly's boyfriend," I verified.

"Kelly's fiancé," she corrected me. "And…you know…we started to compare notes about how you both are when it comes to…you know…to sex."

I didn't like the direction this was taking, but I couldn't stop her now.

"And?"

She glanced at me again, meekly. "Well, you know how Jonathan is always pawning her in public…"

Pawing, I thought, but didn't say. "Yes?"

"Well, Kelly says he's even worse when they're alone. She said he's the horniest guy on earth."

I knew I wasn't going to appreciate this.

"Let me guess," I said. "You felt compelled to dispute that claim."

"Well, I laughed, because I thought it was funny. I asked her if she'd ever heard my nickname for you, and she said *yes*, but she didn't know what it meant."

Shit. As I'm sure you've noticed, Pam usually calls me "H.B." And, no, it doesn't stand for *honey buns*. It's a shortened version of *horny bastard*.

"And did you tell her?" I asked, anxiously.

"No, but I think she figured it out."

More than likely. "And?"

Pam smiled. "Well, then, we had another drink, and we were still discussing...you know...and the next thing I knew, we were talking about having a contest–"

"A contest?"

"Yes, a contest—to find out whose boyfriend is hornier."

"A contest?"

"Well, sort of a bet. We agreed that she would go home to Jonathan, and I would come here. The first one to...you know...complete the act—would be the winner. But we had to make sure that you and Jonathan were both home and...you know...*available*. That's why I called you before I came over.

"I...I really hope you're not mad at me. It was fun, wasn't it?"

Fun.

Silly me, I had thought it was *passion,* pure and simple. Pam had screwed me—no, slam-banged me—to win a bet. I had been used. But I couldn't seem to get angry about it.

"Whose idea was this, yours or Kelly's?"

Pam frowned at my question. "Why do you want to know?"

"Just curious."

"I don't know—I guess it was Kelly's. You're not mad, are you?"

"No, of course I'm not mad. I'm just a horny bastard —who'll take sex any way I can get it. How much did you bet?"

Her frown deepened. "That's between me and Kelly. Look, let me get dressed, then we'll talk about this. I thought it would please you." Pam left the room and returned to the bedroom.

I waited for a minute, then picked up the telephone. I didn't know the number I wanted to call, but I didn't have to know it. I just pressed the *REDIAL* button.

"Hello," Kelly answered. She wasn't even breathing heavy.

"Hi, Kelly. This is Scott."

"Oh, hi, Scott. How are you?" Now she sounded uncomfortable.

"I'm fine. You?"

"Great." Then, after a moment's silence, she added: "It's been an interesting evening, hasn't it?"

"Uh-huh."

"Well, congratulations on your victory. I knew you could do it."

For some reason, I didn't take this as a compliment.

"Tell me, Kelly, was it close?"

"Close? Yeah, it was close, but no cigar," she answered casually. Or evasively, I couldn't tell which.

"What do you mean?"

"What do I mean," she mumbled, as though not certain herself. "Do you you really want to know? Honestly?"

Now *I* wasn't so sure. "Yes, honestly."

Kelly lowered her voice, like she was letting me in on a secret. She said: "There *was* no contest, Scott. Jonathan's out of town. He's in Georgia on business this week. I'm just sitting here reading a book, by myself. But, please, don't tell Pam that. She'll be very upset with me."

I was not pleased to hear this. "You mean, you *contrived* this whole event?"

"I wouldn't say *contrived*."

"Then what would you say, Kelly? You tricked Pam—forced her to attempt a new record for speed screwing—while you sat on your fat ass and popped bonbons into your face. Why would you do such a thing?"

Kelly's not the sort to take such abuse passively. She lashed out at me: "I didn't *force* Pam to do anything! Besides, I don't know what *you're* complaining about. I got you laid, didn't I? You and Pam are back together now, aren't you? You'd still be sitting in a booth at *Jason's*, whining about your non-existent love life—or chasing that tramp from the newspaper—if I hadn't *contrived* to have Pam go home and screw you. You should be thanking me."

"Forgive my lack of gratitude," I said caustically.

"You're forgiven," she shot back. "But, regardless, don't you tell Pam about this conversation. I wouldn't be able to face her if she knew."

"Is that a fact?" Oh, the possibilities...

"Yes, that's a fact. I did you a favor, Scott. You can repay me by keeping your mouth shut. Promise?"

"No promises, Kelly," I said, and hung up.

I walked into the kitchen, took one look at the charred remains of my dinner, then wandered back into the bedroom. Pam was just getting back into her bra. She turned away when she saw me, which struck me as an odd thing to do—all things considered. But then, as I approached her, I realized she hadn't turned out of modesty. She had turned so I wouldn't see her crying.

When I touched her arm, she turned back to me and laid her head against my chest. "I'm sorry, Scott," she said softly. "It was a stupid thing to do. I used you, didn't I?"

I stroked her hair. "No, Pam, you didn't use me. Kelly used *you*. There was no contest."

She looked up at me, puzzled. "What do you mean?"

"I mean there was no contest. I spoke with Kelly."

"When?"

"Just now."

"Just now? So you know, then."

"Know what?"

"That there was no contest."

Hellooo? Earth to Pam. "That's what I said, didn't I?"

She smiled at me, a smile of relief. "Of course there was no contest, H.B. Jonathan's in Atlantis this week. I knew that all along."

"You mean Atlanta."

"Wherever."

"You knew that?"

"Yes. Kelly told me that a week ago—that Jonathan would be in...Georgia this weekend. You know, sometimes she takes me for such a dimwit. She didn't think I remembered that her precious Jonathan was away."

Now *I* was confused. "Then why'd you go along with her bet? Didn't you see that she was setting you up? Setting *us* up?"

Her smile grew even brighter. She wrapped her arms around me. "So who's the fool, H.B.? I've really missed you the past few days, and now we're together again. And it was fun, wasn't it? Besides, now Kelly owes me—"

The phone rang just then, so I never found out the wager we'd been racing for. I picked up the phone, expecting it to be Kelly, exercising damage control.

"Hello?"

There was a moment of silence, then a man's voice: "Is this Scott Jamison?" The voice was familiar, but I couldn't place it.

"Yes. Who's this?"

"Skipinski. Are you alone?"

I put a finger to my lips, telling Pam to stay quiet. "Yeah, I'm alone, Skip."

"I got something to tell you, Scott, but I want you to be clear on one thing: you didn't hear it from me. You got that?"

"I've never heard anything from you, Skip, and never will."

"Yeah, well, I'm taking a chance telling you this, but it's for your own good."

He had my attention. "What is?" I asked.

"Those plates you asked me about. The vehicle is registered to Kyle Hutchinson." He paused, perhaps expecting me to respond. I said nothing. "What's your interest in him?" he asked.

"Do you know him?"

"Every cop and every dopehead in the county knows Hutch. He's a dealer, at least two steps up the ladder from the likes of Gary Greer. In fact, he was probably Greer's supplier. We've seen him in the area a few times lately."

The mysterious gray van, owned by a drug dealer called "Hutch." But what could he want from me?

"You say this Hutchinson guy supplied Greer? Well then,

maybe that's where Greer got the gun. Could the unidentified fingerprint belong to him?" I hoped.

"To Hutch? Not a chance. Hutch has been arrested often enough we'd have made that connection."

"But you know by now that the fingerprint isn't mine. Don't you?" I assumed they had taken my prints from the conference table, or the chair I sat in, shortly after I left the room. It might not have been proper procedure, but what was to stop them? If they really wanted to know...

Again Skip paused, which more or less answered my question. Then he continued in a harsher tone: "Whatever you think you're accomplishing in this case, Scott, you're wrong. If you know anything more than you're telling, you better come clean right now. You try and pull something over on us, and we'll nail your ass—but good. You mess with somebody like Hutch and you're as good as dead. He's a big, mean son of a bitch. The only reason he's still doing business is 'cause no one *ever* testifies against him. He makes sure of that, one way or the other."

I wasn't sure how to take this. "I'm not messing with nobody, Skip," I said. My double negative was intentional—I thought it sounded more sincere. "I'm just trying to find some answers."

"That's not your job. You seem to have a real problem keeping your nose out of places where it doesn't belong. I hope you don't get it snipped off one of these days. Your pretty girlfriend might not find you so attractive then." He hung up, abruptly.

As I set down the phone, I saw that Pam had finished dressing.

"Was that about the lawsuit?" she asked, innocently.

I stared at her. "How did you know about the lawsuit?"

She shrugged. "A little bird told me." Then she looked at me, still naked. "Why don't you get dressed, and we'll go out for dinner. I'll treat tonight. Anyplace you want to go."

"Oh, so now you're rich, huh? Must've been some wager you and Kelly made."

Pam smiled coyly. "Get dressed," she said again.

"In a minute. First, I want to know why you've been avoiding me. The last time you were here, you said you'd be back that same evening. That was fifteen days ago."

"But who's counting, right? Get dressed. I'll tell you why, over dinner."

"Tell me now."

"Aw, c'mon. Don't spoil it, H.B. I have something special to tell you—an interesting little antidote that I overheard."

"You mean *anecdote*."

"Yeah, that too."

"Does it have anything to do with why you've been avoiding me?"

She thought about this for ten or fifteen seconds. Then she said: "No, not really."

"Then tell me that much now. You can save the anti...*anec*dote for later."

Pam frowned, disappointed that I wouldn't let this point go.

"Well, you remember, I went over to Kelly's that night."

"Uh-huh."

"Kelly said she had something important to tell me. Actually, it was an announcement. Or a celebration. Jonathan had finally proposed to her. You should see the ring he gave her."

"I've seen it."

"Yeah, I heard," Pam said, with an edge to her voice. "You and your friend, the reporter."

"Getting back to your story..." I prodded, not wanting her to lose her train of thought.

"Well, it got me upset—her gloating about her engagement. She's five years younger than I am, you know."

Oh, brother.

"And *that's* why you didn't come back? Because Kelly's marrying Jonathan—what's-his-name?"

"Tritschler," Pam answered, thinking I had asked for a name, when actually I was doubting her excuse. "And, yes, that's why I didn't come back. That's why I haven't been taking your calls. Kelly's engagement really got me thinking. What am I doing with my life? *What am I doing with you?* I'm over thirty years old, and–"

"Pam," I said, quietly interrupting her, "we've been over this. We've talked–"

"*You've* talked!" she snapped. "I always end up listening, and nodding my head like some fucking boggle-head doll. I'm tired of it, Scott. Tired of being taken for granted. Tired of you making fun of me, just because I'm not the smartest person in the world.

"I sat there at Kelly's that night, and saw how happy she was—and I went home and just cried. I've cried a lot these past two weeks."

I was suddenly sorry I had provoked this discussion. We had been getting along so beautifully…

"Don't be jealous of Kelly, if that's your problem," I said tartly. "She's happy because she got herself a rich guy. If Jonathan—what's-his-name—didn't have money, she would've never looked at him twice.

"Tell me—is that what you want, Pam? Somebody who can lavish you with expensive gifts? Who can fly you off to Bermuda, or Aruba, whenever you get the urge to go?"

She had to think about that one, but not for long.

"I'd settle for someone like that, if I couldn't find someone who just *cares* for me, and accepts me the way I am. Right now, I don't seem to have either."

Boy, could she stick it to me when she wanted to. Not that I could blame her, though.

I was beginning to feel self-conscious—standing there, arguing, with nothing on. I looked around for my undershorts. Finding them, the red bikini briefs, I debated whether to struggle back into them, or just pull on the sweatpants by themselves. I hesitated, holding the garments just off the floor.

Muttering to myself, I glanced up at Pam. She had her hand over her mouth, but I could tell she was quite amused, grinning at my predicament. I had to grin back.

"What's so funny?" I asked, starting to laugh.

She laughed herself. "You are! You put off doing your laundry until you have nothing left to wear. You burn your dinner in the oven. You can't even walk down the damn hallway without tripping over your own two feet!"

"I was distracted," I said, still laughing.

"Oh. Sorry I distracted you."

"No apology necessary," I said, slipping into the sweatpants.

We stood there, then, facing each other for a minute, in awkward silence. We'd reached an impasse. Neither of us wanted to fight, but we couldn't simply pretend that everything was back to normal.

At last she said, "Maybe I should be going."

"I wish you would stay," I said, humbly. "Stay and tell me your anecdote. We can get a pizza from *Luigi's*, and a bottle of wine."

She seemed to consider my peace offering, then shook her head.

"No, some other night. I promise." She turned to leave.

I followed her to the front door. As she was turning the dead bolt, I finally found my voice.

"Pam?"

She turned and looked at me, sadly. "Yes?"

"I love you."

She tilted her head, as though not certain she had heard me correctly. But I knew she had. Then she looked back at the door knob, reached for it, and turned it slowly. Her hand was trembling, ever so slightly.

"I'd like to believe that, Scott. Really I would."

She opened the door and walked out.

NO VACANCY

IT WASN'T A WAREHOUSE, EXACTLY, but it took a stretch of the imagination to see it as a professional building. I had found it almost by chance. It was tucked away in a heavily wooded tract, across an abandoned railroad line and at the end of a concrete driveway that had originally been poured to accommodate the Model A. I almost turned around when I reached the ancient structure, figuring I had made a wrong turn somewhere up the road.

But there—next to the oddly-modern front door—was a fake-wooden sign that seemed equally out of place. In bright red letters, the sign advertised the building's only tenant: *Geoffrey P. Hufnagel, Attorney-At-Law.*

Terribly peculiar, I thought.

I parked my car and climbed out. Then I took a minute to survey the building. The best I could figure, it had been a small factory at one time. It was low, and long, and built solidly out of brick. The concrete driveway circled around to the side of the building, ending at what must have been a loading dock at one time, but was now bricked-up to match the walls on either side. Those brick walls, I noticed, had been blasted clean in the not-too-distant past. I guessed that the owner had attempted to refurbish and subdivide the building, in the hopes of attracting professional tenants. Only one, apparently, had bought into the concept thus far.

Yet there were no signs on the property, advertising available office space. That's what struck me as the most bizarre aspect, considering that such signs are nearly as common as goose shit in these parts of New Jersey. Maybe, I thought, the owner had simply given up on competing for tenants in this economy, knowing that most businesses could easily find more suitable space in the glutted market.

The front door was open, just as Geoffrey Hufnagel had said. I walked into a respectable-looking lobby area, which appeared as though it had been intended to serve a number of individual businesses. No one was sitting at the stylish, maple-and-marble receptionist's kiosk. And only one of the five doors beyond, the one in the center, was lettered with a tenant's name. Again, *Geoffrey P. Hufnagel, Attorney-At-Law.*

This door was also open. I walked through it into a moderate-sized office, obviously Geoffrey's headquarters. There was a desk, a credenza, a couple of mismatched filing cabinets, and several bookcases of varying sizes and styles. The bookcases were jammed with law books, binders and legal journals. The effect of all that printed material would have been impressive, I suppose, if there had been less clutter to it. The overstuffed file folders stacked on Geoffrey's desk and credenza were equally disarranged. Had Miles been with me, he might have suggested that the office had been ransacked by a thief-in-training: someone who could adequately rifle and fling a room's contents, but who had yet to develop an artistic flair for the procedure.

"Mr. Jamison? Is that you?" A voice came from a room beyond, through a doorway that was partially hidden by one of the file cabinets.

"Yes, it's me," I called back. "Geoffrey?"

I heard footsteps and then saw the attorney as he came through the doorway and around from behind the file cabinet. He paused to close the two drawers of the cabinet that had been hanging open. Then he approached me, side-stepping a packing box on the floor. I detected a slight limp in his gait. He came up to me and held out his hand. We shook, and sized up one another.

"Pleased to meet you, Mr. Jamison," he said, smiling.

"Call me Scott. Likewise," I answered.

I don't know what *his* first impression was, but mine was this: Geoffrey Hufnagel was not as young a lawyer as I had been expecting. He was at least my age, short, with a high forehead, and a pair of glasses with very thick lenses. I noticed the glasses right away because he repeatedly pushed them up on the bridge of his nose, after which they immediately fell back down. This caused him to tilt his head back and squint up at me. The effect was disconcerting.

His clothes were *L.L. Bean*, but the catalog from which they were ordered had been printed, mailed and discarded at least a decade ago. The chino pants and the oxford shirt were both faded and frayed at the edges. His tie, however, was of an interesting, modern design. I complimented him on it.

He looked down at the tie. "A gift from my brother's wife," he said, absently.

"She has better taste than *my* sister-in-law," I noted.

He considered my comment for a moment, then asked: "You mean Donna?"

Of course, I was taken aback. We had spoken briefly on the phone, and now had barely met, and already he was reciting a detail from my personal life that was well beyond the scope of expected, or even assiduous, research. I didn't know whether to be impressed or annoyed. I was definitely suspicious.

"Yes, Donna," I responded. "How do you know about her?"

Geoffrey just shrugged. "My mother probably mentioned the name at some time." He gestured at his high forehead. "I'm cursed with an inability to forget the names of people I don't know, and places I've never been to. I could tell you, from memory, the names and hometowns of every player on the 1971 Pittsburgh Pirates, or the '69 Mets. But even if you offered me a hundred dollars, Mr. Jamison, I couldn't tell you what I wore to the office yesterday, or ate for lunch today."

"I'm not offering," I said dryly. "And please call me Scott."

He pushed his glasses up again. "I wouldn't expect you to."

"So," I said, changing the tone of my voice to indicate we'd had enough small talk, "what's your opinion of Angie Greer's lawsuit?"

He raised a finger, asking me to hold the thought, while he located a chair with only a small stack of papers on it. These he placed on top of another, larger stack, and then he pulled the chair up to the front of his desk. He limped around to the other side, cleared off another chair, cleared off a space on his credenza, and sat down. Then he opened a drawer of the credenza, which I was surprised to see was almost empty. He pulled out yet another file folder and placed it in the middle of the cleared area. He gestured at the empty chair across from him. I sat down.

"What is all this?" I asked, sweeping my hand to indicate the multitudinous stacks of papers and collections of folders.

"Research," was his nebulous response. Then he opened the folder in front of him. He shuffled through the papers inside until they were arranged to his satisfaction. Finally, he turned his head to me, tilted it back and said: "You have an interesting case here, Mr. Jamison."

"Scott. Tell me about it."

"Well, as you probably know, Scott, we have a Good Samaritan Act here in New Jersey. Are you familiar with it?"

I nodded. "Somewhat."

"Well, it supposedly renders individuals—including rescue squad volunteers, such as yourself—immune from civil damages arising from acts committed or omitted while providing emergency medical care."

Nicely phrased. "Yes, I've heard that."

"Good, good. But the act may not apply in your case, for two reasons. First of all, your negligence—assuming for the moment that you *were* negligent—caused no physical harm to your patient, but rather to your patient's spouse. Secondly, courts in New Jersey and elsewhere have ruled that Good Samaritan statutes *only* apply to caregivers who happen upon an accident victim, and not to trained individuals—as you are—who *deliberately* respond to an EMS call for help—as you did."

Already I was lost. "I'm not following you," I said.

Geoffrey swiveled in his chair to face me directly. He raised his hands—like he was about to conduct the metropolitan orchestra.

"The situation is *unique*," he intoned. "Had you been a neighbor walking down the street, and heard Mrs. Greer's cries for help, then you could have entered her home and done anything to help—within reason, of course—and harbored no fear of being held liable for damages. By the same token, you could have continued on your way, simply ignoring her cries, and also been held blameless.

"But that's not what happened. You answered the call, and drove directly to her home. More importantly, you put on your squad jacket and took your first aid kit from your car, which not only confirmed that you are trained to render care in just such an instance, but that you *intended* to render care."

"So?"

"So, at that point, you had a legal duty to act, to provide first aid to that woman. You could not have abandoned her, or refused to help, without fear of reprisal."

"So what I did was right. Right?"

Geoffrey shook his head. "Right, but wrong. Because you were acting as a representative of the Dayfield Rescue Squad, you also had a duty to abide by its regulations—which clearly state..." He searched through the papers in front of him until he located the one which said: "...that you are *not* to enter an unsecured residence. At that moment, when you were on the porch of the Greer residence, you were both *compelled* to act, and *forbidden* to act. At that moment, you were confronted with the classic quandary: damned if you do, and damned if you don't."

This wasn't encouraging. "In other words," I summarized, "you're saying the Good Samaritan Act may not protect me."

Geoffrey pushed his glasses back up on his nose and opened his eyes wide. "That's right," he said, as his glasses fell back down.

"So what do you suggest we do?"

"I suggest we claim immunity under the Good Samaritan Act, and move for a dismissal."

I was certain I had misunderstood him. "Come again?" I asked.

He smiled broadly at my confusion. He started to push his glasses back up, but then decided to take them off altogether. Without them, he was forced to squint. Grinning and squinting, he more closely resembled a bit actor in a low-budget horror movie, than the guy I wanted to represent me in a court of law.

"You see, Scott," he continued energetically, "I have a philosophy when it comes to defense litigation. I always say: *attack the weakest link!*" He said it with such vigor, such conviction, that I looked around the room, expecting to see a pep poster inscribed with the words. I saw only the usual display of diplomas and certificates. I made a mental note to inspect these documents, later.

"Attack the weakest link," I repeated, with none of his enthusiasm. It sounded like a good strategy for playing red rover, but failed to inspire me as a basis for my legal defense.

"Yes!" he said, emphatically. "In any legal dispute, the defendant has a built-in advantage. On one side," he held his left hand out, "there's a crime, or an injustice, that has supposedly been committed. On the other side," he held out his right hand, about nine inches from the left, "is the accused. The plaintiff, or the prosecution, has to build a chain of evidence, linking the two together. If the chain holds, the plaintiff wins his case. But if the chain breaks..." He separated his hands, and let them drift apart, dramatically. "...the defendant is found innocent.

"Now," he continued, "too many defense attorneys expend ridiculous amounts of time and effort, trying to break every link in that chain. That's wasteful. It's quite often counterproductive. And I won't be a party to such nonsense. I believe it's better to blow a single, gaping hole in your adversary's case, than it is to prick it repeatedly. From a distance—which is how a judge or a jury will *always* view a case—a dozen pinpricks are invisible. But even a blind bastard like me..." He squinted again, for emphasis. "...can't fail to see the breach left by a howitzer shell.

"Attack the weakest link," he said again, concluding his opening statement.

"But why the Good Samaritan Act?" I countered. "You said a minute ago it may not apply in this case. Why is that the weakest link?"

Geoffrey didn't answer my question. Rather, he picked up his glasses and cleaned them with the back of his new tie. Then, putting them back on, he stood up. He motioned for me to follow him. "Come," he said simply.

He turned and limped back around the filing cabinet, and disappeared through the doorway at the back of the room. I stood to follow him, being careful not to knock over any of the stacks of "research" lying about. Not that he'd notice...

The light was dim on the other side of the doorway. I hesitated for a moment, allowing my eyes to adjust. Looking around, I saw the framework for several additional rooms. The vertical bracing was in place and drywall had been mounted in a few sections. The work, however, had not been done recently. Dust coated all surfaces uniformly, and cobwebs had formed in the corners.

Geoffrey was about thirty feet ahead. He had stopped walking and turned around, as though waiting for me to catch up. I continued to look around as I strolled up to him.

"What is it with this place?" I asked. "Did the owner run out of cash in the middle of renovating?"

"Not a bad guess," Geoffrey said, "but it's much more complicated than that. You ever heard of ECRA?"

The Environmental Clean-up Responsibility Act—the nightmare legislation of every commercial property owner in New Jersey. I'd handled some research pertaining to its provisions, a few years before.

"Yes," I answered.

"Well, you're standing in the middle of one of its worst casualties. This building was constructed as a munitions factory back in 1912. The mortar shells your grandfather lobbed at the Germans during World War One were probably manufactured here. That's why the place is built like a fort; the outside walls are four feet thick in some places."

Geoffrey started walking again. I followed.

"Really?" I asked, trying to sound interested. I was beginning to regret that I'd brought the subject up.

"Yes, really. And that's also why it's all but abandoned now. Disposal regulations were non-existent back then, so there's no telling what kind of hazardous wastes are buried on this site. Unless, of course, you want to dig it all up."

"Which is what ECRA would require before the building could be sold," I observed.

"Exactly. The most recent owner got caught betwixt and between. He can't sell it, he was forced to stop renovating it, and now he can't even rent space in it."

"Then what are you doing here?"

"I was grandfathered in," he answered simply.

"You're not concerned about the health hazard?"

Geoffrey stopped, turned around, and smiled at me benignly. "We're all going to die someday, aren't we? I'm not worried about the risk here; there's a lot more out there…" He vaguely gestured at the outside world. "…to be concerned about. Besides, I'm here rent-free. I just have to keep an eye on the place, and file a report with the bank once a year."

We reached our destination. It was a room in the far corner of the building, apparently part of the original design. Maybe a lunch room, maybe the working quarters for the factory's clerical staff. Geoffrey opened a door into the room. It was pitch black inside. He reached for a light switch, but turned and faced me before he flipped it. When he spoke, his voice was uncharacteristically meek.

"Can I ask you not to tell my mother about this?" he requested.

About what? Was Geoffrey into something illicit? Or unseemly? Uncertain of what I was promising, I simply nodded. He flipped the switch.

I expected a revelation—brilliant overhead lights suddenly illuminating a breath-taking collection of…of…I don't know…of auto parts, or body parts, or works of art. Instead, the darkness was barely relieved by the glow of a single red bulb of low wattage. The eerie light enabled me to see only one thing: hanging along the length of a horizontal string, like clothes along a clothesline, were black and white photographic prints. Geoffrey Hufnagel's little secret, his mysterious hideaway, was nothing more than a darkroom. He led me inside and closed the door.

He turned on another light, a white one, which more clearly defined the limits and contents of the room. One by one, he gathered the photos from the string and stacked them on a nearby counter top. He motioned me over to view them.

"This is my first love," he announced.

I glanced at the pictures. They were all of a young woman.

"Her?" I asked, perplexed.

He frowned at my misunderstanding. "No," he said, gesturing at our surroundings, which included numerous pieces of photographic equipment and paraphernalia. "This—photography. My becoming a lawyer was my mother's dream. *This* is what I'd rather be doing for a living."

"Oh," I said, returning my attention to the stack of fresh black-and-whites. They looked like high-quality surveillance shots: all had been taken outdoors, from a distance, through a telephoto lens. The compressed nature of the woman's surroundings confirmed that much. Also, the fact that the woman was apparently unaware of the photographer's presence reinforced the impression that he—Geoffrey, I assumed—had been hidden when he had taken them.

I studied the woman's face. She was pretty, in a waif-like sort of way—and remotely familiar. Had I examined her surroundings as closely as I did her wistful features, I would have probably guessed, correctly.

"Do you know who she is?" Geoffrey asked.

I shook my head.

"That's your adversary, Angela Greer."

"Oh," I said again, not completely surprised. Who else would Geoffrey be stalking and photographing that might be of any interest to me? "She looks different than the last time I saw her."

It was an understatement, and Geoffrey chuckled at it. "I would hope so. I took these pictures yesterday, three weeks to the day after her husband had beat her up for the last time." Then, after a moment, he added: "She's a good-looking woman, don't you think?"

I shrugged. "Certainly better-looking than she was three weeks ago," I said, handing the photos back to him. "But I don't understand what good these are to us, and what they have to do with your 'weakest link' philosophy."

"You don't?" he asked, slightly incredulous.

"No, I don't."

"Look at the pictures again," he said, offering them back to me. "Tell me what you see in them, other than an attractive woman. Look at her eyes, especially."

A warning buzzer started to sound in my brain. I couldn't isolate the exact problem, but something just wasn't right here. As I studied the sad, vulnerable face of the woman who was bringing suit against me, I tried to make a fundamental—but crucial—judgment regarding Geoffrey Hufnagel. Was he brilliant, though just a tad eccentric? Or was he simply eccentric?

"I'm not following you, Geoffrey," I said, acting irritated.

He raised a finger to emphasize his point. "Someone is pulling this woman's chain. I can tell a lot about a person by just observing them, and sometimes even more by examining pictures or videotapes. This is *not* a woman to initiate a lawsuit against a man who was only trying to help her in an emergency. She'll fold up like a cheap card table–"

The warning buzzer sounded louder.

"Of course not," I snapped, while my estimation of Geoffrey's abilities began to fall. "Her lawyer, Pressman, is the one pushing this lawsuit. When he found he couldn't make a case against the Dayfield Police Department, he nosed around for another victim, and came up with me. And if it wasn't for that damned squad regulation–"

Geoffrey's eyes lit up, as though something I said had unlocked the entire mystery. "Pressman! That's it!" he blurted.

Instantly, I resolved to find myself a different attorney. I was astounded that Geoffrey could have not realized something so obvious. Of *course* it was Pressman. I was about to scream that at Geoffrey, but I held up as he continued to ramble, as though in a trance, or in the grip of a powerful revelation. For once, I'm glad that I didn't interrupt.

"…before we agree to meet with Pressman on Wednesday, we *insist* that his client be present. We won't even have to file for a dismissal. We'll smash the weakest link then and there!"

Wednesday? Meet with Pressman on *Wednesday*? Had I missed

something?

Geoffrey stopped talking, and noticed my stare of bewilderment. He grinned sheepishly, realizing his oversight. "I forgot to tell you, didn't I, that you're being deposed on Wednesday."

"Deposed?" I was not happy to hear this.

"Yes, deposed. After we spoke on Thursday, I called Pressman's office, to inform him that I would be representing you."

"You did?" I was even less pleased to hear this.

"Yes, and the very next day—*boom!*—there's a messenger at my door serving a deposition notice. I've never received one so fast. I guess Mr. Pressman is anxious to bring this matter to a head."

"And you agreed to a deposition, on such short notice?"

People usually squirm only when they're seated. Geoffrey Hufnagel was standing, but he squirmed anyway.

"Well, I haven't *disagreed*. I wanted to talk it over with you, today. Frankly, I thought it would be a good idea, just to call his bluff. But this is even better: if we insist that Angela Greer be present, we can blow his entire case out of the water and be done with it! I could disaffect her from this lawsuit in a New York minute. What do you say, Scott? The best defense is a good offense. *She's* the weak link in his case, so let's take a shot at her."

Now what was I to do?

"But I don't understand, Geoffrey. If Pressman is—as you say— pulling this woman's chain, then what good does it do to get them in a room together? He'll do all the talking. We'll be no better off than we are right now."

Geoffrey waved that solitary finger at me, as though to negate my argument.

"I never said *Pressman* was pulling her chain. *You* said that. Personally, I think Pressman is just the hired gun. But if we take up his offer, and get Angela Greer in a room, under oath, I think we can divide and conquer.

"You're a big, strong fellow; you can handle any pressure that Pressman puts on you. But Angela Greer won't be able to stand the heat. What do you say, Scott? Let's go for it!"

I don't have much experience in matters like this, so I was unsure how to respond. On the one hand, I was hesitant to blindly follow the advice of this odd man, Geoffrey Hufnagel. It seemed he was too anxious to engage the enemy—on the enemy's terms, no less. That scared me.

But on the other hand, I liked the idea of not dragging out the lawsuit. I had enough other things to worry about already—minor matters, such as my career at DataStaff, my relationship with Pam, and my standoff with the Dayfield Police—to let this annoyance fester. If there was a chance it could be resolved in the next forty-eight hours, why not take it?

Furthermore, Geoffrey had suddenly shown me—just when I was about to give up on him—that he really had a nose for this business. Or at least for this case. With nothing more than the materials I'd sent him, he'd established the nuances of our respective positions. He'd studied the law. And, most importantly, he'd developed a theory that I couldn't reject myself: that Pressman was *just the hired gun*. Something about that explanation appealed to me, though I couldn't put my finger on it.

"Okay, Geoffrey," I said at last. "Tell Pressman we've agreed to the deposition, but only on the terms you mentioned."

He grinned at my statement of approval. "Consider it done," he said.

I picked up one of the photos of Angela Greer. I asked: "Would you mind if I took this with me?"

"Be my guest," he answered, still grinning. "Although I think this one..." He reached for an alternate shot. "...is more flattering."

"No, this one will do."

A half hour later, I was pulling into the entrance way to my apartment complex. I locked my car and crossed the darkened parking lot. It had been a long day. My only thought, at the moment, was to climb the stairs to my apartment, grab a beer, and call Pam. Remembering our encounter of the previous Friday evening, I smiled to myself.

I stopped at the panel of mailboxes that serves my complex. As I fished in my pocket for the key to open my box, I heard, in the distance, the distinctive chime of a delivery truck in reverse gear. It was oddly reassuring. I opened the box and pulled out my mail—bills, junk, and an envelope from the Dayfield Rescue Squad. Official verification of my suspension, no doubt.

Then, all of a sudden, I couldn't breathe. There was a python wrapped around my neck, squeezing so viciously and relentlessly that—within seconds—my eyes felt like they were going to explode from the awful pressure. Dropping my mail, I reached up to claw at the creature, only to find it covered with a smooth, nylon-like material. Gasping, I groped for its head and found a fist instead. It wasn't a snake, I dimly realized, but the forearm of an immensely powerful human. Male, I assumed.

Then I heard a dull thud, and immediately felt an agonizing shock as another fist rammed into my abdomen. The pressure above and pain below were more than my conscious self could sustain, but just before I blacked out I heard a man's voice—up close to my left ear yet still quite distant—snarling, "I'll teach you to *fuck* with me, Jamison. You're a dead man."

NO RULES

22

Bound and gagged.

It's one of those neatly balanced, crisply dichotomous phrases that roll smoothly off the tongue—like: *drawn and quartered,* or: *raped and tortured*—but that don't adequately describe the *terror and agony* (another crisp one) entailed by its composite parts. Yet that's the condition I was in, when I came to a short while later. Bound and gagged.

I was on my stomach, my hands cinched tight behind my back, with my face against a dark, grimy patch of indoor/outdoor carpeting. My kidneys hurt, my neck ached, my wrists chafed, and my head was pounding. Those discomforts alone would have been sufficient to ruin my evening, but in addition I couldn't speak—couldn't hardly breathe—and I had no idea where I was. No morning after had ever approached this awful state, and I hadn't even had the pleasure of drinking myself into it. I retched, but with no outlet for escape, my stomach's contents simply burned in my throat.

"So, the lover boy has returned to us, eh?"

The voice sneered above me in the darkness. It was the same one I had heard from the unseen mass of muscle that had throttled me.

Then I felt another sharp pain as its owner kicked me in the thigh.

"Welcome back, asshole," the voice continued. "Welcome to thief hell, reserved just for stupid fucks who think they can steal from me." Another kick slammed into my upper arm, with force barely insufficient to break the bone. I groaned, and prayed that I would lapse again into unconsciousness.

His steps moved away, and then a dim light came on. I tried to focus on my surroundings. The juncture of carpeting and sloped wood paneling less than eight inches from my face told me I was in the rear of a vehicle, most likely a van. I had almost made the connection when my assailant returned. With remarkable ease he picked me up by my shoulders and flung me into a worn, padded bench attached to the vehicle's wall. I winced as my hands, still tied behind me, took the brunt of my collision with the paneling.

My eyes were still closed as I heard the familiar screech of a metal folding chair being opened. I kept them closed as I heard the chair being set heavily down in front of me, and as I heard it protest a great weight coming to rest on it. Then I heard, and faintly felt—and distinctly smelled—breathing on my face. The fragrance was not appealing.

"Look at me, asshole," the voice commanded. I flinched, and opened my eyes slowly. He was sitting right in front of me—his hairy, meaty face scowling at me. He was big, very big, in the way that offensive tackles, and nightclub bouncers, are big. Once lean and muscular, now overweight but still quite formidable. *A professional wrestler,* Fran had estimated. *One mean son-of-a-bitch,* Skip had warned. Kyle Hutchinson. Or "Hutch," as his friends called him. Both of them.

"You know who I am, don't you?" he asked gruffly. Or maybe he didn't ask, but just told me he knew that I knew. I hesitated, not knowing whether to nod, shake my head, or do nothing. I did nothing, the wrong choice. Quick as a cat and strong as a bear, he cuffed me across the side of my head. I reeled for a moment, and retched again. When I was able to reopen my eyes, I saw, in his oversized paw, the gleaming shaft of a long, sharp blade. A hunting knife, I assumed, but with no perceptible rise in my level of fear. You get to a point, you know, and you just can't go any higher on the shitless scale.

"Not a word," he said brusquely, as he brought the knife up next to my face, spun it around—so that its sharp edge faced him—then slid it under the bandana he had used to gag me. A slight pull and the bandana fell away, cut in two. I spit out the rag he had wadded in my mouth, and retched one last time.

He chuckled at my discomfort. "That newspaper article was dead on, Jamison. You're certainly no Clint Eastwood. Let's just hope, for your sake, that you've got more brains than balls."

He set down the knife and brought a bottle up from his side—a cheap grade of vodka, I managed to see. He slurped an ounce or two, then held the bottle to my lips.

"Here, asshole," he said. "Drink."

What could I do? Refuse? I tilted my head back slightly and he poured the liquid in my mouth. I swallowed quickly, the vodka searing my throat as it went down. It was all I could do not to retch once more.

"Now," he said, taking the bottle back, "you and I are going to have a little discussion. I've gotten tired of following you around, hoping you'd make this easy for both of us. You've left me no choice."

He took another swig of the vodka as I watched in mute apprehension. I had no idea what he was talking about, or what he wanted from me.

"The only thing I haven't figured out," he said, as he set the bottle down, "is whether you and Angie are splitting the money, or whether you just took it yourself. She probably told you that I talked to her last week. She acted like she doesn't know anything about it. But she's a pretty good actress. Don't you think?"

He smiled as he asked this last question. With his teeth bared, he looked even more menacing. If that was possible.

I answered, "I wouldn't know, Hutch."

He actually laughed out loud at this. Then he nodded, as though pleased with a joke I had told him.

"That's funny," he remarked at last. "You two probably rehearsed this scam for weeks, and now you're telling me you don't know if she can act. That's a good one, asshole."

What scam?

"Hutch, I don't know what you're talking about."

Wham. He cuffed me again, even more sharply than before. I reeled, and almost fell over on the bench. When I opened my eyes, I saw that his smile had disappeared. He stared at me for a minute.

"You think I'm just some big, dumb fuck, don't you? Well, let me clue you in, asshole. You fooled Gary Greer—hell, you as good as murdered him, the way you set him up for the cops—but you haven't fooled me. I *know* what's going on. I know more about you than even Angie does."

He paused and nodded at me. "Yeah, that's a scary thought, isn't it? You've been humping Angie Greer for—what? about six months now? But she don't know that you've *really* been dickin' her when she's not even around. She don't know about the blonde babe you got in reserve. And she probably don't know about the money you took. *My* money, asshole."

My head was throbbing. Hutch was giving it a beating, inside and out.

"And you know," he continued, "I'll bet I can guess how much you *thought* you got away with. Gary Greer was into me for fifteen grand, and he was 'sposed to pay me back the day after he got offed. He must've had at least that much at his place the night you suckered him. He was never much of a businessman, but he probably had eighteen—maybe even twenty thousand—all in cash. Am I close, asshole? Is that how much you and Angie stole from me? Or that you stole yourself?"

I shook my head, while warily tracking his free hand.

"You're wrong, Hutch. I don't know Angie Greer. I've never really even met her. In fact, she's filed a lawsuit against me for causing her husband's death."

Hutch roared—a deep but mirthless laugh.

"Oh, that's stupendous, asshole. Angie Greer is *suing* her hero from the rescue squad. You expect me to believe that?"

"I can show you the papers–"

"*Fuck* your papers, Jamison. If you got any papers, they're part of your scheme, no doubt. You two pretend to be strangers—or enemies, even—and the cops don't look into the shit you're trying to pull. Or maybe you've got them paid off, too. Wouldn't surprise me." He stopped, and took another drink from the bottle. He didn't offer me any this time.

"Though, I must admit: it was a neat little plan. If it works, Angie gets rid of Gary, with no questions asked. You get Angie to yourself, *and* the money. Gary's dead, and I'm screwed.

"But I've got news for you, asshole. It's not *gonna* work. I never cared much about Gary, and I don't give a flying fuck about you and Angie. But I do intend to get my money back. *Nobody* steals from me."

Kyle Hutchinson had obviously reached the same mistaken conclusion that Gary Greer had jumped to on that damned evening. He thought that I was Angie Greer's mysterious lover—a shadowy individual who, quite likely, didn't even exist. And he was also convinced that I had stolen money from the Greer house—money that was to have passed from Greer to him. That much seemed apparent to me at this point.

Of course, I knew nothing about any money. As far as I was concerned, just then, it was simply another untraceable piece to an unsolvable puzzle. I was far more concerned about getting myself out of this mess than I was in fitting its fragments together.

But at that point, I didn't know where to begin. Though it was clear that Hutch was ill-informed about certain matters, it was also quite possible that he knew a few things I didn't. I wondered: could I somehow extricate myself from this quagmire, and even come out ahead? Ahead, that is, if you didn't count a few scrapes, bruises and an impending heart attack…

Hutch was waiting for me to say something. I had to be *very* careful. A denial, or anything resembling a denial, would only get me slugged again—or worse. I had to play along—somehow. I asked a question, almost holding my breath as I did.

"So, you don't think Angie knows about the money?"

Hutch slowly sat back and folded his arms across his chest. His action seemed to indicate satisfaction—satisfaction that I'd finally decided to stop acting stupid, and was going to play ball with him.

"You tell me," he said. "I mean, it's not like she didn't know what line of business her husband was in. She must've thought she was too good for him. It's no wonder she started fuckin' around with the likes of you. Not that you're any improvement, Christ knows.

"But let me tell you this, asshole. If you think nobody knew about you two, then you're even dumber than you look. Gary told me himself that he thought Angie was making it with a cop—somebody who came to her rescue one night after he'd beaten the shit out of her. So poor old Gary wasn't too far wrong–"

Hutch stopped talking abruptly, and lifted a finger to his lips. I listened, and heard footsteps outside the van. Then a woman's voice saying: "Don't blame me for being late. *You're* the one who wanted to watch that stupid ball game. The Mets are history, anyway, so why–"

"Aw, shut the hell up," a man's voice replied. "You nag just like your mother, the old bitch."

Then I heard two car doors slam, an engine starting, and the sound of tires squealing—loud at first, then receding. We were apparently still in the parking lot of my apartment building.

Hutch shook his head. "Classy neighbors you have, asshole."

I smiled weakly. The interruption, I feared, would put an end to his rambling dissertation. And he hadn't told me anything I didn't already know.

"So—to answer your question, asshole—no, I *don't* think Angie knows about the money. I took the liberty of searching her house, and found nothing. Course, I didn't expect to find anything there. After you sandbagged Gary, and put on your innocent act for the cops, you simply rode off into the sunset, and took the money with you.

"And, you know something, asshole? You might have gotten away with it. If you hadn't opened your big mouth to the newspaper, you might have pulled it off. But when I saw that article—and I read about Gary putting a gun to your head—then I put it all together. It's just too bad he didn't pull the trigger first. Then we wouldn't be having this conversation, would we?"

Now there was one fucking brilliant observation.

Hutch took another hit from his bottle, and then picked up the knife again. Slowly and deliberately, he polished the blade on his pant leg. Then he said: "So, tell me, asshole. When do I get my money back?"

What could I say? That I had put it in a CD, and there was a penalty for early withdrawal?

"I…I don't have your money, Hutch."

He raised one bushy eyebrow, and one gleaming knife. The eyebrow didn't faze me.

I hastened to continue: "Not here, anyway. But I can get you the fifteen thousand, if that's how much it was."

He narrowed his eyes. "If that's how much it was? What are you telling me, asshole? That you haven't even counted it? What kind of a thief are you?"

Not a very accomplished one, obviously. But I've always been a pretty good ass-kisser. That was the talent I had to count on, if I was going to weasel out of this fix without any additional physical damage.

"I'm not a thief, Hutch. I didn't know until later that Gary Greer was, um, selling for you. And I didn't know until just now that the money he had was yours.

"But if you let me out of here, I'll make sure you get what's coming to you. No offense, Hutch, but you're not the kind of guy I want to have coming after me. I'll see that you get your money."

Hutch smiled, almost benignly. He'd gotten all that he wanted, so far. I had more or less admitted taking the money, and I had groveled at his feet—begging him to let me repay him. The only thing left was to work out the terms. For some unexplainable reason, I didn't think he'd take American Express…

"One thing, asshole. Let's get one thing clear. I never said Gary Greer was selling for me. I just said he owed me money. Do you understand that?" He twirled the knife as he spoke.

"Certainly, Hutch."

"Okay, then," he said, grabbing my arm and effortlessly lifting and spinning me around. "I'm going to give you three days. That's very generous on my part, and I don't expect you to take advantage of my generosity." He cut the rope that bound my hands. My fingers ached as blood circulated freely in them again. Then he pushed me back down onto the bench. I rubbed my wrists.

"Three days," I confirmed. "That'll be Thursday. Where should I meet you?"

He shook his head. "You don't meet me, asshole. I'll be in touch with you. Just don't disappear on me. And don't even think about double-crossing me. When someone steals from me, I get annoyed. Right now I'm annoyed. But when someone double-crosses me, I get angry. Believe me, asshole, you don't want to see me angry."

With that, he reached for the latch on the rear door and—in one fluid motion—flung it open. He looked at me and gestured to the outside world.

"Now get the *fuck* out of my car," he snarled, as though reminding me that we weren't a couple of old pals, having a pop together. I didn't wait for a second invitation.

I half ran and half stumbled across the parking lot, stopping just long enough to scoop up my mail, which was still laying where I'd dropped it. Only when I reached the relative safety of the building's front door did I turn back to look. Hutch's van was still sitting there, in the darkness at the far end of the lot. I used my key and went inside.

In my apartment, with the door locked behind me, I flopped onto a padded chair in the living room. I needed a drink. A cold drink for my pounding head. A strong drink for my shattered nerves. But I was too exhausted, and too rattled, to go fix it. I just sat, trying to make some sense out of this latest—and most volatile—threat to my once-sheltered existence.

I cursed Dorothy McCrae and the article she had written about me. But even as I did so, I refused to accept the notion that a newspaper article alone had plunged me into this mess. Kyle Hutchinson wouldn't have fingered me—would he?—just because of something he read in the paper. There had to be more to it than that.

But what?

At last I turned my head, and noticed the blinking light on my answering machine. Probably more bad news, I thought. Nonetheless, I reached over and punched the *PLAY* button. It was the bravest thing I'd done all day.

A man's voice greeted me: "Good evening, Scott, this is your favorite attorney calling. Just a reminder about the deposition on Wednesday, the day after tomorrow, at 7:30 in the evening. I spoke with Pressman a few minutes ago, and he said he'll *try* to have Angela Greer present. I told him *try* wasn't good enough. So he promised she'd be there. For whatever his promises are worth...

"Anyway, I'll meet you at Pressman's office—it's in the Morris building, on Spring Street in Bedford. I'm sure you can find it. Just bring yourself; I've got everything we need. He suggested that you bring financial disclosure statements, but I told him that was premature. He knew it, too. Can't blame him for asking, though.

"Oh, and don't worry about a thing. It's all under control. Just call me if you have any questions. Otherwise, I'll see you then."

All under control—is it, Geoffrey? My, that's awfully easy for you to say.

NO SHOW

23

MY FIRST DEPOSITION, EVER. IT MIGHT surprise you to learn that I wasn't as thrilled—or nervous even—as I thought I'd be. Geoffrey had done his best to prepare me for our esteemed opponent. Besides, after facing Kyle Hutchinson—with my hands tied behind my back, no less—what did I have to fear from some parasitic lawyer?

"Pressman's going to beat you over the head with the squad regulation that says you should have waited for the police. It's the only thing he has, so expect him to make the most of it. When he's through doing that, he'll probably get real friendly and say those six symphonic words: '*We can make this go away.*' Please, just ignore him. He doesn't have a case and he knows it. He's just hoping you'll roll over and pull out your wallet.

"You can express your sympathy to Mrs. Greer, but that's it. I'll be the bad guy. I'll be the one to say her husband's dead because he shot a cop, and not because of anything you did. That's the whole issue here. The rest is just bullshit."

We were sitting in James Pressman's conference room, Geoffrey and I. Pressman—an alert, well-dressed young man who seemed quite accustomed to giving orders—had ushered us into the room upon our arrival. He had offered no refreshments, which exhibited—I thought—a lack of common courtesy on his part. Even Hutch had shown better manners in that respect.

Pressman had told us that Mrs. Greer was expected shortly, and then had excused himself and returned, I assume, to his private office. As we sat waiting, Geoffrey quietly went over his instructions to me for about the twentieth time.

Then he looked at me oddly, as though noticing a distinguishing feature for the first time. He took hold of my chin, and turned my head to the side. He let out a low whistle. "Boy, that's some bruise you got there, Scott. How'd you get that?"

"I tripped, and fell into a door," I mumbled, turning my head back. Geoffrey just nodded.

A stenographer was also in the room—a middle-aged, plain-faced woman who leafed through a magazine as we waited. Satisfied I knew my role, Geoffrey turned and smiled at her, and engaged her in polite but superficial conversation. He asked her name.

"Sarah," she told him.

"That's a pretty name," he remarked.

Sarah smiled faintly.

We waited for about fifteen minutes. Then we heard a slight disturbance, coming from the reception area. Pressman was speaking—arguing, actually—with someone whose voice we couldn't hear. My curiosity got the better of me. I stood and walked to the door, and quietly opened it just enough to peek out. Geoffrey shook his head at me, but only as a gesture of mild disapproval. Sarah, again, smiled faintly.

Pressman's back was to me, but I could tell from his hunched posture and animated gestures that he was very upset with the person to whom he was speaking. I twisted my head and opened the door just a bit more to get a glimpse of his antagonist. It was a woman, and it took me a few moments to realize it had to be his client, Angie Greer. I recognized her from—I think—Geoffrey's photographs.

By now, Pressman was pleading with her, but Angie Greer was

resisting, shaking her head adamantly. I kept watching her, trying to cultivate the feeling that I knew her from somewhere—and not from the evening when this adventure started. She was so blood-ied on that occasion she could have been most anybody, my moth-er included, and I wouldn't have recognized her. But now, as I watched her refusing his entreaties, I felt certain I had seen her before. And not just from Geoffrey's telephoto shots, but in the flesh.

At last she concluded the argument and walked out. Pressman stood for a moment, probably considering his next move. I silently closed the door and sat back down next to Geoffrey.

Pressman strolled in less than a minute later, smiling as though nothing had happened. "Well," he said in an offhand manner, "my client's not going to be able to make it today. But we can get start-ed with Mr. Jamison here—"

"No we can't." Geoffrey's voice was flat, unwavering.

Pressman tried to act unruffled. "There's no reason, Hufnagel, that my client's absence should delay this proceeding. You'll have sufficient opportunity to speak with Mrs. Greer—"

"We're out of here, Pressman," Geoffrey interrupted. "I specifi-cally stipulated that the plaintiff had to appear in order for this deposition to take place. My client is here, yours is not. Call us when you're ready to comply. We'll try to accommodate you then." He stood to leave, then turned to the stenographer. "It was nice meeting you, Sarah. Have your employer send a bill to Mr. Pressman for this waste of time."

I followed my attorney as far as the door, then stopped and faced James Pressman. He tilted his head, as though defying me to add another insult. I tried to mollify my tone. "Could you tell me, counselor, how long you have known Mrs. Greer?"

I asked the question in absolute innocence, but his scowl indi-cated that he thought my intent to be anything but.

"That's none of your damned business," he hissed.

His vehemence surprised me. I turned to look at Sarah, the stenographer, but she purposely avoided making eye contact with me. I looked back at Pressman. He was still scowling.

"Perhaps you're right," I said. "Have a nice day, Mr. Pressman.

Sarah." I walked from the conference room.

I expected to find Geoffrey waiting for me in the reception area, but he wasn't there. So I continued out into the hallway. There I saw my attorney, waiting by the elevators. He was staring—with an odd, wistful expression—at the floor indicator above one of the two elevator doors. We were on the sixth floor; the indicator he was watching showed that a descending car had just reached ground level.

I didn't think Geoffrey noticed me as I walked silently to his side. I was mistaken.

"I almost caught her," he said, still staring at the indicator. "The doors were closing as I came out of the office. I called to her, but she let them close anyway."

"You mean Mrs. Greer?"

He nodded.

I considered this for a second. "And what if you *had* caught her?" I asked. "What would you have said to her?"

Geoffrey brought his gaze down from the indicator and smiled at me. "It doesn't matter now, does it?"

Just then, we heard a door opening behind us. We turned to see Pressman standing in the doorway to his office. Incredibly, he was smirking at us. "By the way, Hufnagel," he said in a brash tone, "I forgot to say 'congratulations.' It's nice to see you handling one of your own, for a change."

Geoffrey didn't even blink. "Especially since it's a winner," he replied.

Pressman lost his smirk. He licked his lips, and glanced about, obviously trying to think of an incisive rejoinder. "Yeah, well, it's not over yet," he said—which didn't seem particularly incisive, not at all. He ducked back into his office and closed the door.

The doors to the second elevator opened, and we boarded. We were alone in the car. After I pushed the button for the ground floor, I turned and faced Geoffrey. He seemed to be slightly upset.

"What was that about?" I asked.

Geoffrey shrugged. "It seems Mr. Pressman did some research of his own," he said.

"And?"

"And he found out what sort of a practice I have."

What sort of a practice? What did *that* mean? My questioning gaze told Geoffrey that I didn't understand, and would appreciate an explanation.

Again he shrugged. "It's a long story," he said defensively.

"I have time."

"Well, it's nothing to be concerned about. It's just that most of my work is—shall we say—sub-contracted."

"Sub-contracted?"

Geoffrey sighed wearily. "Yes. The story goes back to when I was a junior partner at a large and fairly prestigious law firm in Newark. I'd tell you the name, but it's not important."

"I wouldn't know it anyway," I said obligingly.

He smiled weakly before he continued: "Owing, I suppose, to my ability to remember names and dates, I became the firm's foremost researcher. Whenever one of the partners needed background information to support a case—especially if an applicable precedent was needed—the job would come to me. I could usually find and summarize the necessary material in less time than anyone else. I was the research maven at…" He stopped himself before mentioning the firm's name. As if I gave a damn.

"So what happened?"

"Politics."

Ah, yes. Politics.

"Meaning?"

"Well," said Geoffrey, "to make a long story short, I joined an organization that lobbied for the bill to make assault weapons illegal in New Jersey. I'm sure you're familiar with the law. Unfortunately, that legislation was actively opposed by the firm's senior partner, who just happens to be a state senator."

"And who put the kibosh on your career at this fairly prestigious law firm," I ventured.

Geoffrey raised his palms. "Officially, yes. But the rest of the partners still retain me as an independent consultant. I'm free to pursue my own business, but I haven't had much time to do so."

"So your mother does it for you."

He smiled broadly at this. "In a manner of speaking."

We reached the ground floor and exited the building together. I noticed him looking around—up and down the street—when we stopped on the sidewalk. Finally, he gave up his search and faced me.

"So what's next?" I asked.

Geoffrey paused, and scratched his ear. He seemed to be thinking on the matter. "I'd suggest we wait a few days and see what happens," he said at last. "We still have time to answer the summons—and to file for a dismissal—but something tells me that won't be necessary. After what happened up there," he jerked his thumb skyward, indicating Pressman's office, "I'd say there's an even chance Mrs. Greer will withdraw the suit. I'm just sorry we didn't get a shot at her today."

"So I should just sit tight, huh?"

"Yes, I'd say so. Do you have a problem with that?"

I shook my head. My gesture enabled Geoffrey to see the bruise he had noticed before. Again, he took hold of my chin, turned my head to the side, and examined the injury.

"Did you have this looked at?" he questioned me, in much the same manner as his mother might have asked.

"No. It's nothing."

"Did it happen at home or at work?"

Lawyers. Always looking for an opportunity, aren't they?

"Um, at home," I said, not too convincingly. For just a second, I debated whether to tell him about my encounter with Hutch. I decided not to, not just yet.

Geoffrey let go of my chin and regarded me for a moment. Then, abruptly, he stuck out his right hand.

"Well, I gotta go," he said.

I shook his hand and smiled.

"I'll be in touch," he said. Then he turned and limped up the street to where his car was parked. I watched as he pulled away.

I glanced at my watch, then looked at the sky. It was getting dark. I turned and walked to my car.

NO BRAINER

24

IT SEEMED UNLIKELY—TO ME, anyway—that Kyle Hutchinson was counting down the hours until he paid me a return visit. He had said three days. Two had already gone by, but I managed to convince myself that he'd allow me another 48 hours or so to locate his money. Drug dealers give grace periods, don't they?

Hutch had said that Angie Greer probably didn't know anything about the cash, and I had been inclined to believe him. He had also said that he had searched her house and found nothing. Wasn't it obvious, then, that Gary Greer had left the money somewhere else?

I settled on that explanation, though the thought was not comforting. Roughly twenty thousand dollars, in cash, squirreled away in a locker at the bus depot—and the only person who knew about it was taking a dirt nap.

Yet I was on the hook for it.

That's what I was thinking as I drove home, an hour or so after the truncated deposition. I had stopped in a diner, not far from Pressman's office, and sat gazing into the darkness outside. I couldn't tell you what I had to eat there, or who had waited on me. I had been pondering my situation the whole time.

At least I wasn't worrying about the lawsuit any longer. Pressman was obviously floundering and—from what I had seen—Angie Greer didn't have her heart in it. As Geoffrey had suggested, the chances seemed favorable that that portion of my troubles would soon disappear. My faith in my offbeat attorney—wavering though it had been—seemed to have been well-placed.

I wasn't paying much attention to my driving. My brain was on autopilot, just following the familiar roads back home. Nonetheless, just two blocks before my apartment complex I turned down a side street. I can't say if I changed my route intentionally or because I was preoccupied with the matter, but I found myself pulling up in front of Angie Greer's house. I parked my car in the same spot I had occupied three weeks earlier. I lowered my windows, and turned off the engine.

For several minutes, I sat behind the wheel and just stared at the house. I couldn't shake the feeling that the answers I was seeking could be found within. Maybe Angie Greer didn't know about the money, but what about the gun? Maybe she had an idea—if not definite knowledge—how it had traveled from the glove compartment of a smashed-up car to her husband's hand, seven months later...

Without warning, a voice at my back spoke: "Yessir, that's the place where the man was killed."

I jumped—by now, my nerves were completely shot from the effects of persons unknown sneaking up on me—and turned quickly to see Fay Johnson, the Greers' daft neighbor, standing in the shadows. She approached as I caught my breath, her sheepdog at her side.

"The first two weeks after it happened," she continued, "lots of people came by for a look-see. You're the first that's been here in a few days."

"Oh," I remarked, without much feeling. I hadn't counted on running into Fay the Fruit, who had apparently appointed herself tour guide for the morbidly curious.

"He got what he deserved, believe me," she added, while stepping right up to my window. Then she looked at me, narrowed her eyes, and frowned.

"I know you," she said definitely. "You were *here* that night."

"That's right, Fay," I responded politely. Then I reached out of the window and patted her dog on the head. "Hi, Bailey. Howya doing, pup?" For some reason, I wanted to show the dingbat that I remembered her and her dopey dog quite clearly.

Fay Johnson took a step backwards and looked at me suspiciously. Then she pivoted her head, and examined my car from front to back.

"But you're driving a different car, aren't you?"

Same Fay, still loony. I've had the same car for four years.

"No, this is the same car," I answered simply.

She shook her finger at me. "Don't you lie to me, young man," she scolded. "I remember the car you were driving. You parked it right here that night. It was a *white* car."

"Yes, Fay," I said wearily. "I did park the car right here. But it was blue, just like this car. It *was* this car."

Still she shook her finger at me, and stepped to the side. She leaned over and tapped the finger on my windshield. "And you had a plate on your dashboard. It said *Dayfield Rescue Squad*."

I reached under my seat, grabbed the identifying plate, and dutifully showed it to her.

"That's right, Fay. This is the plate. But the car was still blue."

For me, this game of matching memories was, at best, annoying. But Fay's eyes lit up when I produced the plate, as though I had paid her a very pleasant compliment. She nodded in excitement.

"I knew it!" she exclaimed. She tapped my windshield again. "And you had another plate right next to it! The other plate said...let me think...don't tell me...*Lieutenant!* That's it! Lieutenant!"

Lieutenant? How goofy could she get? I have never been an officer on the squad, so I've never owned one of those identification plates that the officers...

That the *officers*...sometimes affix to their windshields...

Sometimes affix...

Sometimes...

Holy *shit!* I tried to get out of its way, but it hit me like a truck. *Lieutenant!* Fay Johnson—of all people—had given me the answer!

Shouting *"Yes!"*, I threw open my car door and jumped out. Her dog barked, then growled, then whined as I flung my arms around her mistress.

Lieutenant!

It took me a minute to calm down. Fay stood frozen, staring at me in wide-eyed terror. I'm sure she was thinking: *And they call* me *nuts?*

At last I was able to speak in a reasonably even tone. Fay Johnson had given me the central answer to the mystery, but there were still plenty of secondary questions. Maybe she could provide answers to a few of them as well.

"Fay," I asked solicitously, "the night that you saw me, do you remember what you told me?"

Again she narrowed her eyes and frowned. "I didn't tell you anything!" she protested.

This wasn't going to come easily.

"Yes," I coaxed, "yes, you told me a man had left the house just before I arrived. You said it was Gary Greer."

She cocked her head and arched her eyebrow defiantly. "Well, I must have been wrong!" she blurted. "A person can make a mistake, can't they?"

"Definitely," I soothed. "But you must have seen *somebody*. Didn't you?"

She turned and gazed at the house, resting her chin on her palm, deep in thought. "Well, yes, now that you mention it..."

"Yes?"

She turned back to me. "I was in my house by then. I had called the police..."

"And?"

"And he came out the *side* door. But he had gone in the *front* door..." She wrestled with her confusion.

"Who had?"

"The shithead who lived here. Gary Greer!"

I suppressed a smile at her modifier.

"But Gary Greer was still in the house," I reminded her. "It couldn't have been him who came out."

"No, I suppose not. But I *thought* it was him. It was dark, and he had been carrying something when he went in the house. Then I heard him shouting and hitting Angie. That's when I called the police. When he came out the side door, he was still carrying the same thing."

"What was he carrying, Fay?"

"I don't know!" she snapped. "Something…heavy. A satchel, a bag…something like that."

"Then what happened?"

"He got in his car—*your* car—and drove away."

"My *white* car…" I suggested.

"I don't remember," she mumbled defensively. "You've got me confused now. Come, Bailey, let's go in." She turned to walk away.

"No, wait, Fay. Please." I practically begged. She turned back and looked at me impatiently. "Just one more question, please?"

"You can ask your question, but I'm not obliged to answer it if I don't want to." Fay made no attempt to hide her irritation.

"Yes, I know. But can you tell me: have you spoken with Angie Greer since that night?"

"Spoken with her? Of course I've spoken with her—she's my next door neighbor. I've spoken with lots of people since that night, and answered hundreds of questions. I'm not going to answer any more. Good night."

With that, Fay and her dog strode purposefully away, denying me the chance to uncover anything else.

Nevertheless, the pieces had finally started to fall into place. If I could count on Fay's faulty memory, I might be able to work backwards, and find the other answers that had been eluding me. I jumped in my car and drove to my apartment.

Warily, I retrieved my mail and let myself into the building. I took the back stairs, and waited a few minutes before I hustled down the hallway to my door. I refused to be taken unawares.

There was a note on my door. Unfolding it, I recognized the scrawl that read: I'M IN THE AREA ON BUSINESS—JUST STOPPED BY TO SAY HELLO. SECURITY IN THIS DUMP IS TERRIBLE. DAVE.

My brother, telling me something I already knew, as always. I shoved the note in my pocket and unlocked the door.

"Pam?" I called, not expecting an answer. I got none.

Finding my squad directory, I looked up Hank Cindrich's phone number and dialed it. His teenage daughter answered, and sounded *very* disappointed when I asked for her father.

"Don't tie up the line, dad," I heard her instructing Hank. "I'm expecting an important call." Hank barely grunted before he came on.

"Yeah, Scott," he said. "What's up?"

"I need to get into the squad's records tonight," I answered, getting right to the point.

"Tonight? Why tonight?"

"Well, my lawyer screwed up. We have to appear at a deposition within twenty-four hours." That wasn't a lie, was it? Twenty-four hours is twenty-four hours, whether you count forward or back.

Hank groused. "This isn't much notice, Scott."

"I know, and I apologize. But it's very important that I get a copy of the call sheet from that night. And I can't wait until tomorrow to do it."

"Well, I can't let you in the building tonight. I'm in the middle of a project that I just can't leave. Let me call around and see if another officer can meet you there. Are you at home?"

"Yes," I answered. "Oh, and Hank? Could you try Peggy first? And, please, don't call Mike Marder at all. I'd rather not see him this evening."

"I understand. I'll call you back when and if I find somebody." He hung up.

Five minutes later the phone rang. It was Hank. "Karen Weyrich can meet you at the squad building in ten minutes," he informed me. "Don't expect her to be pleasant."

"Karen by herself? Without Carol?" *Was that possible?*

"Carol's working tonight."

"Pity."

"Yeah, I thought that would break you up."

"Thanks, Hank. Oh, one other thing…"

"Yeah?"

"Do you happen to know, offhand, what kind of a car Jerry Boronski drives?"

"Boronski? Yeah, he has an Explorer."

"Is it white?"

"No, it's burgundy."

"Oh."

"But, come to think of it, he drives his wife's car sometimes, and *it's* white. One of those Japanese jobs that all look alike. A Honda, or a Toyota, or a Mitsubishi. One of those. Why?"

"No reason. But thanks anyway, Hank. Now get off the line so your daughter can get a date."

He laughed and hung up.

I grabbed a notebook and headed for the door. I swung it open—and nearly got a fist in my face. The hand was poised to knock, but its owner jumped back a foot when the door came open suddenly. I recoiled at least twice that distance.

It was my brother Dave, returning from his business meeting—or whatever.

"Yo, younger bother," he recovered to say. "Howya doing?"

"I was doing fine until just now. What brings you here?"

"Is Pam here?" he asked, trying to look over me into the apartment.

"No, and I'm on my way out. I don't mean to be rude, but I'm meeting somebody in five minutes."

Dave frowned. "Don't have time to catch a cold one with me?" he asked.

"There's a couple in the fridge. Help yourself." I stepped into the hallway, but held the door for him.

"How long 'til you'll be back?"

Uh oh. "You planning on staying?"

"Yeah, you mind? I don't feel like driving back home tonight."

"What—you and Donna having problems?" For once, I enjoyed asking the question, even though I didn't have time for it.

"Nah. Just thought I'd hang out here this evening. See what's happening in your miserable life. Was also hoping to catch a glimpse of the divine Pamela." He bounced his eyebrows for effect, but the effect was lost.

An idea came to me.

"Tell you what," I said, taking a page from my notebook and scribbling a phone number on it. "Do me a favor. In fifteen minutes, dial this number. A woman will probably answer. Pretend you're looking for someone—but not me. Act confused, or drunk. That shouldn't be too hard for you. Keep her on the line as long as you can. Make up some story, but don't tell her who you are. Would you do that?"

Dave gave me a suspicious glance. "Are you involved in something illegal?"

"Perfectly legal, and nearly ethical. I'll be back in forty-five minutes, maybe an hour. The couch is yours."

"Thanks a lot."

"Don't mention it."

When I joined the Dayfield Rescue Squad, about five years ago, I was fortunate to be assigned to a crew chief who kept things in perspective. Her name was Rosemary Gordon. I'll never forget something Rosemary once told me, almost as an apology for the petty, backbiting behavior commonly exhibited by numerous squad yahoos.

"Scott," she said, "you'll find that we treat strangers better than we do each other."

I was thinking of Rosemary's words as I entered the squad building, and found Karen Weyrich waiting for me. She did not return my smile, and didn't seem to hear when I thanked her for coming.

"I had better things to do this evening than to babysit you," she said. She looked at her watch. "And I can only give you fifteen minutes to get what you need."

"That should be long enough."

"I hope so. Remember, nothing is to leave the building. If you want a copy of a call sheet, I'll make it for you."

"Let's get started," I said brightly.

She grunted, then waddled ahead of me to the records room. She unlocked the door and turned on the overhead light. I followed her in.

Inside was a desk, two chairs and a few file cabinets, but not much else. As I had hoped, there was no phone in the room.

"The call reports are kept in here," she said, touching one of the file cabinets. "They're filed by date. On the edge of each one is a colored sticker. The one you'll be looking for should be yellow."

"What does that mean?"

"Trauma—at home."

I opened a file drawer and saw hundreds—maybe thousands— of sheets of paper, tucked neatly into manila file folders. Each sheet had at least one sticker affixed to it. Several had two stickers. A few had three. All the colors of the spectrum were represented by the stickers.

"What do the other colors stand for?"

Karen sighed, as if to say that explaining the squad's filing procedures went beyond her duties for the evening. Nevertheless, she answered me: "Red means a cardiovascular emergency—heart patients, strokes, GI bleeds. Blue is for motor vehicle accidents. Purple means extrication was required. Green is for overdoses and poisonings. Orange is for hazmat calls. What else is in there?"

"Black," I said, leafing through. Black never appeared by itself—red was its most common companion.

"I'll let you figure that one out."

"What about pink?" There weren't many of those.

"Stork calls."

"And what are the mauve ones for?"

Karen frowned. "Mauve? There are no mauve stickers."

I grinned at her. "Only testing you," I said.

My grin wasn't returned, either. "You're wasting time."

"Right." I scanned the most recent call reports until I found the yellow-tagged call sheet I needed, from three-and-a-half weeks before. I pulled it out and gave it the once-over. Neither of the squad's two lieutenants were listed among those who had responded that night. I handed the sheet to Karen. "A copy of this, please."

The copier was in another room. She looked at me distrustingly, hesitated, then said: "I'll be right back." She hurried off to make the copy.

I continued to search through the call reports. Fortunately, the two code colors that most interested me—yellow and purple—were not that common. By the time Karen returned, I had three more sheets out for her to copy. She looked at them suspiciously. The two with yellow stickers were also from the Greer residence. Karen accepted them without question. But the third one, with both a blue and a purple sticker, she examined carefully.

"What do you need this for?" she asked.

"I was on that call. See?"

"Yeah, I see. So what?"

"I need it to prove my whereabouts on that day," I said, thinking that maybe "whereabouts" was too overblown a word.

She challenged me. "For what?"

"Oh, c'mon, Karen. Stop playing Joe Friday. Just make the goddamn copy."

She snapped, "Don't get smart with me, Scott. I'm doing you a favor being here tonight. And I've already done you too many favors."

Say what?

"You've done *me* too many favors? I don't recall any."

Karen didn't respond to my remark. Not then, anyway. Instead, she motioned at the open file cabinet. "Are you finished?" she asked.

"With this one, yes," I answered, closing the drawer for her. "Now I'd like to look at my personnel file."

"No way," she said, attempting to sound authoritative. "That's off-limits."

"Like hell it is. *Someone* got in there three weeks ago, and gave my squad photo to the newspaper. If they can get in there, so can I. Maybe we should call Hank, and see what he has to say."

Karen obviously found my suggestion distasteful. She scowled, then retorted: "Hank doesn't know his ass from his elbow."

I raised an eyebrow. "I'll mention that to him when I call," I said, as I started to leave the room—ostensibly to find a telephone.

"No, wait," Karen said, caving in. "I'll let you look at your P-file. But I'm only giving you five minutes. Then I'm locking up."

I didn't answer. I just watched while she fished for the key.

Squad personnel records, as I soon noticed, are kept in a single, locked file cabinet with three drawers. The top drawer is labeled "A-G," the middle drawer "H-N," and the bottom drawer "O-Z." I smiled when I saw the label on the bottom drawer. There once was an identical label (or so I'd heard) that had inspired the children's author, L. Frank Baum, to invent a name for his magical kingdom over the rainbow. He christened the kingdom...*Oz.*

Karen unlocked the cabinet and pulled out the middle drawer. She scanned the tabs on the folders within until she found *JAMISON.* She pulled out the file and handed it to me.

I took the file but didn't open it. I hefted it, indicating that it seemed light. "Not much in here, is there?" I commented.

Karen hardly shrugged.

I continued: "You'd think with all the commendations and reprimands I've accumulated over the years, this file would be at least an inch thick."

She glanced at her watch. "You're wasting time, Scott."

Well, not wasting...exactly. *Stalling* was the more accurate term. I started to browse casually through the folder's contents. The usual stuff was included: my application form, a copy of my EMT certification, my blue light permit, and a tally sheet of my attendance at squad meetings and drills. There was another form page which contained information for the squad's insurance carrier—home and work phone numbers, next of kin's names and numbers, life insurance beneficiaries, and so on. All dry stuff.

In the back of the folder were the more interesting items. A copy of Dorothy McCrae's article from *The Dayfield Dispatch* was attached to the minutes of the two special board meetings I had attended in the past few weeks. I noticed that the photo which had accompanied the article was missing.

"See anything you need?" Karen asked impatiently.

"Not yet," I said, pretending to study the notes from the second meeting.

Then, finally, the telephone rang in a room down the hall. I just ignored it. Karen hesitated, then said: "I'll be right back." I barely waved, so absorbed was I in the contents of my personnel file.

From the corner of my eye, I watched her lumber down the hall.

When she turned into the room where the copier was located—the closest room with a phone—I quickly moved to the open file drawer. I stuck a finger into the slot my folder had occupied, and hurriedly leafed through the folders behind it. Through the "K's" and the "L's" and into the "M's". In less than ten seconds, I found the file I was seeking. I lifted it out and opened it. As I expected, it contained the information I wanted.

Now I had to decide how daring I should be. Did I attempt to jot down the information I wanted…did I try to make a photo-copy…or did I simply take it with me? I cocked an ear to listen to Karen's conversation, down the hall:

"Yes, sir, that's what I said. This is the Dayfield Rescue Squad. What's that? Somebody gave you this number and asked you to call? One of our members?"

Karen's words startled me, just enough to cause me to dash my fingers along the edge of the papers I was scanning. Was my broth-er going to screw up his simple task, and blow *my* cover as well as his? I drew my finger back and promptly stuck it in my mouth. Paper cuts are a bitch.

"Well, yes, your friend was right. We're always looking for new members. Could I get your name and number, and have someone call you back with more information?"

I thought: *Way to go, bro.* Pretend to be a prospective volunteer. That would certainly hold Karen's attention. I went back to the file.

"I'd love to tell you more about it, but I'm tied up at the moment. Just give me a number where you can be reached, Mr. Murphy, and we'll get in contact with you at your convenience."

Mr. Murphy, huh? Now there's a safe, innocuous alias. Very common, but not obviously so…like Smith or Jones. I made a men-tal note to compliment Dave when I got back home. Then I took the sheet of paper I needed, slipped it into my personnel file, and returned the second file to its slot. The alphabetical folders looked just as I had found them.

"I understand, Mr. Murphy. You'll be out of town tomorrow and Friday, but you'll be back on Tuesday. The best time to reach you is between 10:30 and noon. I'm sorry, what did you say?"

My brother was doing such a good job of keeping Karen occupied, I decided on the second course of action. It required a big initial risk, but would leave no trace. If only Dave could maintain the charade for another two minutes...

I moved to the desk and opened the top drawer. Lucky me, I found just what I was looking for: the squad's printed stationery. I took a sheet of letterhead and an envelope. I neatly folded the letterhead, stuffed it in the envelope, then slipped the envelope into my note book.

Unfortunately, I didn't notice that the fresh cut on my finger left a small stain of blood on the letterhead.

"No, the work isn't too hard, Mr. Murphy. Dayfield's a quiet town, so we don't get very many difficult emergencies. Look, I really have to go now. No, no—it's not that we're not interested in your help. It's just...what's that?"

I walked down the hall to the room where Karen was still talking on the phone. When I entered, she rolled her eyes at me, showing her exasperation with the persistent caller. Momentarily, she seemed to have forgotten that I was the enemy. But then, when I raised the folder in my hand and pointed at the copier, she narrowed her eyes. I narrowed mine, mimicking her, and turned to the copier.

"Certainly, Mr. Murphy. You're under no obligation to commit yourself. You can come to one of our meetings and talk with some of our members. Examine our rigs, if you like. You can also...what? Oh. 'Rigs' are what we call our ambulances. Yes. Four of them. Could you hold on a second? No, I'm not trying to get rid of you."

I removed a few pages from the folder, made copies, then placed the originals back in the folder. When I finished, I turned to Karen, snatched from her the three call sheets I had selected for copying, and made copies of them also. Then, pretending not to notice her frantic hand gestures, I strode out into the hallway and returned to the records room. Quickly I returned the original sheet I had "borrowed" from the "M" file. Then I sat down to wait.

When Karen returned, a minute later, she stopped in the doorway, folded her arms, and glared at me.

"What have you been doing?" she demanded.

I looked up at her in all innocence. "I've been sitting here, waiting for you."

"Why did you take it upon yourself to make those copies?" She walked over to the open file drawer and peered in.

"You were tied up. I knew you were in a hurry to get out of here, so I just thought I'd save you some time."

She gestured at the file folder sitting on my lap. "Let me see what you have there."

I grimaced. "Boy, you're in a lousy mood, Carol."

"Karen," she corrected me, bitterly. "C'mon, let me see."

I handed her the file folder.

"And those too," she added, pointing at the loose sheets on top of my notebook.

"They're just copies of what's in the folder," I protested.

"Don't give me a hard time, Scott. I don't trust you as far as I can throw that file cabinet." She extended her hand, waiting for me to give her the copies.

"Here!" I snapped, thrusting them at her. "It's nice that you're so willing to help out a fellow squad member in trouble."

She took the sheets and laid them on the desk. She set my personnel folder next to it, then went through every document one by one, checking the copies against the originals. When she was finally satisfied, she handed the copies back to me.

"I've done nothing *but* help you, Scott, ever since this mess started. And I've taken plenty of grief for standing up for you. Carol didn't speak to me for two days after the first meeting–"

She stopped in mid-sentence, as though she had let slip something I shouldn't know.

"You're the one who abstained? I thought Stick Menzel–"

"I didn't abstain; I voted to let you off. Stick voted against you. Jerry Boronski abstained—said it was premature to make a decision one way or the other. Turned out that Jerry was right, considering the lawsuit that was filed against you a few days later."

She was talking—out of school, perhaps—but I didn't want her to stop.

"But you changed your mind the second time around, didn't you? You voted against me then. Am I right?"

She frowned at me and shook her head. "You know, you're dumber than I thought you were, Scott. Yes, I voted to suspend you at the second meeting, but it was for your good as well as the squad's. If I were you—with a lawsuit hanging over my head—I wouldn't have waited to be suspended. I'd have asked for a leave of absence, to give me more time to prepare a defense."

That made sense, although I certainly wouldn't admit it to her.

"But what about Mike Marder, and your roommate, Carol? Why are they so vindictive?" I asked.

Karen shrugged. "I can't speak for Marder. He's on a crusade of some sort, *and* he hates your guts. As for Carol, she simply doesn't like your attitude. For that matter, I don't like it either. But I don't believe you should be punished for it. You're just lucky you weren't–"

She stopped talking, and looked hard at my hand, which was resting on my notebook. My notebook, which contained the folded copy I had purloined. My heart dropped as she stepped towards me and started to reach for it.

She lifted my hand.

"What did you do to your finger?" she asked, her voice considerably softer than before.

Whew. "Oh, it's just a paper cut. That's what I get for hurrying."

Karen eyed me for a moment. "Well, you couldn't have picked a better place to do it. Hold on a sec." She left the room, but came back in just fifteen seconds with an industrial-sized box of elastic bandages. She deftly opened one and started to place it on my wound.

I was amazed by the change in her disposition. A minute before, she had been baiting and browbeating me. But now that I was her patient, she was gentle, almost kindhearted. Again I thought of Rosemary's words: we treat strangers better than we do each other.

Then I thought of something else.

"Say, Karen, can I ask you a question?"

"What's stopping you?"

"In a former life, were you ever a slave on board a galley ship?"

She finished affixing the bandage, then gave me a puzzled look.

"I have no idea what you're talking about," she said.

"I didn't think so."

Sam Malone was on the tube, and my brother Dave was on the couch, when I returned home. Sam was behind the bar, serving Norm a beer. Dave had already had three. He was snoring peacefully, but awoke when I turned off the set. For a few seconds, he glared at me. Then he glanced around, trying to determine if he was still dreaming. Finally, the haze lifted. His glare evolved into a grin.

I walked into the kitchen and looked in the refrigerator. There was one beer left. Popping it, I returned to the living room and raised it in toast to my older brother.

"Here's to the fictitious Mr. Murphy," I said. "You did a helluva job, Dave. I can't tell you how much I appreciate it."

He squinted at me. After a few beers, he tends to squint. "What on earth are you talking about?" he asked.

"The phone call. You played Karen like a drum. Bought me enough time to do everything I wanted to. I'm going to beat the sons-of-bitches now. I've got the ammunition I need. Most of it, anyway."

Dave shook his head. "Who's Karen?"

I looked over at the coffee table beside him. There *were* only three beer cans. In his college days, three wouldn't have even touched him. My brother was getting old.

"Karen. The woman you were talking to at the squad building. Mr. Murphy. You remember?"

His eyes grew wide. He reached into his pocket and pulled out the scrap of paper I had left him. "Oh, shit!" he said. "The phone call! I'm sorry, Scott. I got interested in something on the television, and forgot all about it. I hope it wasn't too important."

Was he goofing me?

I sipped my beer, then shook my head. "No, Dave, it wasn't important at all. Go back to sleep."

I debated whether to wait until morning to implement the next step. At the corporate offices of DataStaff, I could easily find a retired typewriter that would produce safe and very official-looking characters. But I just couldn't sit still until then. When Dave started snoring again, I went into the bedroom, into the closet, and dug out my old Smith-Corona portable.

First, I wrote and rewrote the message, until I had the wording just right. Then I took the typewriter out of the case, and the squad letterhead from the envelope. I winced when I saw the blood stain in the bottom corner. Still, I was lucky: I could simply trim the page a half-inch to eliminate it. Who would notice that the sheet was only ten-and-a-half inches tall, instead of the standard eleven?

I typed slowly and carefully, not wishing to make a single mistake. It was a difficult task. My computer, which allows infinite corrections of infinite errors, has made me lazy. My old typewriter is far less forgiving.

Finally, I pulled the sheet of letterhead from the machine. With more than just a little pride, I re-read the imperious yet anonymous message I had inscribed on it:

AT SEVEN O'CLOCK ON SUNDAY EVENING — THE TWENTY-SECOND OF AUGUST — WE WILL BE HOLDING A MEETING TO DISCUSS THE MOST RECENT DEVELOPMENTS IN A MATTER OF EXTREME IMPORTANCE TO YOU AND TO US AS WELL. THE MEETING WILL BE HELD IN THE COMMUNITY ROOM OF THE DAYFIELD MUNICIPAL BUILDING. YOUR ATTENDANCE AT THIS MEETING IS REQUESTED AND STRONGLY RECOMMENDED.

I did not sign the letter; I just folded it neatly and set it aside. Then I rolled the matching envelope into my obsolete Smith-Corona, and painstakingly typed:

MRS. ANGELA GREER
712 KILBOURN AVENUE
DAYFIELD, NEW JERSEY 07970

PERSONAL AND CONFIDENTIAL

NO ARGUMENT

THE LIGHTS WERE ON AND THE door stood open, but there was no one in the community room at the Dayfield Township municipal building. A small note was taped to the door frame. The note read: *RESERVED - DAYFIELD RESCUE SQUAD.*

The trap was set and baited, awaiting the arrival of Angie Greer.

As for me, I felt like a damned fool—and a nervous one at that. I was hiding in the janitor's closet down the hall, peering out through the tiniest of openings. It was the only vantage point from which I could observe the entrance to the room without being noticed myself. I prayed that the cleaning lady was not working this evening.

At six minutes past seven, Angie Greer came through the double doors at the end of the hallway. I'm surprised she didn't hear me, exhaling in gratitude, when I saw she was alone. She walked slowly and cautiously up the hall, clutching the letter I had mailed her, while looking from door to door for the room to which the letter directed her. She was wearing a simple dress, suitable for office work, and she gripped a small pocketbook that hung from her shoulder. If anything, she appeared

26

even more nervous than I was.

When she reached the community room, she peered in but did not enter. Seeing no one within, she stepped back and looked up and down the hall, obviously confused. Then she noticed the note on the door frame. It seemed to reassure her. She glanced up the hall again, and stared, I swear, at me for a moment. I held my breath, and reminded myself there was no way she could see me. Then she entered the room.

I exhaled, counted to ten, and then quietly opened the door and walked out into the hall. So far, luck was with me. There was no one else around. I strode over to the doorway to the community room and, taking care that I couldn't be seen, removed the note and stuck it in the manila envelope I had brought with me. Then I walked into the room. I silently closed the door behind me.

Angie Greer was sitting on the opposite side of the room's small table, her arms resting on its surface. She stiffened when she realized who I was, and started to rise. She looked particularly frail and helpless—caught in the trap I had set for her—and she anxiously ran her eyes about the room, searching for an escape that didn't exist. For a moment, I felt ashamed for having deceived her.

Then I heard my lawyer's battle cry, resounding within my skull: *Attack the weakest link!* I held up my hand, entreatingly, to try and calm her.

"A few minutes, that's all I'm asking for, Mrs. Greer." My voice failed me, cracking as I spoke the words. I'm no Clint Eastwood, that's for sure.

"I...I don't think I should speak with you, Mr. Jamison," she responded, her voice only slightly more composed than mine. I was impressed that she could think of my name, under the circumstances.

"If that's what your lawyer told you, he's right," I said. "But he's very much wrong about a few other things. Please, just a minute or two."

She stood with her arms crossed in front of her, alternately glancing at me and around the room. I stood in front of the only door, hoping she wouldn't scream. I knew her scream, and wanted never to hear it again. Especially not now.

"I can't tell you anything," she said defensively.

"That's okay," I lied. "Just let me talk to you for a minute. I think you're being taken advantage of, Mrs. Greer. And I want to help you." My voice just dripped with sincerity.

She eyed me suspiciously. "Who's taking advantage of me?"

I know she expected me to say her lawyer's name, James Pressman. So I delayed for five—maybe ten—seconds. This was my payoff line, and I wanted to deliver it with maximum impact.

"Your boyfriend, Mike Marder."

Her eyes opened wide, and then flinched. Her legs seemed to weaken. She grabbed the back of the chair in front of her for support, and then, after a minute, pulled it out and sat down. She buried her face in her hands.

I set my manila envelope on the table. Then I sat down across from her and waited. The weakest link had broken.

At last she asked, quietly: "How long have you known?"

"Only a few days. I was talking to Fay Johnson, and she remembered seeing Marder leaving your house that night, just before I showed up. After that, everything else fell into place." Well, not quite *everything*, I thought. If I knew everything, we wouldn't be in this room right now.

She gazed up at me. For the first time, I got an unfiltered, unblemished look at her. She reminded me of a small bird, recently thrown from the nest.

"Mrs. Greer," I said softly, "I'm going to be honest with you, and tell you everything I know at this point. I hope, for your own good, that you'll be just as honest with me. If you're part of this scam—and it *is* a scam, pure and simple—it's going to come out sooner or later.

"My guess is that Mike Marder has been leading you on—using your misfortune to get at me. But I don't think you know all that's at stake. If you tell me what you *do* know, I'll do what I can to keep you out of trouble. And, believe me, there's *going* to be trouble."

There. I had laid it all on the line, and had given her a clear-cut choice. I could see her struggling with it, for just a minute.

Whom should she believe? Her lover and her lawyer—or me? I half-expected her to stand up and walk out.

But she didn't. Miraculously, she decided, on the spot, to at least hear what I had to say. Well, now that I think about it, maybe it wasn't so miraculous. Especially considering what she eventually told me. And what I eventually found out on my own.

We both knew this much:

Mike Marder had convinced her that I deserved punishment—and she deserved restitution—for what had happened that Sunday evening, four long weeks before. He had persuaded her that I was at least partially to blame for her husband's death. And—willingly or reluctantly—she had bought into his scheme. Together, I assumed, they had hired James Pressman to make the case against me.

But holding precedence over those items was the singular thing she knew for certain, the one fact no lover or lawyer could dispute: I had gone out of my way, and risked personal harm, in an effort to help her when she had needed help. Maybe that was the determining factor in her struggle to decide whether to trust me.

Or maybe, I thought, she was tired of being manipulated.

Or maybe she was working her own agenda.

"What...what do you want from me?" she asked quietly.

"Just a few answers," I said, negating my earlier lie. "For starters, I need to know how long you and Mike Marder have...*known* one another." As I asked the question, I could only think of Dorothy McCrae, and how she might have phrased it.

Angie Greer folded her hands on the table, as though she was going to pray. She lowered her head and stared at her hands. Then she began to speak.

"I met Mike when he came to my house one time, almost a year ago, when Gary was...you know...assaulting me. The police took Gary outside, but Mike stayed in the house with me. He was nice to me—not just patronizing, the way the police usually are. Or were, I should say.

"Don't ask me why, but I refused to go to the hospital that night, or to file charges against my husband. I was surprised when Mike came back the next day. We just talked. After that, he stopped by every once in a while, when he was sure I was alone. Sometimes we'd go for a drive. We didn't really...*do* anything, until a month or two later, when Gary was in jail on a possession charge. I was very lonely, Mr. Jamison."

This background information didn't matter much to me, but I didn't want to interrupt. It seemed to help her to get it out.

"Did Mike ever take you on a squad call?"

She frowned at me. "What do you mean?"

"I mean, when you were with him, in his car, did his squad pager ever go off, and did he respond to the call?"

She nodded. "As a matter of fact, yes. Just once. I asked him not to, but he went anyway. He said he might be needed."

"Uh-huh. And on that call—after he came back out of the house—did another squad member come out and punch him?"

Her mouth fell open. "That was *you?*"

"You didn't know that?"

She shook her head. "No. I remember how shocked I was when it happened. But when I asked Mike about it—after he got back in the car—he said it was nothing. Just a minor disagreement. But I could tell he was *very* upset."

No shit.

"Tell me what happened the night your husband was killed. Mike ran out on you, didn't he?"

She winced when I said this, and I immediately regretted putting my assumption into words.

"I...I'd rather not talk about that," she said, looking away.

I couldn't blame her for avoiding the question. But as long as she was here, I wasn't going to give up on it. It could wait until later.

"Okay," I said, agreeably. "But can you tell me this: What was Mike doing at your house the night your husband died? He was there before Gary came home, wasn't he?"

Angie Greer wrestled with this one. She didn't want to betray anyone, but she *did* seem to want to tell me something. I wondered how far I could lead her, before she clammed up altogether.

She looked down at her folded hands, and answered: "When Gary was in jail, Mike started pressuring me to leave him—to file for a divorce. He brought it up repeatedly. Usually, when he started talking like that, I just changed the subject. I didn't want to

218

think about it. I was afraid what Gary would do if I ever said I was going to leave him.

"But then, a month or so after Gary was released, Mike called me at work and told me he had a better solution. He said we could get Gary out of our lives, once and for all. We could stop sneaking around, and be together."

I had an idea what Mike's "solution" was, but there was something else I wanted to know before she told me. I asked the question like a board-certified shrink:

"How did you feel about this?"

She shrugged. "I had mixed feelings. By that time, I had just about lost hope that Gary could be, you know, *rehabilitated*. But I wasn't convinced Mike Marder was the right guy to turn to." She looked up at me. "Mike has his own faults, you know."

No shit.

"So what was Mike's solution?"

She folded her arms, uncomfortably. It seemed she didn't want to remember this part, let alone recount it for me. Still, she went on. "That night, the night Gary was killed, Mike came over to the house. I could tell from the moment he came in that something was different. That something was *wrong*. Mike was acting very nervous. When I mentioned it, he said: 'I've got the solution with me.' I didn't know what he was talking about.

"Then, out of his jacket pocket, he produced a handgun. 'This is for you,' he said. I couldn't believe it. Mr. Jamison, I was so scared. I told him to get it out of my house."

She paused, and took a small hanky from her pocketbook. I waited silently while she dabbed at her nose.

"But Mike kept insisting. He said, 'Don't you see, Angie? This is the perfect solution! You hide this in the house, someplace where only you can find it. Then, the next time Gary starts hitting you, you retrieve it and *give him what he deserves!* All you have to say is it was self-defense. With his record, no one will dispute your story. Not the police in this town, anyway.'"

I had suspected something along these lines, but it still amazed me to hear it. I had to confirm what I was hearing: "Mike told you to shoot your husband, and say it was self-defense?"

Angie Greer nodded. Then she looked away. Her eyes were moist.

"Did you take the gun?"

She shook her head, vigorously.

"Did you even touch it? Ever?"

Again, she shook her head. "No, I wanted nothing to do with it. Mike tried to make me take it, but I refused. For once, I said *no*. I thought he was crazy."

"Do you know where he got the gun?"

Why did I ask her a question whose answer I already knew? Maybe I was hoping Mike had lied to her about the gun, and that I could expose his lie. In my manila envelope, I had the copy of the call report from that early morning motor vehicle accident—more than eight months before—when the gun had disappeared from its owner's car. Marder had been on that call, with the extrication team. He was one of the yahoos who had torn the vehicle apart.

So now the connection had been made at both ends.

But Angie just looked at me, quizzically. "No, I never even thought about that. I just wanted it out of the house. And him too."

"Then what happened?"

"We were still arguing when Gary came home, much earlier than I'd expected him. Mike and I heard him coming in the front door. We were in the kitchen, where he couldn't see us. Mike panicked. He knew he couldn't get out of the house, just then, so he frantically looked around for some place to hide. Our kitchen has an old-fashioned pantry; Mike went in there and closed the door behind him. He left me alone to face my husband."

The old cliché: the lover in the closet.

"Alone with the gun?" I asked.

Angie looked down, and then back up at me. She was crossing the line now, and she knew it.

"Well, not exactly. I had refused to take the gun. When we heard Gary at the front door, Mike hid the gun—and whispered to me to use it if I had to. *Then* he went in the pantry."

"Where did he hide the gun?"

For the first time, Angie Greer smiled. It was a wry smile.

"In the refrigerator," she said.

"In the refrigerator? In the *refrigerator*? Why there?"

Angie raised and lowered her hands. "I don't know. Because it was nearby, I guess. Maybe he figured Gary wouldn't look in there, but I could get it if I had to. If I had *wanted* to."

In the fucking refrigerator. No wonder the muzzle had felt like ice when Greer had held it against my neck. After working up a thirst, beating his wife, Gary Greer had gone looking for a frosty *Colt 45*. Instead, he had found the real thing.

"And then?" I prodded.

"Then Gary came in the kitchen. He was as angry as I'd ever seen him. Right away I knew he had been drinking. Somebody had given him a ride home, and he had seen Mike's car in front of the house. He started shouting: '*Where is he? Where's the son-of-a-bitch?*' He called me a whore, among other things."

"And you told him?"

"I said there was no one else there. That infuriated him. He started to hit me. I ran. He chased me from one room to another. I tripped over a chair in the living room, and that's when he caught me."

I could imagine what had taken place next, so I didn't ask. But yet another question needed to be answered.

"When your husband came in the house, Mrs. Greer, was he carrying anything?"

Angie Greer cocked her head, a rather appealing little gesture that meant—I guess—that she didn't understand my question.

"Like what?" she asked.

"Like anything. A package, a bag. Anything."

Her eyes lit up. "You know, now that you mention it, he had his gym bag with him when he came in—the one he carried his clothes in when he went to the 'Y' to work out. I might have paid more attention to it, but I was so *scared* at the time. But, you know, it's odd that he was carrying it with him at night. He only used to go work out in the morning."

"Where is the gym bag now?"

Angie gazed into the distance and shook her head, trying to remember seeing the bag in the house. "I don't know. I think he set it on the kitchen table before he started to hit me. But it wasn't there when I got back from the hospital. I don't know what happened to it." Then she sharpened her focus on my face. "Why? What do you think was in the bag?"

"You don't have any idea?"

Her face darkened as she thought. "You don't think..." She tried to avoid the conclusion I had already reached. "...the money that Hutch was asking me about?"

Hutch? Had I mentioned *Hutch* to Angie Greer?

Of course I hadn't, but hearing her say his name made me tense involuntarily. By this time, I was nearly seventy-two hours past the deadline Hutch had given me to make good on Gary Greer's debt. Now, at last, I was making progress toward locating the money, but in those seventy-two hours I had been constantly looking back over my shoulder, and avoiding places and situations where I might be surprised by my oversized acquaintance.

Just two days before, I had prudently, or stupidly—I'm not sure which—withdrawn eight thousand dollars from my savings account and stashed it under the driver's seat in my car. Driving around with a partial payoff under my ass made me nervous, but I figured it might be enough to preserve my well-being, and buy me some more time, if Mr. Hutchinson should have made another unwelcome appearance in my fractured life. But, up to this point, I hadn't seen him or his gray van lurking about my home or office. I couldn't imagine that he had forgotten about me. I assumed he had other business to attend to, and would get back to me in his own time.

"Who?" I asked Angie Greer, playing dumb. I must do that well, play dumb, because she didn't seem to notice the hesitancy in my voice.

"Hutch—Kyle Hutchinson. He's a monstrous, violent man that Gary was...friends with. He came to my house, a few days after the funeral, and told me Gary owed him money—a lot of money. I told him I didn't know anything about it. He threatened me, and then he searched my house."

"And you let him?"

Her expression asked: *How stupid are you?* But she only said:

"It's not a question of *letting* him, Mr. Jamison. Hutch does as he damn well pleases."

I nodded. It was coming together, and it was *almost* making sense. But I could see—immediately—why Hutch had been unsure about Angie's involvement. Did she *really* not know about the money? Or was she playing me like she had played him?

I paused to think about the succession of events. When Gary Greer had returned home that night, earlier than expected, he had seen Mike's car parked out front. Maybe he had seen the plates in the windshield that identified the owner as a lieutenant on the Dayfield Rescue Squad. That's why he had suspected me to be Angie's lover, when I showed up a few minutes later.

...some stupid schmuck from the rescue squad...

When Gary Greer entered the house, he had been carrying a gym bag full of money. It was the money he was to give to Hutch, plus any profit he might have realized for his sales efforts. Just for the moment, I wondered: Had he gotten drunk that night to celebrate a healthy profit, or to console himself on a meager one? Or had he simply gotten drunk for the hell of it? Did it even matter?

More importantly, did Angie Greer know what her husband was carrying?

"You know," I said slowly, "Fay Johnson said she saw Gary carrying something when he came in the house. It must have been his gym bag."

Angie nodded.

I continued: "And Fay said he was carrying the same thing when he left, just after she had called the police."

Angie frowned. "But Gary never left. You know that. He beat me—*God*, did he beat me! He left me lying there in the living room. I thought I was going to die.

"He went in the kitchen, but he never left the house."

I fell silent for a minute. It seemed highly improbable that Angie hadn't figured the rest out by now. She *had* to be playing innocent with me.

"Mrs. Greer," I said at last, softly, "don't you *know* what happened, while your husband was beating you? Isn't it obvious?"

Her eyes welled with tears. She closed them, tightly, and shook her head.

Only then did I realize: She had started to understand—perhaps after Hutch had paid her a visit—but she would not allow herself to see the truth. The truth, on top of all she had been through, would be too painful. Though I had no choice but to do so, she didn't want me to confirm what she had suspected all along. That her lover had betrayed her.

"Um, did you reserve this room?"

Another voice behind me.

Once again I jumped, then turned quickly to see a police officer standing in the doorway. When I realized who it was, I gasped in relief. It was Marty Gustafson, the veteran patrolman who had assisted me on my last squad call, the day before I was suspended. He smiled when he recognized me.

"Whew! You startled me, Marty. And, yes, we reserved this room. Is there a problem?"

Marty shrugged. "Not that I know of. Just turn the lights out when you leave." He looked at Angie Greer, wiping her eyes with her hanky. Then he nodded, and left.

Where was I? Oh yes, the money.

"Mike Marder walked out on you, Mrs. Greer. While you were in the living room, trying to defend yourself, Mike came out of the pantry—back into the kitchen. He knew what was going on—how could he have *not* known?—and he could have come to help you. If he was afraid of your husband, he could have taken the gun from the refrigerator. But instead, he just left.

"And he took your husband's gym bag with him. Didn't he?"

It distressed me to say it, almost as much as it did her to hear it. Not only had my esteemed colleague on the rescue squad stolen the affections of another man's wife, he had taken the man's hard-earned money as well.

I could just about imagine it. He had crept back into the kitchen and had looked for a way out. The side door had beckoned. But first—I supposed—his curiosity had gotten the better of him. What was in the bag on the kitchen table—the bag that had not been there a few minutes before? Could Mike have known there was something other than sweaty sneakers inside? *Had somebody tipped him off ahead of time?*

Angie Greer looked at me—tearfully, helplessly. "I don't know, Mr. Jamison. I don't know what was in the gym bag, and I don't know if Mike took it. I really don't *want* to know." She glanced around the room again. She was very upset.

"I...I really must go now, Mr. Jamison," she stammered. She started to stand up.

I ran my hand through my hair. I realized, just then, that she wasn't going to answer any more questions about that awful night. Whether it was too painful, or whether she was hiding something, I couldn't readily tell. But, either way, I knew I had to change the subject if I expected her to tell me anything else.

She stood, as though waiting for me to grant her permission to leave.

"Mrs. Greer," I said, softening my tone considerably, "there's something I don't understand. Why did you put up with the abuse? For all those months, all those years? You're an intelligent, attractive woman. Why did you allow it to go on?"

She stared at me, not comprehending. "What do you mean?"

Good question, that—and not simply because it knocked me off my course. I was patently out of my element here, attempting to probe the mind of a battered woman.

"Your husband beat you. Repeatedly."

She nodded and—to my surprise—sat back down. Improbable as it seemed, she could more readily talk about her husband's torturous behavior, than the events of the night he had died.

"Yes, yes he did, Mr. Jamison. When he was drinking, he was often cruel...and brutal. I wanted to leave him. On several occasions, I was *going* to leave him—even before Mike Marder came along. But I couldn't.

"You see, he was my *husband*, Mr. Jamison. He hurt me terribly, but he also brought joy to my life. When he was sober, he could be very kind. He could be warm and loving. He made me feel special. I tried for *years* to make him stop drinking. I wanted him to get a decent job, and make something of himself. But he couldn't stay away from the booze. And then he got connected with the wrong people. People like Hutch."

Our discussion was taking a direction I hadn't foreseen—a direction I hadn't even wanted to contemplate. Angie Greer had actually loved her husband, and had stood by him for as long as her strength held out. She had tried very hard to make her marriage work. Only when the pain, and the frustration, and the loneliness became too much to bear did she despair of the task. And that's when Mike Marder came into her life.

I thought, for a moment, of how Sergeant Skipinski had described Gary Greer. Skip had used every slur in the book: *coward...slime...low-life...scum.* And I had found it oddly reassuring to envision the man only in Skip's terms. But Skip had known, and conveyed, only the most visible aspect of Gary Greer. Whereas his wife, Angie, had committed her life to him, and had glimpsed his redeeming qualities—rare though they were. She had hung in there, true to her vow—*for better or for worse*—and had tried to nurture her husband's better side.

So how could I stand in judgment of Gary Greer? And how could I, now, presume to scrutinize his widow's actions? She had tried her best and had failed. Who could fault her, then, for taking comfort from a man who had been kind to her? *And how could I suspect her to be anything but a victim?*

I looked back at Angie Greer. She was dabbing her eyes again. I cleared my throat and she looked up at me, expectantly.

"Um," I hesitated. "Could I get you something to drink? A glass of water? A soda?"

She nodded. "Please. Anything."

I stood and went out in the hallway. I remembered a small lunchroom at the opposite end of the building, so I quickly headed in its direction.

All things considered, I couldn't quite believe how accommodating she had been up to this point. Maybe I should have been more suspicious; it was all coming much too easily. But I shrugged off the thought as I ran through the hallways.

The lunchroom—like the rest of the municipal building—was open but deserted. I fed a dollar into the soda machine, made a selection, then fed in the change to make another one. I hustled back with the two cold cans.

Angie Greer was gone when I returned.

Swearing at myself for having left her alone, I set down the cans and ran back into the hallway. I sprinted for the doors through which she had entered the building, and rushed out into the night. When I reached the parking lot, I hurriedly looked around, and caught a glimpse of her as she closed the door of her car. She saw me too. I dashed across the lot to where she was parked. I caught up with her just as she was backing out of her space.

"Mrs. Greer, wait," I pleaded, walking alongside as she continued backing.

She shook her head, refusing to even look at me. She stopped the car when she was clear of the space, and grabbed the gearshift. In the next second, she would be pulling away—from the parking lot, from me, and from the past she wanted to forget.

But I wasn't ready to let her go. I ran around to the front of her car. I hesitated there. She stared at me through her windshield, wondering the same thing I was: Would I *really* use my body to prevent her from driving away? Then, while her foot and her brain drifted between the accelerator and the brake, I quickly continued my course, around to the passenger side of her car. If the door was locked, I knew, she would be gone in the next instant. The car was already starting to roll forward. I took hold of the latch and yanked it. The door flew open. Angie Greer hit the brake, hard, and shouted at me:

"Leave me alone, Mr. Jamison! *Leave me alone!*"

If she'd continued to shout, she would have quickly drawn some attention. *Unwanted* attention, from my viewpoint. The last thing I needed was to be accused of carjacking a young woman— in the parking lot of police headquarters, no less. I had to say or do *something* to both silence and stop her.

I held the passenger door open, and dropped to one knee on the parking lot asphalt. Looking at her frightened face across the passenger seat, I said, resolutely: "Mrs. Greer, your lover's been lying to you. *He's* going to be facing felony charges, and probably going to jail. Do you want to join him there?"

She bit her lip. Then, in a trembling voice, she answered me: "Right now, Mr. Jamison, I don't know who's lying to me. *You* tricked me to make me come here this evening. So how do I know I can believe anything you're telling me?"

When she put it that way, I couldn't answer her. I couldn't even speak up in my own defense.

"Look," she said, "just give me a few days to sort things out. You've given me a lot to think about. Okay? Just a few days?"

I nodded, and released my hold on her passenger door.

"Fair enough, Mrs. Greer," I said. "But before you go, could you answer just one more question for me?"

"If I can," she replied, quietly.

I paused. For once, I thought before I spoke.

"Could you tell me, Mrs. Greer, what you hoped to gain by filing a lawsuit against me? I know what Mike Marder has against me, but what's in this for you?"

Angie Greer sighed, looked down at her hands, resting on the steering wheel, and shook her head. Whatever the reason she was about to give, it was clear she was ashamed of it. Her voice was even lower when she answered: "The lawsuit wasn't my idea…"

Imagine my surprise.

"…but I went along with Mike. He told me you have a lot of money, Mr. Jamison. He said that Pressman could get you to offer a sizable cash settlement—just to keep the case from going to trial. He said that twenty or thirty thousand dollars would be nothing to you, because you're worth at least a half-million, and probably more." She glanced over at me, and then back down at her hands.

Had I heard her right? Had Angie Greer just said that Marder hadn't pursued this for revenge, but for money? *My* money?

I was astounded…dumbfounded…*shocked*.

I had known all along that *Pressman*—the shyster—thought he could extort a payoff, but I had assumed he was aiming for a few thousand dollars. Just enough to make it worth his effort. File a summons, schedule a deposition, and send a threatening letter or two. All in a week's work for an ambulance-chaser.

Marder, however, had been angling for a bigger catch. He had thought—no, he had *known*—that he was on to something. But how *could* he have known? Who could have told him?

Angie Greer looked at me again, searchingly. "I suppose he lied about that, too," she said.

"What?" I asked, trying to rewind to the last point in our conversation.

"The money he said you had. I mean, you seem like a decent person and all, Mr. Jamison. But you don't look to me like you're rolling in it."

I smiled weakly. "Oh, I'm just loaded, Mrs. Greer," I said, as ironically as I could. "I only act like an ordinary guy so people will treat me like one."

She nodded—quite certain, I'm sure, that I was putting her on. Then she smiled, a meek, endearing smile that told me she would indeed think matters over, in the light I had shone upon them.

"I'm going to leave now, Mr. Jamison," she said. "I really can't answer any more questions. Not now. Would you please close my door?"

Still in shock, I numbly complied with her request. I stared at her car as she drove away. Minutes after she was gone, I was still standing there. Then I started walking, slowly, aimlessly, in the direction of my own car. For the moment, I'd forgotten about the community room and my possessions there. I'd forgotten about my promise to Marty Gustafson to turn off the lights. And I'd forgotten to be cautious.

I wandered around to the back of the municipal building, where the township's off-duty patrol cars were parked in a silent row. Then I stopped walking and stood for a minute, staring at but not actually seeing a vehicle parked beyond the police cars, at the very back of the lot. At last it registered with me, why the vehicle had caught my attention and finally worked its way into my consciousness. It was a gray van.

Run! my instincts suddenly screamed at me. *Get the hell out of here! Don't even look back!*

Of course I should have listened to my instincts, but of course I didn't. Rather, I found myself being drawn to the gray van, like a fish with a hook in its mouth is drawn to the fisherman. Slowly at first, but then with a quickening step I approached it.

I wasn't absolutely sure it was Hutch's van; maybe that's why I ignored the shrieking voice in my head. The vehicle was backed into a parking space, and its front license plate was missing. It didn't seem possible that Hutch would have followed me here, to the front door of the township's police department. It just didn't seem possible. There had to be another explanation.

The lights in the parking lot illuminated the front of the van, well enough for me to have noticed the absence of a license plate, but its rear end was in darkness. I came up to the vehicle, touched its front tentatively, and then crept along the passenger's side, intent on checking for a rear license. I knew I would remember the number if I saw it, if I *could* see it in the dim light. I crept, then I paused before taking the last step around to the back. At last, but too late, my sense of caution was returning. Just before I continued walking, I heard a step behind me.

I spun around, and was immediately blinded by a brilliant white light shining directly in my eyes. I expected a blow to follow, and I cowered before it. But only my eardrums were assaulted, by a harsh, deep voice demanding: "What the *fuck* are you doing back here, Jamison?"

NO SWEAT

27

TELL ME, WHAT DID SKIP HAVE TO BE SO angry about? He had scared the hell out of me, sneaking up from behind like that, and then blinding me with his flashlight. If anyone had a right to be pissed off, it was me. There's no law against taking a stroll on municipal property, is there?

But I have to admit: I was glad to see him. The constant threat I'd been living under—knowing that I might find Hutch's powerful forearm wrapped around my neck at any moment—had taken its toll. I had to relieve the pressure. I had to tell someone who could possibly help me, without getting me killed. Skip seemed like a plausible candidate. After mumbling something about waiting to meet a friend—which I know he didn't believe—I asked him if he could spare a minute; I had to speak with him about something important. He brusquely told me to go wait inside the building.

I never did get to check the gray van's rear license plate.

So two minutes later, I was back in the community room, this time facing the door. Skip was down the hall, checking in with Marty Gustafson, who was dispatching. Skip took his time, letting me wait. I gulped down one of the cans of soda while I sat there. I could have used something stronger.

Skip finally came in with a cup of coffee in his hand. He kicked the door closed behind him, and then glared at me for a second before he sat down. I just smiled.

"Still haven't learned, have you, Jamison?" he said, as he lifted his feet up on the chair next to him.

"Learned what, Skip?"

He didn't answer, but sipped his coffee instead. Then he set it down and looked at me.

"So, what did you want to see me for?" he asked.

I cleared my throat. "I got a visit the other day," I said, gravely.

"I'm happy for you."

"From Kyle Hutchinson."

Skip nodded, and took a pen from his breast pocket. I thought he was going to start taking notes. Instead, he just examined the pen for a minute—checked that the tip extended and retracted properly—and then returned it to his pocket. Then he stared passively at me, as if to inform me that anything I had to tell him was less important than the operating condition of his favorite ballpoint.

"Yeah. What of it?"

"Hutch. Kyle Hutchinson. He paid me a visit."

"Yeah, I know. Monday evening. In the parking lot of your apartment building."

What? "You *know* that?"

Skip shook his head in disgust. "Why is it you think everyone else is *dumber* than you are, Scott? I told you to keep your nose clean, but every time I turn around, there you are—sticking it in somebody else's business.

"You know, you're damned lucky. Hutch could have done a number on you. Could have messed you up but good, not just knocked you around a bit."

All at once, I was terribly confused. "I didn't go looking for that ape," I said defensively.

Skip just shrugged and sipped his coffee.

I asked: "How do you know all this?"

He looked up at the ceiling. "Why do I have to deal with these people?" he asked, though his question obviously wasn't directed at me. "I just wanted to be a cop, not a nanny."

I waited until he finished his soliloquy.

He glared at me and continued: "I shouldn't be telling you this, Scott, but I *think* I can trust you to keep it to yourself. Don't make me regret it."

I swallowed. "You can trust me, Skip."

"Yeah, I'm sure," he said sarcastically.

"How did you know about Hutch coming to my apartment building?"

Skip scratched his cheek. He seemed to be debating whether to tell me. Then he looked at me and said: "We'd been working with the sheriff's office, keeping an eye on Kyle Hutchinson, since shortly after Gary Greer went into cold storage. They thought Hutch might make a mistake, and try to link up with Greer's customers. So they—the sheriff's office—put him under surveillance. We gave them a hand when we could."

I thought about this for a second.

"So you saw Hutch kidnap me that night?"

Skip grinned. "That was a kidnapping?" He looked around the room. "Shit, where's a telephone? We better alert the FBI."

"You saw him strangle me? And drag me into his van?"

Skip shook his head. "*I* didn't see it, personally. The sheriff's department had one guy tailing Hutch that night. When he saw Hutch toss you into the van, he called for back-up. We sent three guys in an unmarked car. They kept an eye on things. When you came stumbling back out, they backed off."

It did not please me to hear this. "Why didn't anybody come help me?"

"*Why didn't anybody come help me?*" Skip mimicked me. "For two reasons, one of which makes perfect sense to me. You had little to worry about; Hutch would've never made it out of the parking lot with you in that van. But our guys saw no need to blow the entire operation just to break up a little chat between the two of you.

"One of our guys got close enough to catch pieces of your conversation. He didn't hear much, but he could tell you were essentially okay."

I was still pissed. "So you let me dangle."

"Dangle. That's a nifty word, Scott. Can I borrow it sometime?"

"What was the second reason?" I asked.

"The what?"

"You said there were *two* reasons why *'your guys'* didn't help me. You only told me one."

Again, Skip scratched his cheek. His voice was lower when he said: "The desk jockeys from the county—and I'm including the prosecutor *and* the sheriff's office in this—had a notion that you were involved with Hutch's operation–"

"*Me?*"

"–and they're still not convinced you're clean. They seem to believe Chico's story."

"What story? Who the hell is Chico?"

Skip snorted. "Now don't tell me you don't know who *Chico* is."

I shook my head. "Never heard of him."

Skip stared at me for a moment, trance-like, as though my denial had created a whole new set of possibilities. Then he snapped out of it. "Well, we can check that with no sweat. Your name would be on the call sheet when he was taken in."

This was getting even more confusing. "Taken in? By the squad?" I asked.

"Yeah," said Skip, nodding. "The squad took him to Bedford Memorial on an overdose call—about two months ago. Chico says you attended to him in the back of the ambulance, and that you asked him a lot of questions that had nothing to do with patient care."

"Wasn't me," I declared.

Skip shrugged. "Well, like I said, that can be checked. If the sheriff wants to bother. Me, I think Chico is lying. You're too stupid to be involved in Hutch's dealings."

"I'm touched by your confidence in me."

"Yeah, but that still leaves the question: why *was* Hutch following you? Since I don't buy the prosecutor's theory, I'd like to hear yours."

I took a deep breath, held it for a second, then blew it out. Did I tell Skip what I'd learned in the past few days? In the past hour?

What did I have to lose?

"Hutch was following me for the same reason Gary Greer put a gun to my head. He mistook me for somebody else. For the guy Angie Greer was screwing."

"Oh," said Skip—as if he was disappointed. As if the simple fact made sense, but he had been hoping for something more.

"Wouldn't you like to know who the guy is?" I asked.

"Is he a runner for Hutch? Or another one of Greer's customers?" In other words, is he into drugs—as either a buyer or a seller? Now *there* was an interesting thought.

But was it possible? Did Mike Marder have a larger part in this drama than that of Angie Greer's lover? The possibility intrigued me. It might explain one mystery: how Marder knew to take Gary Greer's gym bag that Sunday night—when he should've just gotten his tail out of the house.

But it only took me a few moments' reflection to reject the notion. The adjacent puzzle pieces just wouldn't fit. For all his faults—which were multiplying by the minute—there was no evidence Mike Marder was involved in Greer's and Hutch's business dealings. If he had been, Hutch would have caught up with him long before he came after me.

"No," I answered.

"Then I'm not interested," Skip said flatly. "Angie Greer's affairs are not my concern."

Skip was ready to close that door, if I would only let him. But I still felt I was going to need his help. He left me no choice. I had to play my hole card.

"But what if the unidentified fingerprint, the one on Gary Greer's gun–"

"Keegan's gun," Skip corrected me.

"–belongs to Angie Greer's lover. *Then* would you be interested?"

Skip folded his arms across his chest and smiled at me.

"Gee, Scott," he said, "I thought you'd forgotten about that gun."

"I'll *never* forget about that gun," I said in all seriousness.

Skip nodded, then scratched his cheek again. He raised his finger, and almost said something, then resumed the cheek-scratching. It appeared that I'd gotten his attention.

"So you think you know, huh?" he finally remarked.

"I have a pretty good idea."

"Uh-huh. Thanks, no doubt, to something Angie Greer told you earlier this evening—in this very room."

I smiled. "Nothing gets by you, does it?"

He ignored my compliment.

"To be honest, Scott, we're not nearly as interested in that gun now as we were a week ago. Keegan told us the print could belong to his brother. He said his brother took the gun out of his glove compartment and looked it over, about a month before Keegan had the accident."

"So why don't you fingerprint Keegan's brother?"

"Because it's not worth the effort. His brother lives in California. He was just here visiting when he handled the gun."

"But that doesn't explain how the gun got from the car to Gary Greer," I pointed out.

Skip shrugged. "Missing guns turn up in the strangest places. It could have been thrown from the car in the accident, and found later. It could have been someone from the wrecking company who came across it. Or Keegan could have been mistaken; maybe the gun wasn't in the glove compartment to begin with."

"Regardless, if you think you know something about that gun, I'd like to hear it."

I was about to open my mouth when I heard that little voice in my brain. *Not so fast,* it told me. *Don't hand him this one without something in return.*

"Who is Chico?" I asked.

Skip sighed. He had expected an answer, not another question.

"He's a dopehead who lives in the apartment complexes off of Paterson Road. He was one of Greer's customers."

"Was?"

"Yes, was. We, um, had reason to ask him a few questions recently. The sheriff's guys—clever bastards that they are—mentioned your name to him. When Chico heard you were on the squad, he not only remembered you, he started spinning some yarn about the time the squad took him in. Gave them some bull-shit about how you kept asking him about Gary Greer—how much shit he dealt, when the buys were made, how–"

"How Greer carried the drugs and the money," I ventured, interrupting.

Skip stared at me. "Yeah, questions like that. How'd you know?"

"Only guessing," I said. "I've never met this Chico character in my life. Go ahead, check the call sheet. It'll have a green sticker attached to it, but you won't find my name on it."

Skip continued to stare at me. "You'd better not be screwing with me, Jamison," he warned. "I've been on your side through this whole operation. I'd be in deep shit if it turns out you're involved. Almost as deep as what you'll be in."

"I know. But don't forget, Skip: I'm too *stupid* to be involved in Hutch's dealings."

"I'll stand by that statement."

"*Skip?*"

A voice came across Skip's walkie-talkie. He yanked it from his belt and answered: "Yes, Marty?"

"*You better get rolling. We got an emergency on our hands.*"

NO FUTURE

28

"WHAT'VE YOU GOT, MARTY?" Skip spoke into his walkie-talkie, as he swung his feet from the chair and onto the floor. I stood up just as he did.

"A kid with a knife," Marty Gustafson's voice came back. "He's cut somebody, but I don't know who just yet. I have a woman on the line who's in hysterics."

Skip motioned for me to follow him. "I'm on my way," he said into the walkie-talkie, while heading out the door. "Get me an address."

Down the hall Skip sprinted, with me right behind.

"I'm suspended from the squad, you know," I told him as we ran.

"Do you think I care?" he shot back. "You're coming with me."

"You parked out front?" I asked, as we went through the double doors.

"On the side."

"Let me get my first aid kit from my car. Pick me up at the exit."

Skip didn't answer, so I assumed he agreed to my suggestion. I dashed to my car, popped the trunk, and grabbed my kit. For just a second, I debated whether to take my squad jacket as well.

I left it in the trunk.

The red and blue lights on Skip's patrol car were already flashing as he roared up beside me. I barely had time to jump in next to him before he peeled out onto the main road. He flipped on his siren.

"Where we going?" I asked, trying to be casual—if not blasé—about the unfolding adventure.

"Hilltop," Skip answered, just as we heard Marty on the radio, putting out a call for the squad. Marty gave a more precise location than Skip had. Our destination was on Lakeside Drive. The name rang a bell.

"Lakeside," I repeated, remembering out loud. "Billie lives on that street."

"Is that right," Skip remarked, as we flew past a half dozen cars that had pulled to the side. "Maybe we'll see her there."

"If you're lucky," I added, while glancing in his direction. My glance was rewarded: I caught the hint of a smile on his lips.

"I don't mess with married women," he said dryly. Then he picked up his radio handset. "Three to dispatch," he called, "you know anything more?"

Marty answered: "The best I can determine, we got a Romeo syndrome. Juliet's mother called it in. I couldn't tell from her who's been stabbed."

"Stabbed?" Skip asked.

"Stabbed, sliced...I can't say. The woman just kept screaming that there's blood everywhere."

"Ten-four." Skip replaced the handset.

I asked Skip: "What's a 'Romeo syndrome'?"

Skip turned onto Noble Street, which intersects Lakeside Drive right at Billie DeMarino's house. We sped down the street, our siren still blasting.

"It happens often enough," Skip replied, "even in this vanilla town. Some lovesick teenager shows up at his girlfriend's front door, carrying a weapon. Sometimes he brings a baseball bat, sometimes he's got a gun."

"This time," he said, as he turned sharply onto Lakeside,

"Romeo's got a blade. Sounds like he's used it, too."

I watched Billie's house as we took the corner and sped by. Looking back, I saw her running from the house to where her car was parked on the driveway. It reassured me to know my part-ner—or former partner, if you will—would be joining us momen-tarily.

Skip continued: "Let's hope the blood that has Juliet's mother so upset belongs to Romeo himself. I dislike it when the girl's father or—worse yet—the girl herself, gets hurt. But anything's possi-ble."

"There's the house," I said, pointing it out for Skip. "Somebody's on the front porch waving to us."

As Skip pulled onto the driveway and stopped the car, I grabbed my first aid kit and jumped out. I could see, in the dark-ness, that it was a boy—maybe thirteen or fourteen years old—who had signaled us from the porch. As I approached, he opened the front door and yelled in: "The cops are here!" Then he turned back to face me.

"Who's hurt?" I asked, as I stepped up on the porch.

"Nobody important—just the dickhead my sister dates," the boy replied. There wasn't much emotion in his voice. "He slashed his wrist."

"His *own* wrist?" I asked, as I peered in through the storm door. I couldn't see anybody, but I did notice a thick trail of blood on the floor. It ran from just inside the door, through the foyer, to a room beyond.

"Yeah, his own wrist. It was the only one available."

Turning back to the boy, I asked, much too rapidly: "What's the kid's name? How is he? Who's in there with him?"

By this time, Skip had joined us on the porch. The boy spoke to Skip as he answered my questions. "He's in bad shape. My dad's trying to stop the bleeding, but he's not having much luck. His name is Steve Arnushko. My mother and sister are in there too."

I pulled the storm door open, and held it for Skip. "After you," I said, gesturing inside.

"Police!" Skip called.

"In here!" a man's voice replied. "Hurry!"

Skip went through the door. I followed at a distance, doing my best to avoid stepping in the crimson stream that showed us the way.

The room beyond the foyer was the kitchen. I watched Skip as he entered, stopped, and looked about. Then he turned to the right and stepped out of my view, still following the trail of blood.

I hesitated. Of all things, I was trying to remember what my lawyer, Geoffrey Hufnagel, had said about my potential liability in a situation such as this. Clearly, I was not acting as a squad member now, but neither was I a simple bystander who had happened upon the scene. It was ridiculous, but I was frozen: wondering about my status, per the provisions of the Good Samaritan Law.

I glanced back over my shoulder, hoping to see the flashing blue light on Billie DeMarino's car. I knew she was on her way, but she hadn't arrived yet.

"Scott!" came Skip's thunderous voice. "Get in here!"

I ran the final few feet into the kitchen. No sooner did I clear the threshold than the entire scene was presented for me. Skip was on the floor, his knees in a puddle of red, trying to apply pressure to the wrist of our young Romeo. The blood-soaked towel he was using had long since ceased to be an effective bandage.

I glanced up. At the far end of the kitchen were two women—a woman and a girl, actually—holding on to one another while they watched. The girl was crying. The woman she was holding appeared distraught...maybe catatonic. Using her horrified expression as a gauge, I allowed myself to assume that this incident hadn't been on the evening's agenda.

On the floor, next to Skip but edging away as I approached, was a short, overweight, and thoroughly homely man. His pants and the front of his shirt were spattered—no, *splattered*—with blood. He nodded at me, as though expecting me to make good on his failed efforts to staunch the young man's bleeding.

Finally, there was Romeo—Steve Arnushko—himself. He was a big, gangly kid with close-cropped hair. The first thing I noticed about him was how white his skin was, and how cool—deathly cool—it felt when I touched him. He was unconscious, lying there in the blood he had let loose. I estimated he had bled out at least a liter-and-a-half. Maybe more.

In my experience, I've found that most suicide attempts, especially among teenagers, are more properly defined as cries for
help. When the victims injure themselves, usually they do enough
damage only to attain the attention they desperately need.

Steve Arnushko, on the other hand, had been quite serious. His
wound wasn't a cry for help; it was—short of putting a bullet into
his brain—about as earnest an effort to end it all as young Steve
could have made. The chances were looking good, just then, that
he would succeed.

As I knelt over him, I quickly determined that he was still
breathing—but his breaths were coming in muted gasps: very
rapid and very shallow. I searched for a radial pulse on his uninjured wrist and found none. At his throat, I did manage to find a
weak carotid pulse. It was also very rapid—at least 120 a minute. I
peeled back an eyelid. The eye was glassy, its pupil dilated, as it
stared off into oblivion.

"Skip, go get your oxygen," I said, as I opened my first aid kit.
"When the duty crew gets here, tell 'em we need the MAST pants.
And make sure the MIC unit is coming." From my kit, I grabbed a
trauma dressing, a roll of gauze—and a pair of rubber gloves. I put
the gloves on first.

Skip relinquished his hold on the bloody towel, stood and
walked away. When he reached the foyer, I heard him stop and
speak to someone. I recognized the voice that answered him: it
was Billie.

"Chief!" I called to my partner. "I can use your help in here!"

Billie hurried into the kitchen, carrying her own first aid kit. If
she was surprised to see me, there in her neighbor's house, she
didn't show it. She knelt down beside me just as I removed the
blood-soaked towel from our patient's wrist.

It was not a pretty sight. I still can't imagine how he had managed it—*I* certainly couldn't do such a thing—but our young
Romeo had made an incision in his wrist that cut straight through
to the bone. He had severed a number of veins, and had nicked the
artery as well. Blood continued to trickle slowly from the wound.

I slapped the trauma dressing over the incision and squeezed—

hard. Billie helped me secure it with gauze. We used three rolls.

"Did you get any vitals yet?" she asked me.

"Just an approximate pulse count—120 or more. And thready."

Billie pulled a blood pressure cuff from her kit. She worked it around our patient's upper arm and pumped it up. She put on her stethoscope, positioned the diaphragm at the crook of Steve's elbow, and listened. Everyone in the room watched the dial on her BP cuff as the indicator fell toward zero. She couldn't help but grimace as it passed 85 and she still couldn't hear a thump. Then she jerked her head, slightly, responding to a faint, distant echo.

"Seventy-eight, systolic," she said flatly.

Skip returned with his oxygen kit. Right behind him was the boy who had met us on the porch. The boy looked around the room, started to walk toward his parents and sister, then reconsidered. He reversed himself and drifted quietly into an empty corner.

Skip opened the oxygen kit and set it on the floor next to me. I found a mask inside and fitted it to our patient. We gave him 100%—full flow oxygen—and used the pressure valve to force it into his lungs. There wasn't much else we could do until the paramedics arrived.

"Who's on duty tonight?" I asked Billie.

"Jerry and Sylvia. They should be here in ten or less," she answered.

"What about the MIC unit?"

"Coming from Bedford," Skip interjected. "They'll be here in less than that." Then he asked: "How's he doing?"

I just shook my head. It was too late to report the bad news, and too soon to hope for the good.

Skip looked around the room, just as he had done when we arrived. Then he eyed the girl's father. The man was standing back a few feet, leaning against the refrigerator, his arms folded in front of him.

"Where's the knife?" Skip asked the man.

Juliet's father didn't answer. He just looked across the room at his son, who was still standing in the opposite corner.

"It's probably still outside," the boy answered. "You want me to go get it?"

"Yes," said the boy's father.

"No," Skip countermanded. "Leave it where it is."

The boy wavered, trying to decide whom to obey. It only took him a second to decide in Skip's favor.

"So he cut himself outside?" Skip asked.

"Yes," replied the father, softly.

"Did anybody see him do it?"

Again: "Yes. I did."

"*Why* did he do it?"

The man licked his lips before answering. "Because the door was locked," he said.

"Excuse me?" Skip asked, nearly as baffled as I was.

"It was *me* he was after, the son-of-a-bitch." The man's voice was louder now.

"Sir?"

"He stood on the porch and swore at me, brandishing that knife. Said I was ruining his life. If he'd had a gun, he would have shot me—right through the plate glass."

Such hostility. I guessed the cause, maybe four seconds before the man said it, but four centuries after Shakespeare wrote it.

"I had forbidden my daughter to see him anymore. I told her she had no future with this guy." He looked down at the floor, at the motionless young man sprawled in his own blood. "Maybe now she'll listen to me," he added defiantly.

I was mesmerized. All the elements of a classic Greek tragedy— or of a soap opera fighting for market share—were unfolding before me. The girl, Juliet, provided audio backdrop, bawling loudly into her mother's ample bosom.

But Skip, the pragmatist, has no appreciation for high drama. He just kept digging for a logical explanation. "So, because he couldn't get at you, the boy slit his own wrist?"

The man nodded, a little too eagerly. "Yeah, I told him to get the hell out of here, before I called the cops. That's when he said he was going to kill himself, if I didn't let him see Louise..."

Louise, huh? *Steve and Louise.* For me, it didn't quite have the *élan* of Romeo and Juliet.

The father continued: "So I told him: 'Go ahead, you stupid bastard. Do us all a favor.' I didn't think he had the crust to actually go through with it."

Skip prodded: "And then?"

Again the man licked his lips. He glanced at his son. "Then he cut himself. It must be a sharp knife, because the blood came gushing out. Then he fainted."

"You dragged him in here?" Skip guessed.

The man nodded. His voice was soft again when he said: "Yeah, I thought we could help him better in the house." Once more, he glanced at his son.

We heard a siren approaching just then. Within a minute of each other, the MIC unit and the duty crew arrived, and our attention was refocused on our patient. The paramedics quickly started a large bore IV, in an attempt to replace some of the fluid Steve had lost. His condition stabilized, but it hardly improved. The clear stuff the paramedics pump can bring up the pressure, but it doesn't carry oxygen. And that's what our patient needed most desperately.

Jerry Boronski was with the duty crew. He scowled at me when he came in with the litter. I ignored him.

As the kitchen filled with emergency responders, Billie and I became less critical to the operation. We eventually moved out onto the front porch. We lingered there for a few minutes. I was in the process of telling her how I'd been pressed into service when I noticed a faint, metallic reflection coming from beneath the banister at the porch's edge. Curious, I walked over to it. I squatted down to see what was catching the light.

It was a knife, of course, with blood on its edge. Just as I reached for it I heard a voice on the other side of the banister, warning: "Leave it be, Scott. Don't even touch it." It was Skip, standing on the dark lawn, conversing with another patrolman.

I stood up. The two policemen didn't even look at me.

"Is this the knife?" I asked Skip—a rather stupid question, considering.

He didn't answer me right away. He just kept talking, in a hushed voice, with his colleague. Finally, they nodded in agreement at each other, and the other patrolman walked away. Skip turned to me.

He said, "I'm going to be here for awhile, Scott. If you can catch a ride, you can leave. But I still want to talk to you in the next few days."

I was somewhat surprised by this. I lowered my voice and asked: "Do you think there's something funny going on here?"

He stared at me for a second, impassively. "You ask too many questions, Jamison. Now, do you want me to find you a lift, or can you get one from your friends?"

I turned to Billie, who was now talking to another responder. "Chief," I called, "can you give me a ride to the municipal building?"

"No problem, Scott," she called back.

I turned back to Skip. "Billie's going to give me a ride," I said airily.

"Lucky you," he answered.

"Yes, lucky me."

I turned as though to leave, and then turned back as though I'd forgotten something. "By the way, Skip," I said, "you didn't tell me why Hutch's van is sitting in the back lot at the municipal building."

He eyed me coolly. "Who said that's Hutch's van?"

"Is it impounded?"

Skip looked away for a second, then back at me. "I've told you as much as I'm going to tell you, Scott. Just leave now, while you're still ahead."

"Let me guess," I persisted. "You, or the sheriff's department, caught Hutch selling to Chico. The both of them are under arrest right now, and Chico's been singing his head off. That's how you know so much about the conversation he and I supposedly had. Am I right?"

Skip just looked at me. "I'm not saying," he answered at last.

"No, I wouldn't expect you to. I'll just have to go down to the sheriff's department tomorrow, and see what they have to say." I turned as though to leave, hoping he'd stop me.

He did. "Jamison," he called, just before I rejoined Billie.

I walked back to the banister. "Yes?" I responded.

He said, "I told you to quit while you're ahead. You're right: Hutch is under arrest right now, but it's being kept quiet. The prosecutor is working on him, trying to get him to roll over on *his* supplier. If you stroll in there, asking a bunch of stupid questions, you could blow everything. You could cause yourself a lot more trouble than you have right now."

I nodded. This was getting better by the moment. "Is your case against Hutch pretty strong?" I asked.

Skip looked around before he answered me. "Very strong," he said. "Otherwise his lawyer wouldn't be dealing with the prosecutor."

"Any chance he'll get out soon?"

Skip narrowed his eyes. "What's it to you?" he asked suspiciously.

"Any chance?" I repeated.

Skip shook his head. "None. You can tell Angie Greer she can spend the money. Hutch won't be back for it."

I didn't have to act surprised. "What? What money?" I gasped.

He just grinned. Then he reminded me: "You're not as smart as you think you are, Scott."

When we were in her car, my partner wasted no time before asking: "How's the lawsuit coming?"

"I'm not too concerned about it," I answered. "I expect it to go away in the next few days."

Billie turned with a joyful expression. She was truly happy for me. "That's great," she said. "Must be load off your mind."

"Uh-huh. I'm going to call Hank Cindrich when I get home, and request a hearing at Wednesday night's board meeting. I'm going to ask to be reinstated. And then I'm going to resign."

Billie almost drove off the road. "You're going to *what?*"

I shrugged. "I'm thinking of giving it up, Chief. My boss is on my ass. I just don't have the time or the enthusiasm for it anymore."

"Bullshit," she replied. "You'll be back riding with me next week."

"Who's riding with you *this* week?" I asked.

"Miles," she answered, as I had expected.

"Good," I said. "Could I buy the two of you lunch, Tuesday afternoon? I have to check something with the both of you, before the meeting on Wednesday."

Billie glanced at me, and raised an eyebrow. "You're buying?"

"Certainly."

She smiled that winning smile of hers. The one that makes Skipinski melt. "Boy, you must have some good news to report," she said. "Okay, I'll clear it with Miles. Unless you'd rather call him yourself."

"No," I said. "I'd rather you call him. If you don't mind."

"I don't mind. I have to get in touch with him anyway. And I'm sure he won't turn down a free lunch. *Especially* from you."

"Chief, you should know by now," I said unequivocally. "There's no such thing as a free lunch. *Especially* from me."

NO FAITH

29

MILES COATES DID NOT TURN DOWN MY offer of a free lunch. It was raining when the three of us met that Tuesday afternoon, so he couldn't work anyway. The rain was appropriate for the occasion.

In contrast to Billie's earlier reaction, Miles didn't seem particularly joyful to hear that Angie Greer would probably be dropping the lawsuit. When I told him, shortly after we took our seats, he acted rather indifferent. He just nodded and went back to studying his menu.

We were in a small restaurant that Billie had selected. For the first ten or fifteen minutes, we talked about the squad, about work, and about the weather. The three of us talked, and the two of them laughed on occasion. I couldn't join in the laughter; I'd left my sense of humor elsewhere.

I hardly glanced at the menu before ordering. Billie questioned the waitress about three different items, then settled on a seafood combination. Miles ordered something exotic; I don't remember what it was.

They both knew I had something significant to tell them, and they both waited patiently for me to get around to it. A suitable opportunity arrived shortly before our meals did. While they nibbled at bread sticks and sipped their drinks, I told them about my recent conversations with Fay Johnson, Angie Greer and Sergeant Skipinski. Of course, I didn't reveal everything—I notably failed to mention Kyle Hutchinson, and the squad files I'd lifted—but I relayed enough information for them to understand the plot…and to distinguish the villains from the victims. And I *didn't* tell them I wanted this information to be kept quiet; if anything, I inferred the opposite. If Billie wished to repeat my story to her friend Peggy, so much the better.

All the while, while they sat listening in complete absorption, I kept my hands under the table, or under my folded arms. I didn't want my friends to see that they were shaking. As the salads came and went, and as the main course arrived, I kept telling myself that I had made a huge mistake. That there was another explanation.

But no matter how I examined it, it always came back to the same reality, to the same inescapable conclusion. I had been betrayed.

After two bites of my quiche, or my soufflé, or whatever it was I was eating, I couldn't hold it in any longer. I set down my fork, wiped my mouth with my napkin, and turned to my best friend. I asked him: "So, Miles, who else have you told?"

"Told what?"

"That my father left me enough money to live on for the next fifteen or twenty years."

Billie stopped eating and looked at me. Miles did the same.

"What are you talking about?" he asked. His tone sounded defensive.

"C'mon, don't play dumb with me," I said, brusquely. "There's only one reason I've been on the hot seat these past few weeks, and you're it. Most of this would not have happened—there wouldn't have even *been* a lawsuit—if you hadn't opened your fat mouth, and told at least one person something they shouldn't know. I just want you to tell me who else you've let in on my private affairs."

"What *are* you talking about?" Miles raised his voice.

"All this time, I thought I could trust you. I thought you were my friend. My *best* friend. Then you go and do something like this, and stab me squarely in the back. You *told* Mike Marder, didn't you? You told him I went in that house before the police arrived. But even worse—*much* worse—you told him I had enough money stashed away to make a lawsuit worth pursuing.

"How else could he have known? Pressman didn't know. Angie Greer didn't know. Billie here, my partner—whom I'd trust with my life—I've never told. Even *Pam* doesn't know, for Christ's sake. You're the only person I've entrusted with that knowledge, and you managed to use it against me. How could you do it? *Why* did you do it?"

Miles just sat there, shaking his head.

"Now, please," I added, "don't act like you don't know what I'm talking about. Don't insult me, on top of everything else."

Billie glanced at Miles, then turned to me in bewilderment. Her face had gone pale.

"What's going on here?" she asked. "Is this one of your childish games, Scott? If it is, I'm not finding it amusing. Not in the least. What's he talking about, Miles?"

Miles continued to shake his head. He set down his fork, put his hands together, and rubbed them—one in the other. When he started to talk, his voice cracked.

"How...how could it be," he stammered, "that the man I considered a friend, would accuse me of going against him—just because he's got a problem that he can't figure out?" He looked at me, sadly, and continued: "How could you sit there, and *humiliate* me, Scott—in front of Billie—and blame me for causing your troubles?

"I wish to God you'd never told me about the money your father left you. Because ever since you did, you've managed to hold it over me. Not blatantly, but in a subtle way that's absolutely maddening. You're always picking up the tab, playing the role of the big spender—as if to remind me that *you* can afford it, and that *I'm* struggling to make ends meet.

"And now, when it seems that somebody else has learned your precious secret, you show that you had no faith in me to begin with. We *had* a good friendship, Scott, but now you've trampled on it. You've treated me like *shit*, all because you're faced with a riddle you can't solve."

Miles took a drink of water, then stood up. He pulled his wallet from his back pocket, yanked out two twenty-dollar-bills, and threw them on the table.

"I'm finished with your free lunches, Jamison. And I'm finished with you." He turned and walked out of the restaurant.

We watched him go, Billie and I. Then she turned back to face me. She looked down at her plate for a few moments, then pushed it away. Lunch was over.

"Well, Scott," she said as she stood to leave, her voice remarkably calm, "maybe you have more money to your name than I would have ever guessed. But I don't think it can buy you a friend to replace the one you just threw away."

Had I screwed up? Had I falsely accused my "best" friend of betraying a confidence?

I was sitting at my desk, an hour later, turning the question over in my mind. Except for Miles, I was certain I had told no one—had never even hinted—about the money I had squirreled away.

But Mike Marder had definitely known.

How?

I pulled open my bottom desk drawer, and leafed through the hanging folders inside—through files of company projects either on hold, or in doubt, or both. At the rear of the drawer, I located a file folder that has nothing to do with my work at DataStaff. I lifted the file out, closed the drawer, and set it on my cluttered desktop. I glanced over my shoulder before I opened it.

The first sheet in the folder had been there only a few days. It was the page I had copied—surreptitiously—on my visit to the squad building on the previous Wednesday. I scanned it, searching for a clue. But the data revealed nothing—just names, addresses and phone numbers with no apparent connection to the still-missing puzzle piece.

I was about to put the page back when I noticed something else in the folder. It was unrelated to my current predicament—or so I thought—but a resonant chord sounded in my ears as I picked the item up.

It was the prospectus I had received a few months earlier from the Walnut Grove Country Club. Attached to it were my notes summarizing what I had learned—and Fran Hufnagel had wheedled—from our conversations with the slick membership director, Mr. Oswald.

Absently, I browsed through the printed matter. I remembered the three distinct stages of my discussion with Oswald: my initial curiosity, which gave way to an intense irritation, which was finally replaced by a smug—though short-lived—satisfaction, when I had breached his well-polished veneer. I was reliving the experience when a light went on. It wasn't the brilliant, blinding flash of a wondrous revelation; it was just the soft glow of a simple possibility. Like an illuminated light switch that enables you to creep down a dark hallway, just so you can reach it and flip it without walking into a wall. I crept toward that glow.

Mr. Oswald, the membership director of the Walnut Grove Country Club, had been reading off a computer screen all that he knew about me. As we had spoken, that day, I had wished I could see through the phone line, to get a glimpse at the electronic file that was at his disposal. It might have given me the answer that I was looking for right now.

But I had lost patience, lost my cool, and settled for a lousy put-down. This time, I resolved, I wasn't going to let him get away so cheaply.

I picked up the phone and dialed Pam's work number. I was pleasantly surprised when she answered it herself. "Hi, gorgeous," I said, engagingly.

"Hello, H.B.," she replied. "What's up?"

I got right to the point. "Your friend Kelly—what's her boyfriend's name again?"

"Jonathan," she answered.

"Jonathan..." I left it hanging, as though incomplete.

"Tritschler," she said, and which I wrote down. "Why do you ask?"

I ignored her question. "What sort of work does he do?" I'm sure I had asked before, and that Pam had told me, but I honestly didn't remember.

"It's a family business," Pam said. "Some kind of engineering or architectural consultants. For shopping malls, I think. Why?"

Why?

"Oh, no reason. Somebody here at DataStaff is researching the, um, jewelry business, and I thought what's-his-name was in that line of work. My mistake." Pam would buy that, wouldn't she?

"Oh," she said. "Well, at any rate, I'm glad you called. I'd like to see you—soon. We have to talk."

"You're right," I said. "But this week is jammed for me. How about Friday? I'll meet you at *Luigi's*. We'll grab a pizza, and go back to my place. And we'll talk. Okay?"

Pam hesitated. "Well, okay," she said after a few moments. "Seven o'clock?"

"See you then," I said.

I was about to put the phone back in its cradle when I heard Pam calling: "Scott?"

"I'm still here."

Again she hesitated. Her voice was lower when she continued: "You told me last week that you love me. Did you mean it?"

Why was she asking?

"Of course I meant it."

"Okay, then. I'll see you Friday." She hung up.

Women.

A minute later, after I had assembled my notes, I picked up the phone again. When I finished dialing, and heard the ringing on the other end of the line, I reminded myself: *Be brief. Be direct. Say no more than you have to.*

"Good afternoon, and thank you for calling Walnut Grove Country Club," answered a woman's cheerful voice. "How may I direct your call?"

"Mr. Oswald," I grunted, restraining myself from adding a *please.* I didn't want to sound mannerly.

"May I ask who's calling...*please?*" Rub it in, why don't you?

"Jonathan Tritschler," I said.

"Mr. Tritschler, may I tell him what this is in reference to?"

"He'll know."

"Thank you. Hold for a minute…*please.*"

It took Oswald only a few seconds to come on the line. His effervescence was instantly nauseating.

"Mr. Tritschler! How *nice* of you to call! How are you today?"

"Fine," I mumbled.

"Great! That's just great," Oswald bubbled. "And how's your lovely fiancée?"

"Kelly's fine too."

"Wonderful! Have I told you, Mr. Tritschler, that the two of you make a beautiful couple? Have I told you that?"

Had he? The odds were favorable. "Yes," I said.

"Yes, you're a lucky guy, Mr. Tritschler. And Miss Perniciaro is a lucky woman. I envy the both of you.

"But anyway, I'm so glad you called. How can I be of assistance to you this afternoon?"

The one- and two-word responses wouldn't suffice now. I had to bluff my way from this point on, hoping I could fool Oswald just long enough…

"Well," I said, trying to emulate Jonathan's limited tonal range, "my company is planning a new marketing campaign. I need to find a good agency."

"I see," said Oswald, his exuberance not quite so overbearing now. "And how might I help you in this regard?"

"Well, I showed the prospectus you sent me to our search committee, and we're impressed with its design. We'd like to know who created it for you."

Oswald didn't speak for a few moments. I could hear a faint tapping sound as I waited for his reply. I knew the sound intimately. He was at his keyboard, entering commands into his computer.

What was he seeking? Didn't he know, from his own memory, who had prepared and billed him for that ornate printed piece?

"So you'd like to know who our marketing firm is, would you?"

Hmm. Did I detect an edge to his voice?

"Yes."

"Uh-huh. Well, hold on a minute, and I'll get that information for you."

Tap, tap, tap.

"By the way, Mr. Tritschler," he asked in an offhanded manner, "how's that project in Dallas working out?"

Dallas? Had Jonathan been working in Dallas recently? Or was Oswald suspicious, or just being cautious—and possibly setting a pick for me? I wracked my brain, trying to recall any mention of Jonathan's involvement with a project in Dallas. I couldn't remember any, but that didn't mean much. I tend to tune Pam out when the subject is Kelly and/or Jonathan, and their latest escapades.

"Dallas? You mean Atlanta, don't you?" I said, then held my breath.

Oswald laughed in embarrassment—but whether it was real or fake, I couldn't say.

"Yes! Atlanta! How stupid of me! I should have remembered!"

"It's going okay," I mumbled.

"Fantastic!" Oswald exclaimed, his earlier chumminess now fully restored. "That's just wonderful. Ah, here it is. The name of the marketing agency that developed our prospectus is Zimmerman, McClatchie and Associates. They're right here in North Jersey. Would you like their phone number?"

"Yes, please," I answered.

As he recited the number, my heart jumped right into my throat.

The number was identical to the one on the sheet of paper in my hands.

It was the work number listed on Mike Marder's personnel file.

"Tell me, Mr. Oswald," I said. "Is this outfit a full-service agency?"

"Full-service? I'm not sure what you mean."

"Well, if we need some help in finding prospects, could they manage that?"

"Oh, most certainly! They were *very* helpful to us in developing a database. We paid handsomely for their work, but it was worth it. Their lists were of the highest quality."

Oswald was onto a subject he loved to discuss, and I wanted to keep him on it.

"Is that right?" I asked, sounding intrigued.

"Definitely! You see, they do work for a few financial service firms. Don't quote me on this, but it's my understanding they've occasionally had access to customer records. *Complete* customer records. You know how it is, these days, with information going every which way at millions of bits per minute. If you know where to look…"

I wanted to say: *Tell me about it, asshole. It's how I make my living.* Instead, I mumbled: "So you'd recommend them?"

"Without hesitation! Please mention my name when you call them."

"I'll do that."

"Marvelous! Oh, and one other thing before you go, Mr. Tritschler…"

"Yes?"

"For your wedding reception—have you decided which package you'd prefer? I know it's a big decision, and that you and your lovely fiancée must agree on the details, but, as you know, there's only so much time—"

"Yes, I know," I interrupted. "Kelly and I spoke about it yesterday, and we've agreed on the most expensive arrangements. Spare no expense, Mr. Oswald. I only intend to marry once."

Then and there, I made his day.

"Excellent! Tremendous! I'll draw up the contract right away, and send it over for your signature. You're a lucky man indeed, Mr. Tritschler. And Miss Perniciaro is a lucky woman. I envy the both of you. *Immensely.* My profoundest best wishes to you both!"

"Goodbye, Mr. Oswald," I said.

Then I hung up…before I threw up.

NO PROBLEM

THE NEXT MORNING, I GOT AN early start on my work at Data-Staff. I had one of those rare and wonderful projects to complete: a report that I not only found interesting, but which lent itself to my unique talents. That is, it was nearly identical to a project I had busted my hump on two years before, but which had, unfortunately, never seen the light of day. The earlier project had been killed before it got to the review stage.

Thus, all that was required to complete my current project was some snipping, grafting and polishing and—*voilà!*—a Scott Jamison masterpiece was ready for delivery. I walked it into Arnie's empty office and dropped it on his desk, confident he would be dazzled by its perspicacity, when he got the chance to look it over.

During the day, I left two or three messages on Miles' answering machine, and my number on his business beeper. I owed him an apology—a *humongous* apology—but I knew it would take some time before he would even listen to an explanation. I'd have been surprised had he returned my call.

Certainly, I felt terrible about the way I had treated him. But I couldn't let the ache of regret

I felt distract me from the confrontation I was expecting at the evening board meeting. I had to forget about Miles for the time being, and concentrate on the issue at hand.

When the time came, that evening, I double-checked my notes, and triple-checked my appearance in the mirror. I was wearing one of my better ties and my absolute best sports jacket—which is to say: a combination that showed no visible food stains. The board members, I knew, would be wearing t-shirts and jeans to the meeting. I deliberately overdressed for the occasion, based on a piece of advice Arnie had once given me. It's his theory that people pay more attention to what you say when you're dressed better than they are. Of course, I had no first-hand evidence to back up this notion, but I figured it couldn't hurt to try it out.

I drove to the squad headquarters and walked into the meeting room five minutes early. For once, I was looking forward to taking on these people—if any of them were still inclined to give me a hard time.

The board members entered the room from the kitchen and—like contestants on a TV game show—took their appointed places. Most of them ignored me. Only Peggy Nowicki acknowledged me, and she with a wink. That further bolstered my confidence.

Hank Cindrich called the meeting to order. He no sooner finished taking the roll when he opened his notebook and removed an envelope. He looked up at me, nodded, and began to speak: "I received a letter yesterday that's of great interest to all of us. The letter is from a Mr. James Pressman, attorney-at-law. It's dated Monday, the day before yesterday, and it reads:

To the Dayfield Rescue Squad Board of Directors: This is to inform you that my client, Mrs. Angela Greer of 712 Kilbourn Avenue in Dayfield, has this day decided to drop the civil liability suit which she had earlier filed against one of your organization's members, a Mr. Scott Jamison. Mrs. Greer asked me to notify you of her decision, as it may impact upon internal proceedings of your squad.

Mrs. Greer has also directed me to express her gratitude for the prompt and professional care the Dayfield Rescue Squad has afforded her in the past. Please accept, as a token of her appreciation, the enclosed donation to your volunteer organization, drawn on the account of Mrs. Greer.

Sincerely, James P. Pressman, Esquire."

When Hank finished reading Pressman's letter, the room fell silent for several moments. I wasn't sure what to make of that. I was watching Mike Marder out of the corner of my eye. At last, Hank spoke again. "I'll entertain a motion to dismiss the charges pending against Scott," he said. "And to reinstate him to active duty."

"So moved," said Peggy.

"Seconded," followed Karen Weyrich.

"Discussion?" Hank asked.

Jerry Boronski raised his hand. Hank nodded at him.

"I'd like to ask Scott one question, if I may," Jerry said.

When Hank nodded again, Jerry looked at me and continued: "Scott, what were you doing at that suicide attempt on Sunday? You were on suspension at the time."

"*What* suicide attempt?" Stick Menzel asked, but which no one answered.

"I was there at Sergeant Skipinski's request," I answered simply. "I was with him when the call went off."

"You were with Skip?" Mike Marder asked, abruptly.

Without even looking at him, I answered: "That's what I said."

At that, Mike turned to Hank. "Mr. President," he asked, seriously, bringing a smile to Hank's lips, "could we table this for just a few minutes? I have to go check on something. It has to do with the matter at hand."

Carol Hartshorne, the parliamentarian, answered the question on Hank's behalf. "That's reasonable," she said. "We can give him five minutes."

Hank shrugged. "Okay, Mike. Five minutes. Then we vote whether you're back or not."

Mike left the room. In the silence that followed, we could hear him, down the hall, closing the door to the copier room. Then, less than ten seconds later, Peggy Nowicki stood and followed. Everyone in the room sat and watched her as she went. That is, everyone but me. I was right behind her.

Peggy hurried down the hall, opened the door to the copier room and walked right in. As she and I both expected, Mike was on the phone. He looked up at her in dismay. Covering the mouthpiece with his hand, he demanded: "Could I have some privacy here, Peggy?"

Peggy was great; she handled Mike Marder's request with style and verve. Saying: "In a minute, Mike, we'll give you all the privacy you could ask for," she deftly snatched the phone from his hand and, turning her back on him, spoke into it.

"Hello, Mrs. Greer?" she said. She paused for a moment, receiving confirmation that Angie Greer was indeed on the line, and then continued: "This is Peggy Nowicki, the captain of the Dayfield Rescue Squad. We received a letter from your attorney yesterday, and I just wanted to make sure it was authentic. You *are* dropping the suit? Thank you. And thank you very much for your kind donation. We appreciate it. Yes, Mrs. Greer, I know just how you feel. I'll tell him that. Yes. Good night."

Peggy hung up the phone, refusing to look at Mike.

Three of the board members were in the doorway, watching us. Mike's eyes met Carol's. She slowly shook her head. To this day, I don't know if her action was a signal, an answer...or the expression you'd expect from someone who has just realized that she had been played as a patsy. Carol turned and walked away.

To the board members who remained, Peggy said, "It looks like we—the *six* of us—have one more matter to discuss." Then she turned and addressed Mike and me at the same time. "I'd appreciate it if you two would wait here." She looked at us individually, hesitated, and then added: "I *can* leave the two of you alone together, can't I?" She sounded just like a second grade teacher when she said it.

"No problem here," I said brightly.

Mike didn't respond.

Peggy waited a minute, then said, "Mike?"

"I heard you," was his testy response.

"I know you heard me," Peggy said evenly. "But I have something else to tell you. Mrs. Greer wants you never to call her again. From what I've learned in the past two days, it seems like a reasonable request to me."

Peggy turned and left the room, closing the door behind her.

The moment I had been waiting for was finally at hand.

Mike made the first move: he glared at me. I simply smiled back.

"So what do you want?" he growled.

"I'd like to hit you, Mike," I said sweetly, "but I've already done that, and it didn't do much good. So what I want now are a few answers. First of all, I'd like you to tell me if you recognize this."

I reached into my jacket pocket and pulled out the membership invitation from the Walnut Grove Country Club. Still folded, I handed it to him. I watched him carefully as he opened it. His hands froze for just a second when he saw the club's embossed logo. Then he quickly scanned the literature, trying to appear unaffected. He looked at me—defiantly?—as he handed it back.

"Maybe," he said. "The company I work for does a lot of mailers like this."

Ah, yes. He was going to make it as difficult as possible. Having been out of touch with Angie Greer for the past week, he had no idea how much I had actually discovered. I didn't expect, nor did I want, him to simply admit all. There was too much fun to be had in making him sweat.

"I'm going to give you two options, Mike," I said flatly. "And please think for a minute before you pick one."

"You're in no position to be giving *me* options, Jamison–"

"Here's the first option," I said, cutting him short. "You go to the Dayfield Police, in the next day or two, and tell them how Ray Keegan's handgun found its way from his car—almost nine months ago—to Gary Greer's possession on the night he was killed."

Mike squinted at me, an attempt at seeming confused. "What gun? What are you talking about?"

"The gun that Angie Greer says you tried to give her, just before her husband came home that night. The gun that Gary Greer used to shoot a police officer."

He winced at this, but didn't falter. "Angie Greer is lying," he sneered, still defiant. "I don't know anything about any gun."

Like a card game in which you're holding all the high trump, I was thoroughly enjoying this. I continued: "The gun that has an unidentified fingerprint on it. If *I* go to the police, I'll give them my best guess who the print belongs to. If *you* go, you can tell them whatever you please."

The sneer faded, but not completely. His eyes darted from me to the door, as though he was looking for a way out. Then he folded his arms in front of him.

"I still don't know what you're talking about. But, just out of curiosity," he asked, "what's my second option?"

"I'll tell you the second option in a minute. But first, I want to know something else.

"The night you brought the gun to Angie Greer, did you already know her husband would be coming home later, after concluding a major drug deal? Did you find that out from Chico? Or was it simply a coincidence, that you asked your lover to kill her husband on that *very* night?"

"What's the second option?" he asked again.

"The second option is that the next time I speak with Kyle Hutchinson—you know Hutch, don't you?—I'll give him *your* name, and *your* address, and tell him to ask *you* about his missing twenty thousand dollars. If you've never met him, let me assure you from personal experience: Hutch is a rather unpleasant fellow. And if you never thought about the consequences before, let me *also* assure you: You stepped into deep shit when you stole from him. The police, at least, play by rules. Hutch has no rules.

"Of course, I'll only speak to him *if* you decline your first option."

At the mention of Hutch's name, and the missing money— which I had estimated at the high end, for my own reasons—Mike Marder's self-composure crumbled. If I'd harbored any doubts before, I had none now: Angie Greer had *not* known about the money, and Mike had never told her. Except to pay Pressman's retainer, he had kept it to himself.

But now that the truth was out, now that Mike Marder could see how much I had learned—about him, and Angie, and the missing gym bag—he realized in an instant how perilous his position had become. Of course, he didn't know, not yet, that Hutch had been removed from the picture. I especially enjoyed watching him agonize over the thought of what Hutch might do to him.

I'd just played my king to his jack. I couldn't help but smile—no, make that sneer.

"I know *exactly* how you feel, Mike," I said, smugly. "Neither option is particularly attractive, is it? You're damned if you do, and damned if you don't."

It wasn't very smart of me to rub his nose in it like that, but I couldn't contain the extreme cockiness I was feeling. With that same swagger, I continued:

"Tell you what, Mike, let me make the first option even more attractive. If you return the money—all of it—to Angie Greer, I'll go to Hutch and get you off the hook. I'll tell him Gary Greer's gym bag was found in a locker at the YMCA, and it was returned, unopened, to his widow. Hutch won't give a damn—as long as he gets his money.

"Then, in appreciation," I said, waving the membership invitation at him, "I won't tell your employer how you *lifted* confidential information for your own enrichment. On Wall Street, they call that sort of thing *insider trading*. People go to jail for it."

"You can't prove that," he snapped.

I shrugged. "Still, it's an awfully peculiar coincidence, wouldn't you say? Do you want to chance your job—and your professional reputation, such as it is—on it? You'll need a far better lawyer than James Pressman to make your case."

Again his eyes flashed at the door. He licked his lips. He was out of trump, and I still held the ace. And he knew it.

"So," he said in a low voice, "just to clarify what you're saying, but not admitting anything—"

"Be careful now," I interjected.

He glared, then went on: "If I leave the money with Angie, *and* I tell the police where the gun came from..." He hesitated, glanced again at the door, then continued: "...you'll take care of Hutch. And you won't go to my company with your half-baked suspicions."

"My, you catch on fast! I couldn't have summarized it better myself, Mike.

"Of course," I added, "you realize that your career with the

Dayfield Rescue Squad will be over. I haven't studied all the regulations, but I'm sure that stealing personal property from an accident victim isn't considered acceptable behavior."

"I haven't admitted anything yet," he reminded me.

"And I haven't promised anything yet," I reminded him.

Ruefully, he nodded. He looked away, and thought to himself in silence. Then he looked back at me. He extended his hand.

"Okay," he said. "I'm trusting you to keep your word."

I ignored his hand. "You haven't much choice," I said haughtily.

Finally, I had pushed him too far. He drew back his hand, clenched it into a fist, and swung it, hard, right at my face. Yes, he cold-cocked me. Caught me looking and leaning the wrong way, and knocked me off my feet, over a chair, and onto the floor. I saw stars for a minute. And, Christ, did it hurt.

He stood over me, still shaking his fist. "You had that coming, Jamison," he snarled. "Now we're even."

I blinked, and shook my head, trying to stop the ringing in my ears. At last, I was able to focus on him. I knew better than to stand up.

"Not yet," I answered back, my tongue thick in my mouth. "But we're getting there."

I didn't get up for a few minutes. Even after Mike turned and left the room, and slammed the door behind him, I just laid there with my eyes closed. Maybe I had asked for it, but that hardly made the pain in my face more agreeable.

When the door opened again, and I heard footsteps approaching, I hesitated before looking up. Whoever had entered the room stopped and stood over me, and silently appraised me for a moment. Then he spoke: "You know, Scott, this routine is getting old. This is the second time in a month I've walked into a room and found you sprawled on the floor."

I opened my eyes and faced Miles, who looked down at me impassively.

"How do you think I feel about it?" I asked, wincing at the pain.

He didn't answer, but after a few seconds extended his hand to help me up. I took it and he hoisted me to my feet. He righted an overturned chair for me, then pulled up one for himself. We sat and stared at one another.

"Peggy told me you were in here with Mike," he said at last. "She didn't tell me he was beating the stuffing out of you."

I touched the side of my face. Nothing was broken, but I knew another unsightly bruise was developing.

"We weren't fighting," I mumbled. "In fact, we had just struck a deal—to our mutual benefit."

Miles raised an eyebrow. "Is that right? Gee, Scott, you and Mike have some strange customs. Most people just shake hands when they reach an agreement."

Ignoring his sarcasm, I said: "I've been trying to get in touch with you all day."

"I know," he replied. "You want to apologize for what you said yesterday."

"Can you forgive me?"

He waved his hand. "Don't worry about it. You've been under a lot of pressure lately, and I haven't been much help. I can understand why you suspected me."

I started to protest: "But I never should have–"

Again he waved me off. "I said forget about it, Scott. Now that everybody knows about Mike and Angie Greer, I can tell you: I haven't been entirely innocent through your whole ordeal."

"What?" I blurted. "What are you talking about?"

Miles looked up at the ceiling, as though to collect his thoughts. I couldn't imagine what he was about to say.

"I knew months ago that Mike Marder was messing around with Angie Greer. And when you were slapped with the lawsuit, I was pretty sure Marder was behind it."

"You knew?"

Miles nodded. I felt my anger starting to rise, and an intensified throbbing where Mike had hit me. I demanded: "Then why didn't you tell me?"

He raised his palms. "I couldn't. I ran into the two of them—Mike and Angie—a couple of months ago. They were at a secluded bar in Ironport, holding hands and acting real friendly toward one another, when I stumbled upon them. This was shortly after I had been to the Greer house on one of their domestic calls. So when we saw each other in that bar, neither Angie nor I could pretend we didn't know each other. Mike picked up on it."

"Yeah, so?" I asked.

"Mike followed me outside. He gave me the sob story about Angie's abusive husband, told me she'd be in great danger if Gary Greer found out she was seeing someone else. He asked me never to tell anyone I'd seen them together."

"And so," I concluded bitterly, "when your choice was between him and me–"

Miles broke in on me: "I gave Mike my *word*, Scott. None of us knew then what was going to happen later, but even that didn't give me the right to break a promise. If the situation were reversed, would *you* have wanted me to tell Mike something that I'd given you my word I'd keep secret?"

He had me there, that's for sure. "So that's why you've been so cool to me lately," I surmised.

Miles smiled weakly. "I couldn't stand to be around you, to see you wrestling with your problems, while I had some of the answers but couldn't say anything. It wasn't comfortable for me, either."

I considered this for a minute. "Why are you telling me this now?" I asked at last.

He shook his head. "I don't know, Scott. Maybe I'm tired of keeping secrets for everybody. Maybe–"

Miles was interrupted by the door swinging open. We turned as Peggy walked in on us. Her face was without expression, and she said nothing until she was standing right in front of me.

"Give me your hand, Scott," she said authoritatively.

I glanced at Miles. "Why?" I asked.

"Just give me your hand," she repeated.

Slowly I raised my hand to her, palm up.

"Turn it over," she said. I complied, and as I exposed the backside I realized, too late, what was going on. Peggy reached out and slapped my hand sharply. "Consider yourself reprimanded," she said, her face breaking into a grin. "And don't *ever* set foot in an unsecured residence again."

"Not a chance, Peggy," I said, while rubbing the back of one hand with the palm of the other.

Miles cleared his throat, asking for our captain's attention. She turned to him.

"So what happens to Mike?" he asked.

Peggy's grin disappeared. "We deferred it for now. If he doesn't resign, we'll schedule a hearing for him to present his case. Everyone's entitled to a fair hearing."

Miles nodded. "You guys are good at that 'deferral' trick," he observed.

"We try," was Peggy's answer.

NO THANKS

31

ARNIE, MY BOSS, GLANCED UP from his work when I knocked on his door. He signaled for me to enter.

"You wanted to see me?" I asked, even though I knew the answer.

"Yes, Scott," he said, signing his name to some form before looking up at me. "I just wanted to–" He cut himself off in mid-sentence as I came closer to his desk. He stared at my face.

"*Another* bruise? Don't tell me you walked into a door again."

"Nah," I said, touching my swollen cheek. "I had it out with some jerk last night. He's in a lot worse shape than I am."

My boss shook his head. "Aren't you a little old for that sort of thing?"

"I'm getting older by the minute, Arn. I hope we have a decent retirement plan at this sweatshop. I'm ready for it."

He smiled at this. It did me good to see him smile.

"Yes, well, I just wanted to say you did an excellent job on that report you finished yesterday. It reminded me of the work you *used* to do."

Now, how's that for a backdoor compliment?

"You liked it, huh?" I intended to milk this

for all it was worth.

"Yes, I liked it."

"Good. Can I have the afternoon off?"

Arnie's smile widened. I felt absolutely wondrous.

"Just like that?" he laughed.

"Yeah, just like that."

"Why? You have something important to do?"

"*Very* important. I have to go see my lawyer–"

"Oh, yeah," he said abruptly, "your lawsuit. How's that going?"

I told a white lie: "We *almost* have it whipped. We're wearing the bastards down."

"Good," he remarked, "but not good enough. Is that the *only* reason you want to skip out on me this afternoon?"

"Actually, no. I also have some shopping to take care of."

"Shopping?"

"It's *very* important, Arn."

"Shopping?"

"I have to make a purchase, before I get kicked out of the store."

For a moment or two, Arnie didn't recognize his own words. Then a light clicked on, and his face brightened considerably.

"Well," he said, "in that case, go right ahead. And best of luck to you."

"Thanks, Arn," I replied, while turning to leave. I didn't want to give him a chance to reconsider. I was almost out the door when he stopped me.

"Oh, Scott, by the way. About that report…"

"Yes?"

"Amazing, the similarities it bore to a job we handled for NT Technologies, two years ago. You remember that project, don't you? The client killed it before we completed the initial report."

It never comes easy, does it?

"Uh, when was that again?"

"About two years ago."

"Gee, Arn, I can't remember what happened last week, let alone two years ago."

"Well…anyway," he said, waving his hand to dismiss the matter. "Nice job. Keep up the good–"

I was out of there before he finished the sentence.

My next stop was the former munitions factory, where Geoffrey Hufnagel dabbles in law and photography. I arrived without advance notice and found my attorney at his desk, taking notes as he paged through a thick document. He glanced up as I entered, but showed no surprise at seeing me.

"Have a seat," he said amiably. "I'll be with you as soon as I finish this page."

"No hurry," I told him as I sat down. "I just came by to pay my bill, and to thank you for all your hard work."

Geoffrey shrugged. "Was nothing," he said. "Pressman was a fool for even bringing the suit. What some idiots will do for a lousy retainer..."

I looked around the office. Somehow, it appeared less cluttered than on my last visit. I said so to Geoffrey.

"Yeah, I'm cleaning up a little," he admitted. "I might not be here much longer."

"Oh? Where you going?" I guess I wasn't completely surprised.

Geoffrey set his pen down and looked at me. "My nemesis—the senior partner at the firm where I used to work—is retiring next month. The other partners have asked me to come back once he's gone."

I nodded. "Have they made you an offer you can't refuse?"

Geoffrey shrugged again. "There's advantages and disadvantages."

"What about your dark room, and your photography?"

He raised his palms. "That's one of the disadvantages."

"What are the advantages?" I asked. "More money?"

Geoffrey frowned. "Yeah, somewhat. But that's not the main reason I'm considering it. The real problem is, I'm too disorganized to be on my own. And I can't afford an assistant."

Glancing around, I couldn't argue with his assessment. Not directly, anyway.

"You know what you need, Geoffrey? You need a woman to look after you. I'll bet you'd get your act together if you had someone to go home to each evening."

His frown flipped over. "That's just what my mother tells me. Repeatedly. You got anybody in mind?"

Did I have anybody in mind?

"What about Angie Greer?" I had said it, half on impulse and half in jest. But then, when it was out, I was struck with the possibilities. Geoffrey had admired Angie Greer, if only through a camera lens. And the woman certainly had a lot to offer. Maybe it could work, for the both of them. Maybe…

Geoffrey's smile faded. "Angie Greer? No thanks, Scott. I mean, she's an attractive woman and all. And she'd probably make a good wife—for the right guy. But she's, well…she's damaged goods. You know what I mean?"

Damaged goods. As soon as he said it, I knew he didn't mean it. That was his mother speaking. Fran Hufnagel would take one look at Angie's unhappy history, and would declare the young widow off-limits for her son, the prominent attorney. Which very well could be the best thing for the both of them. Angie Greer was in need of someone, but she certainly *didn't* need a mother-in-law like Fran.

"Damaged goods," I repeated, remembering the nervous, confused woman I had confronted earlier in the week. The innocent victim, who had been abused and abandoned by the men she had loved.

"Yes, I suppose she is. But aren't we all, Geoffrey. Aren't we all."

NO SURPRISE

The following evening—
Friday—was a busy one at *Luigi's Pizza Parlor.* All the tables were filled and the crowd at the carryout counter was standing three deep. Why, I can't imagine.

Making matters worse was the fact that Luigi himself was operating the cash register. In all likelihood, his receipts from the previous two evenings had been out of balance by five dollars—*five dollars each night!*—so he had decided to handle all transactions personally for awhile. To his thinking, that would thwart the employee who was skimming from him. If, in fact, he was being skimmed at all.

The problem was that Luigi (a.k.a. Fred—his given name) is not sufficiently nimble to command an electronic keyboard. His fat, stubby fingers often hit two keys at the same time, resulting in charges of two hundred dollars or more for a large pie with mushrooms. As you can imagine, correcting such errors tends to cost time…and customers in the longer run.

Lucky for me, I had called my order in long before I came to pick it up. When Pam and I arrived, we had to squeeze through a mob to get near enough to the carryout counter to claim it. I could see the box with my name on it sitting on top of the oven. But in the hubbub caused by the bottleneck at the register, I couldn't get anybody to wait on me. Most of the employees were preoccupied; the remaining few were watching their boss as he furiously and ineptly fumbled with the keyboard, and his patrons' cash, and their crumpled receipts.

Personally, I was in a great mood—why wouldn't I be?—but all around me I heard grumblings and muttered profanities. It took me a minute to realize what was going on. Then I caught the attention of the young woman who usually works the register. She was standing behind her boss, helplessly biting her nails while he butchered almost every entry that the keyboard required. She rolled her eyes when she saw me, and gave Fred an unambiguous hand gesture behind his back.

I've never seen a riot in a pizza parlor, but the ingredients for one were simmering. Customers were shoving and snapping at one another as their pies cooled and their tempers flared. Yet Fred steadfastly refused to give up his post.

Pam sized up the situation just as quickly as I had. Being far more reasonable than I, she tapped me on the shoulder and whispered a sensible suggestion in my ear. "Let's get out of here," she breathed. "This pizza isn't worth a broken rib."

Perhaps I should have listened to her. After all, I wasn't very hungry, and I had more urgent matters to attend to that evening. But the pizza was only fifteen feet from where I stood, ready and waiting to be whisked away. I couldn't let a few harrumphing housewives keep me from claiming my dinner, could I?

"Hey, Luigi!" I shouted. *"Buona sera á té!"*

In that simple greeting, I had recited half of my total knowledge of the Italian language. But I accomplished my initial objective. The crowd quieted down somewhat, just out of curiosity, and looked at Fred for his reply.

He didn't even look up from his cash register. I noted the beads of sweat on his forehead as he answered: *"Buona sera á té, Scott."*

Now I had the advantage. I still had four or five more words left in my storehouse of Italian vocabulary, but Luigi had completely expended his ammunition. From this point on, he could only pretend to understand what I was saying.

"*Comé il tempo oggi?*" I asked loudly, though I knew better than he did the current atmospheric conditions.

Fred continued to punch the keys on the cash register, pausing only to wipe his brow. He was well aware that his customers, one and all, were waiting for him to answer me. They didn't know what I was asking, but they had every right to assume he did. How could a true *paisan* not know a few simple words of his "mother" tongue?

I stepped forward, and patrons moved to the side to allow my passage. When I was right in front of him, I lifted my hands—in the classic Italian fashion—and remonstrated forcefully: "*Luigi! Su pizza huele como desagüe crudo y tiene un sabor del vómito de perro sobre un cartón.*" I pressed my thumb against my upturned fingers, and shook my hand in Fred's sweaty face. "*Capisci?*" I demanded.

Now the entire restaurant was silent. Everyone was staring at "Luigi," or at me, or was glancing from one of us to the other. Behind me, I heard a woman giggle. I turned and saw her: a middle-aged woman—with black hair, dark eyes and olive skin. She was wearing a brightly-colored dress. I winked at her and she smiled back. I turned again to face Fred.

He was trying very hard to ignore me, but I could tell by the deepening flush of his face that he wasn't succeeding. He dropped a coin on the counter, then lunged at it, just missing it before it rolled onto the floor near my feet. I picked it up and set it on the counter.

I was about to start in again on Fred when he threw his hands up and shouted: "I've got things to do here, Scott!" Then he turned to the young woman behind him and crossly commanded: "Here! You take over! I've got to check on things in the kitchen!"

He glared at me, then stormed off and burst through the kitchen's swinging doors like a bull through a matador's cape. His customers stood for a moment, stunned, then spontaneously joined in applauding my act. The majority of them had understood, if not its content, at least its subtleties. I bowed deeply, left and right.

When we were back in my car, with our pizza sitting safely in the back seat, Pam gave me a quizzical look. "I didn't know you could speak Italian," she remarked.

"I can't," I admitted. "Most of what I said was in Spanish."

"Oh. So what did you say?"

I grinned at her. "I told Luigi that his pizza smells like raw sewage, and tastes like doggie vomit, on cardboard."

Pam giggled, just like the woman who had understood me when I said it the first time. "I thought you were speaking Italian."

"So did Luigi. But he wouldn't know Italian from Klingon."

"What's *Klingon?*" Pam asked.

I looked over at her. "You don't know?"

She shook her head.

"Really, Pam. You should watch more television."

When we got to my apartment complex, I handed Pam my keys and told her to go ahead, that I had to check something under the hood of my car. She offered to take the pizza, but I told her that I would bring it in just a minute. I didn't want it out of my sight.

"Don't be too long," she warned me. "The pizza will get cold."

I waved her along.

Minutes later, after she let me in the door to my own apartment, I saw that she had already set the table. A bottle of wine was on the counter, waiting for me to uncork it. I handed Pam the pizza.

She asked: "Are we going to have our discussion now?" Her tone was serious—almost stern.

"Later," I said. "Let's eat first."

"Then we talk?"

"I promise. Whatever you want to talk about."

She nodded, satisfied. She placed the pizza box on the kitchen table. I turned away to attend to the wine. But all the while, I kept an eye on her.

Pam opened the pizza box. At first, she didn't notice the item I had tucked into one of the corners. Then it caught her eye. She frowned at first and glanced up at me. I pretended to be preoccupied with a corkscrew.

"What is this?" she asked suspiciously.

Innocently, I replied: "What is what?"

She looked at me. Then she picked up the item. It was a small, cube-shaped jewelry box, wrapped in clear plastic. There was a dab of tomato sauce on its side.

I set down the corkscrew and walked back to the table, staring in wonderment at the item she held. "Where'd you get that?" I asked—perhaps overdoing the wonderment part.

Pam pointed at the pizza box. "It was in there when I…

"Oh, cut it out, H.B.. *You* put it there. You know what it is. Don't you?"

"Open it," I invited.

Again, she gave me a suspicious look. Anybody else would have known immediately what was going on, but Pam—bless her—was all innocence. She removed the plastic covering and opened the little box. As you guessed, there was a ring inside. Pam took it from the box and frowned at it—like it was an anchovy that had found its way onto our meat-lovers' special.

"Is this for me?" she asked, her voice absolutely flat.

Maybe I expected a more emotional reaction. Maybe I thought she'd throw her arms around me, or throw a fit, or throw a punch. She only stared at the ring.

"Yes, Pam," I said, launching into my prepared oration. "I'm asking you to marry me. The past few weeks, I've learned just how much you mean to me, and how sorry I'd be if I let you get away. It's time, I've realized, for me to make some changes in my life. But the change that matters more than all the rest, the change that will make everything else possible, is making you my wife.

"I've thought hard about this. I hope you've thought about it too. And I hope, very much, that you'll say yes."

It was the best speech I could manage, but she didn't even glance at me as I delivered it. She just kept looking at the ring. Then, quietly, she said: "It's not as big as the one Kelly got."

I was flabbergasted. She was complaining about the rock?

"Size isn't everything, you know," I reminded her.

"No," she said, trying her best to keep from laughing, "but it helps." She looked up at me. Her eyes were moist, but there was a sparkle in them. She was enjoying herself, making me work through my proposal.

"I've never heard you complain before."

She stood up and put her arms around my neck. "I've never had reason to," she whispered. Then she kissed me, which I took as an affirmative answer. It was a deep, lingering kiss, which lasted longer than a few marriages I've known.

When it was over, she pulled back from me, tilted her head, and said: "I suppose now you'll expect me to get your shackles up."

Do what? Get my *hackles* up? This time, Pam's misquotation had me baffled. I was already dazed, out of breath, and couldn't fathom what she was trying to say. "Come again?" I requested.

"You know, you'll want me to rescue you from that sinking slave ship. Unlock the chains, or whatever."

I could only stare at her, so dumbstruck was I. She smiled, sat back down at the table, and took a bite of our pizza. At last, I managed to ask: "How do you know about that?"

She wiped her mouth with a napkin, ever so daintily.

"You talk in your sleep, H.B."

"I do?"

"Yes. When you're not snoring."

"I snore?"

"Mmm-hmm."

Just like that, I had lost control of the conversation. I'd come into it with the element of surprise on my side, and now she had me backpedaling. And people think she's ditsy.

The telephone rang just then, sparing me further embarrassment. I answered it there in the kitchen.

"Hello, is this Scott?" a woman's voice asked.

"Yes. And you are?"

"Dorothy McCrae." My friend, the investigative reporter.

"How are you?" I asked, though I didn't much care to know. Which was okay, because she didn't bother to answer.

"I'm on my way to police headquarters," she informed me. "We've just learned that a member of your rescue squad has been arrested on a felony charge. I thought you might know something about that."

"I might," I said.

She waited a minute for me to elaborate. I let her wait. Finally, she asked: "Would you like to make a statement?"

I looked over at Pam, still seated at the kitchen table. She had the ring on her finger, and was examining it from different angles. When she noticed I was watching her, she self-consciously lowered her hand from my sight, and took another bite of the pizza.

"Yes, I have a statement to make. Are you recording this?"

Dorothy hesitated. "I will if you want me to," she said.

"Suit yourself," I replied.

I listened as she fumbled with her cassette recorder. In a matter of seconds, she was ready.

"Go ahead," she said.

I cleared my throat, getting Pam's attention. "You can print this..."

"Go ahead," Dorothy said again.

"Okay, here goes:

"Mr. Scott Jamison, a resident of Dayfield and an employee of DataStaff Corporation, is pleased to announce his engagement to Pamela Healy, his girlfriend of the past six years—give or take a month or two. The couple has not yet decided on a date for the big event, nor on anything else, for that matter. More on this as it develops."

I relished the silence from Dorothy's end. Almost as much as I relished the way Pam was smiling at me, just then.

"That's it?" Dorothy asked at last. "Nothing about your fellow squad member?"

"What fellow squad member?" I asked, just before I hung up the phone.

I finished opening the wine, poured two glasses, and carried them back to the table. Handing one to Pam, I sat down. She held it, expecting—I suppose—for me to propose a toast. Instead, I picked up a piece of pizza and took a gluttonous bite of it.

"So," I said, with a mouthful of dough and gummy cheese, "what did you want to talk about?"